First Token

A Story of Life, Love, & Tennis

by Howard Zoldessy

Copyright © 2018, 2019, 2021, 2023 Howard Zoldessy.

Disclaimer: This work is a fictitious creation. Names, characters, places, and incidents are the product of the author's imagination. Any resemblance to actual persons living, dead, or on life support, or any business entities, events, venues, or settings is purely coincidental.

US Copyright Certificate of Registration No. TXu 2-093-396 Effective Date of Registration: June 29, 2018

US Copyright Certificate of Registration No. TXu 2-148-601 Effective Date of Registration: May 23, 2019

US Copyright Certificate of Registration No. TXu 2-274-555 Effective Date of Registration August 9, 2021

(US Registration Nos. TXu 2-093-396 and TXu 2-148-601 and TXu 2-274-555 and TXu 2-380-108[2023])

All rights reserved, including the right of reproduction in whole or in part in any form.

ORANGE TABBY PUBLISHING

Knoxville, Tennessee, USA

Cover Art by Roger Ryskamp
Cover Design by Maria Loysa-Bel Nueve – de los Angeles

International Standard Book Numbers: 978-1-963281-00-2, 978-1-963281-01-9, 978-1-963281-02-6, 978-1-963281-03-3, 978-1-963281-04-0

Printed in the United States of America.

Thank you,

Elizabeth, Rachel, Alex, Monte

Terry Runger

Jen and Steve Frabitore

Connie and Steve Schmidt

Marcy and Andy Bliss

Dedication

First Token is dedicated to the notion of a permanent American Comedy Hall of Fame. The public expression of comedy is emblematic of a free society, a celebration of its liberties and freedoms. Comedy has the capacity to heal and unite, and yet, political correctness is snuffing out our comedic sensibilities. A Comedy Hall of Fame would memorialize more than just an art form; it would protect and sustain a piece of Americana that is now challenged and might well disappear, perhaps leaving behind various imposters. Hundreds of funny and brilliant images shall sadly vanish from Western culture unless they are immortalized within a timeless and accessible public vault. Visualizing an American Comedy Hall of Fame is the first step. Execution is another matter. The project needs a catalyst, so let's find a way to conserve this rich and flavorful slice of the American pie. Let's find a way to preserve our comedic heritage. I propose the following:

The American Comedy Hall of Fame

"When The Going Gets Tough, The Tough Get Funny." ©

The Author's Pledge

Ten percent of the author's meager royalties from this endeavor shall be donated to the International Tennis Hall of Fame in Newport, Rhode Island.

In Memoriam
Izze, a twelve-pound tortoiseshell cat

Table of Contents

Post War	17
April 1956	19
The Closet	19
The Cabot Estate	22
The Library Book	27
The Tennis Exhibition	37
First Kiss	42
Buster	44
Men's Canteen	49
The Day After	65
The Red Maple	72
Mount Flushmore	73
Elizabeth Anne Aughrim	78
Origin of Hitters	86
Jakub Baranski	92
Becky and Dexter	103
Mixed Doubles	114
May 1956	118
The Hamburger Recipe	118
Street Music	122
The Torch	127
Hospitality Manager	132
Abdication	136

Nordic Navigator	140
First Serve	143
Forged by Ice	156
June 1956	**160**
The List	160
July 1956	**165**
Sadie Hawkins	165
The Quiver	170
The Catch	173
August 1956	**177**
Wall of Doors	177
Chad and Veronica	181
London	184
The Hearing	189
Meatballs and Spaghetti	194
First Dance	199
The Terrace	205
September 1956	**220**
Water	220
The Shiksa	227
Second Serve	230
October 1956	**236**
The Letter	236
Perfection	246

The Dream	252
Private Eye	257
The Tea Cozy	259
Box of Tissues	263
Break Point	267
The Velvet Box	273
The Flat	277
November 1956	280
Wet Leaves	280
Mail Slot	285
The Chain	293
December 1956	297
The Nun	297
January 1957	301
The Pretzel Cart	301
British Racing Green	304
February 1957	306
The Mouser	306
Mint Schnapps	314
March 1957	318
The Draw	318
April 1957	321
The Tournament	321
Match Point	332

The Fates	340
May 1957	345
Rheingold	345
Afterlife	350
October 1957	363
Act Five	363
Our Story	371
A Note from the Author	376

Post War

In the formative years of the twentieth century, American policy transformed from protective isolationism to global superpower. In retaliation to Pearl Harbor and the Axis threat, the US committed to foreign interventionism in 1941. The American Century was now in full gallop.

In 1956, the United States entered an epoch of unprecedented growth. Ten years removed from World War Two, twenty years from the Great Depression, the paucity and constraints that characterized those decades faded with the arrant abundance emerging in the 1950s; a golden era for some, misery for others, and transformation for all.

The thriving economy and American optimism engendered the Baby Boom generation, an explosion of breathtaking immensity. After the war, the US population grew by thirty million; four million babies were born in the US in 1955, and ninety-five percent of those babies were born into homes united in wedlock.

In January 1956, President Eisenhower reported to Congress that the US had "broken through to new and higher ground" to extend prosperity with "full employment, rising incomes, and a stable dollar." Six months later, his administration announced a budget surplus of almost two billion dollars. America had become a four hundred-billion-dollar economy, unemployment was about four percent, the housing industry was flourishing, and automobile manufacturing quadrupled from previous years. Americans bought eight million autos in 1955, and seven out of every ten American families now owned a car. On a per capita income basis, Detroit had become the wealthiest city in America. With a top-tier interstate highway system under construction, mobility had become a new American standard.

The tectonic plates of America's social construct were now in seismic upheaval, an undeniable collision buckling the established dynamic. One out of every four Americans was now enrolled in school or college, an all-time record in US history, and one-third of all college enrollees were women. Women also held one-third of American jobs, and in November, women would cast half of the votes in the 1956 presidential election. One week after Election Day, the US Supreme Court affirmed a lower court's ruling that desegregated the public buses in Montgomery, Alabama. Rosa Parks stood her ground against the misery. Ninety-three years after Lincoln's proclamation, the bell of freedom pealed again.

With the sacrifice and hardship of World War Two in the rearview mirror, Americans were pursuing relaxation and amusement. The monumental war-time manufacturing effort carried over into the 1950s, fusing with a national unity that Aristotle had theorized was inherent in a democratic society. The American family was intact, and God was alive and well, as millions of Americans regularly attended some form of organized religious service. For many of the faithful, proof of God's existence had finally been verified. On October fourth, in the year 1955, at the intersection of East 161st Street and River Avenue in the Bronx, the Brooklyn Dodgers won their first World Series Championship.

April 1956
The Closet

He has relived his last day on earth from every aspect and from every angle, at times recalling details he had long ago forgotten, details so precise and minute that every reincarnation adds another deposit into the account. In every recollection he is awake when reveille comes through the speakers at three in the morning. The stale biscuit and powdered eggs are always repulsive—better to die on an empty stomach. The strafing of the beach by the American rocket barrage explodes in his ears and rattles his spine. As always, he checks his gear one last time before going over the side and down the cargo net onto the weather deck of the amphibious landing craft. The sequence of events before descending the cargo net may vary. The craft's churning through the ebbing tide of the Yellow Sea never changes. The blanket of smoke hovering over the Port of Inchon is so thick, it is as though it is stitched into his fabric. The cloud is so dense he cannot see the shore. He cannot see the enemy. He is crossing the water to the edge of the world, to the edge of time.

The craft drops its ramp at the base of the seawall. The splash sprays his face with droplets of water. The moisture crosses the threshold between the landscape of dreams and the tangible world. The sheets on his side of the bed are damp. He lobs a grenade over the seawall and then scales the ladder into a hail of small-arms fire from the North Korean fighters. Three Marines drop. The booming grenades deaden his ears.

His wife Becky rolls onto her right side, but he is numb to her soft, eurythmic breathing. Becky's dreamscape is a baking cottage in the Lowlands. Becky and her grandmother are rolling out dough. Their aprons are tinted with flour dust. The powdered sugar canister is smudged with Becky's fingerprints. The cottage is filled with the aroma of pound cakes. Gramma smells like lavender and talcum. A buzzin' fly lands on the sill. "Shut the widduh, my lub," Grandmother says with a smile.

Amid the chaos and live fire, Dexter Alexander's second grenade finds its mark. It always does. Smoke billows from the North Korean bunker at the base of Cemetery Hill. Dexter continues with the other Leathernecks. It begins to rain. His feet slog through the mud. If he cannot run, he will die. Panic sets in. Enemy mortar fire scatters his platoon. Dexter makes for a cluster of red pines. The mud is deeper now, and he wades through sludge. The hillside below the trees becomes firm. Four Marines follow him toward Observatory Hill. His strides are long and swift. He passes through time, and he passes through his life.

Dexter's gait is slower now. He is standing in a lush pasture of ryegrass and fescue on the ridge of a gently sloping field. He inhales the sweet and spicy scent of curing tobacco. The North Carolina earth is freshly tilled, and two wooden carts piled high with tobacco seedlings are parked at the base of the modest rise in the shadow of a shade tree. His cousin is transplanting the seedlings into the furrows. A team of plow mules grazes just beyond the carts. Another man emerges from behind the sycamore. He is clad in overalls. A North Korean army insignia is sown onto the sleeve of his sweat stained denim shirt. He is armed. "Miles, don't shoot me!" Dexter pleads. "I never hurt you!" Miles aims his bolt action shotgun.

Dexter Alexander opens his eyes; he is paralyzed with fright. His heart is ramming blood through his body. His mouth is dry. The taste is fear. He is not in a hospital. He is not floating in the afterlife. He is at home in bed with his wife. But this dream had been different. A vestige shadowed his soul across the planes and followed him back through the portal. His brother Miles might be hiding in the bedroom closet. Minutes pass. A thin blade of light from the streetlamp descends through the gap between the wall and the Venetian blinds, illuminating the top of his wife's night table. Becky is asleep and lowers the quilt from her face. As their breathing patterns merge, his respiration moderates to normal.

Dexter rises without disturbing Becky. Standing next to the bed, he smothers the impulse to check the closet, knowing the creak of the hinge would wake Becky. In the bathroom he splashes his face with water. With his right hand fisted and cocked, Dexter brushes aside the shower curtain with his left hand. Crossing the hallway to the kitchen, Dexter opens the refrigerator and draws a swig of grapefruit juice from the carton. He relocks the front door bolt. Back in the kitchen, he checks the wall clock. It is now Friday morning, just after two. He stretches out across the living room couch and falls asleep.

"Korea will never go away, hon," he tells his wife over toast and coffee.

"It will over time. You should wake me up next time. Talking about it might help you come back to bed."

"There's no sense in both of us losing sleep." Dexter makes no mention of his brother and the shotgun. "What time am I picking you up tonight?"

"If just Veronica and Gretchen are coming for dinner, probably about eight. If more people show up, I'll just stay over. Call me about four. I'll know by then. I'll look for your ring."

The Cabot Estate

On this bright and buoyant Friday afternoon, Becky Alexander and her employer are flitting about within the culinary hub of the Cabot Estate. The French provincial dining hall is being readied for this evening's gathering. Mrs. Cabot purchased the hand carved walnut dining set in Paris; the chair backs feature interlocking oval rings that do not align with the human spine. Guests display both impeccable posture and diplomatic sensibility, concealing any hint of discomfort. The chairs' nom de guerre, expressed within the secret society of the Cabot daughters and Becky Alexander has evolved. Previously known as those "ill-natured chairs," they are now "those arrogant French chairs."

Directly beneath the kitchen, a steep and narrow stairwell christened "the mineshaft" opens to a wine cellar that even Manhattan's most persnickety sommelier would admire. The grape larder is the trailhead for a cavernous maze of right angles that terminates at two musty chambers. A retired root cellar is the windowless cavity on the left, and a vacant armory is on the right. Becky, being more agile than Mrs. Cabot, insists on traversing that treacherous flight when the cook is occupied.

Hired as a domestic four years ago, Becky's aptitude for detail became apparent early on. Becky now manages all maintenance and hospitality functions on the estate. When Mrs. Cabot learned that a fourth-generation society lady had alluded to Becky's complexion with disparaging language, Mrs. Cabot severed all ties and insisted her acquaintances do likewise. They did.

Becky has penned this evening's menu in triplicate, the cook placed the order by phone, and the chauffeur, Charles, has fetched the provisions. Becky instructed the cook to rouse the baked Alaska from its hibernation. "Then what will we serve on Sunday?" the cook asked.

"Let's serve strawberry shortcake at the hospital fundraiser," Becky replied.

A bond has blossomed between Becky and Veronica Cabot, the older of the two Cabot daughters. Born in the same week in 1930, Becky and Veronica have discovered they have few dissimilarities. Both are tall, slender, quick-witted, and strong-willed. Veronica has mentioned on more than one occasion that Becky could be a fashion model. "She's as thin as a needle and could slice cantaloupe with those gorgeous cheekbones."

Encouraged by Veronica to share her Gullah-Geechee heritage, Becky's bill of fare at the Cabot annual end of summer fest two years ago instantly achieved the lofty status as one of the most celebrated of all Cabot functions. Becky taught Mrs. Cabot, both Cabot daughters, and the cook traditional Lowcountry coastal cuisine. The guests fussed over the shrimp and grits, fried corn cakes, crab rice, peanut stewed chicken, and baked okra and tomatoes. Becky explained to the Cabot ladies that her maternal grandmother, who moved the family to New York during the great migration from the rural south in the 1920s, taught Becky the recipes and the traditions. Only Veronica is privy to Becky's tales of root doctors and herbal medicines, although peppermint tea, occasionally fortified with rum, has become a regular winter afternoon beverage. Veronica's intrigue with the Gullah belief that Lowcountry infants encased in the amniotic sac are imbued with clairvoyant powers has initiated more than one provocative late-night conversation on those nights when winter weather blows and Becky bunks at the estate.

Veronica's younger sister Gretchen is expected home this evening, escorted by her fiancé, Scottie. Separated by only twenty months on the Cabot tree, the sisters hold two of the four cardinal locations on their social compass. Confidantes Regina Ellsworth and Bridget Radcliff round out the core. Three of the young ladies spent their leisure hours in tennis whites. Gretchen sought out museums and archaeology exhibits. Gretchen's passion for investigation has propelled her through two years of law school. Now in her final year, Gretchen is moonlighting as a legal researcher for a patent law firm near her Greenwich Village apartment. Veronica and Gretchen share a strong facial resemblance and a deeply intuitive bond. Their sisterhood does not welcome rivalry or bickering.

Chasen Endicott Cabot was a mere lad when his father acquired the family's Glen Cove estate from a bankrupt Dutch industrialist after the First World War. Until recently, Mr. Cabot's Long Island had been a provincial retreat, an escape from the frenetic pace of the city. That notion changed after the Second World War. Sculptured by a receding glacier ten thousand years ago, the largest island in the continental US emerged as a safe harbor for the American Dream. Blessed by water, the Long Island Sound lapping its northern shore and the slate gray Atlantic Ocean its southern coast, Long Island's population exploded in the ten years after Germany and Japan surrendered to the Allies.

On a field that once yielded potatoes sixteen weeks after planting, America's first mass-produced suburban development sprouted in Hempstead. Levittown delivered a new single-family home every sixteen minutes. Three of America's first generation of shopping malls landed in Nassau County while aviation firms, skyrocketing across Long Island's landscape, crossed the billion-dollar revenue threshold. With a burgeoning commuter class, improved highway and rail lines, and sprawling communities, Long Island redefined the American suburb.

This sun-laden Friday in early April had been rather typical. Mr. Cabot's brief conversation with the Chrysler Building's uniformed elevator operator had been cordial and weather related, as it is every morning. "Good morning, Rita," rang out as Mr. Cabot breezed past his receptionist, bound for his corner office and his grand view of the East River.

"Good morning, sir. Coffee will be on your desk in five minutes," Rita recited robotically, distracted by the carbon paper smudge on her right index finger that had migrated to the return lever of her electric typewriter.

As he does every morning, Mr. Cabot scans Manhattan's East Side. He presumes that the membrane of rush hour vapor, hovering fifteen stories above Midtown, will burn off by lunch. Mr. Cabot's younger brother Emerson strolls in. "Good morning, Em. Anything new?"

"Last night I got a call from our politician friend up in Boston. He claimed he was calling to see if we needed his help with the approvals. Then he casually mentioned fixing up his brother with Veronica."

"What did you say to him?" the senior Cabot asks.

"I told him we're still in due diligence and..."

"No! Veronica! How did you handle that?"

"I told him she's very busy and will be traveling back to London. I gave him nothing."

"Good. Last thing Veronica needs is a rover for a husband."

Mr. Cabot's receptionist delivers that promised cup of coffee. "Mr. Cabot, I forgot to mention this. The jeweler delivered that new watch yesterday. I didn't know if you would be in today, so I told him to deliver it to your house."

"That's fine, Rita. Did you see it?"

"No sir, it was gift wrapped."

"Did I miss someone's birthday?" Emerson Cabot asks.

"Veronica lost her watch, probably on Chad's boat. Becky gave me her wrist-size. I bought it from that Hasidic family on West 47th Street."

The conversation with Emerson is nourishment for a man endowed with the ability to seamlessly navigate variables with sociability, a family trait. According to ancestral mythology, the Cabots are descendants of legendary seamen John and Sebastian Cabot, who were both retained by the English King Henry VII. The clan's rise in America is a documented odyssey of timely investments. After parlaying profits from utility speculation in the Southeast, the Cabots began acquiring real estate during the Panic of 1893. Crafted by three generations, the Cabot portfolio stretches across two US time zones and into Mexico. Under the helmsmanship of the current skipper, the family is planning to cast anchor in London.

After two dozen phone calls sandwiched around a bowl of cold borscht and a slice of warm black bread at a Russian tearoom, Mr. Cabot leaves for home at three-thirty. Before departing, he reminds his brother about tomorrow's tennis exhibition at Northshore Racquet and Golf Club. The doorman flags down a taxi from the endless convoy of yellow Checker cabs for Mr. Cabot's short ride to Penn Station for the four-fifteen, his choice of commute when his chauffeur has other obligations.

The Library Book

Becky Alexander breaks toward the vestibule. She ceases with the second chime as Bridget Radcliff passes through an interior set of double doors. After the third tone, "Good evening, ladies," drifts in from the grand foyer as Bridget bypasses the dining hall's French doors and mounts the circular stairway.

Becky calls out, "Bridget, are you staying for dinner?"

"Yes," reverberates down the natural echo chamber.

"Is Regina coming?"

"She didn't hear you. She's already on the second floor," Mrs. Cabot replies.

"She's faster than the lift. Must have been all that tennis."

"I'm so happy the girls will be home tonight, Becky. Let's plan on Regina and Skip. And let's not forget Chad. I'm certain he'll be here."

Bridget Lowell Radcliff, an ensconced member of the blooming leisure class, owns an ample trust fund that allows her freedom from toil and exertion. Emancipated from responsibility, she often submits to an irrepressible appetite for events destined to command the lead story in the morning paper. In 1955, Bridget attended Marian Anderson's brilliant performance at the Metropolitan Opera, witnessed the launching of the USS Saratoga in Brooklyn, and sat ringside in Yankee Stadium when Rocky Marciano pounded Archie Moore for the heavyweight crown. One evening last month, at a celebrated New York gathering spot, a married Australian tennis star, bewitched by Bridget's blonde locks and vivacious spirit, offered to leave his wife for her.

Unamused by his oleaginous flattery, Bridget directed Casanova's attention to the table where a syndicated columnist was enjoying dinner with a retired diva. "What is the proper spelling of your wife's name?" Bridget asked.

"What in bloody hell for?"

"For the accuracy of a certain gossip column, my dear."

Bridget schedules her tennis matches in the morning and her golf dates after lunch. Nothing supplants cocktail hour. Bridget is the youngest member on the Board of Directors of a Newport, Rhode Island polo club. She owns two Texas-bred ponies but knows little about equine care. Twenty-five years old, Bridget lives alone in a carriage house on her family's estate. As sole heir to the family's holdings, matrimony is not an aspiration.

Mr. Cabot hails a taxi at the Glen Cove station. The cabbie drops him at the east wing of his estate. Mr. Cabot travels the arched corridor that connects the carriage wing to the brown granite manor house. He joins his wife and Becky in the dining hall. Mr. Cabot kisses his wife on her cheek while executing an artfully discreet pinch. "And how is Becky this evening?"

"I'm fine, sir. And you?"

"I'm terrific, thank you. Can I still count on both girls for dinner?"

"Absolutely," Mrs. Cabot cheerfully sings. Becky excuses herself, dashing into the kitchen to rescue the sweet potato biscuits from death by fire, the cook being engaged in the cellar.

"I'm really looking forward to this weekend. The weather looks good for the exhibition. I invited Em…"

"Is he coming for dinner? Is he bringing…?"

"I don't believe so," Mr. Cabot answers, returning the interruption. "They'll be here tomorrow. I'm assuming he'll bring Marjorie, but she always appears to be so bored at tennis matches."

"That's not her fault, Chase. She doesn't play, and they have no children. I'd get bored too if I wasn't living in a tennis household."

"Mr. Cabot, the pool man will be here on Monday, and the cabanas will be cleaned and painted on Thursday."

"Thank you, Becky. Do we have time for a cocktail on the patio?" he asks his wife.

"Sir, your very dry Martinis are on the butcher block table next to the olive tray. Would you like me to get them?"

"Becky, you're always one step ahead of the rest of the family. You should be running our hospitality division."

Mr. Cabot starts for the kitchen, exercising discretion as he puts cocktail hour on ice. He listens for Becky's response to the door chime. "Good to see you, Chad."

"Hello, Becky."

Chad strides into the dining hall, issues a cordial greeting to Mrs. Cabot, and then grabs Mr. Cabot's hand. "I can't wait to tell Veronica that I've been invited to play at tomorrow's exhibition."

"That's wonderful," Mr. Cabot replies. "That's the very least I'd expect from our club champion."

Chad Jensen Harrington personifies his Nordic lineage of blond seafaring men of towering frames and keen blue eyes. Chad is proud of his double-barreled surname and considers an innocent omission of one name an act of negligence. Chad holds a degree from an Ivy League law school and has become a competent litigator for a Wall Street firm. The Cabots and the Harringtons have been acquaintances for two generations, and Chad has been enamored of Veronica Cabot since elementary school. After his sixth-grade graduation reception, Chad informed his mother that someday he was going to marry fifth grader Veronica Cabot. Chad resides at his Manhattan apartment during the week. Unable to resist his passion for nautical adventures or his longing for Veronica Cabot, he beds down at his family's estate on Long Island's north shore every weekend.

Chad's law school graduation gift, a six-week European holiday with two classmates, had been interrupted by an unfortunate encounter with a Spanish maiden. Upon arriving in Paris and learning of the situation ten days after his liaison, Chad solicited his father's guidance by wire. Mr. Harrington assured his son that this very delicate matter would be handled swiftly and quietly. The senior Mr. Harrington instructed the triad to abort their itinerary and return to Spain immediately.

Mr. Harrington expressed his strategy to his Manhattan attorney. "We have to take care of the girl, protect the boys, and keep my wife out of this." Assuming financial restitution would satisfy the first condition, Mr. Harrington ceased all other engagements.

Twenty-four hours later, Mr. Harrington and his checkbook met with a dignitary from the New York office of the Spanish Consulate. Mr. Harrington's attorney then arranged for a wire transfer to a Madrid hospital and a separate wire transfer to an attorney representing the young lady's family.

Mr. Harrington's attorney issued a non-negotiable directive upon greeting the trio of future lawyers just after they cleared customs in New York. "Gentlemen, the Madrid incident never occurred. It shall never be discussed or referenced in any shape, manner, or form with anyone, including yourselves. Is that understood?"

"Yes, sir," resonated as one voice on the sidewalk of the International Arrivals Building at Idlewild Airport. A good soldier, Chad has never discussed Madrid with his father.

Navigating the social platitudes with the Cabots, Chad's eyes are upon the door, and his ears are attuned to the footsteps descending the staircase. Becky returns from the kitchen with two garnished Martinis and one cold glass of lemonade. Bridget and Veronica glide into the dining hall. Bridget tilts her head forward as Mr. Cabot plants a paternal kiss on her forehead. Bridget sips Mr. Cabot's cocktail. "Gin Martini, hint of dry vermouth."

The aura of Veronica Cabot's grace and striking refinement are irresistible. From the moment Veronica enters a room, she exudes a gravitational force that rotates all heads in her direction. Her shimmering red hair and sage green eyes are a striking contrast to the luster of her ivory complexion. It would not be unusual for a lady so endowed to enjoy the role of a centerpiece, but those few who are close to Veronica know that is not her nature. Born to pleasant looking parents, Veronica's preternatural beauty blossomed at fifteen. When she was seventeen, a cease-and-desist letter authored by the attorney who had once been general counsel to the governor had been dispatched to modeling and theatrical agencies as a maneuver to preserve her privacy. The list of gentlemen Veronica has graciously declined constitutes an international Who's Who.

Veronica lives on the family estate with her parents, and she prefers the serenity of her car for her weekday commute to the Cabot office. On the first Monday of every month, Veronica donates her vocal cords, raising funds by telephone for a church charity. In public, Veronica is drawn to witty theater and comedic opera, but in the privacy of home, she adores slapstick comedy.

Mr. Cabot issued a decree to Veronica's primary school administrators that his daughter was not a candidate for the practice of converting left-handed children. As Veronica's tennis game evolved, she capitalized on her intrinsic advantage. Her first serve to the ad box kicks into the doubles alley, and her cross-court, one-handed backhand, juiced with topspin, skips away from a righty's forehand. When Veronica was six, she began her studies under a teaching pro. When she was twelve, she and her father split sets. When she was fourteen, she defeated him regularly. Now, Veronica declines tournaments and tennis ladders to focus on business affairs and fund-raising, which govern her daily docket.

Having no sons or nephews, Chase Cabot has been grooming Veronica to oversee the family's holdings. Chase delights in the paradox that lurking beneath his daughter's fetching charm is a fierce competitor with a cardsharp's deadpan. Last month, Veronica notified a major retail tenant, with whom Cabot endured a contentious relationship, that their request to extend its lease had been denied. Having anticipated their tardy notice to renew, Veronica negotiated a fresh lease with that tenant's main competitor for twenty-five percent more rent. One week after that cunning move, she reduced the rent from a card and gift shop to the vanishing point for three months. The owner's husband had suffered a heart attack, so the shop would be operating with sporadic hours.

In the dining hall, Mrs. Cabot greets her younger daughter. "Gretchen, your auburn highlights are absolutely stunning against that emerald cardigan. My hair was exactly that color when I was your age." The guests are seated according to Mrs. Cabot's dictate. Her husband stands behind his usual chair, at the head of the table. Veronica sits next to her father. Chad is assigned the chair between Veronica and Bridget. The chatter begins with Louise Brough's chances of winning Wimbledon and ends with the Dow Jones hitting 500.

Becky's menu is a fitting match on this eve of Northshore's first of two annual tennis exhibitions; salad and biscuits, baked local flounder with lemon and capers, asparagus, and piped peaks of duchess potatoes. The second round of conversation lands on a more somber topic. The team of advisors dispatched by President Eisenhower to the Republic of Vietnam to aid the French with troop withdrawal appears to be staying on. Bridget shares her father's concerns. "Edgar told Mother and me that this could escalate."

"Oh, how dreadful," Mrs. Cabot comments. "We don't need another Korea."

"I fear Edgar could be right on this," Mr. Cabot reluctantly adds.

The humor elevates as Becky presents Mr. Cabot's favorite dessert. Known as "the delectable dichotomy" within the Cabot trinity, the baked Alaska's frozen ice-cream core, outfitted with a warm sweater of sponge cake and an overcoat of heated meringue, presents a conundrum for the calorie counters. Veronica, Gretchen, and Bridget set a limit of one nibble.

After dinner, Gretchen asks Veronica about her month-long trip to England. "Did you meet any new, interesting men?" Chad's blood pressure elevates.

"I really didn't have time to socialize. The trip was all business."

Chad's arteries relax, his desire to alter the path of the conversation does not. "Scottie, how did you and Gretchen meet?"

Scottie tips his fiancée a wink and then shifts across the table toward Chad. "I had been at the firm for two years. I'd get to work an hour before the partners arrived and stayed an hour after they left. I needed a break, so, one night I stopped at the public library."

Gretchen intervenes. "Scottie caught my eye immediately. It was an overcast night, and in walked this very handsome man in a British double-breasted trench coat. When he walked to the archaeology section, I knew I had to meet him. I grabbed the nearest book and casually approached him at the check-out desk. I conspicuously peered over and saw that he had no wedding band, so, I mentioned that the book he was about to borrow was also on my list. Scottie said, 'Why don't you check it out now and let me know when you're finished.' I smiled and thanked him."

"Smooth move, Scottie."

"I'm really not that calculated, Chad."

"But I am," Gretchen interjects. "I already had that book. I had never been so emboldened. I had to meet this perfect fellow wearing the perfect trench coat. We agreed to meet at the library exactly one week later, at eight o'clock. I got there at seven-thirty, took a seat near the entrance but not too obvious. I was hoping it would rain and we would go out for coffee. I wore my waterproof cloche hat. I was prepared." Becky and the cook are now standing in the dining hall near the door to the kitchen.

"Scottie arrived five minutes early, and he smiled at me the moment he walked in. He was wearing a blue blazer with chinos, and he was carrying an umbrella. He brought me a gift, a study about North American Archaeology. We both forgot about the book I was supposed to give him. We left the library and went out for coffee, but we left when the cigarette smoke got too thick. Walking down Bleecker Street, we heard guitar music from a folk club. We sat in a quiet corner, drank espresso, and just talked.

"It rained when we were in the club. The air had a sweet fragrance, and the streetlights were sparkling off of the puddles. We talked a little on my stoop, and we agreed to see each other on Saturday afternoon. I so wanted to kiss him goodnight, but I didn't. On Saturday we hit two museums and then watched the seals in Central Park." Gazing toward Scottie, Gretchen adds, "And we've never looked back. We're building our library, and that book Scottie gave me will always be the cornerstone."

"Did you know Scottie was *the one* on your first date?" Chad asks.

"I knew before that. I knew when I stood next to him at the check-out desk. I had a feeling of recognition the first time I saw him, like I already knew him. All week I kept asking myself, 'How do I know him? Where did we meet?' I had so many questions I was going to ask him, but I never asked any of them. I just needed to silence my inquisitive mind and enjoy his company. This wasn't a research project."

The Cabot clan knew of that serendipitous encounter, but they had never heard these details. Veronica is enthralled with the notion that a book with hundreds of identical siblings has been deeded by gesture into a cherished artifact. She wonders, *Was it by chance or destiny? If they hadn't met in the library, would they have met somewhere else?*

Gretchen announces that she and Scottie have a train to catch. After the proper goodbyes, the remaining guests agree with Mr. Cabot's suggestion to forego a nightcap.

Veronica walks Chad to the door. "What time shall I pick you up tomorrow?" he asks.

"I'm riding over to the exhibition with Regina," she explains.

Chad leans in to kiss her goodnight, but she offers him her cheek. "I want more from you, Veronica."

"We're friends, Chad. Not lovers."

The Tennis Exhibition

The weather gods have exceeded human supplication, as Northshore's first tennis exhibition of the season has been graced with sunny skies. At two o'clock, new member Hillard Gabriel Abraham submits his paperwork to the club secretary. Dashing through the outer office, the general manager extends his right hand. "I'm Patrick Elliott. It is my pleasure to welcome our newest tennis member." Shifting his fedora to his left hand to accommodate the handshake, Hillard notices beads of perspiration below Mr. Elliott's thinning hairline.

"Hillard, your timing couldn't be more perfect. Our first tennis exhibition is underway. We've got members of the US Davis Cup team, cast members from two Broadway shows, and a few celebrities. Be prepared. It might be standing room only." Hillard now appreciates why he had to park in the rutted field beyond the asphalt lot.

"I'm not really dressed for it, but I would like to see the Davis Cup team hit. Thanks for letting me know, Mr. Elliott."

"Please don't sit in the lower sections, as those seats have been reserved for visitors. Members have been asked to sit in the upper rows."

"Will you be attending?" Hillard asks.

"I can't," the slightly overweight GM responds. "My desk is buried in paperwork. You should also visit the Men's Canteen in the basement of the clubhouse. We've got a real artifact down there, a bar from a Chicago speakeasy."

When queried, Hillard relates that he learned of Northshore's red clay courts from tennis member Steve Andres. Mr. Elliott savors the praise.

"I've heard that Steve is a strong player. It is undeniable that our eight courts are among the best in the northeast." Mr. Elliott ushers Hillard into the hallway. "There's something I would like to mention, and please do not be offended. Northshore had been a restricted club for decades, an unfortunate policy that just seemed to perpetuate. I'm proud to have been the GM when we opened our doors to Jewish members. Please call me Pat, and please don't ever hesitate."

"Thank you, Pat. Please think of me as just another tennis member. I can't understand the policy of restrictions. That's not what this country is about."

"Well said," Pat replies as he and Hillard shake hands again. Pat returns to his office. The club secretary had contained her disappointment when the conversation progressed into the hallway. She had enjoyed Hillard's company.

Hillard's route to the exhibition is impassable, as the walkway is cluttered with spectators sitting on lawn chairs. Cutting across a fairway, then negotiating a passage through a majestic partition of blue spruce conifers, he finds a sliver of grass next to a tapered stormwater gully. Hillard's view of the Davis Cup teammates on Court 1 is unobstructed. Standing in front of a terraced daffodil garden, he fills his lungs with the aromatic fragrance of hyacinth and jasmine seeping from the yellow trumpets. Perched on the lip of the trench, the pointed toecap of his wingtips extending over the concrete valley, Hillard stands motionless. During a break in play, Hillard brushes spruce needles from his left shoulder. The gallery inhabiting the seating sections reserved for members occupies his attention. Rotating his view left, he surveys the club room, a single-story, stone structure with large, half-round fixed windows. The building's veranda is cantilevered over an outcropping of rock and scrub brush. The steep embankment slopes into the daffodil oasis behind him. He theorizes that the spectators on the veranda, under the protection of its green canvas awning, have the best vantage for enjoying the tennis.

The audience politely applauds winners or heroic efforts, but they are silent when a player commits an unforced error or a double fault. Hillard spots a spent paper cup embedded in the row of winterberry hollies that lines the court. During the next changeover, he steps to his right and pockets the trash for disposal later.

Sitting with his family in the gallery's top row, Chase Cabot reminds himself to increase his dinner reservation. He is quite certain that Chad Harrington will join them after playing doubles on Court 7. Mrs. Cabot and her sister-in-law, chatting about everything except tennis, are enjoying the shade beneath their white parasols. The dashing Cabot brothers, shielded from the brilliant sunshine by the Panama hats they purchased at a millinery shop, occasionally divagate into random comments about one deal or another. Veronica Cabot, Bridget Radcliff, and Regina Ellsworth are following the Davis Cup matches on Courts 1 and 2. The ladies are sporting off-white linen dresses and beribboned, wide-brim sun hats.

A Seven Sisters graduate and captain of her college tennis team, Regina Pruitt Ellsworth has postponed setting her wedding date until her name is inscribed upon the championship plaque on the pro shop wall. Regina believes she will lose her conditioning when she and fiancé Skip get married. Blessed with a delicate nose, a wrinkle free, oval face, and prominent dimples, Regina had recently modeled tennis outfits for a national retailer. After that photo shoot, she permanently abandoned fashion to pursue a deeper aspiration. Regina retired her portfolio and changed her look. She wore her ash brown hair in a bouffant bob with a finger wave, ideal for tennis but impracticable for high style. A major shareholder in her family's Suffolk County Savings and Loan, Regina, discusses banking and finance with her father every morning at breakfast.

Regina lacks the confidence in her backhand to drive the ball down the line from behind the ad box. She opts for the safer cross-court route, clearing the lower part of the net. The greater obstacle to the title she covets is sitting two rows below the Cabot party. Regina whispers to Veronica, "I would love to know what Elizabeth Anne is thinking. Both times she beat me in the finals, she had a different plan. I wonder what she'll have for me this year. Just look at her, always analyzing. What do you think is on her mind?"

"No idea, Regina. There is so much going on."

"You seem distracted, Veronica. Are you okay?"

"I couldn't be better. I'm just taking it all in."

Sitting alone, Elizabeth Anne Aughrim has taken notice of the Davis Cup Captain's western grip. She has also detected a subtle difference in his ball toss, sacrificing velocity for placement on his second serve. Bedecked in the latest fashion, a white pleated tennis skirt with a cinched waist and a white sleeveless V-neck top, Elizabeth Anne declined an invitation to play doubles on Court 6 with members of a Broadway cast. Elizabeth Anne has no intention of expending her skills unless it benefits her ambition to become the first member in Northshore's forty-nine-year history to win three consecutive championships in either golf or tennis.

After investing forty-five minutes and relishing every moment, Hillard withdraws. If not for his tan fedora, Hillard would not have lasted fifteen minutes in business attire. He rules out the short walk to the neighboring veranda as the slate walkway is too congested. General Manager Pat Elliott has abandoned his desk. He is now on the veranda, helping his staff with the crowd. Head waiter Dexter Alexander, scheduled to work the dining room after the exhibition and then the Men's Canteen until closing, is covering two service stations.

Hiking along a golf cart path, Hillard discovers a water fountain in front of a cinder block maintenance structure. His olfactory notes three distinct triggers, the wisp of rotten eggs from the fountain's arc of sulphurated well water, the aroma of freshly cut grass enveloping the landscaping shed, and the scent of gasoline oozing from the tractors and mowers. He detects that same petroleum bouquet as he navigates his sports car across the knobby grass field.

Hillard drives a Triumph TR3. When he was twelve, Hillard saw his first English roadster and instantly fell in love. He spoke to his schoolmates about the four-speed manual transmission, the in-line four-cylinder engine, the freedom of the ragtop, and the maneuverability of the rack-and-pinion steering. He vowed that someday he would own one. Hillard bought his TR last October from a Brit who was transferring back to the home office in King's Lynn, Norfolk. Hillard's TR is blue, not British Racing Green—a small consolation for a dream fulfilled.

Hillard revises his schedule. He will feed his cat Buster, review his lease comments for a Monday meeting, set up a hitting schedule with tennis partner Steve Andres, and return to Northshore and visit the Men's Canteen. A mile beyond the gates of Northshore, a bevy of teenage girls in a topless Chevy Bel Air honk, wave, and blow Hillard kisses. Hillard owns a prominent chin, chiseled cheekbones, a high forehead, and deep eye sockets with lashes long enough to swat flies. His wavy brown locks and olive complexion have inspired more than one comment at his parents' shul about Sephardic blood. The young ladies in the honking car could not have known that Hillard is a classic ectomorph, tall, lean, and willowy.

First Kiss

According to Hillard Abraham's parents and grandmother, Hillard was an adorable infant with a striking black mane and delicate, well-defined features. The same three blood relatives swore out warrants against a childless nurse's aide who had snatched Hillard from a Bronx hospital nursery when he was two days old. The newborn, wrapped in a blanket and tucked into a brown paper grocery bag, was within ten feet of the main entrance when the attempted kidnapping was foiled by an observant emergency room resident on a midnight cigarette break. The case was referred to the district attorney, but the family later declined to press charges.

Another notable affirmation of Hillard's appeal occurred when he was twelve. In 1940, his mother took him to a hospital on Long Island for an experimental flu vaccine. The parents in that chaotic clinic had been children during the deadly flu pandemic of 1918. Incredibly, five hundred million people contracted the infection, and fifty million fell victim, including over half a million Americans. By comparison, the First World War claimed sixteen million victims. One calamity overlapping another, the Great War ended six months after the flu took hold. With radios and newspapers reporting that free public trials of this new groundbreaking vaccine would be available on a limited basis, a manic fever ensued. Bolstered by reports that the serum had been bench tested on US military personnel in 1938 and 1939, and the general public would not have access to the vaccine until 1945, parents worked every angle to enroll their children into the program. News of these limited public trails spread faster than that season's infection rate. Hillard's father, who had been earning thirty-two dollars a week, bought a vaccine ticket for twenty-five dollars from a synagogue elder, a well-connected downtown lawyer.

After a tense two-hour wait, an attendant led Hillard and his mother into a small exam room where he was told to jump up onto the paper lined exam table, roll up his sleeve, and wait for the nurse administering the injections. The attendant then left the room, leaving the door partially open. Hillard, fidgeting with anxiety, sat on the table. His mother relaxed on a chair in the corner, smoking a cigarette, speeding through the glossy photos in a home and garden magazine.

A dreamy eyed, freckled faced ten-year-old girl, bundled up against the harsh winter with scarf, hat, and gloves, strolled into the exam room and asked Hillard if she could kiss him. She had no intention of waiting for his response, and he was too shocked to have offered one. She kissed him gently on his left cheek, looked at his face for an instant, and skipped out of the room. His mother's laugh shattered the moment, a shrill alarm on a dark winter morning, an intrusive nudge from the plane of dreams. It wasn't the first time his mother had embarrassed him.

Before the inoculation nurse arrived, Hillard's mind exploded with wonder. His thoughts were private, secured from his mother's trespass. He had never been kissed by a girl who wasn't a relative. Her touch was soft and gentle. He could barely feel her lips. They were a little cool and a little wet. When she pressed against his left knee and closed in, he leaned forward, or she would not have been able to reach him. *Maybe that's why my mother laughed*, he thought. *Because she saw that I wanted the girl to kiss me. Would my friends' mothers have laughed like that? Why did the freckled girl kiss me? Would she have stayed longer if my mother wasn't here? If I turned my face, would she have kissed me on the lips?*

43

The daydream crashed as the dreaded vaccine nurse entered with a rectangular metal pan in her left hand. Inside the pan a white towel concealed the harpoon. The bandage dangling from her left sleeve caught Hillard's eye. The antiseptic cotton swipe, the puncture, and the sting are forgotten details. The image of the freckled girl lingers still.

Buster

Inspired by the Davis Cup teammates, Hillard Abraham longs for his first hitting session on Northshore's red clay. His blue sports car coasts along the driveway that connects the street to the parking lot. The TR3 rolls into the last slip on the left bank of parking stalls. The asphalt lot sits between the apartment building and a two-acre, wooded preserve—one of the last verdant patches in Forest Hills. After sharing an apartment with three male post-graduate students, Hillard executed his first real estate transaction as the sole guarantor when he signed a two-page lease for the corner apartment with a private terrace overlooking the woods. Applying the hand brake, Hillard looks to his right into the urban forest of American beech, northern red oak, and red maple. A natural oasis bravely weathering pressure from the development community, the preserve is a metropolitan jungle teeming with avian life, insects, and ground critters.

Hillard enters the building through the side entrance. Bypassing the elevator, he lopes up the three flights of stairs. Hillard finds Buster perched on top of the recliner in the living room, a strategic intersection for monitoring the human traffic entering the apartment and the bird and squirrel traffic in the tree canopy. After replenishing the feline's food and water, Hillard nestles into a cushioned chair on the terrace. His tools of trade, a black briefcase, a manila folder, and a red ink pen, are within his grasp. Buster joins him, settling into his chair on the opposite corner. They sit on their private terrace for hours, reading the wind, appraising the sunlight, and interpreting the night.

Buster adopted Hillard five months ago. Last November, driving home from an open-air spin on Montauk Highway, Hillard stopped at a gas station and received permission to pump his fuel. After squaring up with the gas jockey inside the garage, Hillard returned to his TR and discovered a young, robust orange tabby with no collar sitting on the passenger seat. The attendant had never seen the cat, Hillard had been the only customer at the station, and the animal was not leaving the car. Hillard presumed that the cat had officially retired from scavenging the potato and duck farms on eastern Long Island and now desired comfort and leisure. A hefty feline with ginger highlights ringing his coat and tail, Hillard asked the tabby his name. The response was received intuitively: Hillard's inner eye saw the name "Buster."

Evaluating the driver's every motion, Buster hunkered down in the recessed leg well of the passenger seat as they drove back to Forest Hills. When they arrived home, the feline jumped onto the narrow bench behind the seats while Hillard secured the roof. With a little coaxing, Buster followed Hillard to the door of the apartment building but would not enter. Buster allowed Hillard to carry him up the three flights to his new residence, a one-bedroom corner apartment on the third floor of a three-story building.

Hillard had no pets as a child, and Buster had never experienced confinement. Their eight hundred square foot cohabitation experiment began with an air of uncertainty. Initially, Buster hid under the bed, but by the third day, he declared possession of the right corner of the terrace. By the end of the first week, Buster hoisted his flag over the entire domain. Hillard employed building superintendent Ed to cut a six-inch arch into the base of the doors that connect the terrace with the living room and the bedroom. Ed also cut a third portal into the laundry closet door, granting Buster unlimited passage to the terrace and his privy. Buster fancies the warmth of the television frame but swats the rabbit ears, causing the antenna to be relocated to the bookcase. When Hillard is spinning his rhythm and blues tunes or playing pop hits on the living room radio, Buster retreats to the terrace or seeks refuge under the bed. The feline is unperturbed when the apartment is filled with symphonies or Christmas carols.

Buster adapted to residential life without losing his feral instincts. Hillard values Buster's inclination to hunt down the wasps and yellow jackets that occasionally invade the apartment. Hillard complimented Buster the first time he witnessed the moggie eat a yellow jacket. Buster earned higher praise when Hillard witnessed the feline leap from the couch, snare another assailant hovering above the coffee table, and land two feet beyond the launch pad. "You're a fierce creature, Buster. I suspect you have some Wampus cat in your bloodline."

Buster's roommate pays each of Ed's two children a dollar per week to play with Buster for thirty minutes every day after school or a dollar a day to tend to Buster if Hillard is traveling for business. One evening, Hillard found a note from the sibling cat sitters. They could not find Buster despite having searched the apartment. After dinner, Hillard observed Buster crawling out from under the couch. The beastie had torn a hole in the cloth underlining and established a secluded napping vault on the cross members of the wooden frame. A week later, Hillard learned that a bag of steamed shrimp constitutes fair game. The forensic evidence led the detective to another feline cave—a hole in the fabric underlining of the queen box springs. After dining on a semi-stale toasted bagel leaking peanut butter and jelly, Hillard tore out the compromised fabric under the bed, the couch, and the recliner. One week later, with the help of Ed and his industrial stapler, they installed heavy duty protective linings. The following month, the tabby purloined a grilled chicken breast from an unguarded dinner plate. Buster refused to turn evidence on his accomplice in the caper, the caller who hung up when Hillard answered the kitchen wall phone.

Last January, Hillard discovered Buster cowering under a terrace chair, immobilized by a red-tailed hawk's piercing screech. According to Hillard's handbook of bird biology, a hawk's talons can exert two hundred pounds of gripping force per square inch. Hillard calculated that his handgrip would be over eleven thousand pounds if men were constructed like hawks. One evening just after sunset, Buster exploded through the living room with no regard for his own safety. Seeking shelter beneath the box springs, the cat caromed off the bedroom door like a billiard ball off a side rail. Upon investigating the source of Buster's distress, Hillard heard a great horned owl hooting in courtship. The following day, a pair of binoculars accompanied the handbook on the terrace's cafe table.

As a child Hillard was fascinated by creatures endowed with the gift of flight. He took umbrage with people who misused the term, explaining that squirrels, fish, and even snakes don't fly. Leaping or gliding is not flying. Hillard studied avian migratory patterns. He marveled at their strength and endurance. He has never revealed to anyone that he has magical dreams about being able to fly. His reconnection to that otherworldly experience may occur within his first waking moments or several days later. Recollection notwithstanding, on the day following a flying dream, Hillard's humor is euphoric. Hillard has yet to fly in a plane; his business meetings and tennis tournaments are within driving distance and he seldom takes a vacation. Fulfilling his aspiration of flying to a distant destination resides somewhere down the road.

Men's Canteen

Hillard Abraham savors the splendor of twilight. The evening mist infiltrates the terrace as the cricket symphony orchestrates the sun's surrender. Lambent specks in the eastern sky wink and flicker. The forest trees cast a shadow that consumes the landscape. A lone lamppost at the end of the parking lot emits a feeble glow, a nimbus crown of soft light. A furry red tree bat whiffles through the lamp's halo, a flapping umbra upon the silhouette, a fluttering overshadow. Hillard's TR resides within that meager field of light. By day, a dwarf red maple shades the roadster from the afternoon sun.

Hillard Abraham returns to Northshore at ten forty-five as the last wave of dinner guests are heading for home. He enters the building through a side door. A weather-beaten *Men's Canteen* sign hovers above nailed to the oak lintel. A low wattage porch light, its globe cloudy with dried insects, oozes a faint vapor of illumination. Hillard crosses the threshold. The loose bottom hinge prevents the warped door from closing flush. He jiggles the door handle, and the bolt clicks into the strike plate.

Hillard travels the narrow corridor, and his six-foot frame nearly grazes the naked incandescent bulbs. Exposed water pipes, encased in whitewashed asbestos insulation, are secured to the ceiling above the light fixtures. The passageway terminates at the Men's Canteen. Hillard's right arm prevents the solid core maple door from closing behind him. On his right, the infamous mahogany bar, a crescent-shaped mountain range rising from the crust, dominates the landscape. Dexter Alexander nods hello as Hillard enters the dark, stuffy grotto.

The air in the canteen is thick and musty. A patina of smoke, alcohol, and bravado has impregnated every surface, impervious to mop and sponge. A gentleman with silver temples is perched upon a stool at the far end of the bar. Wrapped in a Harris Tweed blazer, this dignified fellow is impassive to Hillard's entrance. A large man in a wrinkled white shirt is anchored to a chair at one of the five cocktail tables. The back of his heavily starched shirt faces the bar. This lardaceous man has been swilling beer, and the low ceiling captures his stogie's fuggy vapors, augmenting the stale, inhalable air. The dark paneled walls are decorated with photos of Ted William, Joe Louis, and Sam Snead. Brass wall sconces leak a perimeter of muted yellow light while under-counter fluorescent tubes emit a bluish hue behind Dexter.

"I saw you on the veranda this afternoon. I'm Hillard."

Dexter towels off with a bar nap and shakes Hillard's hand. "I'm Dexter. Can I get you something?"

"I'll have a beer."

"Can or bottle?"

"Bottle, please." Dexter snaps the cap of a German brew and serves up a chilled glass stein inscribed with Northshore's Crest. Hillard delivers his rehearsed opening. "Dexter, I bet you know everyone at Northshore and everything that goes on."

"Sir, I would never..."

"Please, call me Hillard."

"Whatever I see or hear stays with me."

"But everyone needs to gossip a little, so who do you talk to?"

"My wife. She has to know everything anyway."

A voice from the far corner adds, "That is a woman's nature, lads. And we are well advised not to cross."

Hillard is intrigued by the amalgam of English dialects. He hoists his mug in the direction of the voice and proposes a toast, "To the nature of women!" The English gent elevates his highball two inches above the bar. Dexter, now marking the levels of the liquor and red wine bottles in the speed rack with a wax pencil, thinks this could be a long night.

"Dexter, please pour that fellow a drink and put it on my tab."

In an apologetic voice, the gentleman sidesteps the offer. "Please do not be offended. I must respectfully decline. On occasion I know my limits."

Hillard carries on. "Dexter, what is your best Scotch?"

Dexter reaches for a dusky amber bottle on the top shelf of the back bar. "I've never had Scotch, but this is our most expensive whisky." Dexter hands the bottle to Hillard, who studies the label.

"This is an outstanding whisky. I've never seen this Scotch in New York. I just read an article about the distiller. They rarely export. How did you get this?"

"It's been here for years. I heard a story that someone slipped it past customs. No one ever orders it. What's special about it?"

"Single malt, Isle of Islay."

"Been there!" offers the intriguing accent.

"When were you there?" Hillard asks.

"It's been twenty years. I embarked on a whisky pilgrimage to Scotland with two mates from Cambridge. In honor of Epicurus, we called the journey our 'stocious holiday.' The Good Lord must have had robust whisky on His menu when He made Islay. He insulated it with the Gulf Stream, endowed it with rich, brown water and salty peat, and planted the seed for distilling whisky into the minds of the Irish monks who inhabited the island. The peat that's used for drying and smoking the barley instills that deep, distinct tang. The peat is thousands of years old, and only a select few are allowed to harvest that precious commodity. You cannot discount the human element; those cunning Scottish alchemists live and breathe their whisky. I had been told the Scots are closefisted by nature, but that's not what I saw."

"They say the same rubbish about the Jews," Hillard adds. "But the members of my synagogue are filled with charity, generous to a fault. Although I imagine a Scottish Jew would be a tough banker to get a loan from. What is your name, sir?"

"My name is Marlowe. Do you lads know aboot the angels' share?"

"I do not," Hillard answers, shaking his head side-to-side.

"Me neither," Dexter replies.

"It's the whisky that's lost to evaporation. The angels in the Orkney Islands aren't as thirsty. Those elements are a bit harsh. But do not ask me to explain the science. I learned it from a noble publican who let us loiter after he closed his pub. That was my first lock-in. About three in the morning, rat-arsed drunk we were and double parked. The fog was rolling into the harbor, into the pub, and into the lads savoring the liquid splendor."

Dexter probes. "You were double parked in Scotland at three in the morning? Sounds worse than New York."

"No, lad. I had two drams lined up. Some villagers were triple parked. I'm better served when my tongue is tasting and not wagging. I'd be happy to join you for a wee dram of that golden elixir as long as the next one is on my tab."

"And maybe Dexter will join us," voices Hillard, who places the order without pause. "Three pours please, neat."

Closing time is now a secondary concern for Dexter. Imbibing with members is so unacceptable that it was never mentioned when Mr. Elliott hired him six months ago. "I really can't do this, Hillard. I could get fired," Dexter explains while setting up three thick-walled Old Fashioned tumblers.

"Understood. And I apologize. Pour three anyway. We'll drink them." Hillard dares not recant. As a youth he had read about the mystical powers dwelling in Scotland. He has no intention of invoking the wrath of a stillroom spirit, the anger of an ethereal white stag, or the vengeance of a Lowland water-kelpie. Dexter breaks the seal, twists out the cork cap, and pours three servings into the lowball setups. Dexter places two glasses in front of Hillard and one at the far end of the bar, trading out Mr. Marlowe's dry highball.

"Do you drink, Dexter?" Hillard asks.

"My cousin and I snuck some hooch in North Carolina when we were kids. Nowadays, I might have a beer at a picnic. But my wife doesn't like it, especially if her family is around."

"That's it!" Hillard proclaims, "It's his commanding officer. That's why he doesn't!"

Marlowe pipes in. "Lads, there is no better social lubricant. It is a rare and exquisite gift. The Sons of Scotland are a bit of a paradox: rugged people with gentle souls. And so, too, is their whisky. The joy that's aging in those oak barrels has a hardy edge with mellow notes. The Scots respect merit. They never took to aristocracy. But they were not immune from the tide of tyranny and deceit that swept through Glencoe and across the Highlands." Marlowe raises his tumbler and offers a toast, "May the good Lord grant perpetual abundance to the peat beds on Islay."

That sacrosanct moment of anticipation that precedes the savoring of a fine whisky is pierced by a succession of rasps and snores. In a subdued voice Hillard says, "Let's not wake him."

"He'll sleep through it. He falls asleep in that same chair every night," Dexter explains.

"The club lets him do that?" Hillard asks.

"He is the club. That's Mayor Brewster, club president."

Hillard sets down his untouched Scotch and checks on the mayor. The extinguished cigar is soldered by saliva to the mayor's lips. "He's okay," Hillard reports, returning to his barstool's leather seat cushion. "He's out like a light."

"I am not out like a light!" the rotund gent bellows as he lumbers out of his chair, snapping his black suspenders against his rumpled shirt as he re-orients.

"Mr. Mayor, we're about to enjoy some fine Scotch. We poured you a glass if you would like to join us," Hillard offers, gesturing to the unclaimed tumbler.

"What are you guys drinking?" the mayor asks. Dexter hands the bottle to Hillard, who passes it to the mayor. "Sure," says the mayor, who has only scanned the label and is uncertain of the payload. Bumping into tables, fumbling with his black framed eyeglasses, the mayor ambles up to his single malt. He places the bottle, his eyeglasses, and his saliva tipped cigar stub on the mahogany bar.

"Sir, Mr. Marlowe is from the UK. He's a whisky connoisseur. He is astonished that you have such a rare whisky in the canteen, and he's amazed that Dexter has never tasted Scotch but is familiar with the fermentation process."

Taking his cue from Hillard, Marlowe approaches the mayor, "Magnus Marlowe, London."

"Mayor Joe," as they shake hands.

I better keep my eye on these two characters, Dexter thinks.

Hillard rambles on. "I know a Manhattan restaurant owner who increased sales by teaching his staff how to push expensive cocktails. Do you think a program like that could work here?"

His curiosity whetted, Mayor Joe asks, "What's the margins on this stuff?"

"Well, sir, I've only been here a few weeks. I'd venture that a fifth costs you twenty dollars US," Marlowe responds.

"Dex, how much do you charge per pour?" Hillard asks, following the unrehearsed script.

"Three dollars, about twenty-five one ounce pours per bottle," Dexter replies, concealing his distaste for the direction of this screenplay.

The mayor performs a quick calculation. "About twenty-five percent pouring cost. Yeah, I see what you guys mean."

Hillard pounces. "Sir, would you be opposed to Dexter sampling this? Of course, on my account."

"I think it's a good idea, only if Dexter wants to."

Marlowe throws in his support. "Dexter, you should have a gargle. But it must be neat. Always order whisky neat. That's the only way you know you're getting an honest pour."

Dexter now has four concerns, closing time, drinking with members, what the mayor will remember, and explaining this to his wife, Becky. Dexter's pouring technique is classic. He holds the neck of the bottle one inch above the tumbler and pours a fourth serving.

"Listen to that music, lads," Marlowe quips. "That's a liquid symphony, Beethoven in a bottle."

Hillard continues. "Dex, swirl the Scotch. Let's see how the whisky runs down the sides of the glass." Everyone swirls. The blue white back light sparkles off the tawny spirit. "This is a heavy whisky. It isn't runny."

Marlowe adds, "Aye, this one has heavy legs."

Hillard dances on. "The agitation activates the aromas. Now, hold the glass about an inch from your nose and inhale slowly. It's okay to tilt the glass and stick your nose in. If it burns, you're too close. Can you smell the peat? What else do you smell?"

Dexter tilts his tumbler, flaring his nostrils as he sniffs the whisky. "Yeah! I do. I do smell the peat." Dexter inhales again. "I think I can smell orange peel. Is that possible?"

"So do I!" says the mayor. "I smell orange peel. Let me see that bottle, Dex." This time the mayor reads the label. Dexter is pleased that the mayor has called him Dex.

Hillard continues. "Now, let's repeat the sniff test, this time with your mouth open. Your sense of smell might identify different aromatics."

"Nah, all I'm smelling now is my cigar," the mayor reports.

Hillard keeps rolling. "Dex, just sip a little. Don't gulp. Let the whisky coat your mouth and tongue before hitting the back of your throat. When you swallow, you may feel a little heat down your gullet. My favorite part is the finish. Lighter ones just seem to fade out, while heavier ones might linger a bit."

Mr. Marlowe offers the opening toast. "Gentlemen, let us raise our libation vessels." The four glasses clink. "Sláinte!"

Mayor Joe follows, "Down the hatch!"

"L'chaim!" Hillard adds.

"Here's to the bravest sons of guns!" Dexter smacks his lips twice as the whisky glides over the receptors in his mouth. "Wow! Strong…tastes a little like an antiseptic, like iodine…very smoky…I can even taste the peat. I never tasted anything like that."

"Drink a little water, and the next one won't be so harsh," the mayor advises. Dexter is incredulous that the club president is promoting this.

Marlowe extends his right hand. "Dex, you are without doubt a natural Scotch man. Islay single malts are usually too husky for the faint hearted. The journey is sacred, Dex. The destination is sublime. I disagree with those who say writing a script is a solitary endeavor. The best scripts I've ever written were in the company of a bottle of Scotch. My first encounter with a peaty Scotch reminded me of an unwashed root vegetable. It had, shall we say, a distinct hint of soil."

"When I uncorked the bottle, it smelled like a fresh box of bandages," Dexter adds.

With Marlowe setting that table, Hillard steps up. "I bartered a deal when I was a waiter in the Catskills. I taught the bartender how to serve a tennis ball, and he taught me how to serve Scotch. We started out with cordial glasses, but when we got to the sniff test my Jewish nose didn't fit. So, we went to brandy snifters."

Dexter draws his second taste. "Less burn, and my mouth isn't as warm this time. I must be getting used to it. It's really smooth once you get past the peat. I can see why you'd write better with a little Scotch, Mr. Marlow. It feels like my brain went through a pencil sharpener."

"Finish it, Dex. Never waste good booze," the mayor decrees.

"Does that mean it's acceptable to waste bad whisky?" Marlowe asks.

"There is no such thing as bad whisky, Mr. Marlowe."

"Indeed," Marlowe responds.

The mayor drains another tumbler and clears his throat. "When I was ten my father was running for alderman. The night before the election he took me to a debate at the fire hall. They set up bottles of Scotch in a side room, and I could see that the men were laughing when they started drinking. So, I snuck into the Scotch room and chugged the unfinished glasses. I got so dizzy. When we were driving home, I had to hold it down. If I threw up my father would have known that I had been drinking. But when we got home, he missed the driveway, took out the mailbox, and parked on the lawn. That's when I knew he was drunker than I was."

After the next round, the mayor learns that Marlowe is a playwright and theatrical producer from London's West End and that Hillard is an attorney and a new member. Mayor Joe, who had slept through Marlowe's account of the Hebrides, asks about the fermentation process. Dexter mentions the indigenous peat and the conditions that influence the whisky. Hillard throws Marlowe a boyish smirk during Dexter's discourse.

Marlowe offers up another toast. "Lads, you haven't lived until you've had Scotch and oysters for breakfast and stayed pished all day."

The mayor offers Marlowe his hand, "I do like you, Mr. Marlowe. I'm having a swell time. I want you to come back, and we can have this group again."

"And if for some reason I shan't return, you shall find my ashes sprinkled across the Kingdom of the Gaels. The winds shall carry my mortal remains far and wide, from the Hebrides, down to Campbeltown, across the Highlands and through Speyside. I shall spend eternity celebrating the graceful pleasures of the finest whisky known to humanity."

"Mr. Marlowe, Scotland is about the size of South Carolina. Your heirs shall be a busy group," Hillard replies.

"Surely the RAF can squeeze my simple request into their flight schedule."

"To the RAF," Dexter announces. All tumblers chink.

The mayor, clumsy with whisky and slurring his speech, tells Dexter he's doing a swell job and might see a nice Christmas bonus. He asks Dexter to pour four more and charge his personal tab. They knock back that round, and another three or four follow. Squinting in the direction of the wall clock, the mayor hoists his glass. "Gentlemen, it's time for me to throw in the towel." Listing side-to-side, the mayor drifts toward the door.

"We can't let him drive. He's so tight, if we plucked him, he would twang. He's not even wearing his glasses," Hillard says as the maple door closes behind the mayor. "I'm going after him. Let's put him in a cab." Hillard starts for the door.

"He won't drive," Dexter explains. "He lives in that mansion across the street. His family used to own all of this. He walks home every night, and there's nobody on the roads now."

Hillard returns to his stool. "Dexter, I apologize. I hope I didn't create a problem."

"A problem? Hell, he invited all of us to do this again and promised me a Christmas tip. I've never seen him so relaxed. I thought he was going to have a heart attack when Mr. Marlowe told that joke about the monkey and the cue ball. I wasn't sure if he was laughing or choking. I just hope he remembers."

Dexter checks his watch. It is now just after midnight. Marlowe, thoroughly marinated, congratulates Hillard. "Well done, lad. You can chat your arse off with the best. You must have Irish blood. An Irish

Jew, now that's a rare breed. Let's have one more. We're only two shy of hearing the pipes. I hope you lads are enjoying this as much as I am!"

"I am, but I really don't want my wife to worry," Dexter says as his semi-steady hand refreshes three tumblers on Mr. Marlowe's tab.

"Let's just call her," responds the well-fried Hillard before soaking up Dexter's pour.

"She's sleeping," Dexter replies. "We're going to church in the morning. I promised Becky we'd make the ten o'clock service."

"We shouldn't have kept you out this late, Dexter. Let's go home," Hillard says. After Dexter explains that he and Becky share a car, they negotiate the solution. They will pile into a taxi. Hillard will grab an early morning cab back to Northshore to get his TR, and then pick up Dexter at eight-thirty. Hillard will then drive Dexter back to Northshore to get his car.

Walking to the front entrance to wait for the taxi, Marlowe produces an assortment of glasses and the remnants of a nearly spent fifth of blended Scotch. "Lads, we did say we'd have a wee swally for the road. We shall continue our dramming." Marlowe pours three equal portions, and they park on the carpeted steps under the canvas awning.

"I don't think Becky will be mad, but she's never seen me drunk. I reckon there's a first time for everything."

"You're a lucky man, Dex," Hillard comments.

"Indubitably," Marlowe adds. "And take that from a bloke who got locked out more than once for coming home reekin' drunk."

"I am blessed to have her. I was once going to marry a girl who wouldn't have been happy about this."

"What happened? Why didn't you marry her?" Hillard asks.

"Korea, then Inchon."

Marlowe, sitting two steps below Dexter and Hillard, stands and swivels. "You're lucky you made it back. My brother also got drafted. I lost him at Dunkirk."

"Sorry about your brother, Mr. Marlowe. Man, that's tough. I still wake up with the sweats. Sometimes in my sleep, I hear artillery." Dexter draws down his Scotch. "I guess I got drafted. I sure didn't sign up. Spent my twenty second birthday at Inchon Harbor, behind enemy lines. Long way from my family's tobacco farm."

"The girl didn't wait?" Marlowe asks.

"Bernice married my brother right after I shipped out."

"Sorry," Marlowe says.

"It worked out okay. I was putting the chill on me and Bernice anyway. Every day in Korea, I thanked Jesus I didn't marry Bernice. Coming home to nobody was better than coming home in a box to a widow. My brother has the farm now. I wasn't going back there. It makes me sick to think about all that. I was happier than a moonshiner with fresh mash to get away from them."

"You're an honorable man, Dex," Hillard says. "How did you end up here?"

"After discharge, I took a bus to New York. The boys in the 7th Infantry told me the trades were hiring. They were, but I couldn't prove I had experience. Back in Raleigh, they paid me cash. I didn't have a Social Security number then or a license, but I'd been driving a tractor since I was eight. A New York union boss told me they had too many members, but that wasn't it. I knew what it really was. He wouldn't even give me day work. Same dadgum story with other unions. I couldn't get in."

"You put it on the line in Korea, and you couldn't get work. Nice way to thank you." The conversation is again nudging up to that forbidden line, blacks and whites discussing race relations. Hillard pushes it across. "Are you the Jackie Robinson of Northshore?"

"I am."

"That's great," says Hillard. "You should be proud." Dexter mentions that Becky's employers, the Cabots, helped him get the job. "They got you the introduction, Dex. You got yourself the job."

The taxi arrives. The men finish their drinks, hide the glassware in the bushes, and head home, with Marlowe clutching the empty bottle. At two in the morning, the driver stops at a row of garden apartments. Dexter fumbles for his keys as his apartment door opens.

From the front seat, Marlowe declares, "Poor bastart, had a bevvy too many. He's getting grilled. Glad I'm not earwigging that one."

Hillard is the next drop. Hillard offered to cover the bar tab, and Marlowe agreed to pay the cab fare and reimburse the canteen for the pilfered fifth. The generous Londoner also slipped Dexter an enormous tip. Before exiting the taxi, Hillard confirms that the driver will pick him up at six o'clock. Hillard then bids Marlowe and the driver goodnight. With the aid of the handrail, he climbs the three flights to his apartment.

Despite arriving home in the wee hours and a taxi reservation looming, Hillard does not immediately turn in. His constitution requires an audit of the daily events. His motive for visiting the canteen is unnourished, but he will see Dexter again in a few hours. Hillard recalls his impression from the conversation just before the taxi arrived. Dexter is a certified war hero.

The exploits of the 1st Marine Division had been followed by millions. Teaming up with the 7th Infantry Division, the intrepid Marines conducted the first amphibious landings in Korea. That heroic maneuver became the lead-in to the Battle of Inchon, a major turning point that allowed the combined US and United Nations forces to gain control of Seoul.

Hillard surmises that Dexter learned how to navigate the obstacle course of strife and segregation that was everywhere—an undertow in some places, a tidal wave in others. Hillard recalls an editorial he had read about segregated army units in Korea despite President Truman's Executive Order to abolish discrimination in the armed forces.

In those final conscious moments before descending into slumber, when thoughts survive the absence of light and illuminate with insight, Hillard cannot unsee. A nation that needs to enact legislation so blacks and whites can die side-by-side in battle is a lacerated nation. Home of the brave? No question. Land of the free? Sometimes.

The Day After

Hillard Abraham's TR3 collides with morning pockets of ventilation, reviving his credentials. He arrives at Dexter Alexander's apartment at eight-twenty, ten minutes ahead of schedule. Hillard has accounted for securing the top and sealing the cab if Dexter is uneasy about riding in a drophead roadster. That simple procedure will cost them one minute. Hillard backs into a spot in front of Dexter's apartment, shuts the engine, and waits.

At eight-forty, Hillard approaches the apartment. The aroma of bacon wafts down the walkway. Hillard knocks once, hoping that Dexter will open the door. He would rather not deal with an irate wife, although her displeasure would be justified. A tall, pretty lady wearing a salmon-colored dress, hemmed at mid-calf, opens the door. She is the antithesis of irritated.

"Hillard, I'm Becky. Would you like a cup of coffee or some breakfast?" Immensely relieved, Hillard thanks Becky for the offer and starts stumbling with an apology. She tosses him a life preserver. "Dexter told me everything when he got home. It sounded to me like boys being boys. As long as we get to church on time, I have no concerns."

"Becky, if I had a decent voice, I would sing a number from my favorite musical about getting to a church on time." Playfully nudging her by her left elbow, he declares, "I'd rather drive with a pretty girl than with Dexter. Let's go."

Dexter turns the corner. "Hey, get your hands off my wife!"

Becky bolts the apartment door as the two men walk to the TR. Hillard repeats a comment from last evening. "You're a lucky man, Dex."

65

"I said it last night—I'm blessed. Becky gave me headache powders, a cup of coffee, and some dry toast as soon as I got out of bed." Attired in a dark suit and a charcoal fedora with red feathers, Hillard recommends removing the topper after Dexter supports the notion of an open-air ride.

"Dex, there's only one negative about my flip top. I can't wear a hat, so my hair gets messed up."

"I don't have to worry about my hair getting messed up." Lowering himself onto the passenger seat, Dexter reaches over the valley of the TR's V-top door and touches the pavement. "I reckon I've never been in such a low vehicle. If we were any lower, we'd be in a subway."

Spinning along a quiet two-lane country road, Hillard accelerates through a perfectly banked, sweeping left curve. A squirrel with a death wish darts from the woods on the driver's side. The nimble rack-and-pinion steering responds, and the TR veers right, onto the shoulder, out of the arc of the bend, then swerves back after avoiding the critter, resuming its track as if the interruption never occurred. "Man alive, Hill. This thing handles."

"It does, Dex. You've got to drive it sometime. Before we start drinking Scotch."

Hillard uncorks his motive for visiting the canteen. Their first order of business is women. The dialogue then slides into the rumors that the Dodgers and Giants will be moving to California. Their conversation then drifts back to women. The twenty-minute ride ends too soon. As he hoists himself up and out of the chariot, Dexter mentions that after church, he is scheduled to work the afternoon shift. "Are you playing tennis later?"

"Not today, Dex." Hillard reminds Dexter to retrieve the three tumblers that only a few hours ago Marlowe duffed into the shrubs, then he waits for Dexter's 1953 two-door DeSoto Firedome to turn over. Hillard flashes Dexter a thumbs up and then heads east to watch the waterfowl. An afternoon visit with his grandmother is also on his schedule.

Hillard leaves Oyster Cove later than expected. Walking through the parking lot of his grandmother's nursing home, he braces for the pervasive aroma of disinfectant that conceals the decrepit odors of age and frailty. Hillard reports to the reception station and learns that visiting hours have just ended. "I beseech thee, oh fair maiden. Please lower the gate and permit my trespass."

"Last Sunday you were a Texas Ranger, Hillard. What are you going to be next week?"

Hillard finds his grandmother in the dining room. The residents are sitting on sturdy, cushioned chairs on the window side of two long, rectangular cafeteria tables. The seating plan allows the staff unhampered access from the unoccupied side. Two wheelchair bound residents are parked at a small round table. When the staff is not serving the residents, the attendants stand near the wall at the back of the room. Hillard knows a few of the employees and takes time to chat. The conversations usually center on the pennant races or college football. After confirming that no supervisor is within earshot, an attendant known as June Bug, motions Hillard to approach. "Let me tell you what they did this morning."

"Tell me," Hillard says, extinguishing the grin.

"A couple of the old guys were arguing about their length. One guy said he needed a fourteen-inch catheter. Another said sixteen inches.

Another one said they had to order a special one from France. These guys are hilarious."

Hillard carries a chair to his grandmother's table. After kissing her forehead, he positions the chair across from her, on the near corner of the open side, having received permission from the staff to do so. "How's my Bubbe?"

"Feh!" she replies with a shrug of her shoulders.

"Are you feeling okay?"

"Eh!"

"How's dinner?"

"Crap!" jabbers the spunky man with wobbly false teeth, sitting two chairs downstream from Bubbe. Hillard notices dried food stains from earlier meals on the old fellow's faded white shirt. Hillard cloaks his smile and scans the room. Except for the vibrating choppers, the community is indifferent to his presence. Their powers of recognition wander from confused to lucid, then back to cloudy again: their memories have been pruned by time, their minds befogged by age.

As the workers clear the dishes, attentiveness rises. Now fortified, some residents acknowledge Hillard, and a few appear to remember him.

"Why didn't you bring my curlers?" asks a lady in a blue house dress, sitting at the far end of Bubbe's table.

"I apologize. I'll try to remember next time I visit."

"When is Frieda coming back?" asks the dowager sitting in the middle of the far table and twirling her six-carat, costume diamond ring.

"I'll ask them at the front desk."

"What did my doctor say?" asks the doddering old gent with a pronounced Parkinson's shake, sitting next to the diamond ring.

"If I see him, I'll ask him."

The chatter increases. The social director enters the dining room. After reminding the residents of her name and title, she informs her audience that Bingo will be tonight's after-dinner entertainment. A well-groomed resident, sitting between Bubbe and the man with the tottering teeth, lowers her book. She places the novel next to her teacup and raises her hand. "Why is there no story time? We always have story time after Sunday dinner."

The director explains that the lady from the traveling library is running late. "So, let's play Bingo until she gets here, and when she does get here, she'll read us a story."

"Make it a dirty one!" yells the man with the reverberating dentures. The social director ignores the old man. With the help of an aid, she passes out the Bingo cards.

The blue house dress complains. "This is the same card I had last time. This one is bent. I want a new card."

"It's not the same card. You always say the same thing," the costume ring retorts.

"You don't know what you're talking about. And your diamond is fake, and Frieda is dead. I want a new card."

"Give her a new card. I want a dirty story," spouts the stained shirt. The tea sipper, Miss Ethel, offended by his ill manners, shakes her head.

A slight man wearing thick glasses, sitting at the far end of the second table, asks the social director if the doctor will let him drive. The rude man barks, "You're a blind bat. How you gonna drive? By braille?" The social director glares at the offender; Miss Ethel's face is inscribed with disgust. The traveling librarian arrives, and the staff collects the Bingo cards.

Through his chattering teeth, the old man expectorates, "My private part is dead!"

"Mr. Grossman! Please behave yourself," scolds the social director, glaring in his direction. Miss Ethel cringes.

A male attendant, a short fellow with a thick neck and muscular arms, responds to Mr. Grossman's outburst. "Is everything okay?"

"No! Everything will be okay tomorrow."

"Why tomorrow?" asks the attendant.

"Because tomorrow is the viewing."

Miss Ethel comments aloud, "He's so crass."

Mr. Grossman holds aloft his glass of water as if to propose a toast. He swishes his mouth with its contents, breaking the seal of his dentures. He then dribbles his upper set into his right hand and drops them into Miss Ethel's tea. Hillard and the male attendant exchange a glance, both tightening their facial muscles. The social director and the staff respond to the commotion.

"Let's go sit somewhere, Bubbe." Hillard escorts his grandmother to a quiet corner of the social room and guides her into a chair. Bubbe's letters of reference are her arthritic bones and swollen, bumpy fingers. Her résumé is the Romanian poverty of her youth and the one-bedroom tenement where she raised two sons and nursed her husband, a son of toil who lugged ice blocks with metal tongs for thirty years. After thanking her grandson for visiting, Bubbe asks him to persuade the doctor to allow her to have a glass of schnapps. Bubbe falls asleep. Before leaving, Hillard hands a check to a lady in the business office so Bubbe can purchase incidentals from the lobby shop.

The Red Maple

Hillard Abraham arrives home twenty minutes after leaving his grandmother's nursing home. In the waning hours of daylight, he notices paving equipment in a staging area next to the curb cut. He recalls a letter he received from the landlord two weeks ago, informing the residents of work scheduled for a Sunday afternoon. Rolling to the parking area, loose fragments of fresh asphalt ping against the inside of the TR's metal wheel wells. Passing the building and approaching the woods, his headlights illuminate the scope of work. The parking lot has been extended, and six new spots have been added.

Hillard parks in one of the three new slips on the left side-the last space, next to the woods. Walking from his locked car, he freezes upon his disquieting discovery. The pretty red maple is gone. The impotent light from the solitary streetlamp allows Hillard to examine the forensics of the tree's demise. The hewed stump sits almost flush with the grass, and the cut is smooth. The smolder of freshly cut timber lingers near the stump, merging with the fading scent of new asphalt. Sawdust and wood chips surround the stump in an irregular pattern. Hillard counts concentric rings to determine the tree's age, and then he recounts to confirm his findings. The tree was twenty-seven years old, the same age as Hillard.

Entering his apartment, Hillard hangs his fedora on its dedicated peg. This is not the time to chronicle and catalog the tennis exhibition, the men's canteen, and the red maple. It's getting late, his Monday work schedule is taxing, and the events of the weekend deserve thorough interpretation. Some quality rack time and a fresh perspective are in order.

Mount Flushmore

Hillard Abraham's fedoras reside on two wooden hat racks. He will not wear the same hat on consecutive days, and only three hats can be worn in the rain. Hillard never checks his hats. On a dinner date in Manhattan, a chocolate brown wool and rabbit blend went missing. The pilfered hat ruined the entire evening. Hillard has a hat for every occasion except when driving his drop top. All fedoras save one have an assigned hook. A quarantined black wool fedora lives out of sight, cloistered in a hat drum on his closet shelf. He has worn that fedora only once, the day his grandfather was lowered into the sod, destined to dust. Hillard is quite certain the next time that hat will be liberated from its hermitic isolation, he will be departing for an elder's sendoff. On this assumption, his logic shall fail him.

"Why do you wear a hat every day? Is it a religious thing?" a college classmate once asked him.

"A hat creates intellectual gravity," he replied.

"What does that mean?"

"A hat keeps my thoughts from escaping."

Hillard calls his fedoras city hats, a name he created in response to the Western style worn by a Tennessee born attorney who joined the firm a few months after Hillard. Once denigrated in court as a hillbilly by a slick Park Avenue attorney with a spongy case and a Ponzi disciple for a client, this polished Southern gentleman discreetly pursues an avocation that some might deem unorthodox for a legal practitioner. On the flip side, this articulate advocate is an aspiring musician, performing country and western numbers in Greenwich Village folk clubs on open-mic amateur nights, usually Thursday evenings.

After attending one of his performances, Hillard and two colleagues were invited by the singing litigator to join him at a nearby watering hole. Three fedoras and one wide-brimmed cowboy hat entered another establishment in the Village for sandwiches and a round or two. The youngest member of the four, a fellow born and raised in Manhattan, marveled at his colleague's guitar work. "Where did you learn to play like that? And how did you come up with those dog slobber lyrics?

"I'm self-taught. Growing up we listened to the Grand Ole Opry every Saturday night. That's how I learned guitar. When the family got together, my uncles and cousins taught me the mandolin and the banjo. I always wanted to learn the fiddle but never got the chance. I got my first guitar for Christmas when I was ten. I still have it."

"What about those dog lyrics? That was funny."

"I heard that story in Lenoir City, Tennessee. I was settling up with the owner of the local hardware store, and in walked a tiny lady swearing up a big storm. She was wearing a barn coat over her nightgown, the bottom of her nightgown was soaked with muddy water, and her work boots were tracking God knows what. She asked the clerk if he had a mop with a long handle so she could clean dog spit from the ceiling. Naturally, that grabbed my attention. How the heck do you get dog spit on a ceiling? The clerk couldn't resist, so he asked her about it. She said when her husband's two Great Danes stood on the kitchen table and shook their heads, their slobber went everywhere. I didn't laugh out loud, but inside I was bursting. So, driving back to our family chicken farm, I had this image of slobber getting on a ceiling fan, showering everyone with dog spit."

"I saw a Great Dane in Central Park," the young attorney added. "He looked like a small horse."

Hillard jumped in, "Some of your songs sounded more like rock-and-roll than country and western."

"Absolutely. I'm fascinated by the common roots of country, blues, and rock-and-roll." The musician's next utterance came down hard upon the ears of the three city born attorneys. "Gentlemen, I'll tell you why it's called country music. If this republic ever falls, the last vestige of America will be where country music lives."

"America will never fall," countered one of his three compatriots, the only one with veteran status. "Not after what we did in the war."

"I pray that you're right," responded the Tennessean. "But what if? American blood bailed out France, England, and everyone else from Hitler, Mussolini, and Hirohito. If it ever should happen here, who would come to rescue America?"

"There's no power on earth that can match us," replied the veteran. "The presidential oath specifically mentions a foreign or domestic threat. But after two world wars and fighting the communists in Korea, we do tend to forget how vulnerable we are from within."

"That does seem more likely," Hillard said. "Many scholars believe we're destined to emulate the Roman Empire."

"My Constitutional law professor spent half a lecture on the Tytler Cycle. Are you gents familiar with it?" the young attorney asked.

"Never heard of it," the veteran responded. "What is it?"

"A theory that a democratic republic is destined to collapse after two hundred years. That's when corrupt people realize they can siphon off the wealth through the voting process. My professor compared the corruption to a cancerous malignancy."

"I can understand corruption being the downfall of a republic, but this old Marine can't visualize that happening here in the US."

"Tytler was a Scot, wasn't he?" Hillard asked.

"Yes," answered the young man. "He published it in Edinburgh. Our professor made sure we understood the irony of the timeline. Tytler was spouting his theory in 1776."

"I thought he was from Scotland," Hillard remarked. "But if America falls from within, and our Constitution becomes nullified or subordinated, the independent minded states could preserve its principles by reorganizing into smaller entities. From the United States of America to the Untied States of America."

"That didn't work out so well for my Tennessee ancestor's last time. Preserving the Constitution was Lincoln's stated motivation, although he violated its precepts to achieve his victory. Did you ever wonder why Jefferson Davis and the other Confederate leaders were never tried for treason? I'll tell you why. It's because those states had the legal right to secede."

"Perhaps so," the Marine responded. "I hope to God we never see that day. But if we did fall from within, we would need a general to lead those independent states to freedom."

"I would think that a sitting president would uphold the oath of office and do everything in his power to prevent that day," Hillard said.

"But what if the president is part of the corruption?" the Tennessean asked.

"Then we would need a new national sculpture," Hillard responded. "Any president who facilitates the demise of the American republic needs to be memorialized on Mount Flushmore."

The former Marine nodded approvingly. "I revisit the Constitution with fresh eyes every few months. The brilliance in that document is astounding."

"One of the many things I love about tennis is the absence of subjectivity," Hillard added. "The ball is either in or out. In other sports, subjective calls might influence the outcome. And I'm not inclined to view our Constitution with a subjective eye. It says what it says."

Elizabeth Anne Aughrim

The conditions on this dry, overcast mid-April afternoon are ideal for Elizabeth Anne Aughrim. Temperatures are in the low sixties, there is no wind, and the ceiling is gray. Elizabeth Anne is backing her 1955 Ford Thunderbird out of her single-car garage. Her afternoon challenge match with the player ascending the tennis ladder is a welcomed rehearsal for holding off Regina Ellsworth and winning her third consecutive Northshore Club championship. A bonny lass with locks of horseback brown, Elizabeth Anne balances her existence between two orbiting moons: family law and tennis. Approaching thirty and single, she lives alone. Elizabeth Anne's fiancé Andy died in a plane crash three years ago.

Elizabeth Anne's law practice is flourishing. A champion for wives who have been subjugated by philandering husbands, Elizabeth Anne, will not accept a client who has violated the marriage vow. She is implacable and relentless in the courts of law and tennis. Professionally, she is an immovable negotiator, impermeable to a posture based on anything except the law and human decency. The foundation of her tennis game is conquest, a mirror image of her courtroom persona.

Elizabeth Anne's fighting spirit runs in her blood. Her father, a source of pain and humiliation, had been summoned away by addiction, drifting into alcohol binges. Her father disappeared for weeks at a time, leaving Elizabeth Anne and her mother with no money and no food. Elizabeth Anne will never forget the ridicule she and her mother had to tolerate or the taunting she suffered at school. She heard the vituperative whispers that her father was a drunk and she lived in the cabbage tenements with the other shanty Irish. Andy was the antithesis of her wastrel father. He was ambitious, religious, and considerate, embodying her perfect man.

Four months ago, after Midnight Mass on Christmas Eve, Elizabeth Anne insisted on driving her mother home. Mother presumed their destination was the same apartment where Elizabeth Anne had been raised. At three o'clock on Christmas morning, with tears of gratitude flowing, Mother opened the front door to her new home, an ocean bungalow on the Jersey shore. Mother lives peacefully in her two-bedroom cottage with Elizabeth Anne's adoring aunt.

On the tennis court Elizabeth Anne's roadmap has no detours. She probes for an opening and then exploits the exposed frailty. Once she uncovers a vulnerability, the finish line is drawn. She allows her opponents to author their obituaries. Elizabeth Anne subscribes to the Hopman Principle, the belief that snuffing out her opponent's hope during the formative games of the first set is essential.

Tennis discovered Elizabeth Anne when she was fourteen. A stellar student with a photographic memory, Elizabeth Anne offered to tutor another high school sophomore in the library after class. Although the faculty deemed this to be an unselfish act, Elizabeth Anne revealed her motive to no one. Sylvia ran with the well-dressed wealthy girls, and the French and science lessons were an insurance policy protecting Elizabeth Anne from the derisive gossip from the flock of girls for whom snobbery had been a qualification for membership.

Conversing after a session, Sylvia asked Elizabeth for help with a different subject. "How can I wiggle out of working the snack bar at the tennis academy? My father insists that I apply, but it will absolutely ruin my nails, and my boyfriend said it's beneath me." Upon learning that she could earn as much as five dollars in tips working nine to two on weekends, Elizabeth Anne offered to apply. The manager hired her on the spot. Her honesty struck a chord. Elizabeth Anne revealed that she needed the money.

By the end of her first day, Elizabeth Anne was running the snack counter on her own. Quickly absorbing responsibilities and fueled by the unlimited reservoir of caffeinated coffee and cola, the operation hummed under her sole direction. The pristine attire and the gracious civility of the tennis academy awakened a dormant desire. Elizabeth Anne had often fantasized about life among the upper sets, and now she was in their midst. On her second Sunday, after shutting down the snack bar and locking up the money till, Elizabeth Anne walked the perimeter of the courts. Only one match was underway, and she sat courtside to observe the action. Elizabeth Anne established a connection between the older gent's tennis game and his personality; he played with dominance. She deciphered the rules and fundamentals. Elizabeth Anne equated the four-point scoring system to the face of a clock, fifteen, thirty, forty-five, game. Six hours wins the set, and two sets win the day.

After the combatants shook hands at the net, the man approached, "You're Elizabeth Anne, yes?"

"I am, sir."

"Thank you for tutoring my daughter. I hear you're doing a good job in the snack bar. Do you play?"

"No, sir."

"Would you like to learn?"

"Yes."

"The only way you learn is by doing." He handed her his racket and gave her a quick tutorial, covering the grip, footwork, eye contact, and ball strike. He tossed balls from across the net. She made solid contact from both wings. He freed his spare racket from the vise grip of its wood press. Within minutes Elizabeth Anne could sustain a rally. After thirty minutes of hitting, he called her to the net. "You're a natural. I want you to play after work whenever you can. I also want you to read some tennis books I have at home. I'll tell Sylvia to bring them to you. I want you to keep that racket."

"Oh, sir, thank you. But I cannot accept this."

"Yes, you can, and you will. You're not taking it. It's a gift."

"Thank you so much."

Elizabeth Anne studied the books and played every weekend after work. She became the academy's collective protégé. Members enjoyed the opportunity to impart techniques and tidbits with one so eager to learn. Her game soared to a higher level when the club champion taught her serve and volley. Initially, Elizabeth Anne deployed that gambit as a late match ambush, but as her game matured, the tactic became a primary weapon. Her long, lean frame, elastic joints, and iron wrists are tailored for net play.

In September of Elizabeth Anne's senior year, Sylvia's father urged Elizabeth Anne to apply to his alma mater. He offered to write a letter of reference on her behalf. Unbeknown to Elizabeth Anne, Sylvia's father also phoned the dean of admissions. "This young lady is lifting herself up by her own bootstraps, and she will never forget where she came from. She will be an asset to our community." Elizabeth Anne was admitted without an interview and commuted from her mother's apartment for seven years, earning both her undergraduate and law degrees. After class, Elizabeth Anne developed an appreciation for fine clothing, selling designer threads in an upscale department store.

Today's tennis match is an opportunity for Elizabeth Anne to evince her foul mood. Yesterday she submitted reviews of two retired cases. Today, she is seething with outrage.

"I'd like to hear your synopses, Elizabeth Anne. Do you have a few moments?" the managing partner asked.

"I do, sir. In the first case, a businessman with four minor children leaves his family for his wife's married friend. The divorce agreement awarded the abandoned wife and children a paltry monthly sum, just enough to cover their two-bedroom apartment in Queens. The attorney who represented the deserted mother didn't understand the powerful ammunition garnered from a neighbor's deposition. The husband stealing adulteress had been a promiscuous teenager, trading sexual favors with adult men for gifts. When she was fifteen, she had a back alley scraping to terminate a pregnancy."

"What did counsel miss in the depo?"

"The neighbor used the Yiddish term for prostitute to describe the teenager. Counsel thought the word *kurveh* was describing the trollop's physical appearance. Truly wasted leverage."

"Tell me about the second case."

"A married physician with two minor children had been photographed leaving a motel room with his office manager during the physician's lunch break. His wife's private investigator exposed a second and deeper scandal. The philanderer also had a mistress. He even subsidized her nursing school tuition and bankrolled her down payment for a new house."

"In a nutshell, what are your prevailing impressions?" the managing partner asked.

"I'd say that these cases support my contention that there are various shades of despicable. These husbands aren't as loathsome as the Mayor of Casterbridge, but they are reprehensible."

"Wasn't he the reprobate who sold his wife and infant for a bottle of whisky?"

"Indeed. I suspected you had read Thomas Hardy. Both wives settled too early and for not enough money. Shock and pain were destroying them. With the average apartment renting for about sixty dollars a month, another ten or twenty dollars per week could have made a significant difference. The adulteress in the first case accused counsel of being inconsiderate. I wish I had been there. I would have shredded both of them."

"What would you have done differently?"

"I would have given her a dose of inconsideration. I would have planted the seed of discord, exposing the perfidy central to their relationship. Someday the man she stole from a family of four children will leave her for another woman skilled in the same licentious arts."

"What would that have accomplished? How would that have benefitted the best interest of our client?"

"More money, sir. The more I humiliate them, grind them into the stink of their actions, the larger the settlement."

"You are fierce, Elizabeth Anne. You have an advantage over male lawyers who might not get away with that. I don't want you to lose

83

your fire, but I'm sure you've heard at least one sermon about forgiveness being an element of grace. Although the Mayor of Casterbridge committed a heinous act, over time, he discovered a life of purpose. I'm looking forward to reading your complete report."

"Sir, my two passions, law and tennis, have much in common. In tennis, the violent ball strike is concealed within an atmosphere of etiquette and refinement. In the courtroom, I cloak my attacks beneath a curtain of polish and civility. Neither endeavor is a team effort. I'm on my own, isolated on an island, relying solely on my skills and my adaptability."

Before easing her car out into the street, Elizabeth Anne tunes the radio to her favorite program, an hour of Irish music broadcast every weekend. Her ever-present cordovan leather briefcase is on the passenger seat. A brass identification plate, secured at the base of the handle, displays her name, Elizabeth Anne Aughrim. The host announces the next song, a beguiling Irish folk ballad, "The Lass of Aughrim." Elizabeth Anne's ears perk up.

> *If you be the lass of Aughrim,*
> *As I take it you mean to be,*
> *Tell me the first token,*
> *That passed between you and me.*
> *Don't you remember that night on yon lean hill?*
> *When we both met together,*
> *Which I'm sorry now to tell.*
> *Oh the rain falls on my heavy locks,*
> *And the dew wets my skin.*
> *My babe lies cold within my arms,*
> *And none will let me in.*

Elizabeth Anne is numb. Such a cruel irony that she and that mournful folk song share the same name. Reliving the devastation of losing Andy, she escapes to an unlit corner of her living room. Minutes later, she subpoenas her slumbering drill sergeant, who berates her for being weak and orders her back into a state of equipoise.

The Irish streetfighter emerges. Elizabeth Anne drives to Northshore Racquet Club and unleashes an inexhaustible attack of controlled rage. She does not drop one game. The house pro remarks to his maintenance crew, "Elizabeth Anne played every point like she wanted to hit the cover off the ball. She could make it to the semis in the men's draw."

Origin of Hitters

The gossip born of Elizabeth Anne's commanding performance has faded with the light of day. The Northshore maintenance crew readies court one for the weekly showdown between Steve Andres and his hitting partner, Hillard Abraham. Former college teammates, Steve and Hillard are the incarnation of their coach's soon to be published theory, *Origin of Hitters*.

Steve was raised on the red clay of Frick Park in Pittsburgh's east end. When he was nine years old, a dad from the Greek Orthodox Church invited him to Frick for a Saturday morning tennis clinic. A month later, Steve's parents learned that the Gods of tennis had endowed their son with uncommon talent. Initially, Steve's dad was conflicted. Playing sport was an unrealistic endeavor for a young man ordained as a child to work in the family diner. With some convincing from Steve's mom and Uncle Gus, the family found a workable balance.

On Steve's fourteenth birthday, he learned that his father and uncle had traded a jukebox of polka and Perry Como records for one with singles by Elvis Presley and The Platters. The brothers had sold their Pittsburgh restaurant, and the family was moving to New York. After feeding droves of hungry steel workers, serving thousands of kielbasa and cabbage hoagies with a side of golden-brown pierogis, the family bought a twenty-four-hour diner on Fordham Road in the Bronx. Steve became a high school standout in Nassau County. In three years, he lost only one varsity match. Nick was astonished when his son received a college tennis scholarship.

Steve Andres has an unremitting aptitude for tolerating long rallies. Topspin is a primary piece. Forcing his opponent to take the ball at a higher apex is both an indicator of execution and a key to winning. His vulnerability is his backhand slice; he does not generate pace from that wing. The sports editor in his college newspaper wrote, "Steve Andres can play on any surface, including sand or sea." In the same article, an unidentified teammate said that the American Kennel Club should name a new breed after Steve, "The Greek Retriever."

Steve displays his college degree on the wall of his workplace in a Manhattan architectural firm. During his initial interview with the company president, Steve noticed a tennis trophy on the bookcase. "I didn't know you play tennis," Steve commented.

"I do. Even an old codger like me can get out there and still hit a ball. I couldn't help but notice from your application that you played varsity tennis. What have you taken from the sport that helps you in everyday life?"

"Tennis encapsulates the geometry of life. Tennis and architecture are blood relatives."

"Well said. I need that opening filled. Can you start next Monday?"

Raised in the Bronx, Hillard Abraham and his friends walked to elementary school as a group every morning, but on rainy days he walked to school alone. School officials prohibited students from carrying umbrellas into school. A few years back, a child nearly lost an eye when he collided on the stairs with a student armed with a metal tipped umbrella. On inclement mornings, the mothers in the district escorted their children under a caravan of umbrellas. Some mothers formed umbrella pools, taking turns ferrying three or four children. Hillard had learned not to deny his mother the therapeutic slumber required to bounce back from a late-night card game. On rainy mornings, his clothes usually dried by lunch.

87

After school, Hillard and his classmates played in the schoolyard. When they entered the third grade, the high school became the playground of choice. The adolescent boys ruled over the basketball courts but showed no interest in the two paved tennis courts. The girls in Hillard's group claimed the far court for jump rope and hopscotch, and the boys played tag and ran amuck on the other. Hillard and his best friend, Sammy Jefferson, told Sammy's dad about their new playground. Mr. Jefferson, a sanitation worker during the week and a coach at the YMCA on Saturdays, set them up with a collection of old rackets with friable strings and worn hand grips.

Coach Jeff taught Sammy and Hillard the game of tennis. The boys had been hitting on the playground for a year when Hillard's parents bought them new rackets and tennis balls as Christmas and Hanukkah gifts. When Sammy wasn't available, Hillard hit against a wall. The wall in the alley behind the movie theater was the best wall, but sometimes the older kids kicked him off so they could play Johnny-ride-the-pony. The wall behind the church rectory was his second choice until the watchman permanently chased him. The wall at the high school was fraught with risk. The older kids met there to smoke cigarettes. Hillard feared one of the bullies might take his racket.

When Sammy and Hillard were in the fifth grade, Coach Jefferson treated the boys to a tennis exhibition at the Cosmopolitan Tennis Club in Harlem. They were awestruck by Jimmie McDaniel, a giant of a man, six inches shy of seven feet. Jimmie was a champion in the American Tennis Association, the premier outlet for black tennis players. The boys were astounded by the bullet speed of Jimmie's first serve. Soon after that revelation, Hillard was appalled to learn that segregationists said that blacks and whites had to maintain separate tennis facilities. Walking to the subway station, Hillard and Sammy swore they would never allow anyone to tell them they couldn't be friends or play tennis together. Hillard knew his father would back him up.

Tennis had been the ward of the private country clubs, but the sport was slowly seeping into Coach Jeff's urban America. In junior high school, Sammy pursued track and field and became the school's fastest sprinter. As there was no budget funding for tennis in junior high, Hillard continued to compete in tournaments and free clinics. His parents now allowed him to travel alone by subway.

Sammy and Hillard attended different high schools. Sammy became a track star for an out-of-district high school. Hillard's family relocated to an apartment in Riverdale, on the east bank of the Hudson River. Riverdale had two distinct forms of habitation—apartment buildings and single-family Tudor homes with manicured lawns and slate roofs.

Hillard did not play high school tennis. The team was ruled by a clique of boys who passed judgment on classmates who lived in apartments or didn't rotate a splendid wardrobe. The uninspired coach relied on the opinions of this core to determine the roster. Hillard was deemed to be a threat to the hierarchy, and his request for a tryout was marginalized. Throughout high school Hillard ventured by rail and bus to out-of-town tournaments. The money he had earned working in a catering hall, supplemented by monetary gifts from his father, covered his expenses. When he survived to the later rounds, Hillard shared hotel rooms with other boys.

In Hillard's sophomore year of college, the tennis coach dismissed his typewritten request for a spot as a walk-on. The team was set, and Hillard had indicated in his abrupt meeting with the coach that he did not play high school tennis. During the previous summer, Hillard hoisted two Catskill hotel tournament trophies. His self-created training regimen now included calisthenics, jogging, and weightlifting.

Hillard had the temerity to crash the team's first day of practice. The coach had just finished lecturing his team about self-control. "Don't be like Caravaggio," he advised his players, referring to sixteenth century Italian artist Michelangelo Merisi da Caravaggio, believed to have murdered another man over a disputed tennis match. As Hillard approached, the coach barked that practice was closed and told him to leave. Hillard calmly explained that he could beat anyone on the roster. Foaming with anger, the coach ordered the varsity captain to make short shrift of the trespasser. Five games into the set, the coach halted play. The team's best player was about to lose a set to a walk-on at love. The coach offered Hillard number-three singles, "For now." Steve Andres, the projected number-four singles, became Hillard's hitting partner. Hillard learned from Steve that four players, including Steve, were on scholarship. Hillard vowed that he would never again be obstructed by an incompetent like that high school coach or those entitled boys.

Hillard's game has three fundamentals: a savage first serve, an explosive service return, and deep and precise groundstrokes. Accelerating velocity is only one element for success. Taking the ball on the rise and returning it on a linear path within a few inches of the net are other execution indicators. Hillard believes his extraordinary eyesight gives him a physiological advantage. He can see the ball's rotation the moment it leaves combatant strings. He believes he gains a full second covering drop shots. Hillard's ophthalmologist, a weekend hitter, agrees with the notion that only a few players have this acuity.

As a child, Hillard displayed the ability to simultaneously sustain three levels of perception: a predator's focus on the twenty square inch spinning rocket, the one thousand and fifty-three square feet of battlefield across the net, and his opponent's position. After playing four hard court tournament matches in a three-day span in mid-March, Hillard labored climbing the stairs to his apartment or lowering himself onto the seat of his TR. The solution was obvious: a ten-day healing respite and membership at a facility with soft courts.

Jakub Baranski

The temperatures on this Wednesday evening in late April have settled into the low fifties. Hillard Abraham and Steve Andres are hitting under the lights. Regina Ellsworth and Bridget Radcliff, snug and comfortable in cotton tennis sweaters, are relaxing on the veranda. An older gentleman in a blue windbreaker sits in the far corner of the veranda and tucks a Gregorian to Hebrew calendar back into his jacket pocket. The ladies hear a bang from the courts. "Sounds like a bazooka," Regina comments.

Chad Jensen Harrington bursts onto the veranda from the club room. He guides his duffel bag onto an empty chair and joins the ladies. Dexter Alexander approaches. "Would you ladies like another lemonade or maybe a cup of tea? Mr. Harrington, would you like to see a dinner menu?"

"Two teas and one lemonade."

"Yes, sir."

"Regina, please tell me I have the inside track with Veronica. Does she ever talk about me?"

"Chad, just be yourself. Veronica is her own woman."

Bridget adds, "You wouldn't be the first to ask for help with Veronica."

"What is she looking for? Bridget, you're close to her. Does she think she's Grace Kelly? Is she waiting for Prince Rainier?"

"If she wanted a prince, she could have one. You wouldn't believe who she has turned down. She's been chased by European royalty, American industrialists, and big shots from everywhere."

"What does she want? I'm not royalty or a Hollywood star. So, you're saying she doesn't want that?"

"That's not what Bridget is saying, Chad. Veronica rejected the men, not their title or position. All she wants is to be in love and be happy. Veronica has this ideal locked in her heart, and no one has opened that chamber. I'm not sure if she even knows the combination."

"I told Veronica I'll buy her anything, a house anywhere on the Island, whatever she wants. I..."

Regina intercedes, "Chad, keep doing what you're doing. You're surrounding her. Maybe you will unlock that chamber."

"Someday, she's going to realize she's running out of time. The guy who is close to her when that happens is going to be her husband, and that's going to be me."

Dexter returns to the veranda with a tray of beverages. He flips a wall switch, and the lampposts along the slate pathway down to the tennis courts glow with illumination. While transferring the tray to the tubular stand, Dexter notices Hillard firing an ace. "Did not know anyone here could serve like that," Chad announces. "I just found my doubles partner."

Chad grabs his bag and bounces down the steps to the courts. Bridget follows while Regina sips her tea. With his service motion underway, Hillard's concentration is broken. "Excuse me." Hillard turns. His tennis whites are heavy with sweat and clay dust.

"Is something wrong?" Hillard asks, walking toward Chad.

"Herald, I need a partner for men's doubles. You've got a hell of a serve. Are you interested in winning a championship?"

Bridget closes in as Hillard retrieves a ball at the base of the knee-high fence. Bridget whispers into Chad's right ear, "*Hillard*, not Herald. His name is Hillard."

"What about it, Hillard?"

"Hillard, I think you and Chad would make a wonderful team." Bridget's announcement travels across the net. Steve shakes his head in disbelief.

"I'm going to pass."

"You've got to accept. I insist. We'll win doubles, and I'll own both titles."

"I suggest you find another partner." Hillard strides back to the baseline.

"So, you won't be teaming up with anyone else?"

"It's not likely."

Bridget and Chad stroll up the steps toward the veranda and disappear into the club room. Hillard and Steve agree to knock off. After throwing on their gray sweatpants and sweatshirts, they walk off-court. "Steve, do you want a cup of coffee?"

"I'm good, thanks."

Hillard climbs the steps up to the veranda. The solitary man at the far end waves his left hand. His bony face transmits a half smile as his four fingers fan the universal sign to approach. Hillard pivots left and walks the length of the veranda. The fellow stands and extends his right hand. "I am Jakub Baranski."

"Hillard Abraham. It's nice to meet you."

"Please, have a seat. I vould like to talk to you."

Not wanting to disrespect an elder, a thin fellow with pale tones and moderate stature, Hillard accepts. "I will, thank you."

Gripping the chair arms, Jakub lowers himself onto the seat of his corner perch. Hillard places his racket, tennis bag, and towel on the floor and pulls out the chair on Jakub's right.

Dexter walks over. "Hill, can I get you something?"

"Please, Dex. Just some hot water with some lemon. Thank you."

Jakub breaks the silence. "Mr. Elliott tells me there is another Jew here, a man who plays tennis. So, I come to the tennis courts to find you. I can tell you are a Jew."

"I guess it's my curly hair," Hillard responds with a languid smile.

"And your dark color. I'm thinking the only two Jews here should know each other. But I don't mean to get into your business."

"I'm happy to know you, Jakub. I want to think of you as a man I know from Northshore, not just a Jewish man from Northshore."

"You did not see what I saw," Jakub replies with a subtle head shake.

"Where are you from?"

"Poland." Jakub's countenance shifts, and his gray eyes dim. Hillard grasps the veer. "All the tennis players come on Saturday and Sunday. But when I sit here, I don't see you. I don't vant to ask vhere I can find the other Jew. So, I sit here every day until I see you. I know vhy you play on Vednesday night. You don't have to be hide it."

"What are you talking about?"

"Afraid of them knowing. I know why you play when no one else is around."

"Jakub, I have no idea why you would think that."

"If you were in Europe, you would know." Jakub draws a mouthful of water and continues. "I don't have to hide it here in America." Jakub slips his left arm out of his jacket and unbuttons his shirt sleeve. "But I do hide this." He rolls up his sleeve and extends his arm across the table, revealing the Nazi serial number tattooed to the inside of his forearm. "We are the only Jews here. Don't ever show fear, even if they come for us again. They can't take anything else from me. I don't fear them anymore. All they could do now is kill me, and the memories would finally die. As long as I'm alive, those memories are alive. How do you forget Auschwitz and that stench?" Jakub's eyelids hold back the welling tears. "I watched those animals shoot my wife. He tried to rape her. She bit his face…he shot…" Jakub does not finish the sentence. He collects himself. "God bless her. At least she didn't have to live through that." Jakub's sorrow leaks through, and heartbreak invades his face. He removes his glasses and dries his eyes.

"Jakub, you are a man of great courage. People need to know what you and the others had to live through. But only if you want them to know.

You survived, you paid a price that no man should have to pay, and someday you'll be with your beloved wife again. Through all of your pain and anguish, your strength prevailed. You beat the most horrific conditions imaginable."

"You speak with knowing. You are wise for a young man."

"You're the one with wisdom. I read, so my insights are secondhand. If I had been in Europe with you, I wouldn't have had the books or the freedom to read. I've studied enough history to know the cycles of misery that humanity must endure are often the result of policies created by a reigning monarch, a dictator, or a government. Too often, those governments or monarchs are wicked degenerates unleashing evil and dysfunction upon innocent people. They truly abhor human happiness. The tyranny they create is a symptom of a cosmic disease. The tyranny is also a catalyst, motivating virtuous people to sacrifice everything they possess to defeat the evil. It's a perpetual war. Human ingenuity has a way of rising up to beat back the evil dysfunction. It takes great strength, discipline, and willpower to defeat evil."

"Yes, I had to be so strong. And I needed discipline I didn't know I had. My wife would not have survived. They would have broken her. But I know she is on high now, and so are the others. I do not allow myself to cry anymore." Again, Jakub removes his glasses and dries his eyes. "I never cried in the camp. Never!"

"Crying might help you."

"I've cried plenty. After the liberation, I cried for weeks. Then one day, I said, 'Enough!' So, I stopped."

Dexter approaches the table and serves Hillard his hot water. Dexter had heard details of Mr. Baranski's story. His eyes fall upon Mr.

Baranski's death camp tattoo. Dexter retreats to the server's station. Jakub unrolls and buttons his sleeve. He slips his arm back into the windbreaker. "I don't want to trouble that nice man. He didn't need to see this."

Hillard had seen that Nazi brand before. As a hotel waiter in the Catskills during summer break, he observed a daily ritual. After lunch, the survivors huddled together in small clusters under the cover of the unlogged sugar maples. For hours, they sat on lawn chairs and wept, mourning for their murdered parents, for their sisters and daughters, raped and beaten, for their sons, husbands, and brothers, tortured and starved. Every afternoon after lunch, united in sorrow, they relived the inconceivable misery with unlimited tears. A naked arm, a needle, genocide.

As a child, Hillard absorbed the anxiety that permeated the neighborhood and the fear that the Nazis would come to America and drag him and his parents out of their beds and send them to a death camp. The memory of those grieving survivors in the Catskills and the reverence for the millions of dispossessed souls revives Hillard's conviction that those Nazi demons, having slithered back into the crust, are awaiting the next fissure.

Jakub leans back into his chair as Dexter leaves the veranda for the club room. After a few moments, Jakub utters, "I am sorry, Hillard."

"You never have to apologize to me or anyone."

"Hillard, why did the German people believe Hitler's lies?"

"The Nazis used propaganda to foment widespread hatred. Enough hatred to justify genocide. When the brainwashing took root, logic and conscience also fell victim, imprisoned behind the deceptions.

Suggestion is a tool, but propaganda is a weapon. Propaganda can twist your mind, making you believe that men are women, that heaven is hell, and that Satan is God. Genocide is as old as humanity, and propaganda is a harbinger. Without propaganda, the masses cannot be deceived into supporting rampant violence and murder."

Hillard samples his rapidly cooling hot water. "Jakub, the Jewish people have endured a never-ending cycle of bondage, liberty, and then bondage again. The Jews have been persecuted, raped, deported, and systematically massacred. But we're still here."

"That is how it happened in Poland. First, they believed the lies, and then they became part of the mob. One day they were our friends and neighbors. The next day they beat us. They took everything we worked for and sent us to a place worse than hell, and we did nothing wrong. We hurt no one. Any Pole who talked about resisting was arrested and tortured. Only a few thousand were controlling millions." Clenching his right fist, he says, "If only we could have organized. But why us? Why do they hate us?"

"Some say it's because the Jews were accused of betraying Jesus, but Nebuchadnezzar deported the Jews six hundred years before Jesus. I suspect the hatred for the Jews is an ever-transforming weapon kept alive by propaganda. They once said we were hated because the Jews invented the concept of interest. Then they said we invented Communism. There are those who believe that the Jews were behind the Holodomor genocide that killed ten million Ukrainians. If Hank Greenberg had broken Babe Ruth's home run record in '38, they might have added that to the list."

"Who is Hank Greenberg?" Jakub asks.

"A baseball player."

"Really? A Jew?"

"Yes. A sportswriter in Detroit called him The Hammering Hebrew."

"I am not knowing that. So, while Jews were being murdered in Europe, a Jew was playing baseball in America?"

"Yes. But Jews in America weren't being told the truth about the death camps. That information was censored. Don't be too hard on Greenberg. He joined up in 1940. He walked away from baseball for five years of military service."

"How did this happen? Why did God allow Hitler?"

"Those are profoundly complex questions, but there might be some simple explanations. We know that the existence of evil is eternal. We also know that a narcissistic megalomaniac believes his own lies. How else do you explain the insanity of Hitler's military strategy? While still at war with England, he invaded Russia, and then he fell for the Allies' deception. He fortified the Calais coastline, not Normandy. Hitler was a satanic megalomanic. Photos of the Nazi leadership ooze depravity, enough evil to curdle water, to melt sand. But they'll be back. Their formula will change, their image will change, but their intent will not. Only God knows who they will seek to exterminate next and who will rise up to stop them. The brilliant science fiction writers of today believe that future satanic monsters will have weapons of genocide that we cannot fathom. I believe Georgetown University's Professor Quigley is correct when he said that the secret group who wants to run the world engineered the Holocaust to confiscate billions of dollars in precious art, gold, and diamonds from the Jews."

Jakub inhales Hillard's comments. He exhales resignation. "I've seen too much. I cannot disagree."

"How long have you been a member here?" Hillard asks.

"I came last year. My brother lives on Long Island. He married a Hungarian lady he met at the camp. They had a miracle, a daughter." There is a long pause, and Jakub flirts with another breakdown. "When I come to America, I worked in a fish cannery in Boston. I worked twelve, fifteen hours a day. I lived like a pauper in one room. I slept on a cot and ate canned fish for breakfast and dinner. But I saved my money and bought the business. I sold it to the big boys in '54. When I sold, I moved here."

"What do you do now?"

"I invest for my niece, play a little pinochle in a candy store in Brooklyn. I am liking sitting here, watching people play tennis. You are so fortunate to have a home and family, to be able to play tennis." Jakub pauses. He draws in a deep breath, and Hillard detects an asthmatic wheeze. "You are lucky to be free. But that's not true for everyone in America," his eyes rolling toward Dexter.

"I know," Hillard replies softly.

"And you? What do you do?"

"I'm an attorney, mostly real estate. I'm single. I work a lot and play a little tennis when I can."

"What do you like about tennis? Why not golf or fishing?"

"Tennis is the embodiment of my daily battles. Success is based on ability and the terminology speaks to ideals beyond the sport. Think about words like love, match, and service."

"Why here?"

"I like knowing that I can fit in where my parents said I don't belong. 'Stay with your own' is what I heard in my family and in the synagogue. But I don't want that. I love people, good people. I don't want restrictions. And no disrespect, but I play tennis during the off-hours when there are no limits on court time."

Jakub discounts Hillard's explanation. He survived Auschwitz as a mute in a vacuum, understanding intentions without provoking a reaction, viewing every moment within the perimeter of razor wire and armed sentries with peripheral vision. He will not rattle the brotherhood. He will suppress his belief that Hillard has a motive for playing on Wednesday nights. "Hillard, you have your life ahead of you, and you live in a free country. I had opportunities here in America that I wouldn't have had in Poland. Some people in America don't know how good they've got it."

"So true, Jakub. And in spite of everything you've been through, you still found a way to support yourself and help your family. That is a testament to who you are. I do understand why you wanted to meet me. Do you have a radio or television?"

"Tak...I mean yes. I have both."

"Do you ever wonder why there are so many Jewish comics?

"I watch Uncle Miltie."

"We seem to laugh at our own absurdity. Are we funny because of the persecution or in spite of it?"

Becky and Dexter

Dexter Alexander represses the abominable thought of Mr. Baranski witnessing the murder of his wife. Fighting his propensity to project himself into other lives and ponder life without his Becky, Dexter invokes a diversion. He replays the events that transformed his life.

For as long as Becky can remember, her father has been both the clergyman and caretaker for a Harlem house of worship. The nondescript apartment building that welcomes her father's congregation transmits no evidence of housing a religious institution within, except on Sunday. On the morning of the Sabbath, the streets of Pastor Malcolm Reed's Harlem are adorned with families dressed in their church finery, a pageant of handsome families walking to service. The drone of street traffic, a ceaseless workday bombardment of decibels and fumes, gives way to the chords of the church organ wafting down 127th Street.

Loving and charitable, Pastor Reed can be street tough when necessary. When the pious pastor learned of a break-in at the pharmacy on the corner of 127th and 7th Avenue, he worked a tip that led to the apartment of a family with two teenage sons. With the parents' permission, the pastor convinced the desperados to surrender the booty, apologize to the pharmacy owner, and submit to a year's hard labor. The boys agreed to clean the pharmacy's windows every Saturday afternoon and the church sanctuary after Sunday service. The pastor persuaded both sides to accept his brokered deal: cash reimbursement for the broken door lock and no police report.

There is no economy of gratitude in Pastor Reed's heart. His sermons to the children—he considers all of them his children—start and end with gratitude. The pastor instituted church-based mentoring programs. He arranged for a nurse to teach the girls first-aid, and he convinced baseball star Willie Mays to discuss the merits of hard work with the boys. After the lecture, Willie played stickball between the sewer caps on 127th Street.

If illness or injury upends a family's income, Pastor Reed's church arrives with meals and support. The pastor had become known outside of Harlem, developing more connections than the city water department. He wheedled and pressured those connections for help, cobbling together a group of physicians to care for children whose families could not afford medical or dental care.

The pastor initiated a Wednesday afternoon homework group with older students tutoring the younger ones, a fellowship group that convened on Wednesday after work, and choir practice on Tuesday and Thursday evenings. The pastor procured the pipe organ from a Murray Hill church relocating to larger quarters. In September 1953, while unlocking his sanctuary for Tuesday choir practice, Pastor Reed discovered water flowing from the ceiling. A cold-water pipe had burst and became a waterfall. Springing up the four-step staircase, the pastor discovered a puddle closing in on the organ's pedalboard. After moving the organ out of danger, securing trash cans to capture the water, and mobilizing a water brigade to rotate and empty the trash cans, Pastor Reed ran half a block to his apartment and called the landlord.

The pastor tends to all eight of the landlord's apartment buildings. Pastor Reed walks every floor of every building every day. He knows every resident and every family's business. Over the years, the pastor had repaired dozens of bathroom and kitchen leaks, but he had no experience repairing a water line concealed within a wall thirty feet above the finished floor. According to the landlord, the plumber would arrive within the hour.

After an honorable discharge, Dexter Alexander found a job as a dishwasher in a Manhattan restaurant, the Shadyside Oyster Bar & Grill. Although the owner had promised him a promotion to line cook after three months of solid effort, Dexter was stuck in the dish pit despite flawless attendance and excellent production. On a Saturday night in his fifth month, a law school student and his girlfriend bolted on a big ticket. Through the pick-up window, Dexter watched them scamper past the hostess station. Dexter took off in pursuit. The vision impaired old man inside the green shed newsstand pointed out their getaway route. Dexter caught and detained the fleeing criminals until the police arrived.

Under the threat of charges, the thieves agreed to an on-the-spot cash settlement. If their caper had been successful, the waiter, a fellow with a wife, two daughters, and two jobs, would have been responsible for the tab. The damage would have been the equivalent of two days of tips and waiter pay. Although initially disgusted that this future attorney and his pumpkin-faced girlfriend were not punished beyond financial restitution, Dexter later viewed this episode as a watershed event. Without those two, he might never have met Becky.

The following Monday, the owner promoted Dexter to line cook. On Tuesday, the water heater developed a leak. When the plumber responded early Wednesday morning, Dexter and the fry man were the only employees in the restaurant. The wrench toting plumber asked Dexter if he knew anyone willing to join up as an apprentice. Dexter had been earning a dollar an hour. The apprenticeship was paying a dollar and a quarter. Dexter grabbed the plumbing job and agreed to stay on as line cook Friday and Saturday evenings. Dexter's boardinghouse rent was eight dollars cash every Friday night by seven o'clock, or his possessions would be on the sidewalk by eight. The twenty-five cent pay hike put an extra ten dollars into Dexter's pocket, more than enough to cover his boardinghouse rent and his subway fare to Shadyside.

Working assiduously under the tutelage of a senior plumber, Dexter learned the trade. Their team became the company's top crew, the go-to for emergencies. Calling in from a pay phone after finishing a job, Dexter jotted down the address of their next call. Twenty minutes later, the two-man outfit arrived at the pastor's church to repair the water leak. The pastor had arranged for the city to turn off the main valve, and he borrowed a forty-foot aluminum ladder from the local firehouse. The senior plumber, fearful of heights, was unwilling to mount the ladder and perform the repair. Dexter climbed the ladder, chipped a hole in the plaster ceiling, replaced the ruptured elbow fitting, and then repaired the penetration with gypsum compound. He then helped roll up the water-soaked area rug and haul it to the alley behind the building. The grateful pastor identified Dexter as an ideal recruit. Dexter accepted the pastor's invitation to attend church fellowship.

Dexter had been intrigued by the construction of a house of worship within an apartment building. He had never heard of anything like it in North Carolina. The building that houses Pastor Reed's church no longer has a spacious lobby. A demising wall with a double set of doors in its midsection had been constructed across what had once been an oversized lobby, leaving a truncated vestibule on the elevator side and Pastor Reed's sanctuary on the other. To create this Harlem cathedral, the apartments on the first and second floors had to be demolished. The construction supervisor granted two bathrooms a pardon. The floors of the third-story apartments became the chapel ceiling. The windows that once allowed light and air to circulate through the second-story apartments were permanently locked and painted the same pale-yellow shade as the sanctuary walls.

On a cool Wednesday in October 1953, Pastor Reed's daughter, Becky, had been given the afternoon off by her employer, the matriarch of the wealthy Cabot family. Becky's mother had tripped on a roller skate that had been left in the hallway landing, and Mrs. Reed had been laid up with a twisted ankle and two bruised kneecaps. After visiting with her mother, Becky dropped in on her father before returning home to her studio apartment in Queens. She discreetly asked her father about the handsome new member of the fellowship group. After introducing Dexter to Becky, the calculated pastor urged his daughter to return to Queens. He said that a twenty-three-year-old single female shouldn't be traveling alone after eight o'clock. Dexter insisted upon escorting her, and he even paid her fifteen-cent subway fare to Penn Station and her thirty-cent train fare to Queens.

In the half-full subway car, they quietly sat together. Becky gently elbowed Dexter in the ribs to call his attention to a group of five standing passengers sharing one newspaper. "You guys done yet?" the owner of the evening edition asked before he flipped to the next page. After an hour of waiting on platforms and riding the rails, they arrived at Becky's station in Queens. They finally had an opportunity to relax. Dexter mentioned North Carolina and Korea. Becky told him about her Gullah-Geechee roots and growing up in Harlem as the daughter of a pastor. Dexter asked Becky if he could see her again. They agreed to meet on Sunday.

Dexter tempered his anticipation for three days. On Sunday, he traveled by subway and train to Becky's church. He sat alone in the last pew while Becky sang with the choir. Throughout the service, they exchanged smiles. Dexter was now allied with the weather. As rain fell from the heavens, Dexter fell for Becky.

After church service, Becky and Dexter walked to a nearby coffee shop and joked as they made their way through an obstacle course of water hazards. They dodged puddles, tiptoed across a sodden patch, navigated around a rising pool from a severed downspout, and sprinted from the spray of displaced street water from a passing sedan. Becky and Dexter shared a pot of coffee, a cheese Danish, and conversation. "What's the most interesting part of your two jobs?" Becky asked.

"I can tell who lives in the buildings without ever seeing them."

"How?" she asked, sipping her coffee.

"My nose tells me."

"Really? In the Book of Psalms, it says some have eyes but are unable to see. Some have noses but are unable to smell. I can't wait to hear this."

"We enter the buildings from the back. Usually, the building super meets us in the basement just to say hello, and then he leaves. When the job is done, I climb the back stairs up to the lobby. That's when I can tell who lives in the building by the vittles they're cooking."

"I've never heard this before, Dexter. Tell me more."

"If the smell is garlic and tomato gravy, the folks are Italian. The Irish families cook with cabbage. I wasn't sure what the Jews were cooking until we went to fix a leak at a deli. It's brisket. I grew up with collard greens, grits, and fried pork, so the Harlem one was easy, and it's different from the pork smell in Spanish Harlem. I couldn't figure out the German buildings in Yorktown. David, the guy I work with, said it's sausage and sauerkraut."

Placing her cup onto the saucer, Becky asked, "Have you tried any of those foods? Which one is your favorite?"

"I love Italian gravy. There's a pizza guy on Upper Broadway next to the subway. You can watch him toss the dough through the window. He sells a slice for ten cents. What's your favorite?"

"I like all of them. I've learned so much working for Mrs. Cabot. Sometimes she brings in food and extra cooks for their big parties. I take notes and rewrite the recipes onto index cards. Mrs. Cabot has every cookbook in the world. Who taught you how to cook?"

"I watched the cooks in the restaurant and picked it up. I didn't know how much I'd like to cook until I got to Shadyside. It's easy as long as I can read the tickets."

"You must be a natural."

"I think I am. I wonder if the folks in the cabbage buildings know about the Spanish Harlem foods. Do the brisket people know about collard greens and fried pork? Do you know what I mean?"

"I do. I never thought about that. Some people probably just stay with what they know. But New York has everything, so people must be trying different foods."

Dexter paid the forty-five-cent tab with two quarters, leaving a nickel tip. As they walked from the coffee shop, with sunlight sifting through the clouds, Becky recalled a comment a parishioner once said about her father. "A special man can tell a special story."

On the Sunday before Christmas, Dexter gave Becky a present he bought on layaway at the jewelry counter in a Manhattan department store. Becky promised she would wait until Christmas morning to unwrap her gift. Arriving home from Christmas Eve service at the pastor's church, Dexter discovered a red envelope under his door: a Christmas card from Becky. He placed the card on the bureau. He knew then that he needed more than a mental image of Becky's lovely face.

On his initial visit to Becky's church, Dexter parked in the first available seat. On the Sunday after Christmas, he sat in the aisle seat in the second pew. His heart pounded. Becky was wearing his locket. After church, they added a stop to their regular routine. They crossed the boulevard and entered the five-and-dime across the street from the coffee shop. They posed cheek-to-cheek in the photo booth. In the coffee shop, they chuckled at the strip of photos. The waitress found them a pair of scissors; they trimmed the best photo to the inside dimensions of Becky's locket. Dexter buried the second-best into his wallet, and Becky dropped the other two photos into her purse. With their coffee klatch date about to end, Becky asked Dexter a question she had wanted to ask him for weeks. "Dexter, where did you go to school?"

"All of the kids had to go to church school every day after work. Memaw's sister from Philadelphia was our teacher. Miss Dottie came to North Carolina after her husband died. She taught us to read and write, and on Sunday, we studied the Bible. The only time we didn't go was during tobacco auctions. But she came to the auctions with us and taught us the arithmetic. She said if we didn't learn our lessons, we wouldn't fit in. She made us do arithmetic problems at home and bring them back to school." Dexter pauses. "If you gave her a sassy mouth, you got a wood ruler to the back of your hand. She put the fear of God in us. She told us if we did wrong and went to prison, we'd get food that had been chewed by other people."

"Oh, what an awful thing to tell children."

"Yes, but she sure made us think twice about doing wrong. My brother Miles didn't believe her. He said she was lying, that we don't always get caught if we do wrong."

"Can I ask another question?"

"Ask me anything."

"How did your family get the farm?"

"We were sharecroppers for Mr. Isaac. He owned all ninety acres and the pond. But then his wife got sick. We saw her cough blood once when she came to give us some beans she canned. Mr. Isaac lost his heart after his wife died, and he passed a few weeks later. They had no children. We didn't know what to do. Miles told my cousin to fetch the sheriff. Miles made the decisions after Daddy died in a fire. Since Miles was older, Mama said it was his place to run everything."

"Was your father a fireman?"

"He was a moonshiner. He was passed out drunk when the shed went up. He had a mean streak, especially when he was drunk. Not a Christian thing to say, but I think Mama was relieved when he was gone."

"What happened after Mr. Isaac died?"

"His brother came up from South Carolina, and he told us to keep working the farm and to check on the house. He took the dogs and came back with the sheriff a year later with some paperwork. Miles told me to go hang leaf. I didn't know what happened until I got back from the drying barn.

"Mr. Isaac's brother sold us the farm for two thousand dollars. We got the farm, the tractor, the house, the two mules, even the old truck. I worked like the dickens to pay off the note. Miles was always away somewhere. He and Mama moved into Mr. Isaac's house, and Mama told me to stay in the cabin with my cousin. Whenever I tried to talk to Miles about the paperwork, he was as nervous as a getaway driver. When I left for Korea, I told my cousin I'm not coming back to the farm. I hope I never hear from Miles again. This is my life now."

Dexter courted Becky through the turn of the seasons. After Easter service in 1954, Dexter asked the pastor permission for Becky's hand. The pastor had anticipated Dexter's humble petition and supported the union. "Daughter, Dexter is an honorable man, a righteous man. A man with the courage to fight in Korea, a man brave enough to climb a ladder when he didn't have to. He is worth holding on to." Becky and Dexter were married in the pastor's church in October 1954.

The newlyweds moved into a one-bedroom apartment. Dexter secured a full-time job with a Queens plumbing and welding outfit. To the delight of Mrs. Cabot, Becky began to unveil her culinary talent, astounding the Cabot family with the skills she had learned from her grandmother. When Becky and Dexter were about to celebrate their first anniversary, Becky casually mentioned to Mrs. Cabot that Dexter preferred restaurant work. One week later, Dexter was meeting with Northshore GM Pat Elliott, who hired Dexter on the spot.

After pulling two shifts, Dexter arrives home at eleven-thirty. The apartment is empty because Becky is working a dinner party for Mrs. Cabot. At nine in the morning, he will pick her up at the Cabot home. Dexter is counting the hours. At ten o'clock, they will be sitting together on a church pew in Harlem for a mid-week wedding. He checks his Sunday suit and spit polishes his dress shoes. After washing up and brushing his teeth, he removes an envelope from the top drawer of his dresser and leans the photo booth snapshot on his side table against the alarm clock. Nine hours and counting.

Mixed Doubles

The weather forecast for this spring Saturday is the healing tonic for the water-soaked citizens of Long Island and the five boroughs. The rains of April are finally transitioning to the semiarid days of late spring. Northshore's annual mixed doubles tournament shall run as scheduled. Elizabeth Anne Aughrim disguises her umbrage with a façade of enthusiasm. She cannot simply support the philanthropy with a check and duck the humiliation that awaits her. The organizers, Mrs. Cabot, and Mrs. Radcliff would be offended if she does not participate.

Doubles is anathema to Elizabeth Ann; she detests the disgrace of losing to inferior players. Dr. Rick Goldenberg, a practicing surgeon, was Elizabeth Anne's partner in last year's fundraiser. Elizabeth Anne diagnosed Dr. Goldenberg as a classic case of small-man syndrome. He was a wretched partner. Their spineless opponents exploited his feeble groundstrokes, lame service, and fearful net play. During that embarrassing loss, Elizabeth Anne flirted with the amusing fantasy of drilling her partner in the back of the head with an errant first serve as he waited at the net for the point to begin. Despite the humiliation of that experience and the probability of another woeful partner, Elizabeth Anne is resigned to play. She shrouds her fatalism with manufactured avidity.

Elizabeth Anne's humor plummets when she learns that her partner is another physician, Dr. Sanford Rutherford. *Not again*, she thinks, despair now lurking. *I'd rather floss with barbed wire*. At first glance, she approves. He's tall and a bit older, a right hander with muscular forearms. During warm-ups, her attitude rises. He's got a sweeping forehand with good depth and uses an eastern grip on his one-handed backhand, the classic handshake for both power and topspin. Her attitude climbs another rung when he takes practice serves. Before the match begins, they strategize. Dr. Rutherford suggests they capitalize on Elizabeth Anne's dominant forehand. She'll serve first, and he'll defend the deuce court. She's impressed with his manner and confidence and relieved when they win the match and qualify for the second round.

Elizabeth Anne accepts Dr. Rutherford's invitation to join him on the veranda for refreshments. She notices that he wears no wedding band. She wonders, *how much alimony is he shelling out?* His story stuns her. His wife passed away five years ago. The magnifying glass then changes hands.

"I lost Andy in a plane crash. He was a chemical engineer. He was looking at a rubber tree plantation in South America. A bush pilot flew too low. They hit the trees. Andy had to move to Akron for a year, so we postponed our wedding. We were going to honeymoon in Ireland. I wanted him to meet Grandmother." Weepy eyed, Elizabeth Anne continues, "I went to Akron for Christmas, and he drove back to the Island for Easter. He died a week later. They never recovered his body. I still don't know what to do with my engagement ring. I thought Andy's parents could sell it to defray funeral costs. They were devastated. Andy's mom said, 'Andrew loved you so much. You should keep it.' It's in a bank vault."

Dr. Rutherford exhales before speaking. "I'm so sorry to hear that. How long ago did you lose him?"

"It's been three years." Elizabeth Anne's next question is unspoken, transmitted through her eyes.

"Cervical cancer. She was only thirty-one when she passed. Suzanne had been getting tired, so I sent her to a colleague. I expected something routine like a vitamin deficiency. By the time she was diagnosed, the tumors had already metastasized."

"I'm so sorry,"

"Thank you. I don't know what's worse, losing your loved one suddenly or watching her suffer one day at a time." His gaze is now fixed upon a distant point.

Elizabeth Anne brings him back. "Do you have children?"

"No. And to this day I don't know if that was a blessing or not," he answers, re-establishing the countenance. "I really wanted to be a dad, but her death would have been so crushing to a child."

"You're still young enough. You're very youthful for a man in his mid-thirties. Your life's not over."

"Neither is yours."

A middle-aged fellow clad in tennis whites and climbing the steps of the veranda in search of a cold drink passes their table. "Good hitting today, Sandy."

Dr. Rutherford winces. "I'm so sorry, Elizabeth Anne. Most people call me Sandy. Do you want to call me Sanford?

"No, it's okay…Sandy."

Elizabeth Anne and Sandy sense kinship. Both are solitary warriors buried beneath the sediment of memories, haunted by the empty rooms and the lifeless hangers that once draped clothing alive with scent. The endless gulf of time offered small increments of peace. In spite of the pain, and at times because of it, they continued to practice honorably within their professions, seeking justice and rendering care.

Sandy plucks two tickets from a zipped pocket in his tennis bag. "I know this might sound crazy, and you really don't know me. I wasn't planning on going. I had contemplated giving them away. Would you like to go tonight?"

"My goodness. This is the hottest show on Broadway." Elizabeth Anne reads the fine print. "Front -row orchestra! I'd love to go!"

"Didn't your mother warn you about strange men offering you front-row tickets?"

"She did. But I think I can trust you."

In their second and final match, Elizabeth Anne's focus is not on the outcome. She is not possessed by the urgency to win. She and Sandy are strategizing between points. They establish a hand signal for rushing net and a policy for handling shots in the vulnerable middle zone. They breeze to an easy win.

After their match, they firm up their rendezvous and head home. There are no expectations. Guarded enthusiasm counterbalances protective composure. When Elizabeth Anne's taxi arrives, Dr. Sandy is standing under the theater marquee. He opens her door and offers her his hand for an easy exit. After the show, Sandy instructs their cabbie to drive through Central Park before dropping them at the Rainbow Room.

May 1956
The Hamburger Recipe

A warm spell hovering over the Northeast is slowing the pace of people and machinery on this first Monday in May. The train between Queens and Manhattan is running eight minutes behind schedule. Hillard Abraham is going to be late for an eleven o'clock meeting at Cabot Development. At two minutes after the hour, Edgar Radcliff, the investment banker who will be financing the tristate expansion of the emerging chain of hamburger restaurants, expresses his irritation. "Why are you not using a Manhattan law firm? Why are we waiting for this attorney from Queens? We need a heavyweight, not someone who can't even show up on time."

Frank Biaggio, the franchisee responds. "I went to college with Hillard. He's a good attorney, and we trust him."

The man seated next to Frank Biaggio adds, "Frankie's father said to treat Hillard like family."

"And who would you be, sir?" Mr. Radcliff asks.

"I am Ralph Biaggio. I'm Frankie's cousin and the family's real estate agent."

Moments later, Cabot receptionist Rita escorts Hillard into the conference room. Hillard apologizes for running late. Proximity to the air conditioning vents has determined seating. Everyone is sitting on the window side of the conference room, under the registers embedded into the acoustic ceiling. Hillard makes the rounds. "Nice to meet you, sir," he says as Frankie introduces Hillard to the franchisor.

The Cabot team is gracious, Mr. Cabot's right hand is firm and sincere. "Haven't I seen you at Northshore?"

"Indeed, sir. I believe I've seen you there as well."

Mr. Radcliff offers Hillard an insubstantial handshake. "I doubt you've seen me at Northshore. I have to be dragged by my wife or my daughter, Bridget."

Hillard places his binder on the table across from the group and takes his seat. Mr. Radcliff grinds away. "You look like you just graduated college."

"I graduated law school four years ago. My youthful appearance is the result of a birth defect." An uncomfortable hush descends like the curtain of cool air. "When I was a child, I was diagnosed with terminal immaturity."

Mr. Radcliff opens the meeting. He emphasizes the need to move quickly, explaining that their main competitor invested a fortune into a national demographic study and is a year ahead of them. Mr. Radcliff announces his plan for a similar, three-state statistical report. "That study will cost about twenty thousand dollars." Mr. Radcliff then opens the meeting to comments.

Hillard serves first. He steps up to the baseline. "I think we should consider a slightly different approach. That twenty-thousand-dollar study will produce the same raw data and target the same intersections as our competitor's report. Let's just wait for them to make their moves and we'll go caddy corner or one block in either direction.

"When they figure out what we're doing, they'll be more secretive, and that's to be expected. I suggest we do not invest in that study and we adjust our projections accordingly. The markets will fatten over time, and we'll make our numbers as the locations mature. It just might take a little longer, but we'll get there, and we'll control great corner locations."

The silence is momentary. Frankie and the franchisor exchange head nods. Frankie grabs the floor. "So, let me reiterate. You're saying we should let them spend the dough and lead us to the best intersections. Either way, we'd be splitting the market with them, but they're the ones who invest in the study, not us. I like it!"

Hillard adds, "And their return on investment has to include recovery of the money they've got tied up in their study. I would like an unwritten gentlemen's agreement that this strategy is proprietary to Frankie and his family, and it stays in this room." Everyone nods in agreement.

"Ralphie, once you confirm their deals, your job is to find us a comparable location, either caddy corner or across the street. Our preference should always be the going-home side. You've got clout. Your client is a cash buyer. If that's not enough ammunition, let me know. I can help you create leverage. When you've got the deal points worked out, this group will evaluate the merits and give you a thumbs up or thumbs down."

The meeting ends forty minutes ahead of schedule, and the energy level is soaring. Frankie approaches his attorney. "Hill, you gotta come over and see the older one toss the pigskin. The kid's got a hell of an arm. Then Annette wants you to stay for her seven-layer lasagna."

"I'd love to, Frankie. How old is Tony now?"

"He's seven, Angelo is five, and Denise is two. The boys adore her. Denise is our princess. You'll come over, okay?"

"Absolutely."

Street Music

Hillard Abraham tucks his Biaggio family folder into his black leather binder as he enters the Chrysler Building's elevator. The car transports him fifty-eight stories in twenty-nine seconds. "A vertical time machine," he says to the elevator operator. Before descending the stairs to the subway that will whisk him to Penn Station for his train home, a handwritten window sign advertising a new single by an acapella rhythm and blues group draws Hillard into a record shop.

Hillard buys three seven-inch 45 RPM records, chats with the young clerks, and then hustles down the stairs to the subway. Passing through the turnstile, threading his way through the crowd, he narrowly beats the closing doors of the crammed subway car. Clutching the hand strap, Hillard recalls the first time he heard this acapella symphony.

In July 1952, just after graduating from law school and passing the bar, Hillard was assigned his first case, representing a Bronx butcher shop. On his initial fact-finding mission, Hillard observed street-level food markets beneath mid-rise apartment buildings lining both sides of Arthur Avenue. Several food merchants advertised their wares outside. Hillard noted pyramids of fruits and vegetables, stacks of tubers, and even fresh shellfish on beds of crushed ice displayed on homemade wooden structures jutting out onto the sidewalk.

Hillard's client controlled a prime location. The shop was situated in the base of a six-story apartment building and tucked between an appetizing store and a bakery. The butcher shop opened in 1946, and the owner's timing had been impeccable. In March 1943, the US government initiated meat and cheese rationing as part of the war effort. The days of rationing had finally been swept aside in August

1945. Five months later, the savvy butcher opened his doors to a population with a hefty appetite for fresh meat.

On the shop's sixth anniversary, the owner handed the keys to his two sons. The brothers made the thriving business even more solvent with an investment in a new meat grinding machine stationed on a butcher block table below a row of salami stalactites suspended from ceiling hooks. In 1952, the landlord sold the building to a real estate investor. The new landlord had been giving the brothers a case of heartburn. He rejected the brothers' offer to convert their verbal agreement to a five-year written lease and threatened them with eviction. Hillard sent the landlord a registered letter establishing leverage and referencing a case whose linchpin had been the argument of prescriptive rights. Hillard explained to the brothers that some people called it squatter's rights, but that term had no relevance in their case as there had been a spoken understanding and a record of timely rent payments. The letter accomplished the goal of initiating conversation. After three rounds of negotiations and a mild case of internal bleeding, the parties agreed to a long-term lease.

On the last Tuesday evening in July, just after six, Hillard left the shop with his copy of an executed lease. Having tracked sawdust from the butcher shop floor, Hillard stamped his feet on the cobblestone pavers to clear the soles of his Oxford penny loafers. Walking south with his sports jacket across his arm, Hillard waited for a diaper truck to clear the intersection. Turning left, he witnessed about fifteen teenagers gathered on the sidewalks of East Tremont Avenue, waiting for the local singing groups to perform. On this toasty July evening, the girls wore skirts, light colored-tops, bobby socks, and saddle shoes. The boys sported dungarees with rolled cuffs, white T-shirts, and sneakers. A group of older boys burned cigarettes in a narrow vennel between buildings. The concrete alley was littered with crushed butts and spent matches.

The all-boy groups performed in the vestibules and doorways that offered the best acoustics, with tile and glass being the materials of choice. When the shop owners closed for the night, their storefronts became available on a first-come basis. This acapella street opus, an ensemble of individual parts merging progressively into a unified harmony, captivated Hillard. Each group performed one song. The teens ran from group to group and danced in place to the pronounced beat. A mounted policeman occasionally whistled at the teens. His disciplined steed appeared unfazed by the ruckus or the street traffic. A horse-drawn pushcart with baskets of apples, pans of marshmallows, and caldrons of liquefied jelly and melted caramel operated on the street corner three blocks east of the Bronx horse soldier. Several lads ran home to get money. Hillard was fascinated by their ability to catch coins pitched from windows three and four stories above the street.

The music that Hillard heard that day was a revelation as an art form and a glimpse into New York's evolving social structure. This new sound, incubating in their collective gut, had an obvious purpose—an artistic device for wooing girls. Stifled and captive at home, the teens congregated on the streets to seek out the swirling acapella harmonies, music as sweet as buttercream frosting.

The admirers had been a reflection of each group's racial composition. Of the two integrated groups, one group attracted only a few teens. That group was forgettable; they couldn't hold an audience. The other integrated group, with flawless vocals and smooth choreography, drew all the teens. White and black kids, side-by-side, bopped to the music. *I can't be the only person noticing this*, Hillard recalls thinking that evening.

After dinner, Hillard dials Frankie at home. Frankie cuts him off in mid-sentence. "Hold it, please." Cupping the phone, Frankie yells, "I told you guys no football in the house! Don't make me come up there!"

The conversation resumes. Hillard asks, "Should we expect any objections from Mr. Radcliff?"

"I think he has some old ideas on things. He made some stupid comments before you got there, but I knew he just needed to meet you."

"Thank you. We just lost a client who said a legal firm with Jewish lawyers might have communist sympathies. It's been three years since the Rosenbergs were executed. They won't be remembered as traitors. They'll be remembered as Jews who were traitors. It was obvious that Mr. Radcliff had preconceived notions about me. I don't know if it's because I'm a Jew or if it's something else."

"We're dealing with that right now. A lot of people are still suffering in Europe, and they're blaming the Italians. They're lumping all Italians in with Mussolini's Black Shirts. And it's not so easy to fix from here in New York."

"Frankie, nothing will bring Europe back faster than Capitalism and free markets. That's how people lift themselves out of poverty. Capitalism creates wealth, Communism destroys wealth and crushes the human spirit. Do you remember how our philosophy professor ripped Communism apart? He was right. When emotion replaces logic, it's easy to sell an unobtainable utopian fantasy. That's how Communism sells the pipe dream."

"I knew I shouldn't have missed that lecture. The one day I missed that class, he covered Communism."

"One day?! You never made it to his eight o'clock class."

"Not true. I made it to his lecture on Spinoza and metaphysics. God, I needed a lot of coffee for that one."

"You also made his lecture on Darwinism. I remember that because you needed my notes from his lecture the week before when he covered the stoics. You had a great line. You said that since the stoics denied themselves pleasure, Seneca the Younger may not have been the legitimate son of Seneca the Elder."

"Yeah, I remember that. I also remember that Darwin mentioned a Creator in *Origin of Species*."

"You're right. I forgot that. He gave credit to a Creator for initiating the process. If the Communists can edit that out, they will. If they could burn the American Dream at the stake, they would. What are you dealing with in Europe?"

"Pop had to hire two attorneys to help our cousins get their vineyard back in Savoie, France. It's just over the border from Turin. Even though they have a valid deed, this moron French judge denied them what was rightfully theirs. The judge had the audacity to claim that the deed had been issued by an authority that didn't have jurisdiction. That vineyard had been in the family for two hundred years; the deed was valid, and this piece of work told our cousins to take a hike! Pop had to hire a high falutin French firm to get justice. There are dumb bastards everywhere. I don't think Mr. Radcliff is going to be a problem. If he didn't change direction and come around, I wouldn't do business with him. I've got to ask you. How did you come up with that plan to follow those other hamburger guys?"

"By watching a nesting pair of bald eagles up in the Hudson Valley. When the eaglets chirped for food, the parents took turns bringing home dinner. Mom and Dad knew where the fish were by following the ospreys." The call ends with the same enthusiasm that electrified the meeting nine hours before. Hillard spins his new vinyl as Buster escapes to the terrace.

The Torch

The savage heat expected in August catches the express train, and there is little relief from the blistering temperatures of early May. Dress shops are introducing their summer lines sooner than planned. Elizabeth Anne Aughrim, sporting her tropical weather attire a month earlier than last year, responds to her intercom. "Call on line three. It's Sylvia, your friend from college. Should I take a message?"

"No, no. I'll talk to her." The call rings through, "Syl! How are you?"

"We're aces, EA. No complaints. Have you seen the morning paper?" There is a long pause. "Andy's dad passed away. It's in today's obits."

"Thank you, Syl. Let's catch up soon." Elizabeth Anne reburies her deepest fear: word that Andy's remains have been recovered.

One day hence, Elizabeth Anne arrives at the funeral home. She does not sign the guest book. Elizabeth Anne inconspicuously lingers in the back of the long, narrow room as the final wave of friends and family pay their respects. Elizabeth Anne and the grieving widow embrace. "It's so good of you to come, Elizabeth Anne. I can't tell you how often I think about you."

"I think about you too, Millicent."

"Sit, please. Let's talk." Elizabeth Anne adjusts the chairs in the front row. Sitting with her back to the podium, she leaves Millicent a view of the open casket. "He was my strength when we lost Andy. I wouldn't have gotten through it without him."

"You would have, Millie. You're strong."

"The good Lord gave us the strength. We had each other. No one helped you, Elizabeth Anne. You did it on your own."

"I'm still dealing with it."

"You must get past it. I had the best years of my life with Andy's father, and you would have had those same best years with Andy. You can still have those years with someone else. You're too wonderful to be by yourself." With ample tears flowing, Elizabeth Anne and Millicent walk to the casket. "Some people say I should be upset that God called him so early. He was only sixty-one. I'm feeling just the opposite. I thank God that I had him for thirty-seven years. With Andy and now his father gone, I'll be all alone. I have no one."

Elizabeth Anne braves the rush hour mayhem and drives to Sandy's apartment building. The astute doorman, detecting the need for urgency and mindful of Dr. Rutherford's generous Christmas tip, coordinates with the medical group's after-hours answering service. The physician is paged at a dinner conference.

Dr. Rutherford calls the doorman from a lobby pay phone. "You have my permission to park Elizabeth Anne's car in one of the guest spots and to unlock my apartment for her."

"Sandy, how did you get here so fast?" Elizabeth Anne asks.

"Luck of the draw. The cabbie was a great wheelman." Elizabeth Anne delivers an overview of the past few hours. "Where's my pad? I'm writing you a prescription for a cocktail and a good dinner."

Sitting at a cozy table tucked into a quiet corner of a chophouse, Sandy orders two gin gimlets, offering to pay extra for freshly squeezed lime juice. He explains to the waiter that, while studying infectious diseases, he learned that Sir Thomas Gimlette created the cocktail as a tonic for preventing scurvy. Elizabeth Anne recounts the details of the day, from Sylvia's phone call to Millicent's remarks.

"You had a rough day, Elizabeth Anne."

"Thank you for being here for me."

"I want to be here for you. You cleared a hurdle today."

Drawing a deep sigh, Elizabeth Anne replies, "Yes, I guess I did."

"Everyone deals with grief differently. I punished myself after Suzanne passed. I couldn't heal until I separated the sorrow from the guilt. When I peeled away the guilt, I could deal with the heartache. That's when I started to put my life back together. Maybe seeing Andy's mom handling her loss will give you some distance."

The waiter delivers two gin gimlets infused with freshly squeezed lime juice. Tippling her cocktail, declaring the threat of scurvy vanquished, Elizabeth Anne surrenders her tense back to the soft, cushioned leather of the dining booth. "Millie told me to build a life with someone else. I think I've been carrying a torch with no flame. It's time for me to let go."

"Let go in one sense, but never let go in another. Andy will always live in your heart. You'll never forget him, and you never should. Someday we too shall be gone, and the people we've left behind will place us into that special place in their hearts."

"I'm so grateful I've got you."

"We've got each other."

"Sandy, I think I found the magic cure. A gimlet, a warm garlic roll, and your company."

"Let's get out of town this weekend," he suggests as they reclaim Elizabeth Anne's car keys from the doorman. "Doctor's orders. I want you to take it easy, no tennis, no work, let's just relax. I know this quaint oceanfront hotel near the lighthouse in Montauk. And the restaurant across the road serves the best shrimp scampi in New York. I'll pick you up at your house on Friday."

"Sounds wonderful. I love lighthouses. Let's climb the Montauk light and check out the view from the platform."

"I've got a great story for you," Sandy says. "A surgeon in our practice told me his daughter was conceived in that lighthouse."

"Oh, that's great. Does his daughter know?"

"She's too young. But her dad told me when she's older, they'll tell her."

"If she was my daughter, I'd name her Abigail, in honor of the spirit that haunts the tower."

"Didn't know that. How did she die?" Sandy asks.

"Legend has it she was the only survivor of a shipwreck, but she died later."

On Saturday morning, just after six, Sandy is awakened by the damp mist that has infiltrated their hotel suite. Brushing aside the flowing curtains, he peers out of the open window. Elizabeth Anne is on the beach, standing below the high tide line and above the water line. Barely discernable in her white swim robe, she fuses into the morning haze. The disembodied cries from the gulls merge with their forms as they pierce the shroud.

Sandy steps onto the pebbly sand at the top of the beach. He jogs alongside Elizabeth Anne's track, alerting her when his footing is on softer sand, about thirty paces behind her. "Good morning!"

Elizabeth Anne turns her head over her right shoulder, broadcasting a wry smile. "I shouldn't be talking to you, not after what you said at the airport."

"Okay. Must be that amnesia thing. Please, fill me in."

Elizabeth Anne steps out of her sandy footprints. She silences his next utterance with a kiss. "I dreamt we were in a London airport, running to catch a connecting flight to see Grandmother. You called her Judy. She hates that. Her name is Judith."

"I'm so sorry. I'll send her an apology." Sandy leads Elizabeth Anne by hand down the slope of the beach to the moist sand. He recites his message as his right index finger inscribes the grainy dispatch. "Dear Grandmother Judith, please accept my apology. Love, Sandy." A wave washes up within inches of his inscription. "I have it from a very reliable source that the beach postal system will deliver the message when a wave washes the beach clean."

"How will Grandmother receive it?"

"It will be transmitted to her in a dream. Remember, I have this from a highly placed authority."

"You are the best playmate, Sandy. How did I get so lucky?"

"Destiny, sweetheart. We both got lucky."

"Let's get some coffee and come back. Let's make sure the mailman has the letter."

Hospitality Manager

On an overcast Saturday morning in mid-May, Hillard Abraham and Ralph Biaggio are reviewing three land contracts on behalf of the Biaggio family hamburger franchise.

"I had my doubts about tracking someone else's deals. But it's been duck soup, Hillard. We've got three deals now and five more ready to pop."

"It's a breadcrumb trail, Ralphie. Let's surf this wave for as long as we can. Find two more, and Frankie can launch construction."

By telephone, Frankie approves the deals. Ralph leaves Hillard's office with three executed contracts. With the top down and the partially unzipped tonneau cover in place, Hillard motors out of the office lot. Twelve minutes later, he is parking at Bubbe's nursing home.

Hillard's affection for his Bubbe has no conditions, and she has never placed any demands or provisions upon her only grandchild. A seventh grade English assignment required Hillard to write an essay about the one person he could entrust with a secret. The irony of writing that two-page paper in privacy, tearing the transcript stamped with the letter A into shreds and covertly disposing of the evidence into the basement trash cans was not lost on Hillard. One year later, at a family function, Hillard quietly recited for Bubbe what he could remember of that essay. Bubbe then revealed her secret to Hillard. "She wouldn't nurse you. I told her you needed milk, not bottle. She said she wouldn't look nice in a dress, so she did only bottle."

Fifteen minutes after leaving the nursing home, Hillard parks at a coastal trailhead. As he scans the salt marshes and mudflats with his binoculars, the shorebirds trigger the buried impression of a recent flying dream. A few nights ago, Hillard had dreamt that he flew from his terrace to the woods, orbited the trees, and returned to the terrace. It didn't feel like flying, the way birds take to flight, winging through the firmament. He was a vapor with self-determination, an effervescence disobeying gravity.

Hillard arrives ten minutes early for his eleven-thirty meeting with Northshore GM Pat Elliott. Pat clocks in thirty minutes late. "I apologize. We're getting crushed in the kitchen. I didn't expect this large of a crowd for our second exhibition." Now isolated within the hurricane's tranquil eye, Pat unwinds. "At last week's board meeting, Mayor Joe nominated you to represent the club, and the board approved unanimously. I'm officially retaining you. We want to purchase the land that borders our southern property line."

"I'm honored, and I thank you. I'll mail you a representation letter Monday. Let's also get zoning approval now for future development."

"Great idea."

"Do you have time to discuss something else?" Hillard asks.

"Sure. What's on your mind?"

"Making your life easier. Or do you want to get into the land deal first?"

"Your comment about making my life easier has my interest."

"I have a recommendation. It wouldn't surprise me if you are putting in sixty hours a week. Assuming you have the budget, would you consider shifting operations to someone else? Dexter Alexander would be an ideal hospitality manager. I think Mayor Joe would support it. He knows Dexter and likes him."

"How do you know Mayor Joe likes Dexter?"

"I was in the canteen when they discussed a program for increasing alcohol sales. Mayor Joe was amazed that Dexter knew so much about whisky. I think the mayor was calling him Dex."

"Really? He called him Dex? I didn't know that."

"Hiring Dexter would give you some breathing room, and he might be a source for reliable help."

The parallel furrows across Pat's forehead deepen. "That does make a lot of sense. I'd have to get board approval for another salary, but we do have room in the budget." Pat grabs a stack of papers. "I've been working until eight o'clock two nights a week, and my kids are calling me Uncle Dad." Pat sits back in his chair as a round of applause from the tennis exhibition filters in. "I have to get back to the club room. Would you consider meeting me for dinner or a drink? I want to know what younger members think. I've been GM here for seven years, and I don't want to get stale. I don't know how I can repay you, but I'm sure over time, I can funnel more work into your practice."

"That's not necessary, Pat. I'm…" Hillard pauses for a thunderous round of cheers to fade, "…I'm not seeking compensation. I want to build relationships. I'd be happy to meet you for a round or two. Is it okay with you if neither one of us drives and we split the tab?"

"That's fine. Suggest a place and a time. I'll take a cab."

They agree to meet for dinner on Monday at seven o'clock. Pat leans across his desk toward Hillard, wiggling his left index finger for Hillard to approach. Pat speaks in a subdued voice. "Hillard, I promised my secretary Peggy I would mention to you that she's single." Hillard nods his head, shakes Pat's hand, and acknowledges Peggy by name as he leaves the office.

Abdication

"Your parents have not yet arrived, Miss Radcliff. Would you like me to show you to your table?"

Bridget Radcliff checks her watch and confirms that her parents are twelve minutes late for their one o'clock lunch date. "I'll wait here. Are you holding the table I requested?"

"Yes, ma'am. Mr. Elliott told us to seat your party at the table with the best view of court two." Without being entirely disrespectful to her parents, Bridget intends to follow the final match of Northshore's second tennis exhibition. At a quarter after, the hostess guides the family to their table.

"Did you notice how they were looking at my ring?" Mrs. Radcliff indiscreetly broadcasts in the general direction of her disengaged husband, who is trailing the plumed caravan through the club room.

"Mother, I'm sure those ladies also have nice jewelry."

"Perhaps, my dear."

Mother and daughter order tea. Mr. Radcliff orders a Bloody Mary with gin, not vodka.

"Edgar, next time, just ask for a Red Snapper."

"Whatever you say, daughter."

Mrs. Radcliff adjusts her diamond bracelet so that the stones are now fully visible. "Bridget, my darling, will Regina ever win that championship?"

"Not this year. The gap may be closing, but Elizabeth Anne is still the better player."

"What about the men?" Mrs. Radcliff asks.

"Depends if Hillard plays. I don't think he will, but if he does, nobody here can beat him."

"I know him," chimes her dad. "Jewish fellow. I met him at a Cabot deal. He accounted for himself very well. He's strictly a capitalist."

"Hey, Edgar. What if I brought him home?"

With a nod of his head and a shrug of his shoulder, Mr. Radcliff replies. "If that's what you want, I wouldn't stand in your way."

Mrs. Radcliff recoils. "What?!" she snarls. "Don't be ridiculous. We'll have none of that."

After lunch, Bridget struts over to the pro shop. She checks the rankings on the tennis ladder, posted on the back wall between the photos of reigning US National Champions Doris Hart and Tony Trabert. Regina Ellsworth is number one on the ladder, Elizabeth Anne Aughrim is unlisted. The house pro confirms the veracity of the standings. Elizabeth Anne removed her name from the ladder and the tournament.

Rupturing with excitement, Bridget bolts to Regina's practice session on court three. "Elizabeth Anne has scratched her name. It's all yours!"

"She pulled out? Why?"

"I don't know. The pro confirmed it. She's not injured. I read the sign-out sheet. She's coaching a college girl on court eight." Regina

137

meanders off the court, seeking a distraction while processing this earth tremor. She rustles through her tennis bag to look for nothing specific. Bridget then conveys an out-of-context message from Veronica. "Chad is taking everyone out on his boat for cocktails at sunset. Veronica wants us to meet at her house first." Regina confirms that she'll attend, then seeks out Elizabeth Anne.

Chatting with her student at a table under a courtside pavilion, Elizabeth Anne offers some final insight. "Jessie, in a tight match, the difference might come down to what I call pivot points. Those are like the rungs on a ladder. You need to pocket pivot points to win a match. I don't gauge an opponent's serve by speed. I use time and placement. How quickly can I react? And please dismiss the notion that winning the last point increases your chances of winning the next one. Even if that theory holds water, get it out of your mind. Visualize a blackboard. After every point erase it."

"That's what my father says. He played in the 1930s. He wore long pants, and his racket strings were so squishy."

"Players from yesteryear look awkward compared to us. Watch footage of Helen Jacobs or Anita Lizana and listen to the sounds. Today's players are stronger and faster. Equipment and apparel are also improving. Our rackets have more pop, and the sound of the thud is deeper, like a bass drum. Every aspect of the sport is evolving, including strategy."

"Where will it end?" Jessie asks.

"Human physicality and racket technology will keep improving, although at some point the sport will reach its evolutionary zenith."

Regina approaches. Her curiosity is discernable. With racket in hand and sunglasses in place, Jessie thanks Elizabeth Anne for the session and heads to the pro shop.

"Why did you pull out?"

"I'm rebalancing my priorities. I love the game, but now it will have a proportionate place. You've got a good man, Regina. You wouldn't have accepted his ring if you didn't love him. Are you putting aside your life with Skip in pursuit of something of lesser value? I hope I'm not overstepping."

Regina places her bag on the picnic table and sits on the bench across from Elizabeth Anne. A surfeit of emotion is coursing through Regina's blood, shock, glee, irritation, and disbelief.

Elizabeth Anne continues. "Every day I see people throwing away relationships that had been founded on love and trust. Where did it all go? Some people forget that a marriage is a precious, living organism. They take better care of their houseplants. Very few women would hold off a man like Skip. You're putting a condition on the relationship over which he has no control. Do you ever think about his perspective? You're assuming he'll just keep on waiting for you. But he's got limits. Everyone does. What if he changes his mind or meets someone else? What if he perceives his wait as an extension of your selfish motives and decides he doesn't want to be married to a selfish woman? I'm speaking to you the way I would with a client. And I know you're not going to like my summation. You owe Skip an apology for making him wait. Go get married."

Nordic Navigator

Cruising the choppy waters of Long Island Sound, cocktails at sunset is this evening's program for Chad Jensen Harrington's boating party. A few hours ago, Chad's guests politely applauded the long rallies and brilliant shots at Northshore's tennis exhibition. Now, those hands are clutching goblets of beer or flutes of champagne. At the helm of his family's twenty-eight-foot, twin-engine watercraft, Chad's beverage is soft. He never indulges when in command of a ship. A passing Coast Guard bucket acknowledges Chad with a twin horn blast. The skipper and first mate wave, and the party waves back.

The briny is a vital life force for Chad. He has been boating on the Sound since childhood. Acknowledged as one of the best sandbar pilots between City Island and Orient Point, Chad knows the currents and the tricky tides. He has memorized the channel markers, the marinas, and the fueling stations. Chad knows the secluded fishing coves and the oyster beds. In an act of heroic valor when he was sixteen, Chad dropped anchor and abandoned ship to rescue a damaged sailboat. He took command of the vessel and ran it aground before it could sink. During his first year of law school, Chad had contemplated maritime law. He yielded to his father's influence and agreed to concentrate on a more lucrative branch, corporate litigation. Today, he has invited two colleagues from his Wall Street firm to join the excursion.

The revelry usually associated with one of Chad's nautical outings is subdued this evening. Chad blames the squally sea and overcast skies. Bridget and Veronica believe Regina's detached, pensive humor is the curb. Seeking to elevate the mood, Bridget unveils a personal revelation to her two cohorts. "I just read an interview with a famous horse doctor in a polo magazine. He mentioned a surgical device I had never heard of. It's a perfect name for Mother. From now on I'm going to call her The Emasculator."

Regina musters a smile. Veronica's chuckle mutates into a cringe, then a question. "Something is bothering you, Regina. Is everything okay?"

"Elizabeth Anne got me thinking. Maybe she's right. Maybe I am being selfish."

Returning to the Harrington boat slip, Chad's two associates are standing with him at the wheel. "She's gorgeous, old man," one fellow comments. "Veronica is more than I even imagined. When's the wedding?"

"I'm working on it."

Regina Ellsworth is the first guest to depart. She jumps onto the dock moments after the boat is tied down. She deposits her bag onto the front seat of her car and walks to the public pay phone next to the marina's business office. Regina asks the operator to reverse the charges. "Skip, I have something important to say. I have to say it now. It can't wait."

Dr. Charles Wilson had received collect calls before, usually from patients with dental emergencies. Regina's urgent tone has transformed a quiet evening into a fret induced rodeo. Agony is lurking. Skip fears Regina is about to break their engagement. He prepares for a rehearsed assault. "What's wrong? How come you're not on Chad's boat?"

"The boat's not important." Regina inhales, and Skip exhales. "When we went out for dinner last week, you looked so sad when you left me. I know that no one will ever treat me as well as you do." Misery is creeping up Skip's spine into his shoulders, he cannot find his tongue. The chemical composition of the tears in his eyes carry the enzymes of sorrow. Regina pauses. "I've been selfish. I'm ready, Skip."

First Serve

Hillard Abraham leaves his law office at six forty-five. He peers into the shop windows on 71st Avenue and then glides through the Long Island Railroad overpass. He casts his eyes upon the citadel of American tennis, the West Side Tennis Club. Hillard holds this Forest Hills institution and its hallowed grass courts in high esteem. He lives, works, and occasionally plays within this urban pocket.

Hillard arrives at First Serve Tavern precisely at seven o'clock. In the 1870s, the tavern had been a gruff and raspy outpost. The ribald denizens of the second floor gave legend to tales of an opium brothel with secret closets. Like fine whisky, the tavern's history has acquired depth and complexity with age. Pete, a living source of those stories, works in the tavern's dish pit. Raised on the tough streets of Manhattan's lower east side and fluent in Delancey Street dialect, Pete had the privilege of watching Babe Ruth and Lou Gehrig blast home runs into the upper deck at Yankee Stadium. Patrons thirsty for those accounts have learned that a swig of gin helps Pete unlock those snippets of memory.

First Serve's oak door transports those who pass its threshold back to America's second industrial revolution. The tavern's reputation for hosting political discussions is ingrained into its frame and heritage. *RBH 1878* is carved into an oak timber post just left of the towering limestone fireplace. To this day, glasses are raised in the name of President Rutherford B. Hayes. In tribute to Robert Anderson Van Wyck, the mayor who consolidated New York's five boroughs, *RAVW* is incised into the rough-hewn oak mantle above the firebox. First Serve's oak bar, a three-sided rectangle set against the rear brick wall, is the tavern's energy center. The brass footrest bears a stamped date of 1872. An oak mezzanine hovers over the bar, supported by a massive hickory beam that spans the breadth of the building.

"Hillard!" the hostess announces as the lawyer enters First Serve. "Pat is waiting for you at the bar. We've already cautioned him."

"I'll deny everything, Rachel. Did you tell him about the glasses?"

"No. But if you don't, we will. Give me your briefcase and hat. I'll put them in the office."

"Thank you. Please don't let me forget them."

First Serve is a shrine to tennis. The brick walls near the entrance are bedecked with photos of Bobby Riggs, Alice Marble, Bill Talbot, Pauline Betz, and Pancho Gonzales. Hillard wends his way around the oak posts and the crowd. Lead bartender Alex vigorously shakes a Brandy Alexander and throws Hillard a hello nod that's slightly more animated than the other head bobs. Standing in front of the stone fireplace and the photos of Jack Cramer and Althea Gibson, Pat hoists his half-filled beer mug above the canopy of standing room patrons. "This place is a find, Hillard. Monday night, and it's packed. Great choice."

"I knew you'd like it, Pat. Best kept secret in the city, and it's a living tribute to tennis. Do you see that photo of Little Mo on the back of the bar? In '53, I saw her win the finals right here in Forest Hills. She was maybe eighteen. She won all four Grand Slams that year. She was the first female to do that."

"You were lucky to have seen her before the accident."

"I think about her a lot. This place is marinated in tennis. Be careful. A match could break out anytime."

Alex places a cold tankard of beer on the bar. A gent on a barstool hands the pint to Hillard. Pat clinks mugs. "The staff seems to know you. Is it safe to assume you're a regular?"

"I'm here one night a month for a hamburger and a brew, usually midweek. It's mobbed on weekends, and you can't get near the place when there's a big match. There's definitely something very special about the tavern."

"I can feel it. This place is so alive."

Pat's comment is overheard by a passing waitress, balancing a tray of fashionable inebriants. "It hasn't been the same since the glasses," she blurts out as she shifts the liquid cargo to a tray stand.

"Don't listen to Ava. She still hasn't recovered from comedy night."

"None of us have," projects Alex, tinting the brandy's foam with ground nutmeg.

"I love barroom stories. I've got to hear this."

"You will, Pat. And you'll hear the true version. Let's wait until we get a table and get away from these rumor mongers."

"There are several versions, sir," adds Kevyn, whisking by with platters of hamburger patties smothered in cheese and grilled onions, counterbalanced with mounds of paprika home fries. "But it's a fact that the glasses came in the door with Hillard. We're certain that Thalia, the Roman Muse of Comedy, followed him in."

"And she's still here. Every morning we find candy wrappers up in the loft," Ava comments, dodging customers on her way back to the kitchen window for pick-up.

"Let's hope the cops don't show up again," Alex cracks, tossing an eggshell into the trash after separating the yolk for the cook and capturing a half ounce of egg white for a whisky sour.

"Pat, I'm going to tell you what really happened." Hillard draws a quaff of the draught and begins his permutation of comedy night. "My version is gospel. I heard a second-hand account from some college kids last Christmas that included a paddy wagon and handcuffs."

"Last August, during that horrible heat wave, I was meeting a client in the garment district. He gets an intercom from his warehouse guy about a wrong delivery. Instead of shipping him fifty pairs of plastic sunglasses, they shipped him fifty pairs of Groucho glasses. You know, those novelties with a black frame and bushy mustache."

"I know them. I'm trying to imagine where this story is going."

"You can't, sir," adds Kevyn, transporting four Reuben sandwiches, French fries doused with brown gravy, and a pitcher of beer.

A table opens up near the fireplace, and with a subtle gesture, Alex instructs a waitress to seat Pat and Hillard. Hillard relocates the table ashtray to the oak mantle below a set of Big Bill Tilden wood rackets secured to the limestone chimney in a crisscross pattern. Sitting with their backs against the stone hearth, Hillard summons a waitress. "Pat, the Scottish clans who supported Bonnie Prince Charlie were called Jacobites. Tonight, let's be Bourbonites."

"Sounds good to me."

Hillard orders two Bourbon cocktails. "Okay, where was I?"

"Your client just got the wrong glasses."

"Okay, right. So, the owner gets everything rectified and then tells his warehouse man to dump the Groucho glasses. I asked if I could have them. So, I schlep this bulky carton by subway and train to the Forest Hills Station. It was about four in the afternoon; I think it was a Thursday and I..."

Kevyn cuts Hillard off. "It was Thursday, August 25, 1955. I have the news clipping at home." Pat's eyebrows arch.

"It was only the neighborhood insert, Pat. It wasn't the citywide edition."

Kevyn, still loitering, adds, "When I got to class on Monday, everyone knew about it. Cindy, the boss says that business has been up thirty percent since comedy night." Kevyn returns to the pick-up window.

Hillard refreshes his vocal cords. "Cindy said I could leave the box in the office. I came back about nine and put the open carton on a table. Within minutes everyone except me was wearing a pair. Some college boys in the corner tried drinking beer through straws so the mustache wouldn't get wet.

"A college girl at another table said there should be Laurel and Hardy night. I told her I would buy their table a pitcher of beer if they came back dressed as Stan and Ollie. The college kids ran home to change, telling everyone in earshot that the tavern was offering free pitchers to anyone dressed as a comedian.

"Word spread like the Chicago fire. Half the neighborhood came back dressed as comedians. We had Chaplin, Abbott and Costello, and Martin and Lewis. Some guy with a bulbous nose came as W.C. Fields. These people were sitting at home on a quiet night. Then suddenly, there's a masquerade party honoring comedians with free pitchers of beer. The tavern was packed and raucous. Someone called Cindy to help with the crush, and she and her boyfriend flew over."

Pat lowers his tumbler. "Sounds like pure, innocent fun to me. Aside from it costing you a small fortune in pitchers."

"It was innocent, Pat, and the staff explained that only the first pitcher of beer was free. But here's the best part. An old widow with bad eyesight was watching the ten o'clock news report about a liquor store hold-up on Queens Boulevard. The bad guys wore facemasks. She hears yelling in the street, looks out of her window, and sees some college boys wearing the Groucho glasses running into the tavern. She calls the cops and tells them the robbers are hiding out in First Serve.

"Five police cars invade the street, and the cops storm in. Everyone freezes. The cops realize there's no threat, and they unwind, but now the tension shifts to the customers and the staff. There is absolute silence. No one is moving. W.C. Fields stands and announces, 'Ah yes, this festivity is now complete. Let us welcome the Keystone Cops.' The place explodes with laughter. Even the police thought it was funny. The tavern could have stayed open until three in the morning. I left at midnight and there were comedians on the sidewalk waiting to get in."

"Great story. How did the newspaper report it?"

"They used discretion. They reported it as a noise complaint from a private party."

Hillard and Pat place their dinner order. "Hillard, who is that man in the blue blazer?" Pat asks, motioning to a photo nailed to a post.

"That's Jimmy Van Alen. He resides on Mount Olympus. Mr. Van Alen started the Tennis Hall of Fame up in Newport."

"Hillard, as a rule I never associate with members. I'm not concerned now that you're representing the club. Put yourself in my shoes. How would you bring in younger members?"

"I trade places with everyone, the subway brakeman, the cabbies, even the judges. I couldn't do your job, Pat. I could not manage that club. The demands must be immense."

"The challenge for me is the politics. I'm going to confide in you. I had to learn how to function within a pretentious group, people who look down upon those whom they judge to be of lower standing. They believe that wealth defines character, even if that wealth was handed to them. Their superiority is a manufactured pretense. They actually take pride in their insincerity.

"I was raised in a meager home. When my dad was out of work, we struggled. Some nights all we had was cheese and crackers. But every night my mother led us in prayer. She taught us to be thankful for what we did have. If these smug elites knew my background, they would want me replaced. People with a legitimate right to claim moral superiority don't because they have humility. Those who impose moral superiority are illegitimate, and their self-importance is a cover for their inferiority. Their need to exert power is a diversion to hide their weakness. I have to be careful, and I avoid the incestuous gossip from those self-appointed moral authorities by working hard. I never stop moving. I told you more than I should."

"I have seen some of what you're describing, but I didn't know it gets that bad. I don't run with that crowd."

"I'm not complaining, Hillard. I love my job. If Dexter can take food and beverage off my back, I'll be able to diffuse some of the complaints before they erupt."

Hillard transfers an ice cube from his water glass to his bourbon. Pat tears a piece of pumpernickel from the breadbasket. "Pat, I don't know how else I can help. I don't think booking swing bands or bringing in comedians from the Catskills would fly unless your objective was to rack up canceled memberships."

"I can't rock the boat too hard, but I have thought about live entertainment. My wife and I were talking about comedy the other night. Some of the skits on TV get right up to that line of acceptability, but that line is creeping in the direction of the Manhattan night clubs."

"Obscenity is a cheap laugh. Wit is hard work. I'm enthralled by quality comedy."

"So am I, Hillard. Comedy is one of my escapes. Humor is one of the keys that unlocks the humanity in people."

"I have a theory about the science of comedy. Anyone hearing me put science and comedy into the same sentence would tell the bartender to shut us off. I'm ready for another round. Would you like one?"

"Sure."

Hillard's two fingers does not escape Alex's purview. "I think you gents will enjoy this spirit. The distiller finishes this bourbon in American oak."

Pat sips. "Very silky. Good choice, Alex."

Hillard continues. "Comedy is a gauge. A culture that allows freedom of speech is a petri dish for comedy. But if authority becomes threatened, it will censor comedy to the point of defining what is acceptable. That's an aspect of authoritarianism."

"Yes, Hillard. We take that for granted."

"That's what rankles me about cynical comedians. They're parasitic. Cynical comedy undermines itself and erodes the platform it needs for support."

"True, but we tend to self-regulate. A comic that goes too far will lose public support."

"Hopefully, Pat. I walked out on a comedian with a political agenda. His punchlines had a vicious, nasty undercurrent. He was an elitist, attacking everyday people. Later that night, I realized an anagram for the word 'comedian' is 'a demonic.'"

"Oscar Wilde wrote that a cynic knows the price of everything and the value of nothing." Pat scans neighboring tables. He concludes the kitchen is still backed up. "My dad has a sense of humor, and he kept us on our toes."

"We've got one in our law firm. At first, we had to adapt. Now, we pay him back with interest."

"How so?"

"I'm not sure how he got through law school. The first time he sat for the bar exam, he chided a lady from our firm who was taking it for the third time. After he bungled the exam for the fourth time, she sent him a dozen black roses and a dead fish."

Pat raises his whiskey. "Good for her for settling the ledger. I love funny payback stories. I don't know that I'd want him doing any legal work for me."

151

"He couldn't find work after he was fired as a rental agent, so he applied to law school. He probably took the dean of admissions drinking and told him a lot of funny stories."

"Why did he get fired?"

"For showing up late and hungover on a busy Saturday morning. He got his revenge that night after drinking with his buddies all afternoon. The company's home office is somewhere in England. Instead of our normal *For Rent* signs, they use their standard *To Let* signs. So, this clown buys a roll of black electric tape, and at two in the morning, carrying a painter's ladder, he would stick a strip of tape between the O and the L."

"Toilet! He must have gotten arrested for defacing property. How the dickens did he get into law school?"

"The patrol cop who nailed him thought it was funny, so he let the guy slide. The cop did make him go back and remove all the tape. One of his pals who was egging him on that night is now a bartender in lower Manhattan. Half of Wall Street has heard that story."

Kevyn delivers two cheeseburgers, French fries, and two glasses of ice water. Pat flattens the sandwich, and beef juice trickles onto the bottom bun. His first bite elicits approval. "Great sandwich."

After dinner, Kevyn begins to clear the dishes. "When did your shift start?" Pat asks.

"About noon. I'm starved, and I can't wait to get off my feet."

"You're welcome to join us," Pat says as his right-hand gestures toward an empty chair. Alex nods approval as Kevyn informs him she is off the clock.

Settling in, Kevyn asks, "Can Rachel join us? She's also been here since lunch."

"Absolutely," Pat replies. Kevyn's hand signal telegraphs the invite. Via another hand signal, Pat orders two hamburgers. "We want you ladies to have some dinner. I hope I didn't offend you by ordering."

Hillard snaps a response. "If having to deal with me doesn't offend them, there is nothing you could do that could insult them."

"Who says you don't offend us, Hillard?" Kevyn retorts, with Rachel bobbing in agreement.

Pete delivers two hamburgers. Hillard gestures toward the bar, and Alex places a shot of gin on the corner behind a three-compartment garnish tray. Pete snatches his fortification on his return to the grease hub.

"I'm four semesters from graduation. I can't wait to be finished with school." Kevyn offers between chomps.

"I'll tell you what I tell my kids," Pat replies. "You'll start like everyone else, on a bottom rung. Don't plateau, and you'll climb the ladder."

Rachel joins in. "I don't want to get stuck at the bottom. I'm working too hard in school not to get a chance to advance."

"What is your major?" Pat asks.

"Business. I graduated from a high school of performing arts. My father insisted I get a degree in business. An accounting firm in Flat Bush offered me a job when I graduate."

"Excellent. But don't discount those skills you learned in high school. I went to an all-boys trade school. To this day I can tear down an engine and rebuild it. What about you, Hillard? What did your high school specialize in?"

"Schadenfreude."

"I would have liked an all-girls school," Rachel replies. "Fewer distractions."

"I think girls have more to overcome," Pat says. "No offense, ladies, but you'll have limits placed on you just because you're female. Don't listen to people who say, 'Girls can't get into that grad school,' or, 'That company doesn't hire women.' Fight the negativity."

Hillard points to the photo of Althea Gibson. "Just think about what she had to overcome. Althea was barred from tournaments. She finally got to play here in Forest Hills in 1950. She's a female Jackie Robinson. Wouldn't surprise me if she wins the French Championships next week."

The party at the adjacent table has finished dinner. A middle-aged lady, who had overheard the whiskey-enhanced diatribe, turns and addresses the girls. "They're giving you good advice. My husband died ten years ago. I was a thirty-four-year-old housewife with two sons. People gave me idiotic advice. They told me to find another husband. My boys and I moved to a one-bedroom apartment. I slept on the couch, and the boys got the bedroom. I learned calligraphy in high school, so I hustled work from companies that print invitations. I personalized thousands of envelopes from my kitchen table, and my little business grew. Now, I own a print shop. We made it because I believed in myself and didn't follow the advice from people who were basically telling me to give up."

"You're an amazing lady," Pat announces with more than a dash of esteem.

"I was also Gracie Allen on comedy night, and my date was George Burns. Don't you remember?" she asks Hillard.

Breaking Hillard's fall, Pat stands and reaches inside his suit jacket. Pat and the lady exchange business cards. Pat reads aloud, "Royalty Invitations and Printing, Marcy Duchess, Proprietor. I'm honored to know you, Miss Duchess."

"Same here, Mr. Elliott. Goodnight."

When Pat checks his wristwatch, the message is transmitted. The informal gathering breaks for the evening. Ava hands Hillard his briefcase and hat as he sets off for home.

Forged by Ice

Hillard Abraham holds First Serve's oak door open for an arriving couple as he departs the tavern. He embraces the brisk May evening. Hillard saunters past the shops on 71st Avenue. A low-hanging gooseneck lamp creates a disproportionate shadow. The silhouette of Hillard's fedora on the concrete sidewalk is massive. He recalls a vivid childhood memory. He had seen that same shadowy illusion on a chilly winter night; his father's flat brimmed homburg had cast a similar enormous shadow.

Hillard's father worked long hours. He often left for work before the family was awake and returned home when Hillard was in bed. Mr. Abraham's dedication imprinted upon his son; Hillard possesses a herding dog's work ethic. Mr. Abraham had also been Hillard's model for courage and dependability. Gazing into the shop windows on 71st Avenue, more images of Hillard's childhood materialize in his mind's eye.

Hillard will never forget Christmas Eve in 1938. He had just turned ten. Mr. Abraham, who worked as the operations director for a dairy company, had been tasked with rescuing a disabled milk truck during a raging winter blizzard. Just before midnight, the subway delivered father and son three blocks from the paralyzed rig. Bracing against howling, ice-laden winds, the rescue team trudged through fourteen inches of frozen slush and snow. They found the driver huddled under a blanket inside the truck. Mr. Abraham and the driver jacked the truck. Using crowbars for leverage, they removed the heavy-gauge chains from the flat tire. They took turns inflating the new inner tube by hand, and then their nearly frostbitten fingers reinstalled those cumbersome chains.

When Hillard embarked on this rescue operation, his father, testing his son's mettle, told him the mission would be arduous. His father failed to mention the undertaking would also be life threatening. Pedestrian mobility on the icy cobblestone pavers had become precarious, and the footing beneath the jack was nothing short of treacherous. Violent wind gusts from opposite directions slammed into the truck, and twice the jack wobbled. Hillard's body was numb from the frigid conditions, and his mind was numb with fright.

At two o'clock on Christmas morning, Hillard and his father warmed up with coffee at a police precinct in lower Manhattan. The desk sergeant, aware that even the twenty-four-hour coffee shops in his jurisdiction were closed, offered the pair shelter and hospitality. Standing next to the hissing radiators, warming their shivering bodies with instant coffee, Mr. Abraham taught his son a vital lesson. "Keeping the trucks on the road, even under drastic conditions, is imperative. And that's especially true on Christmas Eve. We gave these restaurants and bakeries our word. Our word is our bond."

Mr. Abraham, usually time compressed under the normal pressures of work and life, now had an opportunity to instill a personal canon. With on-duty policemen circulating about, Mr. Abraham explained that the contents of the truck were replaceable, and so was the truck if it came to that. "The driver is not replaceable. Mr. Sawyer is a tough old coot, and I knew he'd wait for help. Abandoning a truck has never happened in the company's history, and it's not going to happen under my watch. Some things are non-negotiable, son. You must have the strength and willpower to make certain things happen. Our lives should be guided by purpose. By being useful to other people, you become useful to yourself." They thanked the desk sergeant for his consideration, wished him a Merry Christmas, and bundled up for their trek back to the subway.

The irony of walking past a prominent Forest Hills church while recalling his father's courage and reliability on Christmas Eve in 1938 is not lost on Hillard. The irony of having to maintain equilibrium at home by avoiding his father has not yet been fully resolved. In the spring of 1939, with Germany invading Austria and war fermenting in Europe, tensions had become elevated in the US. Hillard overheard the elders speak of violence against European Jews. At ten years old, any reticence about speaking up began to evaporate. One night at dinner, with Mr. Abraham working late, Hillard asked his mother why her wardrobe occupied two of the apartment's four closets and why the family needed a housekeeper two days a week. Snuffing out her after-dinner cigarette into a mound of ketchup, his mother offered a terse and angry reply. "My life is to play cards. Now shut your mouth."

A few weeks later, Mr. Abraham had asked his wife not to host more than one afternoon card game per month. The cigarette smoke from four ladies puffing incessantly for three hours saturated the apartment with an unhealthy cloud of smoke that lingered for days. After those card games, Mr. Abraham's modest wardrobe, housed in a hallway linen closet, reeked of cigarette smoke. If time allowed, Hillard's father would hang randomly selected articles of clothing on the towel rack in the bathroom during his morning shower. Soon after Mr. Abraham issued his request, Hillard acknowledged a trio of canasta players leaving the apartment for the second time that week. "I'm warning you, don't tell your father." Hillard was not inclined to deceive his father, so avoidance had become the only solution. Hillard secured an after-school job at the local hardware store. Between sweeping the aisles of the hardware store, regular stops at the public library, and hitting tennis balls, Hillard had his cover for being out of the apartment. All three evasion tactics evolved into his life's pursuits—work, reading, and tennis.

As a child Hillard learned a fundamental lesson. Nothing would be handed to him. He would have to earn what he needed. In high school Hillard was burning with ambition, driven by visions of English roadsters and single-family dwellings with slate roofs. Hillard's study habits and grades were exemplary. He extended his academic success through college and law school, although he believed his contemporaries had mastered one essential tool for success that was foreign to him. They knew how to ask. Upon identifying this conditioning, Hillard began his detoxification.

June 1956
The List

On a balmy, late spring afternoon, Hillard Abraham and the owner of a Manhattan construction company are descending the steps of the courthouse in lower Manhattan. While discussing their lunch options, Hillard spots Chad Jensen Harrington standing alone on the sidewalk. "I was going to suggest grabbing a tube steak and eating in the park, but I see an attorney I know from the tennis courts. Do you mind if I ask him to join us for lunch?"

"Not at all," the builder replies.

After the proper introductions, Hillard invites Chad to join them for a quick bite. The three gents walk along Bayard Street in the direction of the eateries equipped to absorb the frenzied lunch crush.

Hillard mentions a new lease on the Upper West Side. "This will be an authentic Parisian pâtisserie."

"You'll have to tell me that story some other time," Chad recites as he abruptly increases his pace and joins a cackle of Wall Street attorneys five sidewalk segments downstream.

"A rising star in the world of diplomacy," the builder snickers as he and Hillard turn right onto Mott Street and then left under a coffee shop blade sign.

Holding the door, Hillard retorts. "Jack, rudeness is a weak man's impersonation of power."

A vapor of grease, burnt coffee, and perspiration greet lawyer and client as they enter the luncheonette. "Hillard, I'm suddenly in the mood for a hot dog."

Jack springs for lunch: two franks and two soft drinks for one dollar. After re-knotting his tie to conceal a fresh mustard stain, Hillard checks his watch. "We're in good shape. We have twenty-five minutes."

Jack removes his fedora and places it on the park bench, "Sun feels great. I hope the weather holds. I'd like to get in a round of golf on Saturday. I have a feeling you won't be playing golf with your buddy, Chad."

"Even if I did play golf, I wouldn't play with him."

"You don't play golf?"

"I do not. Golf is on my list."

"What list?"

Hillard contemplates a detour. He centers his tie knot. "I don't want to offend you, Jack. I'm sorry I mentioned it."

"You cannot offend me."

"Are you okay with language that belongs in a men's dorm?"

"Seriously! Haven't you ever been on a construction site? Quit fidgeting with your tie and tell me about your list."

"I know some fellows who keep a bucket list, but what I have is a fuck-it list. When I put something on the list, I consider it to be a waste of my time. I either stop doing it or eliminate it from consideration."

"Golf is on that list?" Jack asks.

"Yes. The only way I can relate to a ball is if I'm moving, the ball is moving, and I share that ball with my opponent. And swinging a golf club throws off my tennis serve. Golf is on my list."

"I need to start a list."

"What's your first entry?" Hillard asks.

"There are so many. I don't know where to begin. My wife makes me go to this ridiculous cousins' club every few months so the women in her family can show off their new clothes. The husbands agree that it's a waste of time, but we're afraid to say that to our wives. So, we sit around a card table, drink diluted gin and tonics, and kill time. I'd love to put that on my list, but then I'd have to pay you to handle my divorce."

"I don't do divorces, Jack. But I would like to know what a psychiatrist would say about the men in your family being afraid of their wives."

"I'll go the library and get a book on Freud."

"Don't do that. Not Freud. He's on my list."

"Way to go, Sigmund. Why is he on your list?" Jack asks.

"Some elements of psychoanalysis might be plausible; some might be the ramblings of a cocaine induced intoxication."

"I once fired a guy for drinking a beer while he was running a cement mixer. I'm experienced with intoxication, sometimes my own. What else is on your list?" Jack asks.

"Funny sympathy cards. Just try to find one; you can't. You can borrow that one."

"I'm a demand and supply guy. Who would want to receive a funny sympathy card?"

"Jack, it's a device for the sender. The sender determines who deserves one."

"Who would you send one to?"

"That's easy. When Hitler's secretary Martin Bormann committed suicide, we could have sent this sweet message: 'Dear Herr Bormann, the world is a better place because you're no longer in it.'"

"I think you should give up law immediately and start a line of funny sympathy cards. I'll be your partner."

"We'd have no competition, Jack. We could rate them like they do movies. A one-star is mildly offensive. A two-star is insulting, but just to the dead guy. A three-star ticks off the guy's family, maybe even his entire country. A four-star is so vicious we use someone worthy of a three-star as the return addressee."

"That's brilliant. Do you see that pay phone over there? I'm calling Bellevue. You need help."

"We've got twelve minutes. I'll disregard your last remark."

"Okay. We've got twelve minutes. Is there anything on your list that's kind of serious?"

"I learned to stop listening to advice from those who don't have the insight or experience to give me advice. They think they do, but they don't. I've learned to put that aspect of the relationship on my list. I might even put the entire relationship on my list."

"I definitely need to borrow that one. It works with my wife's brother. After she sees him, she's down in the dumps for hours. The first thing she does is run for aspirin. He drains her emotionally and probably her pocketbook as well. She's better off not seeing him."

"Put him on your list! He sounds like a perfect candidate. But I need to tell you about the reciprocity rule. I'll have to let your brother-in-law know so he can put you on his list. If you guys argue about whose entry is older, I'll be the arbiter. And there is a charge for arbitration."

"How much?"

"A frankfurter and soda."

"Any charge for the mustard stain?"

They pass the stainless-steel hot dog cart on their way back to the courthouse. Jack drops a quarter into the vendor's tip jar. "Our banter completely took my mind off of the hearing. I guess that's a good thing."

"We've done all we can do, Jack. It's in the hands of the judge."

"If we lose, I'm putting you on my list, Hillard. Only kidding. You did a good job."

July 1956
Sadie Hawkins

On a humid Friday afternoon, pierced by intermittent showers, Elizabeth Ann Aughrim reminds herself to suppress her jollity. Her weekend with Sandy Rutherford begins in about an hour. Precisely at four o'clock, Garrett Isadore Douglas, the managing partner, enters Elizabeth Anne's office to discuss two potential cases.

"Izzy, please have a seat. I'm ready when you are to review these cases." Mr. Douglas pulls up a chair. "A lawyer's wife is afflicted with kidney disease; her identical twin sister does not want to be a kidney donor. The lawyer sues his sister-in-law. The healthy sister's husband countersues." Izzy shakes his head in disbelief. "I agree," she responds.

"The healthy sister's husband wants to bring us in. We shouldn't go near this. No judge in his right mind would compel someone to surrender an organ. The healthy sister has children to raise. She won't put her family at risk. The language in the filing indicates all communication between the two families will be terminated unless the healthy sister agrees to donate a kidney. I wouldn't touch this with a hundred-foot pole."

"Tell me about the second case."

"This one is a heartbreak. The parents of a five-year-old girl died in a car wreck. The judge pulled two female attorneys and me into his chambers and told us we were going to serve on a panel to determine custody. Both sets of grandparents were murdered by Hitler, and the only blood relatives are two aunts who despise each other. The deceased father's sister is significantly more intelligent, but she is immoral. She was the neighborhood slut when she was younger. She also has a cunning heart with a history of backstabbing people. The other aunt, the deceased mother's sister, is dumber than dryer lint. She is self-absorbed and self-indulgent, but she was virtuous when she married. To compensate for her sinful past, the immoral one denigrates the dumb one, and the dumb one retaliates by pampering herself with clothes and jewelry. The dumb one has a pair of fangs, so, she's stupid and vicious. Both aunts have three children, and both families could afford a fourth child. One of the attorneys on the panel introduced a third option: a childless Persian lady married to a Brit. This Persian lady adores the child, and I believe she would be a great mother. But the Judge is leaning toward a blood relative. Can you help me?"

"The kidney case is a nightmare. Let's please stay far away from that one. Before I would speak to the judge in the custody case, I would need unequivocal support for the Persian lady. And that includes meeting her and visiting her home."

"I want you to meet her. She is lovely inside and out. Her home is immaculate, and she is as gentle as a lamb. She was educated in England, teaches kindergarten, and gives piano lessons in her home. That's how she knows the little girl. She is in her early thirties, and she can't have children. I'll set up a meeting. I know how to reach her husband. Their last name is Fairplay. I'll take that as an omen." Izzy thanks Elizabeth Anne for her efforts, returns to his corner office, and immediately dictates a letter requesting a meeting with the judge in the custody case.

Elizabeth Anne and Sandy have been dating for two months. They are inseparable on weekends. They connect through coiled telephone cords every weeknight. Last week, she invited him to Northshore for the annual Sadie Hawkins festival. Their rendezvous is set for ten-thirty. The beach traffic on this clammy, mid-July Saturday is congesting all vehicular arteries. Although they planned for delays, Elizabeth Anne and Dr. Sandy did not plan to arrive at precisely the same moment. She parks her Thunderbird next to his Chrysler Imperial. Standing behind his car, Sandy studies Elizabeth Anne as she checks her makeup in her rear-view mirror. She swings out of her car and closes the door. Sandy's duffel lands on the asphalt as they embrace. With a wisp of vapor in the air and droplets of rain in Elizabeth Anne's brown ponytail, they share a lingering kiss in a public venue. "I never thought this would happen again," she says.

"When did you know?" he asks.

Elizabeth Anne leans back, uncertain to what extent she should disregard the blotch of eyeliner on the left panel of Sandy's white tennis shirt. "The day you flew across town in rush hour to get to me." Another cuddle, another deposit of eyeliner, a fresh smudge on the right panel. "When did you know?"

"The first day, on the veranda. I had this feeling of familiarity."

"Familiarity?" Elizabeth Anne asks.

"Yes. You didn't feel like a stranger to me. Everything you said sounded so familiar. It was more than us sharing stories. It was something else."

"I can't believe we're having this conversation in a parking lot. And I can't believe what I've done to your shirt."

"The shirt now has character. Let's go to the veranda. Let's get under cover. But you need to say something. I know that look."

"Andy's dad had Millicent grieving for him out of love. I kept thinking about what you said at dinner that night. When I pass, whose heart will I be in? I want to be remembered because I had been loved. I now know this was meant to be."

Dr. Sandy's right thumb wipes an eyeliner smear from Elizabeth Anne's left cheek. "This was meant to be. There are eight traffic lights between my apartment and the highway. On the morning we met, I made every light. Every light was green. I sailed out of Manhattan, and that never happened before. That was a sign."

Walking to the veranda at their normal spry pace, Elizabeth Anne probes. "I still don't know how you got to your apartment in fifteen minutes. Do you have a helicopter I don't know about?"

"I took care of the cabbie."

"How much did you pay him?"

"Sixty dollars. When I got into the cab, I told him I'd give a fifty-dollar tip if he got me home in ten minutes. That crazy bastard drove on a sidewalk, cut through a taxi garage, drove backwards half a block down a one-way street, and ran two lights. I was so relieved to get out of the cab in one piece that I handed the driver three twenties and never waited for change."

"That's a great story. I think we'll be telling that one for a long time."

Elizabeth Anne and Sandy secure a table on the veranda. "Sandy, you're not with me. Your mind is somewhere else. Where are you?"

"You're right. I was thinking about our conversation. I knew you weren't sizing me up. A man who loses his wife to an illness isn't in the same group as a divorced man. When I became single again, I was repulsed by females who thought of me as a desirable commodity. I didn't want their sympathy or their misconstrued notion that I had performed heroically when all I had done was what any decent human being would have done. I was a thirty-one-year-old physician with no wife or children. You weren't looking at my eligibility, not after what you'd been through. I knew then that I could relax with you."

"I love spending time with you. Let's stop at the pro shop and pull out of the tournament. They'll have enough time to reorganize the matchups. And let's get you a new shirt."

Fanning his steaming oatmeal, Sandy responds, "After we pull out of the tournament, let's go shopping."

"Shopping?"

"Yes. I'm ready to make this permanent if you are."

"I am."

The Quiver

Dexter Alexander passes through the club room doors onto the veranda. "Miss Bridget, is there anything I can get you?"

"No, thank you, Dexter. I'm just waiting for their match to end."

Thirty minutes ago, Bridget Radcliff excused herself from the dinner that followed the Sadie Hawkins festivities. She has been watching Hillard Abraham and Steve Andres grind each other into Northshore's red dirt. When Steve and Hillard lower their swords, Bridget cautiously descends the veranda steps. The metered click of her slingback heels on the slate walkway is a sensual pulse that drives Dexter off the veranda and into the clubroom. Steve receives the same message and vacates.

Bridget's classic beige cocktail dress with cobalt blue piping was the perfect choice. The jeweled comb in her thick fringe cut and the luster of her pearl necklace reflect her natural sparkle. Bridget and Hillard exchange smiles. She then glides directly into his path. Her seductive charm is a powerful intoxicant. "Let's get to know each other, Hillard. Walk with me back to the ballroom, or let's just meet later. Whatever you'd like."

"Bridget, this is so hard for me to say. You've got it all, but we're so…"

"I'm rich, too."

Hillard stays the course. "We're so different. I have a law degree but I'm blue-collar, and I'm Jewish." As an adolescent, Bridget learned how to sidestep her mother's imperious nature. A cigarette in the woods behind the guest cottage or unfinished cocktails swiped from the patio were a piece of cake. A rendezvous with an older boyfriend on a sleepover or a sedative filched from her mother's medicine cabinet became opportunities for developing schemes and techniques. Placing her life of largess in jeopardy by dating a Jew could be a landmine. Her mother's caustic reaction when Hillard had been table conversation back in May would only escalate. Until this moment, Bridget had not considered the reaction within either family.

Hillard chaperones Bridget back to the dinner reception. Standing on the bottom step of the main entrance, Bridget turns toward Hillard and closes in. She is an assault on his senses. He is transfixed by the sparkle of her lip gloss against the porcelain canvas, the curtain of exotic perfume, and the emerald specks in her blue eyes.

"I have no interest in men who are easy to manipulate. That's how I used to play. I knew I had to be straight with you." She inches closer and softly exhales. The current cools his skin, and the scent heats his blood. "We really won't know unless we give it a try. It could be a lot of fun. Are you sure?"

"I'm sure."

"Okay."

The sultry sway of Bridget's hips as she climbs the steps, a sensuous cadence that would have tenderized a weaker man into submission, reinforces Hillard's resolve. His logic has prevailed. Love cannot be cultured in a petri dish. The only currency is undeniable love.

Driving home, Hillard's admiration for Bridget's moxie is eclipsed by his distaste for having invoked a detestable practice. He found his leverage; Bridget's family would certainly oppose her involvement with anyone not befitting their station and heritage. Hillard's quiver, armed with that arrow, became a necessary resource. The feathered shaft hit its mark.

While escorting Bridget back to the festivities, thoughts of a cousin had flashed across Hillard's mind. She had been threatened with disinheritance for dating a Gentile. He knew of other adult children who had been ostracized, even disowned, for breaking the rules of marriage. "A repugnant practice," Hillard had expressed to an associate lawyer tasked with amending a last will and testament with a disinheritance clause.

"I don't disagree," confessed the colleague.

"My respect for the observant converts into disgust when I hear these stories," Hillard explained to his ally. "How can people who had faced the threat of extermination by a German monster expel their own flesh and blood for the crime of falling in love? I guess expendability is in the eye of the executioner.

The Catch

At the behest of an austere appellate judge, Hillard Abraham attended the tryouts for a softball team representing the New York legal profession. Advised by his firm's senior partners to appease the judge, Hillard did agree to play if the Battling Barristers made the post season. The lawyers lost the 1955 semifinal game to the Jersey City Provisions, men who worked in a meat processing plant. One year hence, the Barristers qualified for the title game against the defending champions, the Tapers, the team that beat the JC Pros.

After submitting his line-up to the umpire, the Barristers' manager addresses his team. "Hillard, I want you at shortstop. Bobby, I'm moving you to second base. Let's win this."

With the Barristers clinging to a fragile one-run lead, the Tapers are down to their final at-bat. The defending champions rally, with one out and two baserunners in scoring position, their slugger strolls into the batter's box. The brute's intentions are not inconspicuous. A long fly ball ties the game, a single wins it, and a homerun earns him the headline. The Tapers' raucous rooting section is gleeful with anticipation. Their expectations are moments from realization, pizza pies, cold beer, and cigars at the victory celebrations.

The moment the pitcher releases his first offering, the enzymes of fear dilate his pupils. A floater with no spin or rotation ambles into the heart of the strike zone. On the other end, the slugger's pupils dilate with excitement. The Goliath bludgeons the meatball. The orb explodes out of the batter's box, a meteor minus the plume of smoke. With impact at four feet, the ball is destined to clear the twelve-foot gap between Hillard and the third baseman within two seconds and land in left field three seconds later. Both baserunners break with the blast of the ball, and the Tapers' fans rise and start cheering.

As the slugger's torso uncoiled, Hillard whirled to his right, extended his left arm, and dove into the gap. Within an eyeblink, the energy that propelled him into the gulf runs its course. A greater force is about to restore order, and although it feels surreal, like one of his flying dreams, he is not dreaming. He is suspended over the outer edge of a dirt infield in Central Park, hanging in space with gravity about to intervene.

Hillard's left hand arrives at the intersection of the two primary objects at the precise moment that gravity calls him home. The collision is cushioned by the outfield grass. Miraculously, the ball stays in the pocket of his glove. Hillard rolls to his left, onto his back. He hears Bobby, who is standing on second base, imploring Hillard to throw him the ball.

Required by the rules to stay on base until the impact of bat and ball, the baserunners are stunned. Midway to their next checkpoints, they are frozen on the base paths. Laying on his back, Hillard transfers the ball to his right hand and tosses it with perfect arc to Bobby. The umpire, incredulous with delight, his jelly torso shaking with laughter, calls the runner out. Double play, game over.

At the ensuing pizza and beer celebration, Bobby offers Hillard a celebratory cigar. "Hill, from second base, it looked like you were floating in midair. How did you do that?"

"I'm a little hazy on it. I might have blacked out when I landed. I guess I willed it. I made myself catch the ball."

Hillard draws down his frosty beer. "I'm thrilled we beat those guys, and the Barristers will get a trophy and some prestige. But let's keep it in perspective. This attention is disproportionate to the stakes."

"How so?" Bobby asks.

"It was just a league softball game. Tomorrow, we go back to work, hustling to pay our bills. Breaks like softball or tennis help us keep our sanity. I've got a few tennis trophies at home. They're in my closet. I'm proud of myself for earning them, but they won't put food into my refrigerator or money into my savings account."

"So, you're saying an amazing performance isn't worthy of attention?" Bobby asks.

"No, I'm not. I'm just saying to keep it in perspective. Let me give you an example where the attention is disproportionate in a different way. Everyone knows what Jessie Owens did twenty years ago at the Berlin Olympics, but few know about another incredible performance. An American middle-distance man, eighteen-year-old John Woodruff, was one of the favorites in the eight hundred meters. But John gets boxed in on the first lap. In Hitler's stadium, against runners from countries aligned with the Nazis, they blocked him in. They weren't going to let this black American win.

"John was trapped in fourth place. He couldn't break out, or he would have been disqualified for interference. So, he pulled into the infield and stopped running. He came to a complete halt and waited for the pack to pass him. A runner who stumbles or breaks stride usually finishes last or near the back. Not John. He re-entered the track at the spot where he left it and started to sprint. He was three-wide on the outside when the pack realized he was trying to sprint around them, so they begin to sprint. John was forced to stay outside. The entire field was blocking him from an inside position. John took the lead, lost it, and retook it down the stretch. I've seen film of that race. John Woodruff refused to lose. He was either going to win or drop dead trying. This young black man took on Nazi Germany all by himself, and he beat them. They declared him to be an inferior human, and he beat them all in *their* stadium. And he did it with dignity. Now, let me ask you a question. Did you know about John Woodruff?"

"No, Hill, I've never heard of him."

"That's my point, Bobby."

August 1956
Wall of Doors

Perched on a middle shelf in the bookcase, Buster finds a degree of relief from the steamy August heat. His roommate has placed an eight-inch oscillating fan in the center of the dining table. Four bottles of whisky, backfilled with water and left in the freezer for weeks, are situated around the fan in the four cardinal directions. "I feel for you, Buster. You can't check your fur coat."

Hillard Abraham is enjoying this brief respite. Many of his clients have ventured north to the crystal lakes of the Catskills or the refreshing elevations of the Adirondack peaks. Wearing plaid boxers and a white cotton tee shirt, a slight rustle of wind in the trees interrupts his research. For several weeks, he has been gauging the accuracy of his almanac's sunset table. Two months beyond the summer solstice, tonight's celestial nightshade descended one minute and fifty-eight seconds earlier than last evening's curtain call.

Thirty-four minutes after finishing William Saroyan's *The Time of Your Life*, Hillard decides: he would have ordered a New York rye whiskey if imbibing with the regulars at Nick's Pacific Street Saloon. Now on the other side of midnight, with a gibbous moon climbing the eastern sky, he closes the almanac's moonrise table around a wooden popsicle stick and adjusts the kitchen wall clock. Buster has left the fan's airstream and settles onto his regular terrace chair. After turning off the table fan, Hillard returns to the terrace. His circadian rhythm disrupted by the heat, he rewinds the tide table back to April and his first season at Northshore.

Hillard's brush with Bridget Radcliff in July is another entry in a classified folder. His stance on dating is an evolution entrenched in his moral code. A dalliance to one might be perceived as an affair with a promise to another; therefore, no entanglements unless love is in both hearts. Not infatuation or fancy, irrefutable love. A law school classmate misconstrued Hillard's friendship as a nugget about to bear amorous fruit. She was clearly wounded when he explained their comity was scholastic, not romantic.

It was not destined to work out with a nurse or an aspiring fashion model. During holiday service in Hillard's junior year of college, the senior reverend had noticed Hillard and this eyeful in the synagogue lobby. One week later, the reverend pulled Hillard out of Shabbat service. Conversing with this malted milk quaffing elder requires a bissel of Yiddish and a handkerchief to wipe off the spittle. "Boychik," the reverend sprayed, "She's poison. They're gonifs. Don't get mixed up with them. Can only hurt you. Fershtay?" Hillard certainly did understand.

For several months, the red maple stump had inspired an earnest effort to rationalize the tree's demise. Hillard is not inclined to dismiss events dripping with synchrony as merely coincidental. The dwarf maple was a living organism with a purpose. The tree's abrupt end was not blight, or a lightning strike, or its value as a raw material. Twenty-seven growth rings, Dexter, Hillard, and the tree shared a concordant earthly existence. Kin to a tree, siblings of a sort, all three came into being at about the same time. All three shared a similar composition, mostly water, and a life expectancy of about seventy years. Now, one is gone. Although the tree did not have to be removed to make way for the expanded parking lot, someone made the decision to eliminate the tree, and the pretty red maple was no more. "Why did I not see this before? Dexter was expendable, just like Jakub. They were as disposable as the tree. Saroyan is so right, Buster. Every man is a variation of every other man."

Hillard's logic burrows on. The unveiling of Jakub Baranski's Nazi tattoo is chiseled into Hillard's psyche. "Jakub had to live beyond the limits that test a man's breaking point. Korea may have pushed Dexter close to that line, but he didn't have to cross it. Jakub lost his love, so he immersed himself in work. Dexter's life is teeming with love because of Becky. Work and love, Buster. That's all there really is."

Hillard draws a glass of water. Reaching into the frost encrusted freezer compartment shelf, he lifts the metal lever of the ice tray, cracking the cubes. He deposits the chips into his glass and returns to his chair on the terrace. He approaches another bridge built from assumptions. At their Scotch party back in April, Dexter mentioned that he did not register for the draft and he didn't have a Social Security number or a driver's license. Scratching the top of Buster's head, Hillard ponders aloud. "How could the Selective Service have known about Dexter? Maybe I'm like you, Buster, a little suspicious. It's strange that his girlfriend Bernice switched marital gears like that. I'm no sleuth, Buster, but it sounds fishy. Do you like the word 'fishy?'" The tabby blinks his sleepy eyes, tucks his head into his chest, and tunes Hillard out. "How do we fit in, Buster?"

Hillard revisits his pilgrimage inspired by handbills posted on a barricade surrounding a Manhattan construction site, a wall of discarded doors adorned with leaflets seeking religious recruits. The concept of being born again had appealed to him. In his eighth and final college semester, he registered for Comparative Religions. On ten consecutive Sundays, Hillard attended service at ten different houses

179

of worship. Ten sanctuaries adorned with the sparkle of lovely women, punctuated by speeches filled with imagery and philosophy, left an everlasting impression of chimeric fancies and romantic allusions.

Every congregation embraced him, delighted to share their faith. A few welcoming families invited him home to break bread. On his first mission, a matronly widow with a large brood asked him to dine with her family. Throughout the service Hillard had exchanged smiles with her daughter, a seventeen-year-old Irish angel with deep dimples and blue marble eyes. After the final hymn, Hillard approached. The young lady disappeared behind a wall of offensive linemen, her brothers, cousins, and uncles.

These religious legations revealed an element of femininity that Hillard compared to a vogue fashion parade. He sat near the pews that smelled like the perfume counters at the department stores. The procession of dresses and skirts, viewed with indifference by scholars, a distraction by others, or competition by some, had become an enticement unto itself for twenty-one-year-old Hillard. Wedged between the scruples of Sunday morning service and the healthy desire for the touch of those voluptuous young women, who, by virtue of their roving eyes, were enticed by the same yearnings, the breadth between fantasy and reality became conquerable. The existential benefit from Hillard's definition of being born again had been embedded in a slow-release capsule, delivering its payload incrementally over six years. Within those six years, Hillard found his full voice, one quarter-decibel at a time.

Chad and Veronica

On a cool and brilliantly clear Monday afternoon in late August, Chad Jensen Harrington and Veronica Cabot are motoring home from Northshore's tennis courts in Chad's convertible. Veronica's flaming tassels, amplified by the sunset and swept by the wind, brush across Chad's right arm as she digs through her bag for a hair band. Chad passes through the unlocked, wrought iron gates of the Cabot Estate. He shifts the automatic transmission into neutral. They coast along the five-hundred-foot crushed red brick circular driveway. The speedometer's needle hovers at five miles per hour. On the return, he parks near one of four gently winding slate walkways that converge at the granite trimmed portico. Sitting in the open air with Veronica in his Venetian red-on-white Corvette, Chad cannot contain his obsession. He has loved this elegant and stunning lady for half of his life. Soon the blithe days of summer will give way to winter's dreary and infertile grip. Another calendar cycle will pass into memory. "Veronica, you know how I feel about you. You're twenty-five, and I'm twenty-six. We're not getting younger. If you say yes, I'll drive you to the best jeweler in the city and buy you any ring you want. Ever since I was a kid, I believed we'd get married. Please don't let me wait. Please say yes."

"I really don't want to have this conversation again."

"Why not?" he pleads. "Can't you see that I'm waiting for you to realize I'm the guy you're supposed to marry?"

"This is making me uncomfortable."

"I beg you, please. We both want the same thing. We could have it all. You raise the kids during the week, and on weekends, we'll take them boating and teach them to play tennis. Our kids will know the difference between tacking a sailboat and a Corvette's tachometer."

"But that's not what I want. I've known you forever. I love you as a friend."

"Wouldn't that love you have for me as a friend grow into something more?"

"But what if it doesn't?"

"Then we'd still have a commitment to each other and a family to raise."

"Please don't make me feel guilty. I don't want you to feel like I've been leading you on because I'm not."

"Don't ever worry about that. There's no one else I'd rather spend time with. There are times when I know it's clicking with us, and I know you're feeling it too. No marriage hits on all cylinders. It would work for us. I know it would."

"I'm not sure about that."

Chad exhales, and his tone softens. "What are you going to do? I don't think you're dating anyone, and I know you don't want to be alone. You have too much life in you to be alone. Please, give me a yes. I'd even take a maybe."

"It's getting cold, and Father is going to London. I want to spend time with him before he leaves. I'm going inside."

Veronica gathers up her racket and tennis bag from behind the seat and walks up the winding path. Chad slowly drives off. His vision is locked onto the reflection in his right wing mirror. Veronica disappears behind the picket wall of Eastern arborvitae. The long shadows of late summer inch across the manicured lawn.

London

"Mr. Cabot, would you like a fresh cup of tea?"

"Please. It feels like October in August. When you come back, let's discuss my London itinerary."

Emerson Cabot darts in, clutching an international telegram. "Chase, we've got a scheduling conflict. I'll read it to you. 'Must attend variance hearing concurrent with closing stop no reschedule stop committee not available until Jan stop please confirm.'"

"Easy fix," Chase calmly explains. "You keep your closing on Thursday in Boston, and I'll attend the London closing as planned. Veronica can represent us at the hearing. She has signing rights. We can presume the rumors are correct: they want to limit us on the number of hotel rooms.

"Rita, please reserve Veronica a suite on my floor but not next to me. She needs some privacy. Please make sure we sit together on both flights. And please get her passport from the safe and put it into my hands before lunch. Now, the hard part —please get Veronica on the phone. Becky will know where she is."

Veronica accepts her father's request with no hesitation. "I can use the time to think," she explains.

The limousine leaves the Cabot Estate at one in the morning. The DC-7 is airborne on schedule at three o'clock. From her first-class window seat, Veronica stacks the curtains forward. "If you keep them closed, they might muffle some of the noise," her father suggests.

"I'd rather hear the noise than breathe the dust from those curtains. I forgot to take cotton balls. They drowned out the noise a little when I flew back last time."

Thirty minutes into the flight, Chase attributes Veronica's silence to the early hour. "Did you bring something to read?" he asks his daughter.

"No."

Chase briefs Veronica on the opposing arguments she will encounter at the hearing. His words elicit no response. He restocks, expressing how much he and Veronica's mother are looking forward to Elizabeth Anne's wedding reception.

"I have never discussed anything like this with you or Mother. Chad reminded me that I'm twenty-five, almost twenty-six."

"It's just a number."

"That's what I'm trying to make myself believe. I'm two years older than Mother when you got married. When she was my age, she already had one child. I'm not Bridget. She's been saying since she's twelve that marriage is a trap. I didn't want Chad to know his words upset me, but they did."

"I knew there was something on your mind. Don't let another person's definition of time push you. When we're young we don't realize that life is like a lease. Everyone has an expiration date. I don't measure my life by years. I measure my life by accomplishment. Achievement is my calibration, not time. When I turned fifty I realized it's a blessing and not a curse to be working on your last day on earth. You're only twenty-five. There is plenty of time for you to fulfill all of your ambitions. Your personal decisions belong to you and you alone."

"But we're looking at it from different directions, Father. You're looking back. I don't want to force a decision, and I certainly don't want to make a mistake. I've never had this feeling before —that I'm standing at that proverbial fork in the road. Safe and comfortable has less risk, but I want more. But I also don't want to lose an opportunity."

"The price we pay for a mistake is proportionate to the weight of the miscalculation. What's holding you back? If it's fear of change, think carefully about missing that opportunity. We only get a limited number of them. Think about the Cabot portfolio. The most rewarding projects were the ones we created. We were bold. We created opportunity. Isn't that the essence of this London hotel deal? Tearing down a ramshackle structure and building a majestic hotel with a grand bar and two dining rooms."

"Good comparison, Father. Look at all the opportunities we do turn down."

"Precisely. That's what I mean about real opportunity. You mentioned a fork in the road. We blazed a new trail when we got to that fork. We made a road where there hadn't been one."

The front cabin stewardess offers beverage service. "I'll have tea, please. My daughter would like a cup of coffee."

"Would you like cream and sugar with your coffee?" the stewardess asks.

"No, thank you. I don't want the calories. I always take my coffee black."

As the stewardess disappears into the galley, the plane hits a pocket of turbulent air. Veronica continues when the flight smooths out. "You said not to let time push me, but it does. If I'm going to have children, I have a ten-year window."

"And everything will fall your way in good time. A week before I married your mother, we met with the minister. He asked us if we had given any thought to how we want to raise our children. Your mother answered. She said as we prepare our children for this world, we would also be preparing them for the next. Because of your mother, I am a better man than I ever thought I would be. That's what marriage to Mother has done for me."

"That's why I don't believe Bridget. She says that marriage would complicate her life. But I don't think she believes that. Her money can only buy things that have a price tag."

Chase thanks the stewardess for the beverages and responds. "Her father told me Bridget guards against men whom she thinks might have designs on her money. I applaud her discretion. The world is filled with gold diggers. One bad apple can destroy a family. I suspect she would rather keep her assets secure than put them at risk. Will you allow me to offer a suggestion?"

"Of course. You would anyway."

"That's what we fathers do. It's our job. Would you feel more comfortable in your own home? I know of a red brick colonial with a carriage house that's on the market. It's right on the Sound. The Portuguese ambassador used to live there. Let's put it under contract when we get back."

"No, Father. Thank you, but no. I don't want to come home to an empty house. I want to come home to my own family."

"Do you want to leave Cabot? I don't want Cabot to get in the way of you living your life."

"Leave Cabot? It's in my blood. I would never leave unless you and Uncle Em sell."

"We have no intention of selling."

Veronica sips her coffee. Their seats are now illuminated with the sunlight that has gradually suffused the right side of the cabin. Chase ventures on. "Let's go back to that fork in the road. Things can change in a split second. Around the next bend, there might be another fork."

"Or there may not be, Father. When I find myself thinking that half a dream is better than no dream, I remind myself that I'm a Cabot."

Veronica lowers her chair back, and within minutes her eyelids close. The tension that Chase had seen earlier has dissolved. Chase summons the hostess with a hand wave. He passes her a handwritten note. The stewardess returns with a blanket. "Sorry, sir, we don't have any cotton balls." Covering his daughter with the blanket awakens a memory of checking on Veronica when she was three-days old. Unable to sleep, he delicately placed his fingertips on the infant's back, confirming the heaving of her tiny torso. Chase steps back from his linear view of time. Veronica's twenty-five years is not just a number. His lease is well past the halfway pole and approaching the stretch.

The Hearing

Chase Cabot and his daughter arrive at their London hotel late Wednesday night, and they are greeted by their partner, attorney, and architect. The team reviews Thursday's agenda over an obligatory service of flaky pastries, tea, and decaffeinated coffee. A cable from Rita in New York informs Chase that on Saturday morning, a courier will deliver their tickets for their Tuesday flight home.

The Cabot band reconvenes in a corner of the lobby on Thursday at noon. The attorney provides Veronica Cabot with a brief summary of today's hearing. "Miss Cabot, the local building code limits us to eighty rooms. We're asking for a variance; we're seeking approval for a seven-story hotel with one hundred and twenty rooms."

The architect returns from the bank of pay phones behind the registration desk. His body language implies an update that is not well received. "The panel has been increased to five members. This usually means the variance is likely to be rejected."

"Why?" Chase asks.

"Because the two additions are also on the appeals panel. It's politics."

"I'd like a transcript. Is it too late to hire a court reporter?"

"We sacked that notion, Mr. Cabot. That might create an element of distrust."

"Let's just get through the hearing. We don't intend to postpone construction, but if we have to wait, we will."

The concern is palpable as the two squads leave the hotel, headed on foot in opposite directions. Veronica is oblivious to the occasional crude comment from the gallant men inclined to hurl such sauce from the protection of a crowd. She is preoccupied with revising the planned strategy. The retired RAF officer holds the door open as the Cabot team enters the hearing room at ten minutes to the hour. A building department employee delivers a message to the Cabot attorney. "Sir, please instruct your secretary to sit with the audience. She can sit in the first row if you like."

"We have no secretary. Miss Cabot is a member of the development team. And if you don't mind, she will sit where she belongs, at the head table."

The hearing commences at the stroke of one o'clock. The panel responds to the ten-minute argument opposing the variance with a collective head nod. The Cabot team then presents its position, supported by an independent study and letters from business leaders and cultural dignitaries. A fifteen-minute segment is devoted to opinions from the citizenry. The three public comments are critical of the Cabot request, and all three are utterly baseless. Veronica slides a note toward the Cabot attorney. *Paid by opposition hotels?*

"Yes," the attorney replies, just above a whisper.

The panel calls for final summations, and the opposition group restates its case. Via a hand gesture, Veronica usurps the Cabot attorney. "Thank you for this opportunity. I am Veronica Cabot. The Cabot family's tradition of investment and commitment requires a healthy partnership with the local municipality. I think we can all agree that this project will enhance the district and generate considerable tax revenues. According to the study we submitted, there will be no adverse impact from a seven-story hotel with one hundred and twenty rooms. Please stop me if you gentlemen have questions or comments." Veronica pauses, then continues. "The potential loss of forty rooms jeopardizes the project as planned and significantly reduces the projected tax revenue."

"How so, young lady?" asks the panel member in the middle position, sporting an olive herringbone Norfolk jacket.

"Well, sir, the normal vacancy factor in this market is twenty percent. Without the income from those forty rooms, the operating pro forma does not support sustaining a high-caliber hotel."

From his floor level perch, the panel member on the far left responds. "It is preposterous to believe that Mr. Cabot will change course, young lady. He's closing on the property right now. He's in too deep, and he's too committed. Don't you agree?"

"We certainly are committed to the project, sir. However, if we cannot operate with one hundred and twenty rooms, we will rebrand to a hotel below the designation of a luxury property. We are flexible and could change direction if necessary. If our request is approved, we are willing to provide you assurances that the hotel would be capped at seven stories, even if future projects exceed seven stories and obstruct our views."

The panel member next to the haughty fellow is acknowledged. "Young lady, what manner of assurance would Cabot provide?"

"It would be in writing, naturally. In essence, we would be deeding the sky above the hotel to the city, agreeing never to increase the building height above seven stories."

"Why would you do that?" asks the panel member on the far right, the gent wearing a gray vest below his brown wool jacket. Veronica notices that the stitching on his tan elbow patches is frayed.

"Because those forty rooms are critical to supporting a topflight hotel. If we were to build a cut-rate hotel, our construction expense drops by twenty-five percent. Our operating expenses would also drop, including our lodging tax obligations."

"Exactly how much less lodging tax would the city collect?" the Norfolk jacket asks.

"About thirty percent."

"I would contest that assertion," the supercilious fellow remarks.

"I mean no disrespect, sir. We checked and rechecked the revenue projections. I stand by that thirty percent."

The gray vest announces that the panel's decision will circulate within a week. The Cabot attorney requests a decision now, explaining that Miss Cabot and her father will be flying back to New York in a matter of days. The gentleman in the center unwraps a cigar from the patch pocket of his pleated Norfolk and lights up. As he exhales his first taste, he discloses that he supports the request. The two panel members on his left agree. The request for the variance for seven stories and one hundred and twenty rooms is approved by a three-to-two vote.

Veronica's outfit arrives back at the hotel. They relax in the lobby with tea, coffee, and an array of international newspapers. Upon returning from their successful closing, Mr. Cabot's group is jubilant with the news that the variance had been approved. Mr. Cabot invites everyone for cocktails.

The RAF officer raises his glass. "Mr. Cabot, I want you to know that your daughter displayed grit and aplomb. She won the day."

"Here, here!" resounds.

With the Cabot group occupying a quiet alcove of the lobby bar, Veronica shares her strategy. "Their position was unjustified, and they knew we knew it. But we had to be careful. The panel viewed me as window dressing. I needed them to know that I was acquiescing to their authority. They backed themselves and us into a corner. They needed an escape as much as we did. We gave them the empty space above our seven stories. We gave them air, and as empty an offering as that is, it satisfied their need for a sacrifice at the altar. If I had been too feisty with that pompous gent or had mentioned that they had granted similar variances to hometown developers, they would have thought us arrogant Yanks and denied us."

The attorney seizes the floor. "Miss Cabot, I believe your reference to a thirty percent decrease in taxes was the clincher."

"Thirty percent!" exclaims Chase. "Veronica, where did you get that number?"

"Like the space above the hotel. Thin air."

Meatballs and Spaghetti

Three days after Chad Jensen Harrington had asked Veronica Cabot to surrender to the inevitability of their union, he is perplexed and unsettled. He reschedules his appointments and leaves his office before lunch. In the grand foyer of the Cabot residence, Chad explains to Becky that Veronica has not answered her phone for two days. Mrs. Cabot enters the vestibule. "Chad, we were expecting you." Mrs. Cabot describes how Mr. Cabot had prevailed upon Veronica at the last moment to attend meetings in London, and they left for Idlewild so early Veronica had almost no sleep. Chad's angst dissipates. Mrs. Cabot then relates how thrilled she and Mr. Cabot are for Elizabeth Anne, how wonderful her wedding celebration will be, and how much they are looking forward to seeing Chad Saturday at the reception. Chad floats through the gates of the Cabot Estate.

On Friday afternoon, Veronica and her father meet with their London team. That evening they dine at the home of their business partner. The partner's son, the sole owner of a shipbuilding empire and a very eligible fellow, just happens to drop-in on his parents. "This is an exceptional Cognac," he explains, establishing his justification for crashing the dinner party. "It was bottled in France in 1840, ten years before the Great French Wine Blight." The shipbuilder discovers that antifreeze is not one of the many wonderful properties of such an exotic brandy. "I'd speculate that Miss Cabot may have already found her mate," the mogul utters to his father as he bids his parents goodnight.

On Tuesday, the Cabot's New York-bound DC-7 departs London on schedule. Twenty minutes after take-off, Veronica is reviewing the hotel's construction schedule. Her performance at the variance hearing has alleviated her father's concerns. Veronica shall be the guardian of the family's holdings. Teaching her the secrets to wealth management would be the next phase. Although there is an abundance of time, the capitalization of time and money are two of Chasen Cabot's many virtues.

"There are lessons to be learned everywhere, even under the most trivial of conditions."

"For instance?" Veronica asks.

"What does my favorite dessert teach us about wealth management?"

"I haven't the foggiest. Sounds like one of your famous analogies is forthcoming."

"Why does the ice cream in the center of the baked Alaska not melt even though it's been in a hot oven? The ice cream is insulated by the air pockets in the meringue and the sponge cake. Wealth can do the same thing. Money can insulate us from discomfort. I know many families who foolishly exhausted their assets. Or even worse, they allowed a smooth-talking freeloader to worm his way in and extract their money. They ended up with nothing. They had no idea how to preserve wealth or how to remove the parasite.

"Mother will survive me. She will have security. We're doing this London hotel and Uncle Em's Boston deal to sustain that insulation for generations. When Uncle Em and I are through, the responsibility of protecting the resources shall be under your direction." Veronica sits back in her seat, her gaze shifts several degrees to her right, away from her father. "I hope I haven't overwhelmed you."

"You have, but I needed to hear that. It's distressing to think about you not being here."

"I'm not going anywhere. When my grandfather turned ninety-nine, we had a party for him at his coastal estate in Georgia. A reporter from the local paper asked him about his longevity. He said, 'Young man, when I was in my seventies, I thought I was drinking enough whisky not to make it this far. I was wrong, and so were the doctors who told me to stop drinking.' When the reporter left, grandfather told me a man should never outlive his money or his whisky. I asked him what he missed most from his younger days. 'Your grandmother,' he said. Then he thought for a while and told me he forgot what it was like to taste and smell."

"I'll be your food taster. I'll describe the flavors you're missing." After a few minutes of silence, Veronica chortles aloud, "All that from a baked Alaska."

"I just remembered something else my grandfather said when he heard my uncle tell my cousins not to get married until they figured it all out. Grandfather said, 'If I had waited until I figured it out, you wouldn't be here.'"

"I love that Cabot wit, but I really don't know if that's true. The Cabot men don't take chances, and that has rubbed off. I seldom take a chance."

"On the flight over you mentioned all the opportunities Cabot turns down. We may walk from projects, but that's not to say we won't take a chance. Every general who has ever won a war took a chance. Think about those courageous explorers of centuries past. They took chances. They envisioned new lands beyond the horizon."

Later in the flight, the Cabots order an assortment of tea sandwiches that are served on China with linen napkins. Chase interprets the delicate, square sandwiches as the building blocks of another teaching opportunity. "Do you know what these remind me of?"

"Yes. They remind you of a tea sandwich."

Unfazed, Chase continues, "It reminds me of a family."

"Do you ever run out of analogies?"

"The pieces of bread are the parents; the child is what's inside. The..."

"Are you saying I'm a piece of roast beef?" his daughter cracks.

Chase presses on. "The children are trapped, and when they grow up, they'll serve the same sandwich to their offspring. All children have to rise above the flaws of nurture. Parents who recognize this tend to produce children who don't have to invest a lot of time sorting things out."

"I'll never be able to eat another tea sandwich."

Veronica and her father return home Tuesday evening, nineteen hours after departing London. Veronica's favorite meal awaits-Becky's scratch-made spaghetti and meatballs. Mrs. Cabot joins the travelers in the informal dining room. "Chad was worried about you, Veronica. He came here looking for you. He didn't know where you were. Did you miss him?" she asks.

"I did a lot of thinking."

After dinner, Veronica retires to the bedroom wing. Chase closes the door to his study, pours himself a snifter of Cognac, and telephones his brother. "She's got what it takes. She's like us, she doesn't get infuriated, and she doesn't get boxed in."

Chad phones Veronica Wednesday morning. He asks if she has recovered from the debility of air-travel.

"Nothing is quite as exhausting as international travel."

"Please find time for me. Did your mother tell you I came by?"

"She did. I'm so jammed. I have to run to the office in five minutes and reshuffle my diary for the rest of the week. I'll see you at the wedding on Saturday."

"Did you think about our conversation?"

"Yes. I did a lot of thinking. I'll see you Saturday."

First Dance

Mr. and Mrs. Cabot are traveling to Elizabeth Anne Aughrim's wedding reception in one of their two limousines. Mrs. Cabot remarks, "The marriage bug is quite contagious. These things happen in threes. Regina and Gretchen might be next."

"As long as it's Gretchen setting the date."

The enormous ballroom is bursting with cheer when the Cabots arrive. Joseph Russell, formerly a dishwasher at the Shadyside Oyster Bar & Grill, is manning the bar. Dexter Alexander had instructed Joe to serve every arriving guest a cocktail. A waiter delivers two champagne cocktails to Mr. and Mrs. Cabot.

Hillard Abraham arrives late and stag. Joe exchanges Hillard's fedora for a snifter of Scotch. "Nifty lid, Hill," Joe says as he opens the door to a dry cabinet and places the hat on top of his red wine bottles. Hillard intends to remain innocuous by enjoying some fine Scotch and procuring a few hors d'oeuvres.

GM Pat Elliott, attending tonight's party as a guest, is greeted by a waiter with a tray of Old Fashioned cocktails. "Brilliant move, Dex. The teetotalers must have abstained from attending." As Dexter ushers an elderly couple to their assigned seats, a table near the bar, he and Hillard brush shoulders. Dexter discreetly slips him some skin.

Dr. Sandy's brother, the best man at the intimate ceremony that had been held three hours before the reception, delivers the toast. The guests delight at the newlyweds' inaugural dance as husband and wife.

The party gallops into the homestretch. Veronica Cabot's group of friends and admirers have been enjoying champagne all evening. They are now line dancing to the Charleston. Hillard Abraham is standing at the far corner of the bar at the far end of the lavish reception room. Hillard's back is turned to the dance floor. Veronica leaves her entourage, and Chad Harrington starts after her. Bridget Radcliff intercepts him. "It's nothing, don't crowd her. She hates that." Bridget's counsel brings Chad to a disinclined halt. He ignores Bridget's offer to dance.

Hillard and Joe have been debating a hot topic. Joe, sliding ice cubes from a stainless-steel scooper into two tumblers with his left hand, refreshes Hillard's Scotch with his right. Impressed with Joe's dexterity, Hillard continues presenting his case for the best center fielder in New York. Joe's argument supporting Duke Snyder trails off mid-sentence. A scintillating redhead in a shimmering black gown is circumnavigating the dance floor and approaching his station.

"Hillard." Hillard turns to his right, "I'm Veronica. I don't believe we've ever been introduced." Hillard returns the smile, straightens his posture, and shakes her hand. He is speechless, which is of no significance as Veronica continues. "I believe I have danced with every gentleman at this party, except for you."

"Oh, I get it. You need to fill out your dance card," Hillard quips, smiling through his eyes.

"I certainly opened myself up for that one," Veronica concedes through a demure smile. The band is playing a slow-tempo melody. The dance floor is chock-a-block with couples. The revelers are aware that the curtain will soon drop on this grand party. "Shall we?" asks Veronica.

"I'm honored." Hillard offers Veronica his left arm and escorts her to the fringe of the dance floor. "You need to know that you are proceeding at your own peril. The Arthur Murray folks would have gotten a restraining order if I showed up."

"Don't worry, we'll muddle through."

Hillard shifts from chaperone to trailblazer. Dropping his left arm, he takes hold of Veronica's right hand. He weaves her through the maze of dancers. They stake a claim on a small patch of real estate, five couples removed from their point of origin.

Veronica pirouettes, and they are face-to-face. Hillard delicately places his right hand on the small of her back. His left arm is stiff, and his breathing is shallow. "Relax, Hillard. It's just a fox trot." Veronica places her left hand on Hillard's right shoulder, not quite at arm's length. The soft warmth of Veronica's right hand radiates through his veins. They are gazing and smiling at each other, exploring features of face and expression. They are unfazed by an occasional bump from a neighboring couple.

"Let's strategize," Hillard suggests. "I'm going to step to my left, which would be your right."

Veronica smiles. "Got it."

Hillard then replants his left foot. Veronica dekes left, then coordinates with him, and gracefully glides right. A laugh ricochets, one to the other.

Their dance is brief. The music ends after only a few bars. Chad, roiling with rage, has advanced his observation post to the outskirts of the combat zone. Hillard observes Chad's scowl. Hillard begins to disengage. He ever so slowly opens his left hand in gradual increments. He pulls his right hand from Veronica's spine. Veronica tightens her grip. "No, let's have a proper dance."

"Are you sure? Chad looks upset." Veronica does not reply.

Veronica and Hillard are a radiant pair-flawless proportion with sterling linkage, a tartan of red and black. Another slow-tempo dance floats out of the bandstand. More twosomes have squeezed onto the dance floor, compressing the space between couples. Veronica edges closer. Hillard stretches his right hand across Veronica's shoulders, twirling her long, red coils around his index finger, gently tugging on the rope of hair. Veronica responds. She repositions her hands to the back of his neck. Hillard places his hands upon her slender shoulders.

Bridget joins Chad at the fringe of the battleground. "Just let it play out."

"I don't like this. I'm breaking it up."

With the slow music flowing, his nostrils flaring with disdain, Chad winds his way through the undulating wave of couples. Elongating his frame, hectoring his rival from a superior perch, he barks, "I'm cutting in, tapping you out."

Hillard's trenchant delivery is low and assertive. "I suggest you leave and protect the secrecy of certain Spanish documents."

Diffused through an aural prism, Hillard's words explode into a spectrum of burning outrage at one end and radiant joy at the other. Chad is gut-punched. Seething with contempt, he shrinks into the shame of his callow indiscretion and the looming embarrassment unfolding. Chad yields to the leverage and retreats in the direction of the bar.

Veronica presses her lips against Hillard's right ear. "I like how you handled that."

"Now I've got you all to myself."

"I've been watching you play tennis, Hillard. I wanted to get close, but I didn't know how. I went to London to get away from you. That only made it worse."

"Is this a dream?" Hillard purrs. He draws in her fragrance. "Tell me this is real." Veronica digs her fingernails into the back of Hillard's neck.

The final notes descend onto the ballroom. "Veronica, the band has stopped playing."

"This can't end. I want to stay with you."

"I can't believe I'm saying this. If we leave together, people will talk. What if you change your mind?"

"I don't care what people think. We can't lose this."

"We could meet tomorrow."

"If we're not together I'll be wondering why."

Cuddled within each other's arms, negotiations cease. "Let's go to my apartment. I'm not letting go of you."

Departing the five-by-five parquet plate shift, Hillard admits that the Scotch is creeping up on him. "Hill, I have a driver. He'll drop us."

Walking arm-in-arm toward the ballroom doors, Hillard whispers into Veronica's ear. "It's going to be very hard to sleep on the couch with you in my apartment." As they approach the first set of stairs, Dexter hands Hillard his fedora. Dexter had been observing what he feared could degrade into a nasty confrontation over a beautiful woman.

Dexter trails the couple, escorting his friend and his date to their ride. Standing under the canopy in the night air, watching the '56 Cadillac limo slowly motor down the drive, the silhouette on the rear window a fusion of two, a cathartic wave passes through Dexter.

Chad and Bridget are standing at the bar. "Can I get you folks something?" Joe asks.

"No, thank you," Chad responds softly.

Bridget places her hand upon his shoulder. "Chad, you're going to be okay. The heart heals. Look at Elizabeth Anne. It'll get better…there are others…"

"This isn't going to stand. I'll do anything to get her back."

The Cabots have beheld the enchantment. Mrs. Cabot, unnerved yet trying to appear calm, whispers into her husband's right ear. "Chase, we don't know him, we don't know his people. Chad is sulking at the bar, and the Harrington's are glaring at us. Everyone is talking about this."

Chase leans right and matches his wife's volume. "I know Hillard, he's rock solid. Have you ever seen Veronica with that glow?"

Mrs. Cabot thoughtfully replies, "No."

"This might be it for her. They're a striking couple. I'm happy for her, for them." In a barely detectible drone, he whispers, "I don't give a damn what anyone else thinks." Chase then kisses her cheek and again whispers, "Reminds me of the night I got back from Paris, and I gave you that diamond necklace. You had that same glow."

Dabbing her eyes, his wife replies, "Thank you, Chase."

The Terrace

On this crisp Sunday morning in the waning days of August, Hillard Abraham throws off his bristly wool army blanket as he rises from his living room sofa. He quietly moves about. To his relief, the bathroom plumbing does not wake his overnight guest. He presses the start button on the coffee percolator, and the machine gurgles as steam erupts through the spout. The aroma of freshly perked coffee invigorates the kitchen.

Before he retired to bed, and just after Veronica slipped into one of his flannel shirts and dropped off to sleep, Hillard loaded the percolator and left the bedroom door ajar so Buster could roam. He then transferred a gift box from a shelf in the hall closet to the kitchen counter. Buster hears Hillard filling his bowl. The feline prances into the kitchen.

Hillard steps into the brisk morning. He drapes the contents of the gift box over the back of a chair. A hawk is soaring in a wide circle above the tree dome, monitoring a rabbit. Buster's vision is also fixed upon the bunny. His right ear is pitched at a different angle, funneling sounds from within the apartment.

Veronica Cabot joins Hillard on the terrace. He sets his binoculars on the table and reaches out for her hands. "You're an aphrodisiac, Veronica. Especially in the morning."

Veronica exhales into his right ear, "I know what you mean." The embrace ending of its own accord, Veronica asks, "What were you doing with those?"

"Watching a hawk. The hawk sees the rabbit, but the rabbit is within a foot of safety."

"Please tell me this is not an analogy."

"Just creatures observing one another." After a pause, he asks, "Did you sleep well?"

"I did. I knew where I was when I woke up. Sometimes in hotels it takes me a moment to remember where I am."

"Would you like a cup of coffee?"

"No, thank you. Maybe later."

Hillard notices her footwear, "I like your choice of shoes."

"I kicked my heels under the bed, so I grabbed your sneakers. Oh my, they are so fashionable."

"It's a little chilly out here. I've got a sweater for you."

"Do you mind if I pass on the sweater? Please don't be offended. You're a bachelor. I understand why you'd have a girl's sweater."

"It's brand new. I took it out of the box this morning while you were sleeping. You're my first guest."

Veronica sniffs the bodice. "It is new." She holds the sweater against her frame.

"It should fit," he says. "Becky gave me your size."

"What?! When did you talk to Becky? This is getting too strange." Veronica sits on one of the two chairs. She drapes the sweater across her lap.

Hillard adjusts the matching chair and sits across from her. He employs a calming technique, conscious breathing. "The first time I saw you, my heart exploded. I can't stop thinking about you. I didn't know how to tell you."

"Why?"

"I didn't want to force it. There were so many men chasing you. I didn't want to blend into the background. So, I kept it to myself. I had to hope that circumstances would bring us together."

"What would you have done with this sweater if we had never met?"

"The sweater was waiting for you. No one else would have ever worn it. It matches the color of the dress you were wearing the first time I saw you. You were sitting in the top row, watching the tennis. I had to stop myself from staring. I went to the canteen to ask about you, that's when I met Dexter. But I was so clumsy, and the situation wasn't right. The following morning we were driving in my car, and that's when Dexter told me that you and Becky were close. I asked him not to say anything, not even to Becky. I didn't want anyone to know that I had asked about you. That was back in April. I needed their help in June, and they said they wouldn't tell you."

"How long have you had it?"

"About two months. I bought it in the garment district. I thought it was perfect for you. I didn't know your size, so I left a note on Dexter's front door. He called me at home that night. I went back to the garment district early the next morning and bought it."

"Did you think it would happen?"

"I didn't know if it would. All I can offer you is me. I keep asking myself if I deserve this."

"Do you?"

"I must because you are here."

"So, you got Becky and Dexter involved after your Scotch party?"

"You knew?!"

"There are few secrets between girls. We talk, that's what we do. Becky said you were a lawyer with a sense of humor. She also mentioned Mayor Joe and a theater man from London. I think his name was Marlowe. Someday you'll have to tell me that story. Becky told me Dexter laughed his way through it.

"On the day of the exhibition I really wasn't watching the tennis, I was watching you. You came out of nowhere. I watched you pick up some trash. None of the men I know would have done that. I looked for you at the dinner, but you weren't there. I couldn't get you out of my mind. Some days you were a total stranger. Some days it felt like I've known you forever. The harder I tried not to think about you, the stronger the grip. Why didn't you play tennis when I was playing? At least we would have seen each other."

"I had to avoid the courts when you were there. Being near you and having to keep my distance would have been torture. Does that make sense?"

"Yes, it does. When Bridget said she wanted to go out with you, I felt ill, but I said nothing. I was so happy when she came back to the table and said it didn't work out. When I heard the house pro tell his crew to roll the courts for the Wednesday night players, I just knew he was talking about you. So, I'd go to the club room and watch you and your friend. Only Dexter knew, and he promised me he would keep my secret. Watching you Wednesday evenings changed the definition of secretly dating someone." Veronica studies Hillard's expression. "Am I talking too much?"

"No. Say it all."

"I watched you for months. I wanted to know everything about you. And then it happened again last night. You were standing at the bar. You came out of nowhere. I thought we would dance, I'd give you my number, and we'd go out on a date. Never in my wildest dreams did I think this would happen."

"Are you saying that you want to dial it back? Do you want to slow down?"

"Why? Let's not lose any time. There's so much I want to do with you."

"Dexter was our mutual confidant. He's a remarkable guy. There's something I have to ask you...about my being Jewish. I don't know if that's a problem for you."

"It's not a problem for me. Is it a problem for you that I'm not?"

"No."

"I've heard that Jewish men are supposed to date only Jewish ladies. Are you a Jewish rebel?"

"There is that expectation in the Jewish community. Some people live with restrictions. I do not. There are no social or religious restrictions in my pursuit of happiness."

"So, you're not devout?"

"No, but I am proud of my Jewish heritage. Our rabbi said I'm a culinary Jew."

"A culinary Jew? Are there other types of Jews?"

"Yes. There are pious Jews, casual Jews, cultural Jews, even raucous Jews."

"Raucous Jews?" Veronica asks.

"Yes. For them, the Hanukkah dreidel game is a contact sport."

"You're pulling my leg."

"Maybe. But you do have such a nice leg. Are you religious?"

"I go to Sunday service at least once a month, and I never miss Christmas and Easter. There's something I need to ask you." Hillard braces. "That little guy, what's his name? I don't even know if he is a male."

"That's Buster. He's been here since November. This is his apartment."

"Package deal?"

"Yes. But if it can only be one of us…this is so painful…I'll leave."

"Do you think we can work with Buster about walking on the bed at night?"

"Did he do that?"

"He was on the pillow sniffing my hair."

"I can't blame him." As Hillard caresses her bedraggled red mane, the sun finds refuge behind a sky of puffy cumulus clouds. Hillard asks, "Would you like that cup of coffee now?"

"Not yet. Tell me about those records I saw on the dresser. I've heard those groups on the radio. Is that your favorite music?"

"One of my favorites. It's right up there with Broadway musicals and Gilbert and Sullivan."

"Do you sing?" Veronica asks.

"The only way I could carry a tune is with a set of luggage. Do you sing?"

"No. My sister Gretchen got all that talent. I can't sing either."

"What music do you listen to?" Hillard asks.

"We heard a lot of classical when we were kids. Now, give me anything written by Cole Porter or the Gershwin brothers. If we were going to the theater tonight, and you could choose any movie, what would we see?"

"Great question. Tough choice. We'd see a double feature, *Night at the Opera* and *The Maltese Falcon*. What are your favorites?"

"I love Laurel and Hardy, and I've never told anyone that. When is your birthday?"

"December twentieth. I'll be twenty-eight. What's yours?" Hillard asks.

"I'm a twentieth also. October twenty. I'll be twenty-six in two months. Okay, next question. If we were going out for dinner tonight, where would you take me?"

"Where would you want to go? As long as they serve orange food, I'm okay."

"Hillard! Orange food?"

"Yes. Carrots, oranges, pumpkin, sweet potato, squash, and cantaloupe. I like orange food."

"I never heard this before. You forgot cheddar cheese and apricots."

Hillard returns from the kitchen with two unmatched mugs brimming with black coffee. "Hot enough?"

Veronica sips, "Perfect." She places her coffee on the cafe table. "Hill, what was your childhood like?"

"I have no brothers or sisters. I've been working since I was ten. I've lived in apartments my whole life. My banker told me I'm two years away from buying a home. I like my grandmother better than anyone else in my family."

"Do you have any childhood friends?" Veronica asks.

"I had one friend, Sammy, but we lost touch. My parents wanted to live in neighborhoods with a synagogue. I didn't trust the kids I grew up with."

"Why didn't you trust them?"

"They were always looking for an edge. What about you? What was your childhood like?" Hillard reaches for his mug.

"I can't remember when I didn't have Gretchen, Bridget, and Regina. My parents spent a lot of time with us. They were very generous, but Father's lessons included sensible spending." Veronica folds the sweater into a rectangle and centers it on her left thigh. "Hill, if you could change one thing in your life, what would you change?"

"I think I would duck that question with anyone else. It's not easy admitting that you're lonely. It runs contrary to the image I need to project. I've been wondering if my loneliness is incurable."

Veronica draws in a sigh. "That's something you don't have to explain to me. What didn't they teach you in law school?

"The secret to extracting motives. Presenting the right catalyst is the key."

"Are you extracting my motives?" Veronica asks.

"God no. I have never been in this place before. I'm wide open. Everything is peeled back."

"What do you want that you don't have?" Veronica asks.

"I want what Dexter has. What couples who live in peace and happiness have. I love how loyal he and Becky are to each other."

"I want the same thing, Hill. I think most people do. Gretchen says I'm more loyal than Grandfather's beagles."

"Do you bay like a beagle?"

"Only when I find the right pair of matching shoes. I do hope my wit can keep up with you."

"I suspect it will be me trying to keep up."

213

"Hillard, tell me a secret that you've never told anyone else."

"I have flying dreams."

"So do I! Especially since I had to fly to London three times."

"I don't mean in a plane. I mean flying like a bird."

"Really? With wings?" Veronica asks.

"Not with wings. It's like gliding underwater when you're in a pool. It's like that, but instead of water, you're gliding through the air, exerting no energy. I can't believe I'm telling you this."

"I've never had that kind of flying dream. What does it say about you?"

"One dream interpreter wrote that flying dreamers are showoffs, but that's really not me. I'm fascinated by birds. I guess there's a joke in there."

"You trust me; that means a lot."

"What's your secret?" Hillard asks.

"My fear that I would never know passion. Bridget said I'm waiting for my perfect match, and he doesn't exist. But Gretchen found the one love that she always wanted. I plan on bonding to just one man. That bond is what builds strong families. I know what I want."

"You held out. You're a strong lady."

"I knew what Bridget had on her mind that night. I could say the same about you."

"That I'm a strong lady?" Hillard quips.

"You think funny, Hill. That's a gift. I'm enjoying this. I long for good, honest conversation."

"Honest conversation just flows. When we practice the power of silence, the conversation becomes dialogue. Paul Tillich wrote that the first rule of love is listening."

"Oh, he's so right, Hill. A strong couple needs good conversation."

"I can think of something else a strong couple needs." Their lips meet.

"Hillard, have you ever been in love?"

"A crush or two, nothing close to love. That's a change I would welcome. What about you?"

"Not yet. I'm waiting for the real thing. It would be a change for me too."

"What other changes do you want?" Hillard asks.

"I want to live in my own home with my own family. I also want to lower my skepticism. Is it ironic or logical that I'm skeptical of my skepticism? I have to be more accepting of people who deserve the benefit of my doubt."

"Like whom?"

"This is going to sound so strange, but we are revealing our secrets. I once read a story about a Polish nun who said she heard God's voice. A few months ago, one of the biggest bankers in New York told me he was thinking over an important decision, and God spoke to him. He said it's not an actual voice. It's a feeling connecting his mind, heart, and soul. He's not delusional. Maybe he did feel God's nudge. If he did, I want to know what that's like."

"So, you're looking for affirmation that God is real?"

"I know God is real. That's my faith. I know His teachings, but I want to know God's thoughts. If I hear His voice or feel His touch, maybe I'll understand how He thinks. Does that make sense?"

"It does. I've wondered if God communicates with us through our dreams or with numbers. There's a connection between my dreams and my waking life that I don't understand."

"Hillard, that is so true! I was once looking over a set of blueprints when I realized I had seen those exact plans in my dreams. That startled me. How could that have been a coincidence?"

"It wasn't a coincidence."

"What about numbers? How does God communicate with numbers?" Veronica asks.

"Think about Mount Rushmore. Washington, Jefferson, Lincoln, and Teddy Roosevelt are there because of the gifts they gave us. Their presidential order is one, three, sixteen, and twenty-six; combined that equals forty-six. Is there a message that our forty-sixth president will be as significant? Maybe he'll do what all four did, or God forbid, undo all of it."

"Hill, maybe he will be a she."

"Great point."

"Hill, this is eerie stuff; flying dreams and God's voice. I'm starting to shiver." Veronica cups her hands around the mug. "You arouse me,

Hillard. Dancing with you was magic. I was a runaway train. It felt like the first time I was attracted to a boy. I couldn't help myself then either. I broke from Mother and ran up to him. I even kissed him."

"Where were you when you kissed him?"

"That's the part of that story I don't like. I don't like needles. Gretchen and I were in a hospital clinic getting flu shots."

"Was he in an exam room, sitting on the table, his mother smoking a cigarette?"

Forest Hills, heaven and earth, dissolve into a sensory freefall. Veronica utters, "Oh my God!" Straddling two realities sixteen years apart, random details come flooding back. She remembers Hillard's blue corduroy shirt sleeve and the tile pattern on the exam room floor. Veronica recalls a deeper impression; she knew then that someday she would meet this boy again.

Veronica and Hillard stand and embrace. Drying her eyes on Hillard's bathrobe, she speaks. "I can't believe we found each other. I remember that day like it was yesterday. We were leaving the clinic, and you walked right in front of me. I couldn't take my eyes off you. I felt something for you that I never felt before. When Mother went for the paperwork, I had my chance. I ran into your room. I didn't think about it. I just did it. I only had a few seconds, so I kissed you."

Hillard has yet to find his voice. Finally, "The dread disappeared when you ran into the room. I can still close my eyes and feel your kiss. I wanted to know who you were. I wanted to run after you. You were wearing a hat, so I didn't know you had red hair. I remember freckles. You do have freckles!"

"This is so incredible, Hill. This explains why I'm here with you now. My head feels like it's filled with helium. You have the same face that I saw in the hospital. Whatever guided me into that exam room guided me to you last night."

Hillard caresses the back of her head as they cling to each other and the moment. "I could never explain this because no one would believe it. That doesn't matter. The only thing that matters is that we understand."

"Our mothers and my sister, Gretchen, might."

"Yes. They would. I can see our mothers, a refined bridge player and a canasta yenta."

"They'll work it out. What's a yenta?" Veronica asks.

"We have so much to teach each other. Do you know who the best centerfielder in New York is?"

"You just stop this right now, Hillard Abraham!" Veronica replies with feigned anger.

From an unforgettable moment in a hospital clinic to an embrace on an apartment terrace, their journey has transcended all manner of reason. Two vastly different trajectories with two implausible points of intersection, theirs is a union of incomputable probability. Whether by design or happenstance, ordained or coincidental, it matters not. "I don't know where this is going, Veronica...this is so amazing. I will never forget how I'm feeling right now."

"Hill, promise me you'll be faithful. Please, don't ever cheat on me."

In an increment of time too brief to measure, too swift to record, Hillard's existence has jumped the track. Nothing will ever be the same. His logic has no seat at this table. "I never will."

September 1956
Water

"I'll discuss this with Chase immediately." Emerson Cabot cradles the handset of his beige desk phone and strides past the private washroom in the short passage that connects the two executive offices. His brother is watching the barge traffic navigating the channel beneath the Queensboro Bridge.

"It's been raining like this for three days, Em. Even the East River is waterlogged."

"Chase, our Boston attorney just called. The property on our east side is about to hit the market. If we can get our hands on that piece, we can add rooms and amenities."

Chase pivots abruptly. "The lot with that one-story building?"

"Yes, that's the one."

"Em, call our attorney back immediately. Let him know we're sending a team to Boston to put that piece under contract and set a closing. I know exactly who can put this deal to sleep for us." Just after lunch, on this soggy mid-September Tuesday, Veronica Cabot and Hillard Abraham are motoring up to Massachusetts to nail the deal down.

Departing Boston Friday afternoon with an executed contract in Hillard's briefcase, Veronica nominates a different track home. "Uncle Em taught me to never take the same road twice. We took the Boston Post Road north. Let's take a different route home." Driving south through Providence on the Pequot Path, with the TR's wipers swishing rain, Hillard turns left at a sign for Point Judith. The TR rolls onto a narrow lane with sandy shoulders. They cruise through the fishing village of Galilee, Rhode Island.

Hillard has developed an exercise for teaching Veronica how to drive a manual transmission. Pinkies interlocked, he drags her left hand through the gearbox, taking care not to smudge his fiancée's engagement ring. "It would be so much easier for me to drive your car if I didn't have to shift with my right hand."

"I know, but you're getting really good at it."

Hillard coasts into a hotel lot. "No sense both of us getting wet. I'll park and bring the bags." Veronica signs the registration as Mr. and Mrs. Hillard Abraham. After depositing their luggage and washing up, they walk to the seafood shack they passed on their way to their lodging. The chugging of an old metal hull coal puffer oscillates off the far breakwater. The single-mast steamboat glides through the ocean inlet between Galilee Village and Jerusalem Harbor. The aromatic scent of anthracite fuel wafts across the jetty.

Veronica and Hillard sit side-by-side on the covered patio overlooking the confluence of Narraganset Bay and Block Island Sound. After dinner, Hillard lights up a Cuban cigar. Using the same wooden stove match, he lights the candle in the hurricane lantern that the waiter had pushed aside when he served their striped bass and steamed lobster. The glowing cigar and the teardrop candlelight grow in intensity against the fading daylight. Hillard places his tumbler of Kentucky

221

bourbon next to the lantern. The candlelight sparkles through the amber whiskey. The rhythm of the water lapping against the stone seawall is a soothing contrast to the manic pace of the previous forty-eight hours in downtown Boston.

Veronica transfers a pair of binoculars from her handbag to the table next to her sherry glass. She rests her head upon Hillard's left shoulder. "You are the only person I've ever known who keeps spyglasses in his glove box." Veronica hears a splash, and she investigates with the field glasses. "It might be too dark…let's see what's out there. It's just a fish, but I was hoping for a seal. I wonder what seals do to wash away their troubles. I soak mine away in a tub."

"I'm glad you're using them. I bought them in the Hudson Valley. I had been watching the ospreys diving for carp. Then I saw a Scarlet Tanager near the summit of Mount Algonquin. He had this brilliant, bright red body with jet black wings. That tiny creature migrates to the Andes every winter. That's over eight thousand miles round trip, and he weighs about one ounce."

"That is amazing."

"I agree. I'm glad I had my camera that day. Look to your left, over there. Can you see the light from the Point Judith Lighthouse?"

"I think I see it…I do, it's faint…every ten seconds or so."

"A German U-boat torpedoed one of our merchant ships near that lighthouse in May '45, killed twelve men."

"Never heard that. My God, Hill, that's only eleven years ago, and look how close they were to our shore."

"Germany surrendered a few days later. I hope people never forget what this nation had to do to preserve its freedom, how close we came to losing it."

"Hill, make sure you show me that bird photo."

"I also took a shot of ducks in formation."

"Do you mean a raft of ducks?"

"Oh, are we an expert on the names of bird groups?

"Maybe I am, Hillard. Did you know that a group of crows is called a murder?"

"I knew that. Do you know what a group of owls is called?"

"Ha! A parliament. You can't trick me, Hillard Abraham!"

"Do you know what they call a flock of cardinals?"

"There's no such thing, Hillard. There's no official name for a group of cardinals."

"You're too clever to trick. But we need to come up with a name."

"I just did. A Vatican of cardinals."

At ten in the morning, Veronica and Hillard are back on the road, drinking black coffee in paper cups with fold-out handles. Their conversation loses ground to the hammering of rain pelting the ragtop. Their dialogue resumes when the torrent softens into a drizzle. They arrive in Queens at four in the afternoon. That evening, they dine on the terrace, enjoying a dinner of roast chicken, baked sweet potatoes, and a salad of garden vegetables they bought that morning at a Rhody stand in Shelter Harbor. A station wagon adorned with window decals advertising the family's itinerary of amusement parks and natural wonders pulls into the lot. The family of five scampers for the side entrance. "Hill, do you remember your family vacations?"

"We didn't have any."

"Let's see the world together. We also need to go back to the Island tomorrow to check on the house. Still not sure what to do with the attic, let's not turn it into a storage room. Can you go with me?"

"I have to get to my office in the morning. I need to call your father to discuss this Boston deal and the lease agreement for our house." Last week, after gently interrogating Hillard under the auspices of that nuptial custom, Chase Cabot made him an offer. Cabot Development will buy a red brick colonial on the Sound that once belonged to the Portuguese Ambassador and lease it to Veronica and Hillard for five years. The tenants will have the option to purchase the house anytime within that five-year term. "Let's see the house on Sunday. Does that work?"

"Perfect. When you speak to Father, he may want to discuss Churchill. I heard him mention to a banker a new book about Churchill. He also told the banker that his future son-in-law has a terrific sense of humor. Father retold your joke about terminal immaturity."

"So, he's stealing my material? Did the banker laugh? I need to know if that line needs work."

"I thought I heard a chuckle, but you never know with a banker. They have as much personality as an eggplant. It's a very good line. Maybe it just needs some follow-up."

"Okay. How's this? One of the disadvantages of terminal immaturity is that my family will be oblivious to the onset of senility."

"Actually, that might be an advantage. We'll all be so conditioned to your terminal immaturity we'll know how to care for you when senility sets in."

"Now I know what you're planning to do with the attic. That's where you can lock me away like Mr. Rochester did in *Jane Eyre*."

"You are so good at extracting motives. You'll be comfortable up there. The walls will be rubber, your Scotch will be in plastic bottles, but you can't smoke cigars up there. Absolutely no matches. Every afternoon, I'll take you out for a walk. I'll make sure your straitjacket is British Racing Green. I'll take good care of you."

"I can hold my own with your father, even if the topic is Churchill. I think he and I will be more relaxed now that we've had that obligatory talk. He knows that I would put you and our children first, that I would put myself into the line of fire."

"You mean take a bullet for your wife?"

"Yes."

"Really? You would take a bullet for me?"

"Yes."

"That's less complicated than taking a bullet from me."

"We've gone from fashionable straitjackets to murder in fifteen seconds. My days are numbered."

225

Buster scurries off the terrace as the first boom of thunder rumbles over the building. Veronica and Hillard move into the living room. Sitting on the couch, bare feet propped up on the coffee table, they watch the veins of lightning zigzag across the night sky. After a few minutes, the yawning sets in, circulating from one to the other. "I'm falling out, Hill. Let's get some sleep. Where's Buster?"

"He's in the bedroom. It's past his bedtime. I bet he's already on your pillow."

The Shiksa

Veronica Cabot parks her silver Mercedes-Benz 190 SL in the asphalt lot at Bubbe's nursing home. While escorting Veronica to the social room, a gum chewing aide answers Veronica's query. "I'm sorry, the staff won't allow Mrs. Abraham to sit on the patio."

"That's a shame," Veronica replies. "This September Indian summer might do her some good. What if I wheel her?"

"They won't allow that either."

Undeterred, Veronica asks, "Does your facility allow residents to have their own wheelchairs?"

"You would have to discuss that with our administrator," the aide replies as they enter the social room. They pass an old man sitting alone on a sofa. He is balancing a cane across his lap. Veronica wrinkles her nose at the cloud of flatulence.

The aide directs Veronica to the far corner of the room. Veronica finds Bubbe crumpled in an armchair. The old lady is gazing out of the picture window that overlooks the patio and the hedge wall. "Bubbe, I'm Veronica. I hope my visit is convenient. I wanted to meet you before the wedding. I brought you some flowers and these magazines. Hillard told me red roses are your favorite."

The nurse transfers the bouquet into a vase. Bubbe's arthritic fingers reach into the paper bag. Veronica tilts it, and the top magazine slides onto Bubbe's lap. Bubbe's hand grip has weakened with age and disability, but her grasp of wit has not. A male attendant carries over a chair. Veronica thanks him and sits beside Bubbe. The old lady studies Veronica's face, "Bootiful." Veronica blushes. "Mine boy is happy mit you. Don't matter, you are shiksa." Veronica doesn't know what that means, and she expects laughter when she discusses her nursing home visit with Hillard later.

Mr. Grossman, aided by his cane, hobbles over, "Want to see my teeth?"

"I…I don't think that's such a good idea," Veronica responds, her dilating pupils shifting towards the male attendant, now rushing over. *Hillard warned me about him. Can't wait to tell him. He'll double over.* Veronica exchanges smiles with Miss Ethel, sitting comfortably in a rocker with a book across her lap.

Bubbe rattles on about the food and not sleeping well. Veronica nods and smiles. Bubbe asks Veronica to come back later and sneak in some schnapps. The old lady's expression then becomes serious. "Mine boy likes jokes, take careful." Imprinted in her recall, impervious to memory loss, is a Hillard prank executed on the morning of his bar mitzvah.

"He came down from the bimah and say he had to leave to do tennis, but his friend, who look like him going to wear his clothes and read Torah. I believe, then I knew he was joke. My brudda Lenny says, 'He's meschugener, a crazy.'" Bubbe holds up two withered, bent digits. "I don't talk to Lenny for two years!" Bubbe drifts off to sleep, then springs back. "Mine boy is a mensch. You got a good one."

"I'm so lucky. Thank you. I'll take good care of him."

"I'm too old now…so tired. Maybe God don't want me."

"No, Bubbe, God loves you. He wants you to see your grandson get married."

"Oy vey iz mir." Bubbe squeezes Veronica's hand. "You are kind. He's getting a good one." Veronica watches Bubbe fall asleep.

Driving home to her parents' estate, Veronica reflects on her visit with Bubbe. She certifies Bubbe's bar mitzvah story as another affirmation that Hillard was meant for her. She dissects the phonetics of her new vocabulary, making mental notes of the context in which they were used so Hillard can translate when they speak later. "She's had such a hard life, Hill," Veronica comments during their regular eight o'clock call. "She told me she's old and tired."

"Yes, she's had a hard life. She's an amazing lady. She never gave up. Never accepted the conditions imposed on her by tyrants. Chased from village to village, her family got tired of running. They left Romania when she was a kid, with just the clothes on their backs and no money in their pockets. They lived on morsels for two weeks. This is her last phase. Her strength and spirit carried her. She'll be relieved when this is over. Aging is tough, especially if you're alone. If we make it to that age, please don't hide the Scotch."

Deprived of each other by convention and circumstance, the fifteen-minute phone call intensifies Veronica's yearning. Hillard's absence is insufferable. She has not seen him since Sunday.

Second Serve

Two days after visiting Bubbe's nursing home, Veronica Cabot parks her 190 SL next to Hillard Abraham's TR3. She does not see Buster through the terrace screen. The tabby had been lapping water when he heard the hum of her machine's twin Solex carburetors. He scurried from the kitchen through his arch onto the terrace for confirmation. Racing back through his portal, Buster leaped onto the coffee table, catapulted over the recliner's seat cushion, and landed on the headrest. Buster's calm and relaxed appearance as Veronica greets the tabby belies his preparation.

Veronica places a brown paper bag on the kitchen counter and deposits her olive-green suede purse and an overnight bag onto the bedroom dresser. She kicks off her pumps, returns to the kitchen, and opens a can of cat food. Buster rubs his head against her ankles, snagging her beige stockings. His intentions are not inconspicuous. Veronica holds him in her arms. Buster's purr reverberates through her chest cavity.

After feeding Buster, tending to his litter box, and washing up, Veronica unloads the bag of groceries. She deposits a decomposing slice of pumpkin pie into a paper grocery bag and dumps the mess into the incinerator chute in the hallway.

Returning to the apartment, Veronica finds Buster is again perched on top of the recliner, campaigning for her affection. Responding to his expressive meow, she scratches the fur between his ears with her tea green fingernails. "You know something, Buster? Hillard told me when you first moved in, you were a little standoffish, so he thought about changing your name to Dubious. You've never been shy with me. I think you're a ladies' man. Dubie is cute, but Buster is perfect." Buster double blinks in agreement. Veronica elects to stay in her copper brown business suit. She'll change into flats when she and Hillard walk to First Serve for dinner.

Veronica and Buster are on the terrace when Hillard arrives home. She had heard the honking of Canadian geese, grabbed the binoculars, and watched the migrating chevron pass across the vision field. "It's been too long, Hill."

"I know, sweetheart. I'm writing a new chapter for Dante's *Inferno*. Not seeing you is the tenth circle of Hell. Are you sure want to go out for dinner?"

"Yes, later."

Two hours hence, they are about to leave the apartment. Veronica checks her look one last time. Now attired in her contingency outfit, a teal blue, narrow-waist sheath dress, she spots an oversized manila envelope on the bookshelf. "What's in that envelope?"

"Open it."

She slides the envelope out. "Not thick enough to be another tennis sweater." Veronica un-twirls the red string that secures the flap to the metal grommet. "The Scarlet Tanager! What a gorgeous creature. We're getting this framed. We're hanging this in the study, between the built-ins."

The pulse in First Serve Tavern is throbbing. The unbuckled Friday night crowd is free from chores and responsibilities. Veronica and Hillard work their way to the bar. Before they place their order, two champagne cocktails arrive. Bartender Alex beams a grin. Veronica has been briefed. She knows the names of the staff, the story about the glasses, and the connection to the world of tennis. Alluding to the photo of Maureen Connolly, Hillard mentions that he watched Mo win the championships in Forest Hills in '53. "I saw her too! Best groundstrokes I've ever seen. I was in London in July '54. I watched Little Mo win Wimbledon two weeks before the accident. What a tragedy. I felt sick when I heard."

"I know. Everyone did."

A newly hired waitress leads the couple to the table next to the fireplace. She pours them a second coupe and wedges the half spent champagne bottle through the cubes into a tableside ice bucket. The regular staff stops to chat. Veronica asks them about school and future employment opportunities. Ava asks Veronica if she knows the story about comedy night. Veronica smiles. "Yes, I've heard it."

"But did Hillard tell you the real story?"

"I won't know until I hear your version. One evening, I'll come back without him."

"That's a deal."

Rachel serves dinner. Veronica cuts her sandwich in half. "Great hamburger, Hill."

Pete emerges from the back of the house. He delivers two glasses of ice water stamped with a greasy thumbprint. After dinner, Hillard excuses himself. He asks bartender Alex to give Pete the uneaten half of Veronica's hamburger and a shot of gin. While Hillard is at the bar, the new hire asks Veronica, "Is it true? Does it really happen in a split second?"

"It's magic. There are so many ways it can happen, but one thing is for sure. One moment, it's not there, and the next moment, it is."

"I needed to hear that."

Walking home arm-in-arm, Veronica and Hillard window shop on 71st Avenue. "Hill, First Serve is everything you said it was. Nice people and nothing pretentious. The champagne was such a sweet touch. Pete reminds me of that character from the Laurel and Hardy movies, that gruff felon who just broke out of prison."

A public bus accelerates through a light on Queens Boulevard, belching gray exhaust. Hillard waits for the noise and vapors to clear. "I've known Pete for a few years. When he and the other old timers ramble on, I have no idea what's real and what's imagined. Some of those old fellows were really good at things they never did."

Thirty minutes later, Veronica and Hillard are on the terrace, bundled under Hillard's wool army blanket. They are drinking in the night sky. They hear the rustling of fallen leaves near the base of the tallest oaks. "Raccoons," Hillard speculates. "Can't be a púca."

"A *púca*? You've seen *Harvey* too many times."

"Every time I walk past that lamppost, I check for a six-foot rabbit."

"Cut two ear holes into your old brown fedora. I think that would be a good fit for him."

The chatter fades. They are absorbing the serenity. Hillard soughs. "It's so peaceful, you'd never believe we're in the middle of New York City. If conditions are right, on a very quiet night, you can hear the moonlight."

"What does moonlight sound like?"

"Like the scent of a soft glow, like the taste of a dream."

"When Gretchen and I were young, we would invent magic lands. We'd sit on the back lawn, stargazing. Sometimes we'd take blankets like we're doing now. Gretchen could pick out a star and describe the people and animals that lived there. One night, I said that maybe the stars aren't just stars. Maybe they're really something else."

"Like what?"

"At first, I wasn't sure. But then I remembered that silly game we played in the dungeon. That was the first name for the basement. Later on, we called it the catacomb. We'd turn out all the lights and see how far we could get in total darkness. Gretchen would bring a stick of chalk to mark the spot. When Father found out, he made us stop. He said we could get hurt. The pitch-black basement gave me an idea about the night sky." Veronica pauses for a moment. "I haven't thought about this in years. Sitting here with you, watching the night sky, brings it all back.

"Hill, close your eyes and clear out the clutter. Visualize the most brilliant night sky you've ever seen, a sky with countless stars. Put that image away into a mental compartment. Now, visualize yourself sitting alone in a room of utter, pitch blackness. It's so dark it makes no difference if your eyes are open or closed. You cannot see the dimensions of the room. The room could be small, or it could be an infinite, endless space. Adjacent to this dark room is another room of equal size, and that room is filled with intense, blinding light. A pinhole in the wall that separates the rooms appears. This tiny pinhole allows a spec of brilliant light to enter the room of utter darkness. And then a second pinhole appears, and then a third, and a fourth. And before long, there are millions of individual pinholes and millions of tiny specs of pure, white light. Now, go back to that image of the brilliant night sky and don't think of those stars as objects emitting light. Think of them as portals to a different place, twinkling light emanating from a different dimension. Light from a different plane of existence, right next to ours, filtering through."

"That's brilliant. An exercise like that changes our perceptions. That's a technique for learning how to see the unseen. I have never thought of the stars as anything except energy radiating heat and light. You can apply those gymnastics to anything. You could change your understanding of reality, even your belief system. And you thought of that as a child. We should develop that skill, resurrect that game."

"You mean go back to my parent's house and walk in the basement?"

October 1956
The Letter

Dexter Alexander's DeSoto circles the block a second time. His nightly quest for a parking space becomes more tolerable when he catches the subtle movement of his living room blinds and then spots Becky's '51 Nash station wagon parked under a streetlamp. Dexter's promotion required the couple to purchase a second car. The Nash set them back eight hundred and fifty dollars. Peeking out from behind the blinds, Becky watches Dexter ring the block a third time. Her concern fades when their neighbor, a night watchman, turns on his headlights and vacates a spot as Dexter's sedan approaches.

In a well-orchestrated maneuver, Becky kisses her husband and then slides behind him, helping him remove his jacket. "Thank you, Beck. Figures October first would be chilly. I hope we can get away with snow tires on just your car."

"Don't worry about that now, Dex. I'm so glad there's nothing at the club tonight, and we can have dinner together." Passing through the kitchen, Dexter's olfactory captures the aromas. His face transmits his discovery. "We're having your favorite, pot roast, mashed potatoes, cornbread, collard greens, and apple crumb cake."

Dexter melts into the sofa. He pulls his feet out of his shoes without untying them. "Feels so good to get out of those canoes." Elated to be home with his wife, he draws in a whiff of Becky's menu. "I've had a hankering for your cornbread." Dexter reaches for the newspaper resting on the glass-top coffee table.

Becky sits on her rocker across from Dexter. "I asked Mrs. Cabot if I could slow cook the pot roast in her kitchen. She said, 'Becky, that's your kitchen too.' There's so much excitement in her house. Their children are happy, so Mr. and Mrs. Cabot are happy. They're different now. I saw the same thing in my parents when you and I got married. They're happy for Veronica and happy for themselves. And something else that I can't put my finger on. Maybe they know that someday they will be grandparents. Veronica wants children, but I'm not sure if Gretchen does."

After dinner, Dexter relates a new pressure at work. "I had to break up a big fuss in the kitchen between the head chef and the grill man. That's all I need, a race war."

"Sounds ugly. Did it calm down?"

"It did. I had to pull each one into my office separately and let them cool off. I really don't like the chef, but I couldn't let that influence me. No one likes him. He's a slippery critter. He cheats at cards. I heard a story that he was the guy who would fill empty premium whisky bottles with cheaper stuff for the manager that was there before Pat. This guy reminds me of a grunt I served with in Korea. He cheated, too. Even at solitaire. I fixed it by bringing up one of the refrigerators from the canteen and putting it near the grill station. Problem solved."

Becky's proud smile transforms. Her taut lips and furrowed brow signal her next utterance. "Dexter, a letter came this morning before I went to work. I wanted to give it to you after you had a chance to relax. It has a North Carolina postmark."

237

"Dang! It's them! I reckon it has to be. How did they find me?"

"Stay calm. Don't go to your worst thoughts first. Read it, see what's going on." Becky crosses the area rug and hands him the letter.

Dexter studies the white envelope. "It's from Pastor Vincent Greene, Durham, North Carolina." Dexter opens the letter and examines the contents. He hands the handwritten pages to his wife. "Becky, please read it to me." Dexter exhales and slumps into the couch.

Becky returns to her spindle back rocker. Leaning forward she slips on her cardigan sweater. Becky transfers her knitting from the coffee table into a basket on the floor and places the envelope on the corner of the table, usually reserved for her bindle of yarn. Becky begins.

> *"September 23, 1956*
>
> *Dear Dexter Alexander,*
> *My name is Pastor Vincent Greene. I have known your family for some years. I am writing you to let you know what has happened. I went to the library at Duke and got your address from the telephone books. Folks around here tell me you went to New York. I do believe you are the same Dexter Alexander, brother of Miles Alexander. If you are not, please return this letter. If you are, I am sorry to tell you these events. Your mother passed away two years ago. Her heart gave out, and she's buried at the people's graveyard next to the AME Zion Church east of Raleigh."*

Becky anticipates a spoken response. There isn't one. "I'm so sorry, Dexter. Are you okay?"

"I'm okay."

Becky's gaze pierces the veil. Dexter's monotone utterance and tense facial expression betray his words. She continues.

> *"Your brother Miles borrowed money from a bank and never made payments. He gambled and drank away the money and left. We heard he went to Mexico or France to hide. No one knows where he is at. Before he left, Bernice took up with another man and went with him to Florida. She took their two little boys to her sister in South Carolina, but the sister has four of her own. Now the twins are in a foster home here in Durham. The boys stayed with their aunt for a year and want to go back and live with her and the cousins. Auntie said she will come back for the twins when she can afford it."*

Becky's hands fall onto her lap, then she wipes her tears. The living room is drenched with heartache. Becky crosses the oval area rug and sits next to her husband. "I'm so sorry, hon. Do you want me to keep reading?"

"Yes, please."

At her husband's side, Becky reads on.

> *"The bank tried to talk to Miles. He chased us from the farm, and he threatened us with his shotgun. The bank is going to auction off the farm. The sheriff will be there in case Miles shows up. The banker said if you wanted to come back and work the farm, he would make a deal with you. Your cousin said you were the hardest worker on the farm. People say that Miles was jealous of you and cheated you out of your share of the farm. Folks say he would get drunk and brag about how he got you out of the way. Did you know that he pretended to be you and signed you up at the draft board? Bernice knew about that and kept quiet."*

Dexter's eyes are shut tight. Becky squeezes his hand. "Do you want me to go on?"

Dexter nods and takes a deep breath. "I might as well hear all of it." Becky flips to the second page.

> *"Everyone around here who remembers you is proud of you. They say you are a war hero. Please let me know if you want to come back. If you desire, I will go to the bank with you. Again, I am sorry to bring you this news. I hope God blesses you.*
> *Sincerely, Pastor Greene"*

Dexter breaks the silence. "I'm sorry, hon. I'm sorry I brought this into our home."

"There's nothing to apologize for. You did everything right. You are an honorable and righteous man. Pastor Greene said they all know you are a war hero." Becky places her hand on his shoulder, "Are you okay?"

Dexter musters a half-smile. "I had a feeling Mama was gone. You know how you can feel certain things?"

"I know that feeling. I'm so sorry about your mother."

"I should go to Mama's grave and pay my respects. I figured Miles had something to do with me getting drafted. I didn't want to face it. Cain all over again."

"I'm so angry I could crack on that man till I run out of words. What a low-life rat. By God's grace you came back from Korea. If he was a good man, you would never have left the farm. We wouldn't be together. Look at it that way." Dexter nods in agreement, his eyes brighten. "The twins are the tragedy now. Those boys are your kin, and I'm their aunt. They don't even know us. What are we going to do?"

"I don't know. Maybe I should talk to Hillard. But their wedding is around the corner. I don't know if I should bug him with this."

"You and Hillard are friends. Besides, it's family, and that comes first. Even if their father is a rotten man. When you decide the time is right to visit your mother's grave, I'll go with you. We can take a bus, maybe a train."

"I'll call Hillard. I don't want anyone else to know. He wouldn't even tell Veronica if I asked him not to. If those boys really want to be with their aunt, maybe we can help her keep them."

"That sounds like the right thing, but we have to be careful. Their mother could show up anytime and take them away. This could get very ugly if the parents come back after we help the boys. They could accuse us of interfering. I've heard stories from my father about relatives adopting children when the parents died. But I don't know what happens when the parents just walk out. Let's see what Hillard says."

"We have to write Pastor Greene back. We don't even know their names or how old they are."

"Don't write him back until you talk to Hillard. We need to pray for those boys. We need to pray for guidance so we know how to help them."

Becky returns to her knitting. "Why don't you watch TV or read?" Weary from work and now riled and distressed, Dexter's sullen exasperation will not be allowed to loiter. He reaches for the novel on his side of the coffee table, Ralph Ellison's *Invisible Man*. A tale of blue yarn denotes his spot. "It's funny, Dex. My cousin told me she feels invisible now because she's over forty and men don't check her out anymore." Dexter looks up. "Gretchen told me when she and Veronica go places, everyone notices Veronica. Gretchen said she feels like she's invisible. They look so much alike; the only difference is hair color."

Dexter closes the book around his right index finger. "Skin color, hair color, it's different, but I guess in some ways it's the same. But I don't think anyone ever got sold into slavery because of hair color. We're not skin color or hair color. We're just people, and most of us just want to be left alone and live our lives. Does Veronica know? Does Veronica know that Gretchen feels invisible when they're out together?"

"I doubt it. Veronica would be hurt. I think Gretchen keeps it to herself. I don't know why Gretchen decided to tell me. I guess she knew I would understand and that I'd never say anything to Veronica."

Becky resumes knitting the sweater destined for a patch of real estate beneath the Christmas tree. Dexter sits motionless. The book straddles his lap. Becky reads the signs; she feels his distress. "Dexter, you won't be able to relax until you talk to Hillard. I bet he's home. Why don't you call him?"

"Thinking about it. What if Veronica is there?"

"Doesn't matter. She and I have been so close, you can trust her. She may not even be there. She's been at their new house a lot. Call him."

Dexter dials the rotary phone that shares the kitchen counter with a new four-slice electric toaster. Hillard picks up on the second ring. Hillard explains that he is home with Buster and Veronica is furniture shopping in Manhattan. Dexter relates the contents of the letter.

Hillard asks him to read it to him, word for word. "Dexter, I'm going to have my office send you a letter of representation. I want you and Becky protected. Don't worry about fees. The firm is going to be your buffer. Your brother is malicious and devious. He needed to suppress you. His criminal acts are thought out in advance. You don't think the way he does, and you don't know what he's capable of, especially when he's desperate. He could make all sorts of wild and unholy claims. If they performed an autopsy on this guy, they would probably find a defective heart.

"We have to make sure the money you send will actually benefit the boys. They might skim your money. We don't know if the aunt is part of it. I'll call the pastor. Let's start there. We might be able to trust him to buy the boys clothes, shoes, and books. I'll get the banker's phone number. Your criminal brother may have forged your signature on God knows what. I can get a bank loan, a contract, or even a deed vacated in court once we prove forgery.

"I'm going to tell you something. If your brother surfaces or if I can find him, we're going to press charges and put his ass in jail. Impersonating you with the Selective Service is a criminal act. He sent you to Korea. He was signing your death warrant. It will be my pleasure to hang the bastard."

"Hill, let's talk about that."

"Okay. Let's take it one step at a time. Can I ask you a question?"

"Go ahead."

"Did you suspect he was responsible for you getting drafted?"

"I had a feeling, but I wasn't sure because I couldn't have done it to him. But sometimes I felt like he was touched with something. I once had a dream that he snuck into our apartment when I was out and tried to get fresh with Becky. I've had other dreams."

"What do you mean he was touched with something?"

"He did some mean things when we were growing up. He hurt other kids, and he once hurt the dog."

"How did he hurt the dog?"

"He burnt the dog with stove matches."

"What?! Dex, that's beyond mean, that's evil."

"Yeah, I guess."

"Dex, be like the woodpecker that insulates its brain from the shock."

"Never knew that about them. How do they do that?"

"They retract their tongues to withstand the pounding. It's evolution. You must have the same skill, or you would have lost your mind by now."

"I've got to go, Hill. I want Becky to know she married a woodpecker."

Dexter re-cradles the receiver onto the holster and rejoins Becky in the living room. "Glad to see you're smiling. What did Hillard say?"

"He said not to worry and that I'm a woodpecker."

"A woodpecker?! Either you're joshing me, or Hillard's been getting into the Scotch." Dexter outlines the conversation, explaining the letter of representation and Hillard's plan to call Pastor Vincent and the banker.

"See, Dex, it's all going to work out. No matter what your nasty brother did, you got past him, and you got through Korea because the Lord has a plan for you. It's always been in His hands, and now He'll help the boys."

Perfection

The battle between the defending champion Brooklyn Dodgers and the New York Yankees has unleashed an endemic of World Series fever. An enhanced mode of transmission is typically the source of such a virulent strain. The New York subway system and the burgeoning television industry are the agents of infection. With the series tied at two games each and the home teams having won all four previous matchups, the pivotal fifth game, in Yankee Stadium on October eighth, is likely to determine the champion. For millions of Americans, baseball is a religion. For millions of New Yorkers, baseball is a military endeavor. For more than a few, baseball is oxygen. Today, the emotional fever is conspicuous and highly contagious. Just after lunch fans will begin tracking every pitch on radio and television.

Hillard Abraham has arranged to watch the game at First Serve Tavern. The twenty-one-inch console television from the owner's living room has been drafted into service. Fifteen patrons are huddled around the TV, including Hillard's guest, Joseph Russell, bartender and kitchen man from Northshore Racquet. A devoted Dodger fan, Joe and his grandfather, Poppa Russ, watched dozens of Dodger games from the roof of Joe's childhood apartment building. They still talk about the day they saw Jackie Robinson steal home against Chicago in May 1952.

"Why are they called the Dodgers?" a waitress asks.

"They invented the game of dodging trolley cars," Joe replies.

"Really? That sounds like a crazy thing to do."

"Welcome to Brooklyn."

Pete shuffles out from the kitchen. His bent frame, cloaked in a greasy apron, settles in behind the cluster of fans. A Dodger supporter, sitting on a chair, notices the six-inch paring knife in Pete's left hand. Gripping a half-peeled potato in his right hand, Pete appears ready to uncork a fastball. In his Delancey Street lexicon, the old-timer reminds those who can understand him that Babe Ruth was raised in an orphanage. "Da Babe, numba tree, had no mama, no poppa. I tink he's foist on da list of da best. Best damn ballplayer. Mantle ain't nuttin." Cindy the owner emerges from the office to check on the television reception. Pete hobbles back to the grease pit. "Back to woik," he mumbles.

The image of Yankee starting pitcher Don Larsen taking his final warmups evokes a bold prediction from a Brooklyn fan. "The Dodgers are going to win. Larsen is a better playboy than pitcher. Every nightclub bartender in Manhattan knows him, and he got rocked earlier in the series. He probably had a hangover."

A Brooklyn fan throws a dagger. "Larsen lost twenty-one games two years ago. He led the American League in losses. He stinks!"

The jabber at First Serve ends as the game begins. After the third inning, with no runs on the scoreboard, the television camera pans the grandstands. A fan wearing a Yankee cap offers an astute observation. "The black backdrop that's usually in center field is gone. I go to twenty games a year. I know the stadium as good as I know my subway stop. I'm telling you guys, the backdrop ain't there." The backdrop, a vision aid that provides hitters with a dark background for following the incoming pitch, had been removed to create additional capacity for the overflowing crowd. The group agrees that the missing batter's eye gives the pitchers an advantage.

With two outs in the bottom of the fourth, Mickey Mantle parks one into the lower bleachers in right field for the game's first hit and first run. "You know," says the Yankee cap, "If there's one person who is emblematic of America, it's Mickey."

"What do you mean?" asks a Dodger fan.

"He's like America, he's young and strong. He's a phenom. Just like America, he's capable of anything."

It is now the top of the ninth inning. Twenty-four Dodgers have batted, and not one Dodger has made it to first base. The city is holding its breath, jubilation in one borough, humiliation in another, history in the balance. When Dodger catcher Roy Campanella grounds to second for out number two, the fans in Yankee Stadium rise. Everyone in First Serve is also standing. The Dodgers, down to their final out, send up a pinch hitter. Brooklyn's immediate desire is to fracture history before it's written at their expense. Larsen is exhausted, fatigued after throwing almost one hundred pitches, and taxed from the weight of the moment. He shakes off Yogi Berra's sign for a curveball for fear that his weary arm will hang the pitch. Relying on fastballs and still hitting Yogi's targets, Don gets ahead in the count, one ball and two strikes. He delivers another fastball. The batter doesn't take the bait, believing the pitch is outside the strike zone. The charitable umpire calls strike three. Fans everywhere explode with joy, shock, and amazement.

Don Larsen has pitched the greatest game in baseball history —a perfect game in the World Series. No hits, no runs, no walks, no baserunners-twenty-seven consecutive outs. Team loyalties, intense and territorial, dictate fan response. Brooklyn's rabid fans view the result through a prism, with unmitigated disgust at one end and appreciation for the historical impact at the other. The deservedly smug Yankee pinstripes view Larsen's perfect game as just recompense, with a side helping of trepidation. Brooklyn can win the next two games, and the Dodger roster is loaded and angry. And yet, beneath the fervent affinity and cult-like attachments, Don Larsen's achievement momentarily supersedes affiliation. To the extent that's permissible under the unwritten rules of fan conduct and governed by individual constitution, Larsen's perfect game is a staggering event. On this day, the fans inside First Serve had the good fortune to have witnessed baseball history on live television.

After the game, Joe and Hillard walk over to Queens Boulevard. Joe's allegiance surfaces, "What a tough loss, but I guess I'll be telling my grandkids that I got to see Larsen's perfect game. I think it hurts more to see them lose on TV. Do you think Brooklyn can win the next two?"

"Yes," Hillard replies. "I think that Yankee fan was right. That backdrop wasn't there. They probably took it down for extra seats. But that doesn't diminish Larsen's perfect game. Both pitching staffs had the same advantage, and even with that advantage, the chances of throwing a perfect game are astronomical. And Larsen did it in the World Series, against the defending champs, a team stocked with great hitters."

"Hey, Hill, I need to get a pack of smokes. Do you want anything?"

"I'll go with you. I'll check the magazine rack."

Leaving the candy store, Joe lights up. "I can't believe I just paid a quarter for this pack."

"That's another reason to quit."

Joe and Hillard shake hands. Joe turns left on Queens Boulevard and heads to the subway. Hillard turns right, bound for his office.

That evening, Hillard calls his friend and Dodger fan Frankie Biaggio. "Hello, Annette. This is Hillard. How's it going?"

"To tell you the truth, Brooklyn is on suicide watch. Ma told me everyone on her block was crying. I'll get Frankie. He's in the living room. Hold on, please."

Frankie picks up the phone. "Hill, don't give me any crap about your Yankees."

"Would I do that? All because you called me from the bar after the Dodgers won the series last year, you automatically assume I'll stoop to that level."

"Let me tell you something. Everyone here in Bensonhurst is in shock. It's not as bad as Pearl Harbor, but man, people are in disbelief. I keep telling everyone it was just one game; we can still win the next two."

"I agree with you. It's far from over. But it was incredible."

"I'm trying to make sense of it. There is absolutely no logic behind this. Larsen is just so-so. He's probably the weakest arm in their pitching rotation. How did this happen? You're big on philosophy and interpreting events, even though sometimes I think you're off the walls. What do you think?"

"The historians have to wait until the series is over to define it. If the Dodgers win, the perfect game will lose some of its luster. If the Yankees win, it will be glorified for all time."

"Yeah, I agree. Doesn't make me feel any better, but I agree. Larsen is proof that there's greatness in every one of us."

"Exactly. Look at it this way. For millions of Americans here in New York and everywhere, baseball is more than our national pastime. There are sixteen teams, and each team is a religious denomination. The stadiums are giant houses of worship. The players are like family; millions of fans listen to the games on the radio, and millions check the box scores in the morning papers. Today, perfection was achieved under conditions that defies logic. If baseball, and all that it represents, is a measure of who we are as a nation, maybe on some level, Larsen's perfect game is also a measure of who we are. In spite of all of the dysfunction, in spite of all that is wrong with this country, there is so much that is right. So maybe right now, in October 1956, Larsen's game is telling us that perfection is achievable. We know what's wrong and what has to be fixed. Everyone deserves a fair shot at the American Dream, and segregation needs to end forever. While Larsen's game is celebrated, let's not forget that someone had to lose. For every Yankee heart filled with joy, there is a Dodger heart that is breaking. That's inherent in a meritocracy. There has to be a loser, and that's acceptable as long as everyone has a fair shot. And if you don't win today, maybe you'll win tomorrow because the opportunity to achieve success, even perfection, doesn't go away. As long as we're a free people with self-determination, we have that same shot that Larsen had. A Dodger pitcher could throw a perfect game tomorrow. It's not likely, but the opportunity to pitch a perfect game tomorrow exists. So, what's the better situation? One winner and one loser or two non-winners sharing an outcome not based on merit but based on a perception of equality that is simply a disguise for average?"

"For a Yankee fan, you're a pretty smart guy. I told you I should have made more of those philosophy classes."

"Oh no, here we go again. You're a Dodger fan. I don't think you could have absorbed more than three lectures anyway."

The Dream

"That's all Father has been talking about, Hill. Uncle Em put the game on in the conference room, and everyone in the office was listening. Father said it was amazing. I'm glad you got to watch it."

"It was amazing. A perfect game in the World Series might never happen again. So many amazing things have been happening. It doesn't feel right for us to catch up every night by phone. Not being together is unnatural."

"I know. Only twelve more days. I can't wait to get this over with so we can relax. Gretchen told me she's now thinking about eloping." Veronica Cabot draws a deep sigh. "Let's hide from the world this weekend. Just us."

"Only four nights until Friday. We can do it. Did you go shopping?"

"Wait till you see my new red bikini."

"You're killing me."

"Good. I wouldn't want it any other way."

After a few more rounds of banter, their regular eight o'clock phone call ends at eight forty-five. Fifteen minutes later, Hillard Abraham is sitting in front of his Ratheon twelve-inch black and white television for the nine o'clock news. During the first commercial break, he opens a magazine he had borrowed from the law firm. He flips to a story about medium-range ballistic missiles. Hillard recognizes an image depicted in a color photograph. He had seen that identical likeness a few nights ago in a dream. Or was it a dream? Hillard turns off the television. Sitting in silence, the dream experience filters back into his consciousness.

Four days hence, on Friday afternoon, Veronica and Hillard reconvene. Embracing in the kitchen, Hillard heaves a sigh.

"Are you okay? Is anything wrong? Are you getting nervous?"

"No, not at all. I've got to tell you about a dream I had. I don't even know if it was a dream. I didn't want to tell you about it on the phone."

Hillard sits in the recliner, his feet upon the carpet. Veronica settles on the sofa directly in front of him. He reaches for the glossy magazine photo.

"I will never have any secrets from you. I can't discuss this with anyone else. No one would believe it. People would say I was insane and should be locked up."

"I'm getting upset, Hill. What's going on?"

"Don't be upset. It's not about us, but I guess, in a way, it is. Do you remember when we were talking about dreams and symbols right here, on the terrace?"

"Yes, of course. Right before we became lovers."

Hillard hands Veronica the magazine. "I saw this image, this exact image, in a dream. But it was more than a dream. It's so hard to explain." Hillard breaks eye contact as Buster crawls out from under the sofa. The feline clears the front skirt panel, leaps onto the center cushion, and then onto the top of the back pillow. Veronica turns her head right and acknowledges Buster with a smile. Veronica repositions from the front of the seat cushion to the back.

253

"I was in bed. I guess it was about two in the morning. I..."

"When? What night?"

"I'm not sure. I think it was Sunday night, Monday morning. I was sleeping on my back like I usually do. Then it happened. I left the bed. I started to ascend. I could sense that I was rising above my body, leaving it behind. I floated through the roof of the building, and I kept climbing out into space. Then, I met an escort. I don't know what else to call him. He was floating with me. I can't tell you when I became aware of his presence. He was very old and wearing a white robe with a rope for a belt. He was almost transparent. I think he was made out of light. I couldn't feel any wind, and yet his white robe and long white hair were flowing. There was no other light. Just black. The stars and planets were tiny dots of light. We stopped ascending. We were just hanging there, floating. The earth, a blue orb, was over my right shoulder. I looked over at the earth, then back at my escort. I spoke with him, but not with words. My question was conveyed by thought. 'Where do I fit in?' I asked. He gestured with his left arm. A brilliant red beam of light, as thin as a needle, traveled from his hand to the earth, illuminating a funeral. A man's body was laid out on a narrow platform in the shape of a cross. His body was clothed in a gleaming white gown. The platform was draped in white satin, the top in red satin. Men in ornate gold and white robes were spaced out evenly in a circle around the table. One of them, wearing a gold helmet and standing directly behind the body, was holding a golden staff.

"I then started to descend, and almost instantly, I was back in my body. I have vivid recollection of my ascent, almost no memory of my descent. I remember thinking that now that I was back from the heavens, back in my body, I should go back to sleep. I don't know how much time elapsed or how long I was out of my body. After we spoke on the phone Monday night, I was thumbing through the magazine, and I saw that photo. That's when the dream or whatever it was came back to me. That photo is exactly what I saw when I was floating with my escort, and I looked over at the earth. Did I see that photo somewhere, maybe at the newsstand, and dream this up? Or did I have one of those divine experiences you mentioned? Should I be ecstatic or concerned about losing my sanity?"

"Oh, you lost your sanity a long time ago. But that has nothing to do with this." Hillard vents a laugh. "I would say that maybe you had a vision. Maybe your escort was a figment of a dream, or maybe he was an angel. It's a beautiful story, Hill. From what I can remember of my Sunday school lessons, the men you saw were wearing vestments, and the helmet was a bishop's mitre. I can't remember the name of the staff the bishop was holding."

"So, you agree that whether it was a dream or a real experience, it was religious?"

"How else can you interpret it? All the symbols are there. You asked your guide that one universal question. Where do any of us fit in? The more I think about this, the more remarkable this is. Can you remember how you were feeling? Did you feel safe?"

"Good question. Yes, you would think floating a million miles out in space with no space suit would be fear inducing, but I felt secure." Hillard closes his eyes, "I never felt threatened or vulnerable."

"That says it all. I think you had one of those amazing experiences. You were baptized in space! I'm so happy for you."

"I'm still not sure why a Jew would have that vision."

"Jesus was a Jew. We could start there."

"I think this will stay with me for the rest of my life. This will give me something else to sort out. I was a little concerned about what you would think. I certainly wasn't going to keep it from you. Buster knows about it, but he ain't talking."

"No, you're wrong. He'll discuss it with me. We'll probably just agree to humor you."

Private Eye

Lurking in the elongated shadows of autumn, the morning frost surrenders to the solar eye. The ice crystals meet their October end as vapor ascending from the rooftops. The husky aroma of burning leaves is in the air, uniting with the discharge from heating plants. Building superintendents are running their furnaces just long enough to snap the morning chill. The boilers rumble out of their summer hibernation.

Hillard Abraham is packing for Europe, sorting out last-minute details. His fiancée is heading up a meeting in the Cabot conference room. Veronica Cabot is reviewing details with the staff who will cover her workload during her two-week honeymoon. When she returns to her office, she finds Chad Jensen Harrington waiting for her. He closes the door behind her. "Veronica, you must come to your senses before you make a terrible mistake. I have the evidence. He's a gold digger."

"What?! Chad, what are you talking about? Why were you standing behind the door? I don't appreciate this. Why didn't Rita tell me you were here?"

"Because she treats me like I'm a member of your family, that's why. You've known me for twenty years, and you've known him for only a few months. You're about to put everything at risk for a guy you barely know. A guy who's a gold digger."

"I need you to leave my office. I'm not going to allow you to insult me or Hillard. I never expected such lowbrow behavior from you."

"Me a lowbrow? *You're* about to marry a lowbrow. I have proof. I hired the best detective firm in the city. Did you know that his father quit school in eighth grade and started out as a milkman?! A damn milkman!

They also interviewed people from his Jewish church. His mother has been shooting off her mouth. I can show you an affidavit that his mother said, 'We always wanted Hillard to marry a rich girl.' She's been telling people that your family should give him one of the Cabot hotels as a wedding gift! His mother might have made it through high school, but she has the vocabulary of a guttersnipe. She can't hold a conversation. Have you met her?"

"Yes. I met her once."

"She can only speak in clichés. She's repulsive. This isn't matrimony for them. It's matrimoney. I'm telling you, Veronica, they've set you up. He's not good enough for you. He's lying to you about being that boy in the clinic. Everyone knows that story, and everyone except you knows he's a lying Jew. Call this off!"

"I want you to leave my office. I always suspected you had a vulgar side. If you don't leave, I will call Father."

Chad barrels out of her office. Veronica closes her door, sits at her desk, and sobs.

The Tea Cozy

Becky Alexander places the serving tray on the bureau in Veronica Cabot's bedchamber. Brushing aside the crushed velvet curtains, she cracks open the French doors for fresh air. Veronica emerges from the depths of her walk-in closet, draped in a terrycloth bathrobe. Veronica transfers an armful of dresses and skirts onto the Baroque bench. "I should have purged years ago. I'm supposed to be getting married in less than a week, and here I am cleaning out my closets today. I'm trying to stay busy and not think."

"Whoa! What do you mean 'supposed to be getting married'? Are you getting cold feet? Almost every bride does. It's a big change."

"Chad said some very unsettling things about Hillard and his family. Then Bridget asked me to dinner and said the same things that Chad said. They both said he is marrying me for money. Bridget said if she knew Hillard was the son of a milkman, she wouldn't have been interested in him. She asked me if I really want his mother and father to be grandparents to my children. She said just because Hillard was the first doesn't mean I should marry him."

"What did Hillard say about this?"

"He doesn't know. I didn't mention it to him last night. I knew his family was of humble stock. I didn't know his father had been a milkman."

"You're not marrying his father. You're marrying Hillard. There's nothing dishonorable about being a milkman, and he worked his way up into an office job. Chad is playing dirty pool, and so is Bridget. Sounds like they're working together. They were both born with money. They don't think like someone who had to climb up from having nothing. Hillard doesn't strike me as being after your money."

"I'm letting this get to me. It shouldn't bother me, but it does. Does that mean I'm not ready? Do you have time to talk?"

"Of course, I brought two cups. The gutter man is supposed to be here in fifteen minutes. After I show him what gutters to fix, I'll come back." Becky removes the tea cozy and pours two cups of peppermint tea. The radiator's well-timed clang provides a moment of relief.

"Father knows you can't get that fixed. He just likes to pretend he's boss."

"God knows we've tried. The boiler man said just get used to it. Your mother told your father to get earplugs. We know who the real boss is."

Sitting in velvet armchairs, the small talk dissipates. "Becky, you know that people have been telling my parents that I should postpone the wedding. I didn't care what they said until yesterday. My parents haven't said anything. I know that Father has no reservations. Not sure about Mother. I know that outsiders like to stir the pot, and I know I'm strong willed. I've been able to lock out the nonsense before, but this is different. I can't lock this out. Did you have doubts?"

"I did let some of the talk get into my head, but most of those people had bad marriages. Goodness, I haven't thought about this in years. I knew Dexter's heart, and what my father said was so true. He said the only thing that matters is what I thought."

"Until yesterday I had no doubts about me and Hillard. I can't discuss this with Gretchen. Somehow, it would get back to Mother."

"I won't mention this to anyone, not even Dexter." Becky transfers the saucer from her lap to the tray, "These people don't know what you've got with Hillard. They don't know what's in your heart. You're in love with him. Chad and Bridget have no right to say anything. Do you know what I mean?"

"When Hillard and I got back from Boston, Uncle Em told me to watch out for the negative Nellies. If Hillard knew I was discussing this, he might think it's coming from me."

"I bet there are people on his side telling him to pull back."

"I wondered about that."

"It's easy for me to say that you shouldn't give the outsiders another thought, but I'm not in your shoes. This is the biggest decision you'll ever make. No one should tell you what to do. Whatever you do is between you, your heart, and Hillard. If I had listened to the people who told me to hold off, I wouldn't have what I have with Dexter. Me and Dexter fit perfectly together. We fold into each other like a pair of socks. We really don't even need the company of others. I see that with you and Hillard. I think your parents see it, too."

"That's the part that's destroying me. I love him, but now I have doubts. Are my eyes open now, or am I seeing something that's not there?"

"Oh, before I forget. I finished your index cards. I wrote down all the ingredients and even the pots and pans you'll need to fix each recipe."

"Thank you for doing that."

Becky hears a vehicle passing over the crushed red brick drive. "Gutter man is here. I'll come back in a few minutes. Do you realize if you cancel it, you'll lose Hillard? If I had cancelled the wedding on Dexter, I would have lost him."

"I know. That's why my heart is breaking."

Box of Tissues

As he does every evening after dinner, Chase Cabot is relaxing in his study. An aromatic wreath of cherry pipe tobacco, rising from his leather recliner, flares out against the plaster ceiling. A snifter of Cognac rests on his side table. Chase Cabot has learned to identify the members of his household by their knocks. Tonight's tap is different. It's subdued. "Father, can I speak with you?"

"Of course. You don't need to ask. For you I am always available."

Veronica closes the door and crosses the study. She inhales the male scent, the Spanish leather, the tobacco, the smoldering wood, and the old books. She repositions one of the four bridge chairs and slides it next to the recliner as Mr. Cabot places his newspaper across his lap. "I've had so many conversations with you in this study. And every time I came to you for help, you had a solution. I need your help now. In six days, I'm supposed to get married. I think I want to call it off. I feel like such a fool, putting you and Mother through this."

"Why do you want to call it off? What's happened? And don't ever be concerned about your mother and me. We will always stand behind you and Gretchen. What's troubling you?"

"I need more time. I need time to think. There's too much revolving around in my head. If I leave for London, can I take over the hotel project?"

"I am seldom speechless. You have caught me completely off guard. Before we go any further, and please understand I will do whatever you need me to do, I need to know what's behind this. Unless it's too personal and you don't want to discuss it. I also need to know that you haven't been hurt in any way."

263

"No. It's nothing like that. Can we just leave it as a case of very cold feet?

"If that's what you want, then yes. I will always respect your wishes. But don't ever forget that your mother and I are here for you, always. I can understand why you want to get away. That tells me you've been thinking this through. I'll have to discuss this with our London partner, but I'm sure we can find a place for you in the project. How is Hillard taking this?

"I haven't told him yet."

Mr. Cabot inhales a lungful, then puffs his cheeks as he exhales. "This is going to hit him like a ton of lead. He's clearly in love with you, and you seemed so happy with him. If you were not, your mother and I would not have approved." Chase hands his daughter a box of tissues.

"I'm so conflicted, Father. I think all I need is time, but I don't know if Hillard will understand that."

"He might if you explain it."

"If I tell him some of my reasons, I'm going to hurt him. I don't want to hurt him."

"Hurt him? How do you think he's going to feel when you tell him you're calling off the wedding? I don't get any of this. I thought you two were well suited for each other. Maybe I'm getting old, and I'm not understanding. You should discuss this with him. Is there any possibility that you might change your mind after you speak with him?"

"There are certain things that aren't going away."

"I cannot break through your circle of thought, and whatever your reasons are, they are clearly very personal. I confess that I don't understand, but that's not important. Your mother and I will do as you wish. All of the arrangements and plans can be undone. All I need is your final say so. Do you want to wait until you speak with Hillard?"

"No, Father. You have my word now. I'll tell Hillard tomorrow. After that you can let everyone know."

Chase checks the mantle clock. "It's only eight-fifteen. Why don't you talk with him tonight? Is he home?"

"Yes, he's packing for Europe." Veronica can barely finish the sentence. Tears are flowing. "This is so horrible. I must be a horrible person to do this to him."

"No, my dear. You are protecting yourself. You have your reasons. I can ring Charles. He can drive you over to Hillard's apartment. I think you should have that talk with him tonight. I'll ride with you. I'll wait in the car."

"Thank you, but no. You don't have to come. I'll go now. I feel sick. I pray that I'm doing the right thing."

Veronica kisses her father on his forehead. She drops her moist tissues into the waste basket as she walks across the hand knotted Moroccan area rug. Chase dials Charles on the intercom phone and explains the circumstances. Chase taps his pipe against the inside of the firebox. The spent tobacco tumbles onto the frost-colored ashes and the charred hackberry limbs. Toting the box of tissues, Chase turns off the light and closes the study door. Ascending the stairs to inform his wife, he stops at the first landing. Chase Cabot looks out over the grand foyer, the reception chamber for the many joyous events they have celebrated over the years.

Break Point

Hillard Abraham dials Veronica Cabot's private line. He assumes she is shopping and they'll connect by phone when she returns home. At eight-forty, he hangs up after five rings. At eight-fifty, he hangs up on the fourth ring. Succumbing to his anxiety, he dials her line during the first commercial break in the nine o'clock news. As Hillard hangs up the receiver, the Cabot limousine pulls into the apartment lot. Veronica takes notice of Hillard's TR, parked in its usual place, and the illumination from his living room lamp. Charles escorts her to the entrance. "I'll be parked right alongside the walkway. Right over there, Miss Veronica."

Hillard's apartment is in a state of controlled chaos. Cardboard moving boxes obstruct the walkways. Shipping wardrobes, loaded with clothes and shoes, are stacked three high in the bedroom. Metal frame wood milk crates brimming with record albums line the wall between the living room and kitchen. Corrugated boxes of books and files are clustered around a hand truck in front of the bathroom. A pile of clothing and a random collection of kitchenware on both sides of the door are awaiting their next life via the Salvation Army truck.

Clad in solid blue boxers and a flannel shirt, sorting through seldom used kitchen drawers, Hillard hears the knock. He bypasses the bags of trash sitting on the kitchen floor. He takes the longer route through the living room. There's no need to check the peephole. He's quite certain superintendent Ed is on the other side of the door.

Hillard's fiancée is now before him. Her eyes are red. Hillard has replayed that moment a thousand times since, and he is still not certain how she was dressed. He remembers a beige trench coat. *Yes, it was definitely a beige trench coat.* "What's wrong? You've been crying, and you look drained. Your parents—are they alright?" Clutching a handful of tissues, Veronica enters his apartment. Turning away her head from Hillard she cancels their normal greeting. "I didn't know where you were. I was worried. You don't need to be driving at night. I'll drive you home."

"Charles drove me, he's waiting downstairs." Hillard braces, for what he's not sure.

Buster peers out from inside a cardboard box. His assignment had been to inspect each box before transport. He vaults over the wall of the carton requiring the most scrutiny, a box of fluffy bath towels. Buster retreats to a strategic position beneath the dining table. The tabby rubs his orange face against the edge of a chair leg, waiting for his people to settle.

Hillard closes the door. Veronica is behind him. He emits a long exhale against the back of the door. Hillard rotates back into the room. Now facing Veronica, he detects a slight change of expression, but he cannot get a reading. Different emotions are simultaneously occupying the same space. There are no words or movements, just silence. "Do you want to talk about this? Would you like to sit down?"

"Yes, please." Veronica crosses in front of him and sits on the edge of the sofa. Her knees are locked, and her hands are in her lap.

Hillard shoves a box of files and books under the coffee table. Rotating the recliner, he sits on the edge of the seat cushion, three feet from his fiancée. He breaks the silence. "I promise you that I won't try to extract your motives." A smile crosses Veronica's mouth. "Just a smile? I was going for a full laugh." The smile creeps up to her eyes. "Whatever you have to say, just say it. Please."

"Hill, do you have any doubts? Any fears?"

"About us? No. I know there will be ups and downs, but we'll get through them. That's what strong couples do."

"My heart is saying one thing, my head another. I need some time."

Hillard closes his eyes, and he reminds himself that men don't shed tears. "Are we postponing this or cancelling it? Have you fallen out of love?"

"I think I still love you. It's me. I'm not ready."

"Is there anything else going on?"

"Like what? Am I late? I'm not. We were always careful."

"But you were ready yesterday and the day before that. What's changed? Has something happened?"

"Yes and no. Can we leave it at that?"

"No, we can't. I have a right to know. Why have you changed your mind? If you remember, you were the one who set the date, and you were the one who wanted an October wedding. I asked many times if you wanted to slow it down. You said you didn't want to."

"I know. I let our passion take control. I feel like such a fool, Hill. Look at what I've done."

"What we've done." Veronica nods in agreement.

Buster leaps from the floor onto the sofa and springs up to the top of the back cushion. Buster nudges Veronica with his head, and he purrs with her first stroke. "Buster, I'm going to miss you so much." It shall be weeks before Hillard interprets every shard of irony that just opened his chest like polished steel. He had excelled at avoiding relationships, and he was not inclined to date for the sake of dating. He would have none of the specious explanations, the indignities, and the ensuing emotional damage people inflict upon friends and lovers. Despite his safeguards, he wasn't immune.

Hillard rises from the recliner. With his head turned away, he wipes his eyes as he reaches for a box. "I put your shoes in a carton and folded your dresses. Do you want to take them?"

"No. Please give them to charity."

Hillard places the carton on top of the Salvation Army pile and returns to his spot. "It's going to take me a while to understand this. I'm trying to keep my composure. It's hard."

"I know. I need to go, I can't stay. I'd better leave before I end up in bed with you."

"What's so bad about that?"

"I think I just need a little distance. Maybe I'll go to London."

"London?!"

"I'll work on the hotel."

"Will you go alone?"

"Yes. Do you want the ring back?"

Hillard had not noticed that his fiancée is no longer wearing her engagement ring. He finds an analogy: be as strong as the diamond.

"It's your ring. I gave it to you."

Veronica draws a deep sigh, and Hillard notices an awakening in her eyes. She wipes her red nose. "I need something of us. Can I keep it?"

"You're confusing me. Are you breaking up with me or not?"

"You're a big part of my life…you're a part of me. I just need to get away. I just need some time."

"I'm still confused. Are we engaged or not?"

"I need to step back. But I still want you in my life."

"How can I be in your life if you're in London? That doesn't make sense."

"Wouldn't you stay in touch with me?"

"I don't want you for a pen pal. I want you for my wife. It's one thing if you're keeping the ring as a memento, another if we're still engaged, delaying our marriage." Hillard rises from the recliner and walks to the terrace window. He glances at Veronica's reflection in the glass. Her eyes are fixed upon him, her face anointed with pain."

"Where is the ring now?" His exhalation fogs the window.

"You want it back, don't you?"

Hillard walks around the coffee table and sits next to her on the couch. He places his left hand upon her back, between her shoulder blades. "The best reason to get married is to be with someone you love. But now you've got doubts. I don't know why or what's happened, but you have the right to change your mind. This is torture for both of us. I think we need time alone. Keep the ring. Do whatever you want with it. Didn't you say Charles is waiting for you?"

271

"Yes."

"I'll walk you out."

"No. Please don't do that. That'll just make it harder."

Hillard's hands are now on his knees. He looks down at his stocking feet. Hillard blinks away a drop. "When you leave, I'll try to remember our last kiss, our last embrace."

"Hillard, don't do this to me." Veronica rises from the couch. Hillard holds the door open. Veronica halts her departure when their faces have aligned. Her eyes are tinged with tears. Veronica nods goodbye, and Hillard returns the gesture. Hillard watches Veronica walk down the hall and out of his life. She opens the exit door and disappears into the stairwell. Hillard mirrors her path. He opens the hallway door and listens for her footsteps as she descends the flights. The fading echo surrenders to the closing of the lobby door. The cold and compact cinder block shaft is now silent and still. "A vertical tomb," he softly utters.

From the corner of the terrace, Hillard looks south, back toward the street. He catches a glimpse of the limo's taillights in the narrow line of sight between the trees and the neighboring apartment building. *And just like that, she's gone.*

The Velvet Box

The morning after the breakup, Hillard Abraham summons his old friends: strength and willpower. He cannot be broken. Just after five, he prepares a list of people he needs to notify. His law firm's senior partners are the first entry. His father should be in his office by eight. Hillard does not have a strategy for telling his grandmother. *Maybe not telling her is best.*

A few minutes before his ten-thirty coffee break, Hillard informs the firm's hierarchy. There are no questions. *Were they expecting this, or are they just being considerate? I guess most people will just talk about it when I'm not around.* After work, Hillard unboxes and uncrates the contents of his apartment. Unwilling to tolerate disorganization, he restores the kitchen and puts the furniture back into place. While unpacking the honeymoon suitcase, disbelief short circuits his instinct to logically dissect events and circumstances. His hunger to understand is unnourished. Reliving their conversations, reopening the doors to their planned and spontaneous rendezvouses offers no clues. One comment runs on repeat. After their trip to Boston, Veronica said taking a bullet for her was less complicated than taking a bullet from her. "That wasn't so complicated, Buster. Point blank, and I never saw it coming."

Hillard had gone several months without anyone knocking on his door. Veronica had her own key, as did the super and his kids, and a fair amount of security measures were in place to prevent salesmen or roving preachers from wandering the hallways. The rap on his door this evening truly startles him. He quashes the impulse from that vein of hope that this knock will erase the unerasable. Suppressing those conceits is now essential to Hillard's health. He conjures up an impression of building superintendent Ed and establishes a line of reason. *I've disturbed a neighbor and the super is responding to a noise complaint.*

Clad in boxers and a light blue business shirt, Hillard has no reservations about responding to Ed's ten-fifteen house call in such informal attire. He flips on the light switch just left of the door.

"Dexter! Come in, please."

Dexter wipes his shoes on the mat. There are droplets of rain on the shoulders of his black leather jacket and in his curly hair. Dexter's demeanor is gaunt. His shirt is partially untucked. "Dex, what's wrong? You didn't wear a hat, and you look troubled. What's going on?"

"We need to talk. Do you want to sit?"

"No, tell me now."

Dexter steps into the apartment. Hillard follows that lead and retreats, maintaining the same three-foot separation. "She didn't call you, did she?" Dexter asks.

"Who?"

"Veronica. She told us she was going to call you. I wanted to wait until tomorrow, but Becky told me to get my ass over to you now."

"Dexter, what the hell is going on?"

"If she calls you while I'm here, I'm just gonna get up and leave. Check your phone. Is your phone off the hook?"

Hillard exhales. In the kitchen he lifts the receiver. "I've got a dial tone. I'm completely confused. Where's Veronica? What's going on?"

Dexter pulls out a dining table chair and sits. Hillard again follows Dexter's lead. "You're not going to like any of this. She came to our apartment about seven-thirty. She asked me to do something that I didn't want to do. I'm sorry, Hill. I have to do this." Dexter reaches into his jacket pocket and places a black velvet ring box in the center of the round table." Dexter looks away. "I don't know if you want me to stay or if I should get out of here and leave you alone."

Dexter fills the silence. "She didn't call us; she just came over. She said our line was busy. Becky was on the phone with her mother. We heard a knock. I looked out of the window and saw their limo. She was upset. You could see she was crying. She said there was no one else she could ask."

"So, she had you do the dirty work. She should have done this herself."

"She can't. She said she had a ten o'clock flight to London."

"You're kidding? She's gone?"

"Yup. She said she was going to call you from the airport. That's why I waited in my car until a quarter after. I didn't want to be the one to tell you."

"It's okay, man. I guess it was all a pipe dream anyway. What right did a guy from Queens, a guy who lives in a one-bedroom apartment….?" Hillard turns his head and puffs his cheeks as he exhales. "Go home to your wife. I'm okay. You were put into a terrible position. You and Becky are truly friends." Hillard extends his right hand across the table. Their handshake hovers above the ring box.

"Hill, I know this hurts. Try not to beat yourself up. It's not you. I'll call you tomorrow." Descending the stairs, Dexter recalls his first visit to the building. Hillard hitched a ride home from Dexter when the TR had to be towed from Northshore's parking lot. The dram of peaty Scotch whisky that followed the ride did not dull Dexter's olfactory.

Dexter inhaled brisket on the second floor and tomato gravy on the third. Tonight, he is in no mood for a demographic analysis.

Hillard turns off two light switches and two lamps. His eyes adjust to the darkness. Buster emerges from under the sofa. The feline ambles to the windows that overlook the terrace. His four-beat gait is a silent passage. Buster hops onto the baseboard heating vent for a better view of the parking lot. Hillard walks into the bedroom. Needing a distraction from the burning heartache, he reaches for his quarantined black wool fedora, hibernating in a hat drum on top of the dresser. Buster and Hillard watch Dexter's DeSoto back out of a parking spot. Hillard tilts the brim of his fedora over his left eye. "Well, Buster, I guess we didn't fit in."

The Flat

Upon arriving in London, Veronica Cabot checks into the same hotel that housed the Cabot team back in August. On four hours of sleep, she reports for work the following morning and works until six in the evening. She maintains this pace for several days. On her fifth day in London, she receives a wire from Rita, the Cabot receptionist. Veronica had forgotten to confirm her safe arrival. During her second week, the hotel's general manager offers to show her one of their furnished studio apartments.

Veronica sets up her one-room homestead in a wing of converted hotel rooms. The furnishings are sparse: a single bed, a cafe table, and two chairs are in the center of the room, a butler kitchen is off to the right, and a tiled bathroom with a tub and no shower is on the left. Behind the cafe table, a wood burning fireplace dominates the wall between the bed and the kitchen alcove. The window in the butler's kitchen is bolted shut, and Veronica's scenic view is a brown masonry wall inches from her ground-floor window. A fixed window above the bed allows for some natural light. The hotel's proximity to work, the on-site restaurant, and the daily maid service augment the meager lodging.

By the end of her second week, Veronica informs her colleagues that she has acclimated to London time. Deconditioning her ears from the ring of Hillard's eight o'clock phone call has fallen beyond the parameters of her circadian clock. That's going to take more time. Immersing herself in work and coming home exhausted is her blueprint. The few times she broke, she quickly collected herself and renewed her focus. Although she purchased a new diary in a London stationery shop two days ago, she had to refer to her now retired diary for the name of a commercial washing machine installer. She noticed the memo that she and Hillard would have been checking into their Monaco hotel that morning. She soaked in a hot bath and wept.

Veronica had been encouraged by her staff to accept an invitation to a party in Knightsbridge. According to the invitation, Alfred Edenton III, the son of a member of the British Parliament, shall be receiving guests at eight o'clock. Quite aware that his beguiling American guest had recently arrived in London, Veronica's invitation included a handwritten inscription authored by her host. Mr. Edenton III offered to send his driver to meet her at the hotel. On Saturday evening at eight-thirty, a ravishing redhead in a black cocktail dress breezes into the affair, scorching the eyes of the debonair gentlemen in attendance. Veronica becomes the source of heat and light. Unattached sons of old money, seeking to engage her in conversation, orbit through the ring of black ties and dinner jackets. Veronica deposits several calling cards into her purse. At nine-thirty, she thanks her host for such a lovely evening. "Leaving so soon?" he laments. "The night is so young."

"Please excuse me, Alfred. I had accepted a previous engagement, and it would be most ungracious to disregard that commitment. I've had a lovely evening."

"With your permission, may I ring you at your office? Perhaps we could dine together one evening."

"Yes, I would like that. Thank you."

Veronica declines Alfred's offer for his driver to drop her at her next engagement. She asks the fellow on the door to secure a cab. Thirty minutes later, attired in her cotton pajamas, Veronica reviews the calling cards. She discards all but two. On the following Monday, the names embossed on six of those calling cards phone her office. Having anticipated that formality, Veronica instructed her secretary to inform those gentlemen callers that Miss Cabot is unavailable. By day's end, six salmon colored message memos are paper clipped in a tidy bundle and placed on the corner of Veronica's desk. She reads and then bins all six.

November 1956
Wet Leaves

On a wet and dreary day in early November, Hillard Abraham learns that his grandmother has been diagnosed with pneumonia. Under the double protection of a fedora and an umbrella, he walks from his office to his apartment a few minutes before his usual lunch break. Bypassing his apartment, he unlocks his TR and drives to see his Bubbe. The only unclaimed spot in the nursing home's parking lot has been engulfed by rainwater. The stormwater drain near the end of the lot is clogged with wet leaves; the rising tide has swallowed this corner stall. As there is never any available street parking and he is time compressed, Hillard backs his TR up to the pool. With the rear tires in the soup, he kills the engine. Hillard confirms that the steering wheel is straight, the hand brake is off, and the door locks are set. He swings out from behind the steering wheel, his feet landing on dry pavement. One shove against the front bumper is all that's required to initiate the alternative to rain-soaked feet. The car rolls with a slight downslope into the spot. The curb breaks the maneuver.

Hillard Abraham's grandmother is asleep when he arrives. She is breathing with the aid of an oxygen tank. A nurse informs him that Bubbe is being treated with a sulfa drug, and she is responding. Hillard leaves Bubbe's room and takes the back stairs down to the basement. He borrows a hard bristle push broom from the janitor. Standing on the sodden earth, Hillard clears the stormwater drain of the blockage.

The drain gurgles, and the pool recedes. After leaning the broom against the side door, Hillard exits the lot with dry shoes.

Hillard leaves his law office just after eight. He has embarked on a plan to accelerate his savings. He is working longer hours, taking on more clients, and practicing personal austerity. The senior partners' initial concern for his well-being transformed into support. They are in unity with his desire to buy his own home. The partners hold Hillard in high esteem. They value his natural aptitude to relate to his clients, to comprehend personalities and psychologies. He had expressed to his managing partner on more than one occasion a distrust of attorneys who display a counterfeit curtain of empathy. "I think they're in it for the fees," he had conjectured.

"Without fees we might as well close up shop," his boss countered.

"If we take care of our clients, the fees will take care of themselves," Hillard replied.

In mid-November, Hillard met with his banker. The following day he withdrew from Northshore Racquet. After touring three south shore tennis clubs, he joined a club with four red clay courts, four soft green courts, and four hard courts. Hillard discussed the change of venues with his hitting partner, Steve Andres. Steve also withdrew from Northshore and submitted his application a few days later. The two comrades confirmed their suspicion: the annual membership fee at a tennis club is negotiable. The hitting partners plan to resume their weekly battle at their new combat theater in March. On Saturday afternoons, Hillard has been scouting the towns and subdivisions within a fifteen-minute drive of his new tennis club.

Hillard and his banker had determined that Hillard would have sufficient funds for a healthy down payment and closing costs in about a year, so he renewed his apartment lease for twelve months. "Maybe we should have moved, Buster. Her scent is still here."

The banker encouraged Hillard to sell the engagement ring. "It'll fetch a tidy sum. Diamonds appreciate quickly. Trade your equity in the stone for equity in your house."

"I'll list it as an asset on my mortgage application. But I can't sell it, yet."

A few days after joining his new tennis club, Hillard receives a phone call from Northshore GM Pat Elliott. "We're going to miss you."

"I'm going to miss you too, Pat."

"What about the three land deals?"

"Nothing's changed. I believe we're scheduled to close those deals in February."

"Great. Will you be able to attend meetings here?"

"Yes. But it might be a little rough if Dexter is setting up the reception room for Veronica's wedding."

"I'm really sorry about what happened. Are you okay?"

"I'm okay. Thanks for asking. Would you mind transferring me to Dexter?"

"Before I transfer you, I want you to know that after the Board of Governors meeting last week, Mr. Cabot asked me if I had spoken to you. He wanted to know how you were doing. I told him I'd be calling you to discuss the land deals. He said in spite of what happened, he hoped you would continue to represent the club. He was sincere, Hillard."

"Let's close the land deals and go from there."

"Okay. I've got to tell you something else. I've got a message from the girls at First Serve."

"What did they say?"

"They said they miss seeing you, and even though you're a little older, they would date you. They're sweet kids."

"When did you go there?"

"Sunday night. My kids love a good hamburger. That son-of-a-gun Pete wouldn't leave us alone until I bought him a gin."

"Yeah, that sounds like Pete. I haven't been there for a while."

"Let me know if you want to meet me there for dinner. It's on me. If not there, anywhere you want."

"Thanks, Pat. We'll figure something out. Do you mind asking Peggy to transfer me to Dexter?"

"Sure thing. Hang on." Hillard's line crackles during the transfer.

"Hillard?"

"It's me, Dex. Are you and Becky okay?"

"Hell yeah. What about you?"

"I'm okay. Before I give you some great news, I want to thank you again for what you did. Not everyone would have known how to handle that. Here's the great news. Pastor Greene just called me. The boys are okay. They just turned four. They need clothes. They're growing like weeds. The pastor is a good man. He'll administrate whatever money you send. I told him the firm is sending a bank check made out to him for fifty dollars. My secretary is sending that check out later today. I want to pay half, Dex. I want to help these kids out.

"The pastor said the boys could use twenty per month, ten per boy. We can trust him. The banker doesn't believe any documents had been forged in your name. That's a big relief. The sheriff said the stories of Miles going to Guadalajara were just rumors that Miles started to throw everyone off. The sheriff thinks he's in France under an assumed name. No one has heard from Bernice. Her sister said the guy Bernice ran off with probably did her in. One last thing before I forget. The sheriff's brother-in-law is a stone carver. He can make your mother a headstone for under fifty dollars. This is all good news; could have been much worse."

"Yeah, this is good news. Becky will be happy to hear this. Thanks for helping me and the boys out. I've got to run."

Mail Slot

By her third week in London, Veronica Cabot is yearning for friends and family. Given the sudden nature of her departure, she recognizes that re-establishing those connections shall be incumbent upon her. After work, she buys a box of six note cards with matching envelopes at the same shop that sold her the diary. That evening she pens notes to her parents, Becky Alexander, her sister Gretchen, and friends Regina Ellsworth and Bridget Radcliff. She assures everyone that she is well and making her way. She implores them to write her back at her hotel address. The tendency to look upon her barren left hand, to note the absence of a stone weighing one tenth of an ounce, is fading, so too is the ring's outline against her finger. The unrestrained passion for the only lover she had ever known shall remain cloistered. She banishes any thought of mailing that last card to an apartment in Queens. Veronica glides a thank you note to Cabot receptionist Rita into that sixth envelope. In the morning, Veronica deposits the sealed envelopes on her secretary's desk with a memo to please post them.

Veronica will always regard her fourth week in London as a defining chapter in her life overseas. On Tuesday, she accepts Alfred's dinner invitation. They agree to meet in the lobby of the hotel on Saturday evening at seven o'clock. Veronica has been longing for correspondence from her family and friends. She had asked the front desk to instruct the carrier to drop her mail through the slot in her apartment door. By the end of that fourth week, Veronica diligently checks the floor beneath the mail slot. After returning from a Saturday department store outing with a new dress and matching shoes for her dinner date with Alfred, she almost loses her traction on her first piece of mail. The slick, glossy cover of a popular American magazine is a poor substitute for a floor mat. Veronica deposits her packages on the bed and picks up the magazine. She smooths out the creased cover. "I apologize, Mrs. Eisenhower. I didn't mean to trip on you." Veronica recalibrates the time required to receive a letter from the US.

Veronica and Alfred meet in the hotel lobby five minutes after the hour. Alfred is wearing a handsome dark blue suit, a white shirt, and a solid blue necktie. A tan camel hair overcoat is draped across his left arm. Veronica extends her gloved right hand. "May I?" he asks.

"Yes." Veronica offers him her left cheek. With Veronica on his right arm, they depart the lobby. Responding to Alfred's hand gesture, the valet relinquishes his grip on the passenger door of Alfred's Jaguar XK140. Alfred closes the door after Veronica folds her black cashmere coat into the cab.

Arriving at their destination, an opulent restaurant across from Piccadilly Circus, an attendant holds Veronica's door open as a valet hands Alfred his ticket. After checking their coats, the Maître D' commences to guide them to their table. Their destination is the premier corner table in the exclusive garden room. With a subtle nod, Alfred issues a nonverbal command. The Maître D' alters the route. They travel through the long and narrow congested bar, down the spine of the bustling main dining room, and past seven occupied tables in the intimate, semi-private garden room. Along the way, several guests recognize Alfred and momentarily cease their tableside conversations in anticipation of his acknowledgment. He ignores them.

Alfred asks Veronica for her cocktail preference and then orders a bottle of champagne. After Alfred approves the label and vintage, the waiter pours two flutes. Alfred proposes a toast to their new friendship. The crystal stemware clinks and rings. Veronica takes in the courtyard garden, backlit in a soft, golden hue. "Quite a beautiful setting, Alfred."

"I agree. And it is rare for the setting to be eclipsed by the beauty of one gazing upon its splendor. You are a beautiful lady."

"Thank you. And I am in the company of a handsome man."

"Thank you. I am a direct fellow; I prefer not to waste time. That is a family trait and has been for centuries."

"Centuries?"

"Indeed. My lineage has been traced back to an earl who defended his shire against the Danes before the Norman Conquest over nine hundred years ago. A member of my family has served in the House of Lords since the fourteenth century. As an only son, peerage dictates that someday, I shall inherit that seat from my father. Someday, I shall serve in the House of Lords, and someday I shall have a son who shall succeed my place in the House of Lords." Alfred awaits Veronica's response.

"I did not know your family's history. That is beyond impressive."

"Yours is as well. I believe the Cabot line can be traced back to the fifteenth century. It has been verified that your ancestors, although Venetian, crossed paths with English royalty. Historians have confirmed that the Cabot name appears in records from the court of King Henry VII. That, too, is impressive."

"I believe you know my family's history better than I do."

The waiter halts his approach, awaiting direction from Alfred. "Miss Cabot, would you like to order now, or would you prefer to savor the champagne and suffer my company?"

"Alfred, please call me Veronica. And yes, I'm enjoying this. I haven't even read the menu. And I did have a very late lunch."

"Superb." Turning his head slightly to the right, he addresses the waiter. "We shall order shortly." The waiter departs. "I must confide, ever since I was a child, my family and my dearest friends have called me Alfie. You have your choice, Alfred or Alfie."

"Thank you for your confidence. I like them both."

"I will confide something else. I am thirty-one years old, and by nature and custom, I am extremely selective. As a younger man, I resisted my family's desire to arrange unions. If you and I agree to keep company, there is a probability I shall offer you a proposal."

"I am stunned, Alfred. Absolutely stunned. I never expected to be having such a serious conversation on our first date. Until very recently I was wearing an engagement ring. I'm sure you know that."

"Yes. I am aware."

"We don't know each other, Alfred. I've just learned about your family's history, and you apparently know something about mine. But we just met. Please, let's just enjoy the evening."

"I completely understand. I had presumed that my future title was a sufficient starting point. And that is not something I readily share. I told you that I am very direct, and I know what I want when I see it. Please don't ever doubt my sincerity or my intentions, and my intentions are quite honorable."

With an appropriate peer, Alfred summons the waiter. After the order is placed, Veronica dominates the discussion, and all of the conversation is centered on her hotel project. Alfred reveals that he is familiar with the fundamental details of the project, the Cabot partner, and the partner's various business interests. The couple seated behind them lights up. Veronica fans the air. The residual smoke, drifting in her direction, is clearly an irritation. Alfred's scowl gains the attention of the Maître d'. A waiter clad in a white dinner jacket responds to his captain's finger snap and delivers an ashtray and a verbal request to the offenders. Initially, the smokers are annoyed. After learning who lodged the complaint, they extinguish their cigarettes and apologize.

Moments after dinner is served, Alfred discovers his lamb is undercooked. The waiter responds to the glare of discontent. "Please return this to the chef. This is not acceptable. Did you inform the chef of my preference?" The waiter issues an earnest apology. He then begins to remove both entrees while assuring his guests that the chef will expedite their replacements.

Veronica intervenes. "That's not necessary. My dish is fine. This beautiful plate of cold salmon can wait right here until you fix the lamb." Veronica declines an aperitif, and the dinner date tapers down. After settling up with the hat check concession, Veronica notices that Alfred's tan fedora has a stingy brim.

At ten-thirty Veronica is back in her flat, reviewing the evening. The hat is her first impression and elicits a chuckle. *Hillard wouldn't have worn that. He likes a wider brim. It did look out of place. And Hillard wouldn't have admonished the waiter like that.* She yearns to discuss her date with Becky, Regina, and Bridget. They would have been so amused that Alfred mentioned marriage on the first date. Then it occurred to Veronica that she and Hillard had discussed marriage on their first date. *Well, it wasn't exactly a marriage proposal, and it really wasn't a formal date.*

On the morning after her date with Alfred, Veronica rises with the clang of the Sunday church bells. After brewing a cup of peppermint tea, she writes her impressions of last evening's dinner date on a yellow legal pad. The gossip she would have shared with her allies by phone must now be written. Maintaining good notes will preserve the account. Describing Alfred and noting his several references to parliament reminds Veronica of the banter she had exchanged with Hillard in Rhode Island. She writes, "a parliament of owls." Veronica places the pad face down and draws a hot bath.

In the middle of Veronica's fifth week in London, she receives her first correspondence from home, a letter from Regina Ellsworth. Veronica opens the letter after a bath, a light dinner, and clearing her mind of work-related pressures. Regina reports that she and Skip will be getting married in June and that she has been working in Skip's dental office two days a week. Veronica responds aloud to Regina's inquiry. "No, Regina. I have not heard from Hillard. And we are not in touch." Veronica postpones her written reply. She sets the letter on the cafe table.

The day after receiving Regina's letter, two more pieces of mail arrive: a letter from Gretchen and an oversized picture postcard from Bridget Radcliff. Veronica flips to the color photo of a polo match. Bridget's message is short, sloppy, and written on an angle.

> *It's polo season in South Carolina! Are there cocktails in heaven? You did the right thing.*
> *Love you,*
> *Bridget*

Veronica smiles. *She probably wrote it after two Martinis.* Gretchen's letter is set aside until later. Veronica replies to Regina's letter. She emphasizes that she is just beginning to branch out. Veronica explains that she may not be able to attend Regina's wedding in June, but she would like details about Regina's bridal registry. Veronica does not take the bait. She ignores Regina's query about Hillard. Veronica has set her course; she shall remain steadfast.

A pleasant surprise awaits Veronica when she reports to the Cabot construction office on the last workday of her fifth week. The retired RAF officer, who had attended the variance meeting back in August as a member of the Cabot team, is chatting with the secretary in the outer office. The RAF gent insists on taking Veronica to lunch. They agree to meet at a fish-and-chip shop. Veronica writes the address into her diary as the retired group captain leaves her office.

Veronica's lunch date greets her as she enters the shop. "Miss Cabot, this is the best chippy in London. I eat here once a week." Within a few minutes of placing the order, the bustling kitchen serves up their meal. Veronica scrapes off some of the breading. Encouraged by her host, Veronica samples and enjoys the mushy peas.

"I will definitely come back here," she reports.

After the meal, the older gent explains that he and his wife hold a season box at a West End theater, and he does not particularly enjoy live performances. "I usually fall asleep," he confesses. He also reveals that he and his wife have decided that Veronica should attend instead. "You'll like Betty. She's regular and a good sport. But you are herein forewarned, she bawls her eyes out at the sad parts."

Veronica happily accepts. "Thank you. I love theater, and I'm looking forward to meeting Betty."

That evening, Veronica dines alone in the hotel restaurant. After asking the waiter to return the cocktail and a calling card sent to her table from someone in the lounge, the dining room manager assures her that will not happen again. After dinner and a warm bath, Veronica reads her sister's letter. Gretchen writes that the family is well, Scottie is interviewing for an opening in a Washington, D.C., law firm, and she is considering either a private wedding ceremony or just eloping. Gretchen offers to contact anyone stateside on Veronica's behalf.

Veronica's sixth week in London is dominated by plan meetings with the city's review board. Although the process differs from plan review in New York, the nuts and bolts are almost identical. Returning to her office on Thursday afternoon, Veronica discovers a handwritten note and a dozen assorted roses in a turquoise vase on her desk. "Veronica, let's enjoy each other's company this weekend, Alfie." After dinner, Veronica strategizes. Her response to Alfred must be thoughtful and well measured. Just after lunch on Friday, a messenger delivers a bottle of Cognac and a note to the residence of The Right Honorable Alfred Edenton III.

> *Alfie, the roses are beautiful, thank you. I hope you will allow me to take a rain check. I had accepted an invitation from our partner. Their son is taking us on a tour of his new shipbuilding factory.*
> *Enjoy the Cognac,*
> *Veronica*

The Chain

On the twentieth of November, Frankie Biaggio and an associate arrive at Hillard Abraham's office at nine in the morning to discuss another business venture. Hillard's secretary summons him on the intercom. "Hill, Mr. Biaggio and Mr. Monella are here."

"Please show them to the library. I'll meet them there."

Moments after Hillard arrives, Frank Biaggio grabs Hillard's right hand. "Salvatore, say hello to Hillard. He's handling the hamburger deal for us. He'll let us know what he thinks about your idea." The three men settle into leather chairs around a glass coffee table in the law library. Frankie slides the morning paper off to the side to make room for an ashtray. Then he dives in. "Both of you guys are family. We can talk freely, okay?" Salvatore and Hillard acknowledge Frankie with a nod. "Before we start let me say I'm sorry she burned you that way, Hill. Happens to the best of us. Annette said you'll find someone else who won't stab you in the back."

"I appreciate that."

Frankie scans the headline. "Doesn't seem fair. We're about to celebrate Thanksgiving, and the Russians are murdering the Hungarians. The Commies are no better than the Nazis."

Hillard responds. "A lot of people are saying the US abandoned Hungary. Another mess."

Frankie lights up his filtered cigarette. "Hill, we want to develop a pizza pie concept. After we open about twenty-five stores, we want to become the franchisor. We want to build this into a chain. You gotta handle the paperwork and the leases after Cousin Ralphie bird dogs

293

the locations. You've seen how the delis and sandwich shops deliver to the office buildings in Midtown. We want to do the same thing with pizza, in the city by runner and in the suburbs by car. What do you think?"

"It's a great idea. Has execution challenges delivering hot pies in the suburbs. I think you might want to consider opening in the apartment and office districts in the city first. I have no doubt your pizza pie will be the best in town."

"We haven't figured out the suburb piece yet. We have a great idea for the crazy rush in the city. Coupla weeks ago, this delivery guy carrying bags of deli sandwiches almost flattened me and Pop in the lobby of the bank building. Same day, we saw another guy on a delivery bike almost run down a bunch of businessmen. Those business guys didn't seem too upset. It's like everyone expects delivery guys to be outta control. So, Sal came up with a name that tells people that we're delivering food and we're outta control."

"Sounds good. You will need a catchy name. What's the name?"

Frankie, smirking, defers to Salvatore. "We don't have a good name, Hillard. We've got a great name. But we're not sure we can use it. We also have a great slogan and a great advertising gimmick."

"Why can't you use the name?"

"It might be a little off-color to some people. But it'll be really funny and even clever to others."

There is a pause. Sal and Frankie exchange prankster grins. "What name do you have?" Hillard asks again.

"Kamikaze Pizza."

"You guys are crazy; we can't use that."

Salvatore continues. "Wait, the best part is our slogan—'We Kill Ourselves To Be The Best.' What do you think?"

Hillard is shaking his head, holding onto to a sense of professional decorum.

"Wait till you hear about our packaging. Our pizza pie boxes will have the Japanese flag, but instead of that red dot, the flag will have a pepperoni pizza pie."

"Gentlemen, we'll be sued and put out of business by injunction within a week of opening, and that's just for starters. I love the concept, but please, let's come up with another name and advertising plan."

"We figured you were gonna say that," Frankie confesses. "We have a coupla backups. Sure wish we could use *Kamikaze*."

"Let's reverse the situation. As Italian Americans, how would you feel if a Japanese businessman opened pizza pie stores in Japan and he used a name that you would view as derogatory?"

"Like '*Mafioso* Meatball Company of Tokyo?' I'd laugh my ass off, Hill. So would Sal." Salvatore jiggles his head. "Yeah, we get it," Frankie admits. "But you gotta confess, *Kamikaze* is funny. Now we gotta come up with something else."

Hillard refreshes all three coffee mugs. Salvatore plunks four sugar cubes. Frankie crushes his cigarette into the ashtray. "Sal, we should have slipped some anisette into Hillard's coffee. Maybe we could get him drunk, and he'd approve *Kamikaze*."

Hillard rises. "Will you fellows please excuse me? I want to see if the receptionist was informed of any psycho ward escapees in the area. Gents, I've got to get back to work. This is entirely too much fun."

The brief meeting ends. Hillard walks Frankie and Salvatore to the elevator. They agree to meet in Hillard's office before Easter with a new name and advertising plan.

December 1956
The Nun

Veronica Cabot receives a steady flow of mail in early December, including two additional magazine subscriptions purchased by her parents. Her mother's first letter had been somewhat abrupt. Mrs. Cabot expressed concern for Veronica residing in a public hotel. In her second letter, her mother reported that Veronica's father has a mild case of the flu. Mrs. Cabot had also mentioned that she and Veronica's father might fly over for Easter. "You're not going to be with us for Christmas, so we will try to see you on Easter. Did you remember to pack your bible? Have you been going to church?"

Veronica has been proud of her provident, simplistic life, obeying all of her self-imposed edicts. Having been accustomed to a bleachy clean bathroom, Veronica purchased cleaning materials from a local ironmonger shop two days after settling into her flat. She scrubs her facility almost daily, usually before drawing her bath. The aroma of disinfectant, gleaming porcelain, and a sparkling mirror are essential to Veronica's domestic balance. The hotel manager arranged for his housekeeping staff to launder her washables for a reasonable weekly fee.

On a chilly December evening, Veronica discovers a letter from Becky hiding inside a fashion magazine. Discipline intervenes, and she abides by her practice of reading all fresh mail after her bath. An hour later, she tears open the letter. Becky writes that she and Dexter are well, and when the weather breaks, they hope to travel to North Carolina to visit his mother's grave. Veronica reads and then rereads Becky's closing,

> *When couples break up, folks usually choose sides. We're going to stay close to both. Christmas won't be the same without you.*
> *Love,*
> *Becky*

Veronica immediately pens her reply.

> *Dear Becky,*
> *I just needed some time. I need to tell you something I've never told anyone else. The night before my confirmation I couldn't sleep, so at three in the morning I went down to the kitchen for a glass of water. Then I sat in Father's recliner in his study. I had to move the newspaper and that's when I saw a story about a young Polish nun who had just helped Jews escape the Nazis during the Warsaw Uprising. She led them through the sewer system and then placed them into safe houses. Sister Anna risked the same horrors as the Jews if the Nazis caught her. Sister Anna's strength gave me strength, she was the most courageous woman I had ever known. Five years later, I was in a campus library pulling research materials for a history paper. When I got back to my room I realized that I made a mistake, I transposed a reference number from the card catalogue and one of the books I checked out was the wrong book. But then it hit me like a bolt of lightning, the wrong book was the biography of Sister Anna. That was the first and only time I read a book cover-to-cover.*

The night before her confirmation, Anna told her father that she wanted to be a nun. He told her to live in a convent before making that decision. He told her to eliminate all possessions and all distractions, even family ties. She did, and that's how she knew what was really important. A year later she took her vows, devoting her life to Christ. When she was eighteen, she was in Warsaw, saving strangers from the death camps. Now I know why Sister Anna's story is in my life. I have told this story of Sister Anna to no one else, not Hillard, my parents, or Gretchen.

I needed to get away from everything and everyone. I needed to isolate myself. I did move too fast. I should have listened to Hillard. We're not building this hotel quickly. It takes time to build something that will last, something that will stand up to everything that Mother Nature and humanity can throw at it. I pray that Hillard forgives me. I cannot describe to you how much I miss him, how much I love him. Please do not discuss this with anyone, not even Dexter. I know you won't. I trust you.
Love,
Veronica

In the morning, Veronica asks her secretary to mail the letter. After work, Veronica buys a birthday card and a red pillar candle at the stationery shop.

That evening, Veronica lights her candle and writes a note inside the front flap of the simple birthday card.

Dear Hillard,

Please understand, I had to do this. You have a forgiving heart, please forgive me. Please come to London and stay with me. I will never stop loving you. Tell Buster I love him. Happy Birthday.
Love,
V

Veronica slides the card into the mail slot at the post office around the corner from the Cabot construction office.

One week after mailing Hillard's birthday card, Veronica eagerly checks the postman's daily offerings. She has been planning their itinerary, identifying theaters, parks, museums, and restaurants. She hopes Hillard will be comfortable in that small bed. *I'll make sure he's comfortable.* On December twentieth, Hillard's birthday, Veronica finds the card on the floor of her flat, "RETURNED" is stamped across the envelope. Sitting on the bed, she utters, "It's really over." Veronica places the letter on the cafe table, lights the candle, and draws a hot bath. The following morning, while Veronica is at work, the housekeeper unlocks the door and immediately checks the cafe table for another gratuity. The maid spots the birthday card. *Silly girl, she didn't use enough postage.*

At the behest of the Cabot partner, Veronica attends Christmas mass at Christ Church in Kensington. After service, the partner's wife mentions that their son, the shipbuilder whom Veronica had met briefly on her last trip to London, had asked about her. Veronica accepts an invitation to a dinner party at their home in February.

January 1957
The Pretzel Cart

Mr. Chasen Cabot, now fully recovered from the flu, instructs his receptionist to change the location of the Biaggio meeting to Mr. Radcliff's office. "Rita, I don't want the Biaggio attorney to be uncomfortable." Two days later, with a bone-chilling wind whipping in from the East River, the meeting is scheduled to commence at the stroke of noon. Mindful of his tardy appearance at their initial conference back in May, Hillard Abraham arrives ten minutes early. He has not seen or spoken to any member of Veronica Cabot's circle since their October break-up. Hillard intends to keep the meeting strictly business. Mr. Radcliff's secretary greets him. "Mr. Abraham, if you make a left at the water cooler, the conference room is the third door on the right. There's a coat closet inside the conference room."

Hillard discovers that the second office on the left belongs to Mr. Radcliff, and Mr. Cabot is sitting in one of the two visitor chairs. "Hillard!" rings out as Mr. Cabot rises from the chair. "Excuse me, Edgar." In the hallway, Mr. Cabot offers Hillard his right hand. "I am truly sorry for the discontent that we've caused you and your family," he says in a soft register. "I have the highest regard for you. I think you know that. And I also want you to know that you can call me anytime to talk about whatever is on your mind."

301

Is he baiting me? Hillard's code of etiquette, wrapped around a moral obligation, demands a response. "How is Veronica? How is she doing?"

"Don't you know? She told us she sent you a note."

"I haven't heard from her."

"That's indeed strange. She told us in a letter that she had mailed you a birthday card."

"I've heard nothing."

"I understand." Rather than circle the cul-de-sac, Mr. Cabot heads for the main thoroughfare. "Should be another productive session today."

The décor in Mr. Radcliff's office suite is so achromatic that even the conference table is gray. The meeting commences at ten minutes after the hour. Frankie Biaggio attributes his late arrival to a traffic jam on FDR Drive. Mr. Radcliff welcomes the group as his secretary serves coffee and tea. He then turns the meeting over to Hillard, who reports that Frankie Biaggio now has ten sites under contract, three additional locations are in the pipeline, and construction on all locations will commence in thirty days. Ralph Biaggio adds that their competitor has not yet deciphered their site selection strategy of follow-the-leader. The franchisor provides a financial overview, and Hillard explains that a calendar with all critical dates will be mailed to everyone in about one week. The meeting ends with the attendees breaking into smaller groups.

Ten minutes after leaving Mr. Radcliff's office, Frankie and Hillard reconvene at the pretzel cart on the corner of Madison Avenue and East 53rd Street. Frankie asks the vendor to crisp up his soft dough pretzel on the open flame. Hillard asks for extra mustard. With heated pretzels in hand, walking east into the brunt of the wind, Frankie asks, "Have you heard from her?"

"No, it's over. I've got a feeling she'll settle down in England."

"This going to make you stronger."

"Yeah, I guess."

"Mr. Cabot has regrets, Hill. I saw it in his face."

"What's going on with your pizza pie deal?"

Frankie reports that they've got a new, innocuous name, and they're negotiating with an Italian company to import wood burning pizza ovens. Hillard accepts Frankie's invitation to come to his house and play football with his boys when the weather warms up. Walking to the subway, Hillard notices a mustard stain on his blue paisley tie.

That evening at dinner, Chase Cabot informs his wife that he had seen Hillard. "It was good to see him. But he said he had not received any mail from Veronica."

"That is strange," Mrs. Cabot replies.

"I don't know if we should mention it to Veronica."

"Only if she brings it up, Chase. If she doesn't, don't mention it."

The following morning, they receive a short letter from Veronica. She reports that in February, she will be attending a party at the home of their partner, and she expects to see their son, the shipbuilder.

British Racing Green

On the last Monday in January, New York's snow removal equipment is running around the clock. The city is plowing itself out of a knee-deep winter shroud. The vicious winds, obstructed by the natural screen of hardwoods and underbrush in the forest behind Hillard Abraham's apartment building, have created a landscape of snow dunes. Only the black leather grain vinyl top of Hillard's car is visible. The TR is entombed in frozen powder.

Buster has abandoned his normal observation post. Dissuaded by the rim of snow on the edge of the terrace, he will monitor spring's thaw from a more comfortable post. A bath towel, folded to match the dimensions of the flat crown of the baseboard heating vent in the living room, has become Buster's winter nest. Hillard finally has the opportunity to wear the black dress boots he purchased after Thanksgiving in the recently opened Roosevelt Field shopping center. The leather boots, a taller brother to his black wingtips, serve a dual purpose. Hillard's professional dress code remains intact, and his two roundtrip winter treks between home and office are less treacherous. Energized by Mr. Cabot's comment about a card from Veronica, Hillard has been walking home every weekday morning at eleven-thirty to check his mailbox. After grabbing a quick lunch at home, he returns to work by twelve-thirty.

The affairs of Thursday, January 31, 1957, shall be recorded by those within Hillard's sphere as a series of portentous events that alter one's path. At precisely eleven minutes after eleven o'clock, Hillard receives a phone call from a gentleman employed by the same company as the chap from whom Hillard bought his blue TR3. That afternoon, a dream comes true: Hillard signs the bill of sale and ownership documents for an almost new TR3. The color denoted on the registration is British Racing Green. His new Triumph, designed for the English market, is equipped with a steering wheel on the right. The following day, a new member of the firm, having heard the office gossip, makes an offer to buy Hillard's blue TR. They close the deal after work.

"The gearbox is a little stiff," Hillard explains to his tennis partner a week later. "It's just my second week, and the odometer has only four thousand miles."

"How do you like shifting with your left hand?" Steve asks.

"I'm getting used to it. It's like learning to hit forehands from the left side." The natural progression of the conversation takes a detour, and there is no mention of how comfortable Veronica would have been driving this TR. Hillard also skips the part about stalling it out twice and missing second coming off the line at a stop light.

February 1957
The Mouser

On a gray, chilly morning in early February, Veronica Cabot celebrates the progress report. The Cabot Hotel project is ahead of schedule and below budget. She treats herself to breakfast in the hotel restaurant. Veronica asks the hostess to seat her in the lounge. "I've always wanted to sit at a bar." Within a few minutes, a waiter delivers the morning newspaper, a white linen napkin, and a steaming cup of black coffee. Veronica reads the morning's lead story about the imminent resignation of US Secretary of State John Foster Dulles. The waiter returns to the lounge with a freshly baked scone, a dollop of clotted cream, and a soufflé cup caulked with strawberry jam.

Wrapped in her cashmere coat and a lambswool scarf, Veronica walks to the construction site for a meeting with her general contractor and a building inspector. After the meeting, with her field notes in hand, she strolls the perimeter, reviewing the inspector's comments. Veronica notices two iridescent orbs within the shadow of a two-hundred-liter metal drum still emitting heat from an early morning bonfire. As Veronica slowly approaches, the feline's eyes televise fear. Veronica halts her advance. Speaking in a sweet feminine register and with a measured movement, she lowers her stance. "You must be starving. I wish I could get a better look at you." The cat's apprehension transforms into reluctant curiosity, and its pupils relax.

Veronica blinks her eyes, but the scavenger does not respond. She blinks again and again. The street cat blinks back. Veronica had learned from Buster that a blinking cat is transmitting signs of trust and affection. The feline emerges from the shade of the drum into partial light. "You certainly look like a boy. I bet you're a tomcat. I know I'm not supposed to feed strays, but I'm not going to let you starve. And besides, you're a watchman, keeping the rats out, so let's just call it compensation." Veronica returns five minutes later with a small tin of fishy cat food and a can opener. She dumps the smelly contents onto a section of cardboard and slides the food back into the shadow. She does not see the mouser, but she can feel his presence. Veronica returns a few minutes later with a coffee can filled with fresh water. She deposits the cardboard dinner plate into the metal garbage drum. Every morsel of food had been consumed.

Veronica instructs her foreman to purchase a case of cat food from petty cash and feed the cat every morning. Together, they glue four footers onto a piece of plywood and fashion a food and water station. The foreman creates a permanent spot for the homemade feeding table near the fire drum and alerts his crew to be careful when in the vicinity of the cat. Within a few days, Veronica gains the cat's trust. Slinking out from the security of the shadow, he allows her to touch his peachy nose. "You don't have to be afraid of me. You are a very handsome boy, and you're a long hair! You certainly are in need of a bath. What should we call you? You're a little dubious, so how about Dubie?"

Veronica arranges for a veterinarian to intercede. With the foreman's help, the vet sedates and then traps the cat. The following day, Veronica receives the report. Dubie has a bad case of ear mites. Three days hence, Dubie begins his life as a member of the firm, returning to the Cabot office for sleep and sustenance after his daily patrols. Dubie has no intention of allowing the dread he had induced within the rodent population to be compromised by his speckled rhinestone collar.

A few days after the company mascot has settled in, Veronica seeks out appropriate attire for the dinner engagement at the home of the Cabot partner. Returning to her flat, she finds a picture postcard of Miami Beach and a plain white envelope with no return address on the floor under the slot. She reads the postcard, "Cocktails on Collins. Love, Bridget." Veronica postulates, *Would that be Collins Avenue or her new beau?* Invoking her pertinacious manner, Veronica suspends her curiosity. After a bath, she opens the envelope. Flipping to the last page of the handwritten letter, she reads the signature, "Love, Chad." She reads from the beginning, "February 2, 1957. Dear Veronica, I am so glad you listened to me and came to your senses."

Veronica rises from the bed, calmly walks to the stove, turns on the front jet, and ignites a corner of the four-page letter. "Yes, Chad. I have come to my senses," she utters as she flicks the burning letter into the fireplace. Feeding the flame more fuel, the envelope follows.

While getting dressed for work on the morning of February twelfth, Veronica recalls her part in an elementary school skit honoring Abraham Lincoln. That spawns the memory of signing the hotel registration in Rhode Island as Mr. and Mrs. Hillard Abraham. She shifts her focus to this evening's dinner party.

At twenty minutes after six, Veronica's cab arrives at the Kensington town home of Mr. and Mrs. Thurlow Fairfax. On her first visit, back in August, Veronica and her father admired the Ayrshire rose bushes below the bay windows. This evening, the pruned canes are dormant, awaiting their next growth cycle.

Veronica is greeted by Ackley Fairfax, the couple's only child. A tall and dapper fellow with brown features, light brown hair parted on the right, and a light complexion, Ackley escorts Veronica into the drawing room. As the evening wears on, it is apparent to even the service personnel that the dinner party is merely the backdrop for Veronica and Ackley. After the customary greetings and introductions, followed by the chatter that one would expect before and after a Beef Wellington dinner served in the home of a distinguished London family, Veronica and Ackley drift into a quiet corner of the study. The room is furnished in iron and dark oak. "How did you become a shipbuilder?" she asks.

"Five years ago, when I was twenty-three, my grandfather on Mother's side left me his entire operation. I tripled production in two years."

"That's remarkable. How did you do that?"

"I expanded into the Iberian Peninsula. I bought the controlling interest in a Portuguese yacht building facility. That gave me the base I needed. I upgraded everything, and sales exploded. I haven't looked back."

"That is quite amazing. How often do you travel to Portugal?"

"Once a month. I've got a good plant manager. At this point I might be more inclined to visit for the scenery and the food. Portuguese cuisine might be the best kept secret in the gastronomic world. Have you seen Portugal?"

"Can't say that I have, but I almost lived in a house that once belonged to the Portuguese ambassador."

"Maybe someday you will allow me to take you to an authentic Portuguese restaurant."

"Are there any here in London?"

"A few. But I was thinking in Lisbon."

"Oh really! What is it with you English gents? You don't waste time, do you?"

"I merely was offering to share a special place with you. I would insist on a chaperone."

"Really? A chaperone? How about a letter from my mother?"

"I apologize. That was an absurd comment. You Americans are certainly more direct than we Brits."

"Perhaps, but not from my perspective. But we certainly do inspire raucous behavior."

"You must be referring to Bill Haley and the Comets," the shipbuilder responds.

"I am."

"Why does American rock-and-roll cause such rowdy behavior? His band creates absolute mayhem. His fans block traffic and shut down the rail lines. It has been a borderline riot ever since he's been here. Tonight, he'll be bringing his bedlam to the Odeon in Birmingham. He played Nottingham last night, and they still haven't recovered."

"I'd say it's a reaction to repression. Young people are expressing their freedom. Maybe it goes a little too far, but banning the movie *Rock Around The Clock* here in London doesn't make sense. That feeds their sense of repression."

"That's a very wise observation. Would you like a Cognac? Last time I offered you one, you responded as if I was offering you arsenic."

"Yes, please. I was preoccupied last time. That's the power of love."

"I know that now. I did not know it then. I was once besotted beyond rationality," Ackley confesses, pouring two snifters.

"Is it impertinent to ask you with whom?"

"Not at all. She was a librarian at the Oxford Bodleian Library. I was twenty-one. I was, shall we say, dizzy in love with her."

"Why are you not with her now"?

"It just didn't work out."

"Was it because she was a working a girl? We Americans are direct, aren't we?"

"There are certain expectations, certain standards that must be upheld."

"So, you sacrificed your own happiness?" Ackley does not respond; a pensive pallor permeates his face. "I apologize. I never should have asked you that."

"I confess to this day that I may have regrets. Over time my family might have accepted her."

"Did she know that you loved her? Have you tried to contact her?"

"She was in love with me. I looked her up two years ago. She's married with a son. Her husband is an alcoholic. Can't even hold employment."

"She would have had a good life with you. Any woman you marry would have a good life."

"Are you interested?"

"You intrigue me. It takes a great deal of courage to admit that you walked away from what might have been true love."

"Didn't you do the same thing?"

Veronica sips her Cognac. "Maybe."

"We have that in common. That's a start."

"Maybe."

Ackley perceives an opening, "Let's have dinner on Saturday. There is an authentic Portuguese kitchen in Shoreditch in the East End. What time shall I call?"

"Would that be the sixteenth?"

"Yes."

"Oh dear. I had accepted an invitation from Alfie for dinner that evening. I hope you will allow me to take a rain check."

"Alfie? Who is Alfie?"

"Alfred Edenton III. It would be so impolite if I were to cancel on him."

"Indeed. You must not."

The following afternoon, Veronica dodges two phone calls from Ackley. She leaves her office a few minutes before seven. Her spirits rise when she discovers a letter from Becky on the floor of her flat. The postmark bears the date of February 4, 1957. After her bath, Veronica opens the envelope. Folded within the one-page letter is a black and white print of a woman handing Jesus her veil. Veronica sits on the edge of her bed and reads Becky's letter.

> *Dear Veronica,*
>
> *I loved your story about Sister Anna. I have told no one. But a curious thing happened in church today. We had a guest speaker deliver the sermon, he spoke about those special people with strength and compassion. People with the courage to sacrifice even their own safety and comfort to help those who are suffering. The pastor then spoke about Saint Veronica, who wiped blood and sweat from the face of Jesus as He walked to His crucifixion. Veronica, if you help someone with their pain, you take away some of your own.*
>
> *Love,*
> *Becky*

Veronica slides the note and the print back into the envelope and tucks them into her bible.

Mint Schnapps

Hillard Abraham salutes the mercantile aspect of Valentine's Day. The sentimentality others celebrate on this day is once again an indulgence he will not taste. He ventured out on February fourteenth twice. On both occasions he employed the technique of transfer. Those dates became sustained tennis rallies, with conversation replacing the groundstrokes. The first dram of Scotch energized the dialogue. The second round displaced the awkwardness. Initially, he classified those social endeavors as trifling outings with an expensive price tag. Over time his recollection of those engagements has evolved from contrition to empathy. *Those girls were just as bored as I was.*

Two Mount Rushmore birthdays notwithstanding, Hillard views February as a frigid, four-week inevitability that galvanizes hotel occupancy in Florida while punishing ordinary folks with high heat and utility bills. In some alternate reality, in another dimension, Hillard and his bride exchanged cards in the morning and firmed their plans to dine on lobster and champagne at home.

On this Valentine's Day, Bubbe's nursing home is Hillard's first telephone call of the day. At six in the morning, while brewing his percolated coffee, the nursing station reports that his grandmother is back on oxygen. Her bronchitis and that nasty cough have not improved. Hillard informs the nurse that he will visit after work. Yesterday, while helping his grandmother with her breathing exercises, Bubbe asked him about Veronica. "Where…is…red?"

She's not falling for the story. Savvy old lady, she knows.

During his ten-thirty coffee break, Hillard receives a call from a long-standing client, Jack, the builder. "Have you finished editing that construction contract?" Jack asks.

"I'll have it for you tomorrow. It's a terribly drafted document. I had to insert so many revisions in red ink it looks like a napkin from a party at Dracula's house."

The conversation turns personal. "Sorry to hear what happened to you, Hillard. Could have been worse, could have happened on the day of the wedding."

"Thanks, Jack. I'm moving on."

"Absolutely. Have you added anything new to your list?"

"I have, Jack. I'm done trying to invent powdered whisky."

"When I was a kid, we camped on Schroon Lake. My parents served us powdered milk and powdered eggs. They never figured out that we fed our breakfast to the dog. I'll pass on the powdered whisky. By the way, I'm calling Bellevue. You still need help."

"Be careful, Jack. Or I'll tell your parents about feeding the dog."

"No sweat. I'll just blame it on my brother. But seriously, Hill. I've got to ask you this. If you knew when you met her it was going to end this way, would you have done anything differently?"

"I wouldn't have changed anything. For the first time in my life I was really alive." Hillard's intercom buzzes. "I've got another call, Jack. Stay away from cement mixers." Hillard's index finger transfers the connection.

"Hill, your father is on line three."

"This can't be good. He never calls me here. Put him through, please."

"Hillard, I'm sorry to tell you this...your grandmother is gone. She passed about an hour ago." There is silence. "Hillard?"

"Yeah...I'm here. I feel sick. I'm not surprised, but I feel sick."

"Of course. I'm running out to meet the rabbi at the funeral parlor. Someone has to go to the nursing home as next of kin. Can you do that?"

"Sure."

A vacant overcoat and fedora, incognizant of time and sensation, navigate the slush and the traffic. Recalling that day, Hillard does not remember walking home from the office or driving to Bubbe's nursing home. The crepe paper Valentine's heart taped to the front of the reception station desk is the catalyst. Hillard had not made the connection until that moment. *Fitting. She was filled with love.*

Hillard has long subscribed to the power of levity, the notion that spontaneous episodes of comedic expression have the capacity to transform the intolerable into something endurable. Walking down the corridor to Bubbe's room, acknowledging the condoling expressions of the staff, Hillard passes Mr. Grossman's room. "She's not dead!" the old man blurts out. "She's faking! She'll do anything to get the hell out of here."

That evening, Hillard flips the switch for the law office night light and then locks the door to the suite. Before hitting the street, he briefly chats with the janitor. The bars and restaurants on the boulevard are vibrant and crammed. The street peddlers have vacated the intersections, and their empty flower stands remind Hillard to deliver a check in the morning to the florist. The funeral parlor's director had accepted his father's request to allow the family to supply the floral arrangements.

Hillard buys a pint of mint schnapps from the corner liquor store. At home that evening, he toasts his Bubbe. "God, how did she drink this stuff?"

A few days after Bubbe is laid to rest, Hillard discontinues his midday mail surveillance. He concludes that Mr. Cabot was merely being kind. There had never been any correspondence from Veronica.

March 1957
The Draw

To the relief of the gentlemen members at Hewlett Bay Racquet Club, Steve Andres and Hillard Abraham decline the opportunity to participate in the men's ladder. Steve and Hillard resume their weekly workouts in early March, agreeing to hit on Saturday afternoons until evening temperatures hold steady in the mid-sixties. Their matches draw the attention of both male and female members, arousing their competitive spirit. For the first time in his three-year tenure, the house pro books out every teaching slot.

On their second hitting session, with the first set locked up at six, the pro joins the ten or so spectators. During the next changeover, with Steve leading seven games to six, the pro asks if they have a few minutes to talk. "Sure, Kenny, what's up?" Steve asks.

Kenny explains that he just caught wind of a new tournament to be played over two weekends next month. "The field will be the best thirty-two club players in the metro area. Most of the matches will be played at different clubs on the Island. The winner will bring a lot of prestige to himself and his club."

"Why are they doing this?" Steve asks.

"To promote tennis at the club level here on the Island. We've got great courts. We need to make a little noise."

"Who qualifies for this? And who selects the players?"

"The players have to live in New York, New Jersey, or Connecticut, have amateur status, and won at least one tournament in the last three years at a club that has voting rights in the USLTA. The house pros and the general managers will nominate the players and then vote. I'm hearing that both of you are a lock. It wouldn't surprise me if you met in the finals."

Conversing after their second set, also won by Steve, the gladiators agree that the talent separating the thirty-two players is microscopic. Every match will turn on one or two crucial points. They also agree that they need to immediately embark on a stringent training schedule. Game on.

Hillard arranges to hit every other day under simulated tournament conditions. His makeshift team is comprised of former college teammates who stayed in tennis shape and his network of Catskill hotel pros who live downstate. On days when his racket is on ice, Hillard runs two miles and works out in a health club near his apartment. Whisky, ice cream, pizza pie, and bagels are temporarily verboten.

One week into his program, Hillard receives a call from Steve, who has also plunged into a customized fitness schedule. "Hill, Kenny just called me. He has the draw. They kept it at thirty-two. First matches are Friday, April twelve. The quarters are Sunday, the fourteenth, and the semis and the finals are the following weekend. There's something about this that reeks. You need to win five matches to win the tournament. Chad Harrington is the top seed; he'll play his first four matches at Northshore. He has a cakewalk to the finals, and they still haven't announced where the championship match will be played. All the big hitters are in the lower half of the draw, including both of us.

If we get off our backsides, get into shape, and do what we're supposed to do, we'll meet in the semis."

"I guess Chad's daddy groundstroked a check. I didn't know the luck of the draw has a price tag."

April 1957
The Tournament

Hillard Abraham's preparation on the eve of a tournament rests upon four crucial pillars. Eat at least one orange vegetable and a single protein, either fish or chicken, drink at least three glasses of water, avoid caffeine, and sleep for eight hours. The proper diet and the avoidance of coffee are controllable, anxiety-induced insomnia is another matter. An eruption of insomnolence can be more daunting than a lefty with a wicked serve. At one in the morning, on the day of his first match in the tournament to determine the best club player in the region, Hillard is slumped on his living room sofa. The ticking of the wall clock in the kitchen reverberates like a jackhammer. He removes the batteries. Returning to the sofa, Buster's purr chases him back into the bedroom. At one-fifteen, his anxiety spikes. *Four hundred and sixty-five minutes until my match. This is just great.* Hillard finally falls asleep at one-thirty. Five hours later, he leaves his apartment for a seven-thirty warm-up.

Hillard's match starts precisely at nine, and he squanders the first three games. His mood and commitment awaken during the second water break. In the fourth game, his first serve finds its savage roots, and his ball strike rolls out of bed. Hillard wins that pivotal game with one ace, two winners, and one unforced error. He breaks his opponent's serve and will in the fifth game and cruises without losing another game. After the match, while tightening down the wing nuts on his tennis press, an attractive chestnut brunette in her early twenties asks Hillard if he gives lessons.

"I'm not a teaching pro," he replies.

"They don't have to be tennis lessons."

"I'd have to think about that."

"Here's my name and number. I just graduated. I'm living with my parents, and they never ask me any questions. Call me."

Hillard has twenty-six hours to recover. Before driving back home, his TR motors to the site that will host his second-round match. He studies the parking lot, the court surface, the trajectory of the sun, and the effectiveness of the windscreens. He assumes the match will be played on either court one or court three, in front of the four rows of bleachers. He does not bother to inspect court five, a solitary hard court with no spectator seating situated in the wooded area behind the pro shop.

After dining on a grilled chicken breast, a baked sweet potato, and two fresh carrots, Hillard is sitting on his recliner, listening to a comedy album, when the phone rings.

"Hillard, this is Kenny. I hope you don't mind. I got your number from Steve."

"I'm glad you called. How are you? Is everything okay?"

"I want to talk to you about your match tomorrow. Do I hear laughter? Hillard, I'm sorry. I didn't know you were having a party."

Through a chuckle, Hillard explains. "That's Redd Foxx's comedy album. Hold on, Kenny, I'll turn it off." Thirty seconds later, the call resumes.

"Long story short, Hill. The guy you're playing tomorrow is a ringer. He has the talent level of a top three seed. He had a full scholarship in California and was a college standout. After school he was a house pro somewhere in LA. He's a big man, well over six feet. He's a very powerful righty with a minimal backswing. He crushes the ball and hits everything flat. He just moved here; I mean literally last week."

"How does he qualify for the tournament?"

"This is how we know it's a setup. They've been trying to hide him. The organizers reserved the right to offer one special exemption. Now, get this part: he was working for an advertising company in Southern Cal. He moved here to work for a Madison Avenue public relations firm owned by Harrington Enterprises. It's pure luck that we found this out. My girlfriend's dad coached against him in California."

"So that's why I never heard of him and why none of my tennis buddies know him. I'll need a strategy."

"Can't help you there, Hill. I just know he's tall, thick, and powerful." Hillard thanks Kenny for the scouting report and dials Steve Andres.

"I'm hearing he's strong as a bull. I bet you're faster than he is, Hill. Run him, run him till his legs fall off. Your drop shot is your friend. Go corner to corner on rallies. Take what's there, and don't go for too much. You've got to get a good read on his serve. If you can get him to neutral, you'll be able to break him. Make him work hard on his service games. I've seen guys like him, guys with endomorphic bodies that club the ball. I'll bet you a steak dinner his winners come from his forehand side. Make him hit backhands on the run." Steve awaits Hillard's response. There is only silence. "I've said enough. You know what's going on. They're scheming to take you out. Take care of business, Hillard."

Hillard opens the terrace door. He inhales the evening, natural ventilation for his seething anger. His reptilian rage is clamoring for freedom. Sequestered within its cage, controlled by a time lock, that vault is set to open tomorrow morning.

Thirty minutes before his second-round match, Hillard reports to the tournament representative. Hillard learns that his match will be played on the isolated hard court behind the pro shop, and the umpire originally scheduled to oversee the match has been reassigned. "Under these conditions, the players will officiate," the representative explains.

"The rules allow for no umpire provided both players consent. I do not consent."

"Well, you're just going to have to consent. Unless you want to consider forfeiting."

"Under no conditions will there be a forfeit, and under no conditions will this match be played without a chair umpire. Tournament rules require you or another tournament official to umpire. I have justified concerns about you sitting up in that chair. Your ignorance of the rules indicates you are either incapable or unworthy. I am going to ask the house pro to umpire. He's a member of the USLTA and completely trustworthy. He is also allowed by rule to certify the official scorecard. I don't know what you do for a living, sir, and I don't care. But you need to know that I am an attorney, and I have represented the New York State Sheriffs' Association in court. I will not tolerate conditions that I deem to be unfair or unjust."

After a brief warm-up, the house pro, serving as the umpire, flips a coin. The blonde Californian selects heads. Hillard wins the toss and defers. The gentleman's initial first serve, a rocket, is long. Hillard's backhand return of the second serve, hit deep into the server's backhand corner, is unreturnable. Hillard's down-the-line forehand return on the next point misses the corner of the baseline by an inch. His forehand return on the first serve of the third point explodes over the low point of the net and ticks the vinyl sideline tape just past the service line. Hillard's underlying strategy, to react and respond until he can get a solid read on this ox, is about to be amended. Hillard will take an early, calculated risk. On the fourth point of the first game, Hillard correctly anticipates a wide first serve into the left service box. He nails the backhand return down the line for another clean winner. Down two break points, the blonde ringer adjusts his service location. He moves three inches closer to the center mark. Hillard correctly anticipates serve and volley. He pounces on the first serve. Hillard's cross-court forehand return is too low and too hot to handle. Hillard's revised game plan is intact. Break him early.

During the first changeover, Hillard could not have known that his methodical evisceration of this mountebank from California would achieve a rarefied personal distinction. Such speculation during the match would have required a degree of self-consciousness, and that switch had been turned off. Today's match will later be analyzed as an aberration, a contravention to the notion that a tennis match is a battle of attrition, one player clawing his way to a win. That manuscript had been the norm for Hillard.

In today's match, Hillard was a spectator, viewing the play remotely. His perceptions possessed a sense of foreknowledge. His anticipation of his opponent's shot and the shot itself were one and the same. His feet moved at the speed of thought. Time and motion were bending to his will. He once had a brief encounter with this sensation—that catch in Central Park in a championship softball game. He envisioned the flight of the ball before the slugger hit it.

That evening, Hillard evaluates his performance against his personal doctrine of tennis, his list of goals, and aspirations. He acknowledges that today's match might be the first and only time in his life that he will have checked all thirty boxes. A sobering humility intervenes. Under different conditions and in a different venue, the player from California could win a rematch. Returning to his apartment after depositing a garbage bag into the incinerator chute, Hillard hears his phone ringing. "Hey, Steve. I heard you won your match."

"I did, but I had to go three sets. My left hamstring is acting up. I knew you were ready, Hill. Those clowns are already making excuses…the move from California was too taxing…he's been living in a hotel…he's not adjusted to our time zone, blah, blah, blah. You destroyed him. I'm proud of you." Steve delivers a blow-by-blow account of the critical points in his match and advises Hillard to get plenty of rest for his two o'clock quarter-final match.

"How bad is your hamstring?" Hillard asks.

"Nothing that an Epsom salt bath and my wife's avgolemono soup with orzo can't fix."

The venue for Hillard's quarter-final match is a grand tennis club in Manhasset. After warmups, a waiter attired in a white shirt and black bow tie serves each player a tray with a thermos of ice water and paper cups. Hillard recognizes his opponent's name but not his face, and with good reason. This older fellow, a married father of two, had not won a tournament in four years. In his last nine tournaments, he lost in the first round and left the courts long before the top seeds were scheduled to report. After warm-ups, Hillard's foe unties both sneakers, peels off his socks, and slips on two knee braces. An elbow sleeve on his right arm soon follows.

With Hillard leading four games to one in the first set, the older chap limps to the bench during the changeover. The umpire descends the four rungs of the wooden ladder that connects his perch with the red clay to investigate. The injury is a torn calf muscle. The umpire serves notice. The afflicted player, clearly in agony, is allowed a five-minute injury timeout but cannot receive medical treatment. Hillard agrees to allow a second five-minute medical timeout and offers to remove any objections to medical intervention. His opponent retires, and Hillard moves on. Hillard's hitting partner, Steve Andres, awaits in the semifinals.

The night before their match, Hillard and Steve agree that the older fellow with the obvious injuries was to have been fodder for the rogue from California. The conversation rolls around to their looming match, only fourteen hours out. "It's really a shame we have to meet this way in the semis, Hill. With the crap that Harrington has been saying about you, there's no question that you deserve the right to kick his ass more than I do. I want you fresh for the final. I want you to humiliate him."

"Please don't do that. I want you to play hard. You can beat me, and if you do, you'll kick his ass. I just hate the thought of having to go back to Northshore."

"It doesn't matter where you play him or on what surface. You could play him on the moon, and you'd beat him. Jump on his second serve, throw in some kick on your first. Disrupt his rhythm, and he becomes an unforced error machine. I can't believe that jerk gets to play all five matches on his home court. He's a lock in his semifinal. He's playing his doubles partner. Anyone who understands how they rigged the seedings knows his semifinal is a sham. I can think of seven or eight players that should have been seeded above him, and that includes that guy you took apart from California. I'll see you tomorrow."

Hillard runs down to his mailbox. In the lobby he chats with a second-floor neighbor about New York City retiring its last electric trolley car. Back in his apartment, he settles into his recliner with a newspaper and two magazines. Moments later the phone rings.

"Hill, this is Joe. How you doing?"

"Hey, Joe. I'm good. Haven't seen you since Larsen's perfect game. How are you?"

"I was good until you mentioned Larsen. Hey, Dex gave me the day off, and I scored two tickets to tomorrow's game at Ebbets Field. Podres is pitching for Brooklyn. The Pirates are tough. No one runs on their right fielder, Clemente. Not even Jackie. Wanna go?"

"Man, I'd love to, but I've got a tennis match tomorrow. I really appreciate you asking me. I do want to see a game in Brooklyn, and everyone is saying they'll be gone by next year."

"Yeah, they're leaving. Wait a minute, are you in that tournament?"

"Yes. The semis are tomorrow. The finals are at Northshore on Sunday."

"I'll ask Dexter if I can work the club room on Sunday."

"We can't talk about Sunday. It's bad luck. I was just reading the sports pages. Let's check the schedule." They agree to meet at Ebbets Field on Sunday, May fifth, and watch Hammerin' Hank Aaron and the Milwaukee Braves.

On the morning of Hillard's semifinal match with Steve Andres, Buster hears a sound that awakens the memory of a soothing voice and spiked fingers. The feline scoots through his arch onto the terrace. He watches a Mercedes-Benz 190 SL park near Hillard's TR. Buster races back into the living room and leaps onto the recliner's padded headrest. Transmitting signals of buoyant anticipation that only a cat fancier could interpret, Buster rotates his ears in the direction of the door tumbler. His vertical pupils lock onto the thumb bolt. Hillard, fresh from his morning shower and wrapped in a towel, pays little attention to the beast perched upon the recliner. Buster pays even less attention to Hillard. Leaving a trail of water droplets as he passes into the bedroom, Hillard checks on his TR through the window. Taking notice of the red Mercedes, he initiates a conversation with his roommate. "I always thought she would have looked better in a red one. Silver didn't do her justice." Gifted with the patience of a predator lying in wait yet equipped to discern only shades of blue and green, Buster's expectation drifts off into a long, blissful nap. Hillard loads his tennis bag and locks his apartment.

Hillard parks his TR in a shaded area of a paved lot in Long Beach, Long Island. Forty-eight hours before his semifinal match, Hillard had received notice from teaching pro Kenny about a change of venue. "Hill, the tournament director is changing the location of your semi. He just learned that the club up in Westchester is restricted. Several members have complained about you. Your match with Steve will be back on the Island."

There is no pre-match conversation. Three vanilla rallies serve as warm-ups. Steve wins the coin toss and proceeds to lose the first game of the match. Hillard serves the second game, and his initial first serve is wide of the T by three inches. Steve nets the mediocre second serve. Hillard wins the second game at love and breaks Steve in the third game. Steve is lackluster in every facet, his serves lack pace, and his groundstrokes are either long or finding the net. When he manages to keep the ball in play, he hits with no depth, gifting Hillard the opportunity to hit winners. During the change of sides after the fifth game, Hillard murmurs, "Stop tanking." Steve's racket responds. He promptly loses the next game at love and then ends the first set by serving a double fault on the first of Hillard's three break points. Hillard wins the first set six games to one.

After serving the first game of the second set, Hillard glares at Steve during the exchange of balls. Steve returns a wry smile, loaded with topspin. Steve manages to hold service twice and create the illusion of a competitive match. With the set tied at two games apiece, Hillard runs it out, breaking Steve in the sixth game and again in the eighth.

That evening Hillard dials Steve's number. "You shouldn't have done that. It's a violation of everything we love about the game."

"This is different. They've made this political. Besides, the way you were locked in with your serve, I wasn't going to beat you. After you blow Harrington off the court, we've got to lean on house pros and GMs to clean this up. Tournaments must be fair, and results must be based on merit. There cannot be this backroom fixing going on. Take care of business tomorrow."

After an early dinner of tuna fish and half a cantaloupe, Hillard is unwinding on his terrace, writing notes in the margin of a contract. He feels a shock, a sting on the underside of his right forearm. A yellow jacket has left a calling card. Hillard grinds the intruder into the concrete with the bird biology book and then runs to the kitchen for Bubbe's remedy. He pours white vinegar onto the sting site. The venom and the red blotch are traveling. He applies pressure with his left hand, attempting to squeeze out some of the toxin. The swelling is now creeping up past his elbow and down to his hand.

"Buster, I'm docking your pay," Hillard announces as he throws on sweatpants and a business shirt and hustles down to the local pharmacy. The pharmacist explains that diphenhydramine is the best treatment, but Hillard will need a prescription. Hillard pleads his case, but the pharmacist holds his ground. He cannot dispense without a prescription. "Sir, I'm desperate. Look, I'll make a deal with you. I'll barter my legal services." The pharmacist places an open bottle of the antihistamine on the counter in front of Hillard and turns his back to type out a prescription label. Hillard swipes a swig. Walking back to his apartment, Hillard reminds himself to return to the drugstore in a few weeks to review a lease for a second pharmacy location. The medicine induces an urge to sleep. Hillard sets his alarm for seven o'clock and climbs into bed.

At nine o'clock that night, Chad Harrington receives a return call from the detective agency he had engaged last October to besmirch Hillard and his family. "I have no new updates for you, Mr. Harrington. I've checked with all our sources. I've got nothing new to report."

Last month, when Chad learned of this prestigious tournament, he engineered every advantage he could envision. No expense would be too great. No principle would stand in his way. He had instructed his hired gun to research every facet about Hillard Abraham's tennis background. "I need your agency to go back as far as you can. Let's find out what he didn't like as a kid. Every kid has one area of his game that's weak. You've got to find out what that was. The further you go back, the better. Talk to his coaches, his teammates, guys he played in college. But stay away from that guy he practices with because they are friends. You get the picture. I need a report in two weeks. I want it delivered verbally. I'll take notes. I don't want anything from you in writing. He already got his hands on something I thought was out of reach. I exposed him to the girl who was supposed to marry me, but he got in my way. It's time to finish him off."

Match Point

No amount of caffeine can open the antihistamine curtain. Despite two cups of coffee, a set of twenty-five push-ups, and a shower in frigid water, on the morning of the finals, Hillard Abraham's head is in a fog. He has been here before, after similar stings or during pollen season as an adolescent. Under those conditions there had been no pressing need for a quick recovery. Now, he is in dire need to break through the haze and resuscitate his dulled sensibilities. His right arm has ballooned to a grotesque proportion, the sting site is various shades of red, and his hand grip is restricted by swollen tissue and discomfort. He dismisses any notion of swallowing an aspirin or an allergy pill. He will have to overcome this naturally, summoning whatever it takes to get through. Borrowing a lesson learned from Jakub Baranski, Hillard pulls a white long-sleeve undershirt from his winter drawer and snips the sleeves by two inches.

Hillard takes a second shower in artic water before getting ready for battle. He tries to convince himself that the swelling is subsiding and that he has gained a bit more gripping function in his right hand. Self-deception won't make it so. Only divine intervention could restore Hillard to peak tennis condition. Before leaving his apartment, his left hand slaps his face as hard as he can tolerate. Hillard drives to the championship match below the speed limit, hugging the right lane.

The first set is over in forty minutes. Chad Harrington cannot believe his strategy and preparation have been this effective. The oral report he received from his detective, combined with the scouting assessment assembled by his private coach, have been spot on. His coach reiterated their game plan moments before the match. "Abraham loves pace. Slow it down. Shorten your backswing and your follow-through. Use underspin and throw off his timing with your backhand slice. Go for flat winners when the opening is there. Serve exclusively to his backhand. Don't serve to his forehand unless serving for an ace. When he was a kid, Abraham had trouble with the elements. He was uncomfortable when the wind played tricks with his ball toss or when he had to adjust to direct sunlight. Hit lobs when the sun is in his face. Line up at least three feet behind the line for his first serve."

During the change of sides after the first set, and still groggy from the antihistamine, Hillard trickles ice water down the back of his shirt, shocking his spinal cord. He had played the first set as if he and Chad Harrington were in different time zones. He lost two of his three service games. Hillard had been one stride away, his reactions one moment behind. Winner after winner passed him. His sneakers were made of lead, and his perceptions were processed through a filter and then rebroadcast on a delay. He had been thinking, not doing, and suspension of thought had become impossible. There will be no resetting to what should have been. Adapting is the only antidote.

Under normal conditions Hillard would not have lost the first set. He would have won every service game. He would have played brilliant defense, strategically extending points until Chad Harrington committed an unforced error or Hillard hit a winner. But the conditions that exist today are exceptional. Only Hillard is aware of his injury until Joseph Russell arrives during the break with a large pitcher of ice water and paper cups. With his head tilted down for privacy as he fills Hillard's thermos, Joe asks, "What happened to your hand? Did you get into a fight?"

"I got stung. Don't say anything. I can barely grip the racket."

"I'll be back." Joe carries his tray to the other bench. "Mr. Harrington, can I pour you some cold water? Can I run up to the clubhouse and get you a fresh towel? Is there anything I can get you, sir?"

"Thanks for the water."

Joe extends the break. He pivots and walks back to the umpire's chair. "Sir, I'm out of cups. I'd be happy to bring you back a cup of water."

"Please do. At the next break."

"When is the next break?"

"After the next two games. You'd better go now."

Hillard elevates his focus, igniting his fury and his hatred of losing. He will break through the pain and the antihistamine fog. Adrenalin is flowing. The pain is the fuel feeding Hillard's rage. The source of that pain, standing on the other side of the net, shall be repaid with interest.

Wake up! Hillard silently screams as he walks to the baseline for the first point of the second set. His toss is perfect, and his ball strike emits a pop and a thud. His violent first serve, although long, achieves a goal. His opponent moves in two steps for the second serve but then retreats. Chad assumes the ready position three feet behind the baseline. Hillard's second serve bites the clay and kicks high. Chad blocks the forehand return to midcourt. Hillard executes a drop shot into the ad box off his backhand side. Chad sprints to his left. His lunging backhand flicks the ball back with no change of direction. Hillard bunts the ball to open court.

Chad sets up five feet behind the baseline for the second point. Hillard spins a first serve that kicks into the ad court doubles alley. Chad's backhand lands behind the deuce box. Hillard tests Chad's sprint stamina, his midcourt forehand into no man's land lures Chad into expending effort and oxygen. Chad's outstretched forehand doesn't clear the net. Finally, on the third point, Hillard detonates his first ace of the match. He wins game point on a screaming cross-court forehand.

Chad holds serve. Hillard is unwilling to invest in the effort required to neutralize Chad's service. Hillard's strategy of tactical conservation has inherent risk. If Hillard's service falters, if he should drop even one service game, he might lose the match. Hillard concedes the second game of the second set. He'll look for a break opportunity in the eleventh game of the match with the sun at his back. A male voice pierces the decorum on the change of sides, with the score tied at one game apiece. "Only five more, Chad."

As promised, Joseph Russell returns. Joe's service cart is stocked with two buckets of ice, a large metal pitcher of water, paper cups, and white hand towels. Joe transfers one of the ice buckets and two towels to the table next to Hillard's bench. Joe fills the ice bucket with water. Hillard covers the bucket with a white towel, leaving a slight opening. He dips a cup into the ice water with his right hand. His left hand reaches into the bucket and grabs the cup. Hillard appears to sip the water, but he ingests nothing. His right hand remains submerged in the cold bath, numbing the pain. After engaging Chad Harrington in conversation, Joe offers the umpire that promised cold drink. That buys Hillard another thirty seconds. Joe then appears to struggle with the cart. He kneels down and straightens the two swivel wheels. "Do you need help with that, young man?" the umpire asks.

"No, sir. I've got it."

Walking back on the court for the third game of the set, Hillard flexes the rejuvenated extrinsic muscles of his right hand. His grip strength is improving. On the first point, Harrington anticipates another kick serve. He lines up inside the baseline, angled toward the sideline. Hillard's flat serve targeting the T catches Harrington leaning the wrong way. Harrington again positions himself a foot inside the baseline for the second point. Hillard handcuffs him with a body serve and then wins the point with a deft volley. Harrington never saw Hillard take net. With Harrington on the baseline for the third point, Hillard serves an ace. At forty-love, Hillard abandons his second serve. That backfires, he double faults. Hillard quickly snuffs out his opponent's belief. His first serve on the fifth point is a guided missile.

Hillard's college coach had taught him to ignore spectator comments or gestures, to be immune to both cheers and jeers. During a match on the grounds of a hallowed East Coast university, Hillard heard, "Go home, Jew boy." That slur broke his concentration. He repressed the urge to look into the stands. He refused to reward the male defamer with the gratification of having distracted the enemy. Transferring his rage to the man across the net, Hillard's return of serve from that moment on had been epic. He torched every return. Rocket fuel coursed through his veins; the ball exploded off his strings. One forehand return from the ad box on an attempted serve and volley knocked the racket out of his opponent's hand. That memory had become a useful motivator during the balance of Hillard's college career and beyond. That episode fades in comparison to Jakub Baranski's actions on this day.

Jakub Baranski had become more than a daily fixture on Northshore's veranda. His place within the deepest recess of the canvass covered porch had taken on an air of permanence. Although General Manager Pat Elliott maintained an open seating policy, both the staff and other members honored the accepted notion that the far corner seat belonged to Mr. Baranski. He had become an appendage, as perennial as the wrought iron furniture and the slate floor. Except for the short walk from the parking field to the veranda, Mr. Baranski had never been seen anywhere else at Northshore. After bathing his hand and then discreetly toweling off just before the start of the fourth game of the second set and leading two games to one, Hillard receives Jakub Baranski's nonverbal message to look in his direction. Sitting alone on the top row of the viewing stands, attired in a short sleeve shirt, Jakub Baranski holds his Nazi tattooed left arm aloft.

Chad Harrington's first serve of the fourth game would have been an ace against a lesser opponent. Hillard's forehand flail produces a looping return that lands behind the left service box, near the corner of the baseline and the sideline. Chad, running around his backhand, hits a cross-court forehand. Hillard can only muster a defensive backhand that lands behind the right service box. Chad's cross-court answer has the trademark of a winning shot. Chad relaxes as the ball clears the low part of the net. Reaching for the ball tucked into his pocket, Chad nudges toward the service line for the next point. Streaking across the court at the speed of blur, Hillard's strings meet the ball an inch before it kisses clay on its downward arc. From a point of origin rarely seen in a tennis match, a longitude four feet off the court and a latitude between the service line and the baseline, Hillard's forehand travels around the net post and lands just inside the baseline. Love-fifteen.

Chad's ball toss on the second point is low and off center. His first serve hits the bottom of the net. Hillard's exceptional visual acuity detects a subtle tell in his opponent's service. Harrington's toss arm stays higher on a spin serve, almost parallel to the court. He drops his toss arm to his left knee on a power serve. Harrington adds four extra pre-windup ball bounces to his next serve, and he doesn't fully drop his toss arm. Hillard reads spin serve, and Harrington's left shoulder telegraphs the destination. Hillard pounces. His return is deep, near the center mark. Chad's forehand lands midcourt with moderate depth. Hillard's clean forehand strike drives the ball deep behind the ad box. Chad slides into his backhand, and his momentum pulls him off-court. Chad scrambles back to center court. Hillard hits a forehand winner back into the ad box corner. Chad looks to the chair for help. "In," the umpire announces. Love-thirty.

Chad Harrington's coach, seated in the bottom row of the viewing stands, clenches his fist. The message to bear down is conveyed. Chad's first serve, just inside the center service line of the deuce box, has too much velocity. Hillard's return is long by a foot. Fifteen-thirty.

Chad drops his toss arm low and jumps into the next serve. The projectile arrives flat and heavy. It departs Hillard's side of the net with accrued interest. Fifteen-forty.

Pondering the consequences of losing his serve manifests into reality. Chad double faults the last point of the fourth game of the second set. Chad accepts the reality with minor resignation. This match is going three sets. After Hillard holds serve, Chad Harrington strategically struggles with his serve in the sixth game. Chad's gameplan is obvious: hold service in the first game of the third set and keep the scoreboard pressure on Hillard. The score of the second set matches the first: six games to one.

Chad opens the third set with a dominant serving performance, or so he thinks. Hillard's observations are panning out. The depth of Chad Harrington's toss arm cables his intention. Hillard is willing to trade service games until it's time to strike. With each player holding serve and the score knotted at four, Hillard drops the hammer. He blisters the first two service returns of the ninth game, controlling both points. Hillard can now taste it. At fifteen-thirty, and Harrington deep, Hillard pulls his left hand from his two-handed backhand, his drop shot ticks the net cord and skids left, fifteen-forty. Harrington's toss arm drops low on his next serve, and he violates his coach's advice. Hillard nails the forehand return.

Hillard Gabriel Abraham serves out the match. There is no handshake. Once again Hillard shall treat Chad Harrington as a non-entity, underserving of etiquette and protocol. After thanking the umpire, Hillard peers into the stands. Jakub Baranski's subtle head nod and facial expression carry something deeper than approval. Dissecting that image while replaying the match from the serenity of his terrace that evening, Hillard will later conclude that Jakub enjoyed a sense of vindication, perhaps a degree of retaliation. From the veranda, Joe Russell flashes a thumbs up. Bridget Radcliff, who had been sitting with Chad's parents and two colleagues from his law firm, is engaged in small talk with Mrs. Harrington. The chestnut brunette who had watched Hillard's first round match smiles and waves. Hillard's response, a smile of recognition, does not escape Bridget.

Reviewing the match with Steve Andres by phone later that evening, Hillard mentions two standout impressions. "I knew Harrington was a cheat and a schmuck, but I didn't realize what a self-absorbed narcissist he is. We played twenty-four games, and it never occurred to him that I was wearing long sleeves for a reason. Please don't let anyone else know about that defect in his service motion unless it happens to be his next opponent."

"Where are you going to put the trophy?"

"I don't know. How much do you think Harrington would pay to buy it from me?"

"Not a dime. He'd be more inclined to hire a second story man to steal it from you."

"You're right. I'll lock it away. In the scheme of things, it was just a tennis match. It won't put food into my fridge or money into my savings. But this one feels good, really good."

The Fates

On a damp and foggy April evening, Veronica Cabot and the wife of the retired RAF officer who had lunched with Veronica in November attend a witty musical revue at the Fortune Theater in Covent Garden. After the show, Veronica and Betty dine in a brasserie near the playhouse, a West End hotspot for the theater crowd. A tuxedo clad maître d' escorts them through the standing room throng to the only available seating, a cocktail table in the heart of the bar. Veronica ignores the amusing chatter pitched in her direction from this older and erudite fraternity. She nonchalantly accepts their highbrow allusions and innuendos. She is unfazed upon hearing that she is a sweet dish or a tasty morsel. Moments after their waiter serves the ladies a round of Chardonnay, Veronica overhears a bartender's greeting. "Mr. Marlowe! Good to see you, sir."

"Betty, did you happen to hear what that bartender said? Did he call that man Mr. Marlowe?"

"I'm sorry. I wasn't listening. I was reading the menu."

"It's a common name, probably just a coincidence. But this is the theater district, and the Mr. Marlowe in Becky's story was from London. And he was a playwright or something."

"Who is Becky?"

"Do you see him?"

"See who?"

"Mr. Marlowe," Veronica answers, just above a whisper.

341

"Yes. He's wearing an ascot."

"An ascot? Really? Uncle Em wears one every so often."

"Who's Uncle Em?"

Mr. Marlowe, now engaged in conversation with a well lubricated gentleman whose face is an arboretum of bushy gray whiskers, is standing only a few feet from Veronica's chair. "Excuse me, Betty. There's something I must do." Veronica rises from the table and approaches the gentleman. The bar chatter lowers in volume. The patrons are now absorbed in this interaction. A luscious, tasty morsel, in her mid-twenties, has initiated conversation with a middle-aged man of means. "Mr. Marlowe, my name is Veronica Cabot. I live in New York, and I'm here on business. I know this is probably a long shot, but about a year ago, a Mr. Marlowe from London was drinking Scotch whisky with friends of mine at a tennis club on Long Island. Are you that Mr. Marlowe?"

"I am sorry, Miss Cabot. I have no recollection of that."

"Oh well. I'm sorry to have bothered you." Betty offers an empathetic smile as Veronica returns to the table.

"Oh wait! Is one of your friends a very large gent? I believe they called him the mayor."

Veronica spins back. "That's Mayor Brewster. You are that Mr. Marlowe! You must be him." The bar crowd is now thinking this could get extremely interesting. "Do you remember Hillard Abraham?"

"Indeed. I did not know his surname. We shared a hackney that evening. If I recall he's a tall, thin chap with wavy black hair. He looks a bit like American actor Tony Curtis."

"I never heard that one before, but yes, that's Hillard."

"And Dexter, the chap who was a Tommy in Korea. We had a smashing good time. Are they here with you? Bring them over! I insist."

"No, sir. Hillard is in New York."

"Please convey my best to him. May I send a round to your table?"

"No, thank you. I know Hillard would love to know that I ran into you, but I'm afraid our relationship is a little strained at the moment."

Mr. Marlowe notes a trace of dejection, but a gentleman does not pry. "Well, as soon as that ship is righted, please offer my best."

"I'm afraid it may not get righted." Veronica's expression drops in tone and measure. Betty offers a subtle head nod in Mr. Marlowe's direction, indicating the topic should stay off limits. Mr. Marlowe's discernment overrules. It's time to probe. Veronica and Betty accept Mr. Marlowe's request to join them for a cocktail. The cagy theater producer asks if they would like a taste of a peaty Islay Scotch in tribute to that whisky fest with Hillard. The table grows cold and silent.

"I do not intend to encroach upon your privacy, but I have read many scripts in my life. I have trained myself to look for clues. Have you and Hillard had a dustup?"

"It's much deeper than that."

"Think of me as a well-intentioned interloper. There might very well be a resolution in one of those scripts that will help you patch things up." Veronica explains it all: the ardent affair, the cancelled wedding, her move to a simple London flat, and the returned letter. The

343

graybeard, who has been gradually moving within earshot, continues to close in. Perhaps this soap opera can benefit from his wisdom, as foggy as the evening mist after four vodka Martinis. Veronica is undisturbed by the gray intrusion. Peering over in his direction, she is momentarily distracted by the shrubbery in his ears and nose and the wire awnings above his eyes. Mr. Marlowe drills a little deeper. "So, it's a lover's quarrel?"

"I wish it was only a quarrel."

"I see. I only spent an evening with those lads, and as you would say in America, we were quite spiffed. But every so often you meet someone who is instinctively attuned to the human harmonic. For those so endowed, there is no such thing as distance. There are no strangers."

"This is really not helping me, Mr. Marlowe. I know what I've lost." Flashing a hand signal, the gray hedgerow orders another cocktail.

"But look at what he has lost. Don't lose sight of that. Remember this, my dear, love is the most precious commodity on earth."

The eavesdropper chimes in. "He's right, miss." Veronica smiles in the gray's direction.

Mr. Marlowe asks, "Did you try to call him? Maybe he never got the card. Did you send him a wire?"

"A wire would do the trick, miss," offers the earwigger.

Lowering his voice and his cadence, Mr. Marlowe continues. "This has the anatomy of a playscript. You are the one who left. It's up to you to end the conflict. The sooner you do that, the better. Some men, when wounded in love, become vulnerable. They become clay for the Fates.

They cannot bear the weight brought down upon them by the vicissitudes of life. I've seen many a good man twisted by the Fates into a sotted knave of low value, eroded by drink. That device belongs in the third or fourth act. Miss Cabot, if you don't mind my saying so, you must author the resolution. You must script the fifth act. Think of your time here in London as the intermission. Aside from life itself, nothing is more important than love. There can be no life without love, and no love without life. Love solves the mystery of life, and yet, love is a mystery. We are because we are loved." Mr. Marlowe savors a taste of his whisky. "There's a fragile line between a tragic ending and a happy one. Miss Cabot, write yourself a happy ending. I love a good romance."

"So do I, miss."

May 1957
Rheingold

Joseph Russell separates the curtains ballooning into his living room. Peering north over Lefferts Avenue he rotates back into the apartment. "Weather still looks good, Hon. But fans are showing up early. If we beat Milwaukee today, we'll be tied with them for first. Could be a sellout. I better go. I'm meeting Hillard in front of the bar at noon, but first I have to buy the tickets. I'll see you later." Joe kisses his apron clad wife, prances down the four flights of stairs, and hustles over to the ticket windows at Ebbets Field.

Joe tucks two tickets into his pocket. Avoiding the fan traffic on Bedford Avenue, he cuts through an alley, turns left on Stoddard Place, then right on Montgomery Street. He finds Hillard two doors down from their meeting place.

"Hey, Hill, let's get a cold one."

"I just left the bar. I don't know if I should go back. I don't think they want me there."

Joe's expression changes. "You were the only white guy, right?"

"The second I walked in, everybody shut down. It wasn't trepidation. They were glaring at me. I was invading their turf. All I wanted to do was grab a beer—maybe talk a little baseball until you showed up."

"You can't blame them, Hill. A bunch of black men hanging out can't relax around whites."

"I get that. But they don't know me. I have no malice toward anyone there."

"It is sad. I know you're a good guy. They were reacting to you without knowing you."

"You're right. They didn't give me chance to fit in."

"They've been through too much to trust whites. It's all about trust. Look at the history. Hell, until Jackie came along, we couldn't get into big time baseball."

"Yeah, I get it. I hope we can heal. If we can't, this country could get split apart. Someone with a motive could use it as a wedge."

"We can fix this. I've been in that bar dozens of times. Rudy owns it, and Caesar is his bartender. If you go in there with me, if they see we're friends and that I trust you, they'll trust you."

"You sure about that?"

"No. But it's worth a try. If you don't go back in there, they'll never know that you're a good guy."

"Yeah, you're right. It would be easier to just walk away. We can't let misunderstanding win."

Hillard holds the door open, and a miasma of cigarette smoke and beer filters out. Joe enters first, and Hillard follows. Every patron is a black man, and every man is dressed in a suit. Several men are wearing hats. The interior is long and narrow. The dark wood bar is situated along the left wall, and a row of booths with red vinyl benches runs along the wall on the right. Every barstool is occupied, and every booth is full. Customers stand in the narrow passage between the bar and the tables, clogging circulation. Every man is holding his ground. A cloud of tobacco smoke hovers over the bar, trapped by the low ceiling. The chatter at the front of the house lowers in volume as Joe and Hillard enter. Hillard releases his grip on the handle, and the self-closing door seals off the light from the street. The entire back bar is mirrored. The reflected image reveals glasses of beer, ashtrays, pencil thin smoke trails, and two dozen eye sockets, all pupils focused upon the two arrivals. "This may not have been such a good idea, Joe," Hillard says in a shallow tone. Hillard places his hat back on his head. "Might as well fit in." Joe, who has no intention of removing his gray tweed flat cap, nods affirmatively.

"Hill, would you like a beer?"

"I would love a beer. But not a Miller, Pabst, or a Schlitz. They're from Milwaukee. I don't want to consort with the enemy. I would like a Rheingold."

"You mean to tell me I'm drinking beer from Milwaukee?" says one of the two men standing just left of Joe and Hillard.

"Maybe," Hillard replies. "The only way you can be sure is if you drink a Rheingold, a Schaefer, or a Piels. I think they're brewed here in New York."

"Damn! I'm switching right now. Thanks for telling me this. Hey, Caesar, you got a New York beer?"

Nothing escapes Rudy's purview. "Caesar, you better load up with Rheingold and Schaefer. There's gonna be a run."

"Hill, follow me, I'll order," Joe says over his left shoulder as they navigate their way to the bar. "Caesar, I need two beers, please. Not Milwaukee beers." The patrons in earshot smile and nod.

"I got this." Hillard peels off two singles from a modest roll. Joe steps to his right as Hillard hands two bills to a patron on a barstool, who hands the currency to Caesar. Committed to middleman status, the man passes two glasses of beer back to Hillard. Two quarters and two dimes soon follow.

"Do you mind? I'm sorry to be a pain in the ass," Hillard says as he gives the middleman a quarter.

"You're cool with me," says the man as he places the coin on the bar and flicks it with his index finger across the oak bar top toward Caesar. The bartender nods a thank you.

The general chatter has returned to full volume. Hillard responds to the shift and his self-consciousness evaporates. Hillard senses an intimacy beyond the low illumination. Now he understands why the Venetian blinds are tilted for privacy and why there is no music. Inside this island, this inelegant bar hidden within an array of storefronts and street traffic, these men are free. They are free to relax, free from the imposed social and economic constructs of limitations and restrictions. They are free to pay homage to those brave and noble soldiers fighting on their behalf, Jackie Robinson's Brooklyn Dodgers. Hillard glances at his image in the mirror, in that gap between Caesar and the tall beer taps. The likeness in the glass, taken at face value, had been viewed as a symbol of repression. He had been dismissed as a source of misery. He had been excluded by the colony of men who gathered in the bar to escape that exclusion. Across the threshold and back on the street,

Hillard could graze any pasture or board any train. These men did not have that freedom. Beyond the threshold they would again be relegated by the guard rails. Hillard tugs on Joe's shirt. "The bridge is not going to get built by cowards," he says in a low voice.

"It's just going to take some time, Hill. Just time."

The two men within earshot hear that exchange. They rotate their shoulders to create a circle of four. "I don't believe in magic spells," Hillard announces, "But if we start drinking a New York beer, we might bring Brooklyn some good luck." He then mentions that the Braves are on the final leg of a four-city road trip, "They might be a weary team," he adds. That launches a full hour of Dodger fandemonium.

On Hillard's subway ride back to Queens, the chatter is baseball centric. An inquisitive passenger in a mechanic's uniform, with a lunch pail on his lap, asks about the game. "Man, Henry Aaron humbled us today," responds a fan sitting on the bench across from the lunch pail.

Hillard, standing in the middle of the car and gripping a hand strap, unrolls his play-by-play scorecard. "Listen to Aaron's line score, five at-bats, four hits including a titanic home run, four runs scored, and two more runs batted in."

No one debates the summation spoken by the man with the lunch pail. "Wish we had him. Aaron's a one-man wrecking ball."

Afterlife

Dexter Alexander deposits a dime into the bus station pay phone. Twenty minutes later Pastor Vincent Greene's truck pulls into the parking lot of the Durham terminal. Passing through the main entrance to meet their ride, Becky Alexander asks her husband the same question she asked him yesterday. "Are you sure you don't want to see the boys?"

"I don't trust Miles. He might be hiding somewhere. Let's just pay our respects to Mama. We need to let sleeping dogs lie. I'll be happier than a dairy farm kitty to get out of town without seeing him."

The night before their bus trip to North Carolina, Dexter called Pastor Greene to confirm the arrangements. They conversed for an hour. "There were a lot of secrets in my family, pastor. There were some things you weren't supposed to talk about. I didn't know what those secrets were, but I knew you couldn't talk about them."

"Your mother protected you, Dexter. She wanted to keep you safe. That's why she woke you up at dawn and made you go to work. That's why she had her aunt come down from Philadelphia to keep an eye on you."

"I did work from sunup to sundown. It was expected of me."

"That was the only way she could keep you away from your father and Miles."

"I hardly ever saw my father. He was usually out moonshining."

"He wasn't that way when you were little. He changed when he found Miles in the woods with another boy. I knew that boy's family. When

351

they found out about their son, Diego, they moved away. Your father didn't come home much after that. He stayed out in the woods."

Becky sits between the two men on the single bench of the pastor's red Ford pick-up. She scrunches up against her husband, maintaining a three-inch gap between herself and the pastor. There is no conversation. Fifteen minutes into the drive, with the afternoon sun behind them, Pastor Greene wipes his nose with a handkerchief. "It's only hay fever, but it's getting worse as I get older. When I was a boy, the doctor told my mother I'd grow out of it. I'm sixty-one. I still haven't grown out of it." The pastor turns his head to his left and sneezes onto the partially open triangular vent window. Becky slips her right arm around Dexter's waist and grabs his right hip. The gap between Becky and the pastor is now four inches. "When you're young and you get sick or hurt, you know you're going to heal. But if you get sick or hurt when you're old, you really don't know if you're going to get better. And if you do get better, you don't come all the way back. A little bit of what was ailing you stays with you."

The truck motors on. A directional sign is the justification Becky needs to break the silence. "Wilson, forty miles."

Three-mile markers later the pastor asks, "How does it feel to be back home?"

"Doesn't feel like home to me," Dexter replies. "New York is my home."

"This sure feels like New York. It's colder than I expected," Becky offers.

"Folks around here call this whippoorwill winter," Pastor Greene explains. "And we'll call the next chilly spell cotton britches winter."

Again, there is no chatter and very little traffic. Pastor Greene waves at a man on a tractor. A few minutes later, the pick-up turns left onto a dusty dirt road. Dexter rolls up his window. The truck rambles down the bumpy road for five minutes. The pastor pulls into a gravel lot and shuts his engine. Dexter rolls the window down. "I'll wait by my truck. Please take your time. Watch out for the squirrels. I mean it. They're very aggressive. We call them Mississippi squirrels." Becky looks at her husband. She doesn't know if she should laugh or cry.

Dexter reads her expression. "I'll protect you, hon."

Becky and Dexter cross the powdery dirt road. Gripping the metal pipe banister, they climb the brick stairs. Standing in the shadow of the one-story, red brick church, Becky reads aloud the sign nailed to the arched wooden door. "African Methodist Episcopal Zion Church, established 1934. Pastor Lonnie J. Spady."

Dexter studies the lay of the land. He surmises that the oldest graves are next to the church, at the top of the rolling hillside. Taking Becky's hand, he leads her down the modest slope. He finds his mother in the last plot in the middle row of three curved banks of graves and markers. They stand at the foot of Mama's resting place. Dexter gives voice to the headstone. "Lettie Mable Alexander. Born 1898, died 1954."

"Dexter, Mama was only fifty-six. That's so young."

"She wasn't in good health. At least now she's in heaven. She didn't have peace in her life. She does now."

Becky hands Dexter the red roses they bought at a farm and flower stand inside the bus station. He places the roses at the base of the gravestone. The roses settle upon the earth. A gentle breeze separates the cluster of buds, and the bouquet fans out across the grave. Dexter and Becky stand together in silent prayer, their heads bowed in reverence.

The male mourner crouches to regather the roses. He is unconcerned about grass and dirt stains on the knees of his blue business suit if he should lose his balance. He twists a supple stem around the other eleven roses and anchors the bouquet with a flat stone. He places another stone on top of the marker. He had learned that custom as a child. "Next time, Bubbe, I'll leave you a bottle of schnapps."

Standing in silence, Hillard Abraham finds comfort in the contemplation that only Bubbe's bones are under the earth. Her spirit and loving heart are imperishable and ungraved. Hillard checks his watch. He inhales the rebirth of the landscape. The canopy of young leaves, a translucent lime umbrella infused with a fresh coat of chlorophyll, softens the shadows. Walking from the grave to his car, he is struck by an eerie impression, a hunch that he is being watched. He rotates his vision. Two mourners are behind him, and a groundskeeper is on his left. To his right a Hasidic rabbi in a black suit is floating through the plots, scouting out his next almsgiver. Nothing appears unusual or out of place. The feeling persists. Again, he scans his surroundings for the source of this strange sensation. Hillard whispers audibly, "Nothing behind, nothing on the left, nothing in front, nothing on the right. Pretty weird for this to be happening in a cemetery." He takes a few steps, refreshing the sight angles into the clusters of trees and shrubs. He runs through the process again. "Nothing behind, nothing on the left, nothing straight ahead, nothing…" he freezes. Someone appears to be standing on the far rise next to a massive sycamore. The figure begins to move. Hillard cannot determine if the silhouette is approaching or retreating. He cannot establish a fix through the swaying tree limbs and the oscillating light.

After a few moments, he is certain the shape is moving in his direction. The human form emerges from the shadows.

Moored upon a square of earth, standing motionless, Hillard follows Veronica Cabot's path. She descends a modest ridge, crosses the roadway, and then glides along the upslope of the asphalt sidewalk. Within a minute, or two, or three, they are standing face-to-face, in silence. Hillard's arms are at his side. Veronica, wearing a forest green cashmere topper coat that swings just below her waist, a pair of khaki cigarette pants, and brown ballet flats, is clutching a white paper bag. "I think I should speak first. I have so much to say to you. I don't know where to begin. I'm so sorry about Bubbe."

Hillard utters a soft "Thank you," barely audible over the swishing of the trees. And then there is silence. He nudges in the direction of his TR. His movement is a barely perceptible twitch.

"If you walk away, I will understand." Hillard is mute. "Please don't leave. Is it possible for you to forgive me?"

"Why did you leave? You never told me. You kept me wondering. You never gave me a chance to fix what was wrong. That was a cruel thing you did to me."

"I couldn't tell you. But all I needed was time."

"Why did you leave? And why did you return the ring after we agreed you'd keep it?"

"Do you still have it?"

"Yes. What did you think I was going to do with it?"

"Sell it or give it to another girl."

"Another girl?! It took me twenty-seven years to find you. Did you really think I could replace you in seven months? I guess replacing me was a snap. You didn't value us the same way I did."

"I valued us more than you know. Do you remember my story about the room of light next to the room of darkness?"

"I remember."

"Please try to see this in a different light. I wasn't running from you. I was running from myself. I had to leave the light. I had to hide in the dark."

"My heart only sees it one way, that you ran out six days before our wedding. And you still haven't told me. Why did you do it?"

"I got scared. Please, can we move past it?"

"What scared you? I need to know. I have a right to know."

"Some people said you were after my money, my family's money."

Disgust invades Hillard's face. "Oh please…and you believed them? You left me over hearsay! I don't care about your money, and I don't want to know about your money. It's none of my business. But you believed them. Where was your faith in me? You once said you were loyal. Where was your loyalty to me? So, you thought of me as a man without principles. This is so insulting, but I'm glad I know it now. I need to know, who said this?"

"The Harringtons. Chad said you wanted to marry a girl with money. That your father had been a milkman."

"So what? Harrington and his old man know nothing about my father. Do they know he served in Panama when he was eighteen? Do they know he was born in a cold-water tenement and shoveled coal for a nickel a day when he was six? And through it all, he never complained. If old man Harrington had any principles, he would have told Chad boy to bring that pregnant schoolgirl back from Spain and marry her. I can't believe you didn't defend me or my family. I wouldn't spend a minute with a woman with such little respect for me. I thought I knew you, but I was wrong." With his eyebrows tilted in, his lips pursed with anger, Hillard turns and strides off. Veronica lunges for his left sleeve.

"No! Please don't go. You do know me. You know me better than anyone. I had to shut myself off." Veronica's eyes are wet, and her lips are tight and compressed. "I knew what was in my heart. I needed to know what was in yours. I needed to know if you still loved me or missed me as much as I missed you. I needed to know if you would be there for me when I figured things out. Please don't leave. Please give me a second chance. Please."

"Did it occur to you that this testing of my love might cause me to stop loving you?"

"If you couldn't forgive me after I explained it to you, then you didn't love me enough."

"That's some strange logic. What if I was involved with someone else? Did you ever think that you might be intruding?"

"I spoke to Becky last night when I got home. She said she didn't think you had a girlfriend. It's easy for me to say that if you were involved, I would have kept my distance, but that's not true. I would have fought for you."

"So, you flew from London not knowing if I was in a relationship?"

"Yes. I couldn't get here fast enough. What I want to say to you can only be said in person. I knew you wouldn't be with someone else because I couldn't be with someone else."

"So, this was one big test?"

"Think of it as a confirmation."

"Either way, you set the terms. That's a hell of a way to test me. I thought you were my partner, that we would look out for each other. And then with no warning, we had nothing. You ripped my heart out of my chest and put it on a stick to see if it keeps beating."

"My heart was on a stick right next to yours."

"What else did you have planned for me? Were you going to drop me out of a helicopter to see if I bounce?"

"We're connected by something that's beyond us, and all the signs are there: meeting in the clinic when we were kids, meeting as grownups, and running into Mr. Marlowe in London. Something is putting us together, Hill. We're supposed to be together. Nothing can keep us apart."

"Mr. Marlowe? The guy from the canteen?"

"Yes! Think about how amazing that is. What are the chances that he and I would be in the same London restaurant on the same night at the same time? He likes you. He told me to send you a wire. I went one better. I got on a plane."

"You put me through so much misery. That's hard to forget, hard to forgive."

"It was misery for me too. I lost myself to our passion. I had waited so long our passion consumed me. Someday all of Cabot will be on my shoulders. I'll be responsible for the entire family. I pulled back when I couldn't see how the pieces fit together: you, me, and Cabot. I needed to see it from a distance. I thought about us every day, every hour of every day. And then it came to me. It was so obvious. I need you for me, I need you for my family, I need you for Cabot. I wish I had listened to you when you asked me if we should slow down."

"That's what you say now. Six days before we were supposed to get married, you told me I was expendable. You borrowed me like a library book, and when you were finished, you dropped me into the return bin. I can't go through this again."

"If you walk away, I…" In a hushed voice, her green orbs downcast, the corners of her mouth drooped, Veronica murmurs, "Please don't leave. I felt so alive when I was in your apartment. It was just the two of us. It wasn't about how many rooms, how much money, what cars we drove. It was about us, just us. It's still there, Hill. If you want it. I would marry you today."

"You still want to marry me?"

"I've wanted to marry you since I saw you in the clinic."

"I can't marry you until I get stock in Cabot Development. I'll also need my name added to all of the deeds. I'll save you the legal fees, I'll draft."

Reconnecting to their banter, Veronica recites, "You just stop this right now, Hillard Abraham."

Hillard's eyelids close as he exhales. "If I walk away, I might regret it for the rest of my life. If I let you back in, I run the risk of you doing this to me again. And if you do this to me again, I'll regret for the rest of my life not having walked away."

"Do you think I would have come all the way from London if I didn't love you?"

"You ran from me twice. The first time you skipped away. The second time you took a plane. There seems to be a pattern here."

"It's not a pattern. It took courage for me to walk into that exam room and courage to come here today. I had to find you, Hillard. You could go to the other side of the earth, and I would find you. I don't want to be without you. You're the only man I've ever loved."

"I've been planning my life, and now I'm supposed to throw those plans away because you want me back. Sometimes you have to walk away from people you love."

"Do you still love me?"

"I've been managing pain and disappointment for seven months. I've learned how to live with it."

"Neither one of us has to live with it anymore. We can fix it right here, right now."

"We cannot erase the last seven months." Hillard turns his gaze toward the sycamore on the gentle slope. That voice of reason, the impulse of logic that has illuminated every passage, that has simplified every argument to its core, is silent. His heartbeat is not. "Part of me wants to punish you, and you can't blame me. You really destroyed me, Veronica. There's been no healing."

"There's been no healing for me. Let's heal together. I sent you a birthday card. I invited you to come over and stay with me. I thought you returned it, and I was crushed. But I used the wrong postage. The card was never delivered."

"So, your father was telling me the truth. He said you sent me a card."

"I wrote to my parents every so often. I had to keep my distance. They were so down and concerned. Father would call me at the office. The first thing out of his mouth was, 'Have you heard from Hillard?' Father can see it. That's why he sent us to Boston. He knows you are the perfect fit for me."

"When anything is new, it has a luster. You took that away from us."

"I did. But now we're battle tested. This will make us stronger than we were before. Mr. Marlowe called it our intermission."

"If I tell you I need seven months to think this over, would you wait?"

"Yes."

"Seven months from today. Let's meet right here."

"I will wait for you. Seven months, eight months, whatever you need. I'll wait for you."

"And when we meet after seven months, how will you feel if I tell you I just got married?" Veronica lowers her head. "That is what you put me through. There were so many other ways to have handled this. For starters, you should have explained it to me. We always discussed everything, then out of the clear blue, you shut me out and ran off. I was a disposable commodity. You broke my heart, and now you've come back to break it again."

"I give you my life, Hillard. I will never leave you. Please forgive me. Do you still love me?"

"I don't know if I can trust you. There will be challenges. There will be valleys. Are you going to bail on me when we hit a bump?"

"I don't know what else I can say to you. I thought if I explained it...you're my other half, I need you...I can't believe this is happening. We're in a cemetery, and I'm losing you."

"You're not losing me." Hillard holds out his hands, the paper bag falls to the sod,

Veronica buries her face into his shoulder. "I've missed you so much. I never want to be without you."

"Marriage means taking an oath, till death do us part. Are you really prepared to say that?"

"Yes."

"But that doesn't rule out homicide."

Veronica's sob and laugh merge. "We would meet again in heaven."

"What's in the bag?"

Veronica pulls a sweater out of the bag. She unbuttons her coat, revealing the tennis sweater Hillard gave her. "The first week I was in London, I bought you this sweater. It looks like the male version of my sweater. My flat had almost no heat, so I slept with your sweater. I still have your apartment key."

"Your key won't work. Someone told me you were after my money, so I changed the locks."

"I'm never going to hear the end of this."

"That's how I heal."

"Heal away, I can take it." Nibbling on Hillard's right ear, she whispers, "I know another way we can heal." Their passionate embrace, a curious departure from the rituals usually witnessed in a cemetery and yet aligned with the issuance of forgiveness, lingers. Entwined as one, on a parcel of earth imbued with the contiguity of two planes connected by the voyage of soul, where love and sorrow merge into a personification of infinite and unique proportion, the bridge spanning seven months of separation, seven months of managing heartbreak is so conceived.

A disembodied voice pierces the waking dream. "Excuse me," descends from no specific direction, penetrating the reunion. The Hasidic rabbi, standing beside them, tips the narrow brim of his black hat, "I also do veddings." The muffled laughter and the spontaneous joy of the moment shall long be remembered by Veronica as her most cherished affirmation.

October 1957
Act Five

The Cabot Estate is basking in the autumnal sunlight, glowing in the radiance of late October. An unhurried breeze weaves through the amber and crimson tree crowns. Drifting mountains of billowy cotton clouds, stratified with gray veins of vapor, fashion a scene worthy of a John Constable landscape. On the precise month and day, they were to have been joined in matrimony, one year removed, Veronica Cabot and Hillard Abraham are to be wed.

Two wedding options had been presented to their parents: elopement or a civil ceremony. With the original plans bridled to the essentials, the brokered agreement satisfied the couple's thirst for balance and harmony. After four months of peacefully invoking the art of compromise when their domestic opinions differed, Hillard and Veronica extended no negotiating voice to their families. The pair's vow to maintain their allegiance to each other, to uphold the sanctity of self-determination, had been infrangible. Wishing to exorcise the misery that Veronica set loose twelve months ago, today's nuptials shall take place in her father's study. Mayor Brewster readily accepted the couple's request to serve as officiant. Dexter Alexander assured Hillard that a Speyside Scotch would be teed up and a taxi for The Honorable Mayor would be on standby. Tea sandwiched between a noon ceremony and an afternoon flight, a scratch-made buffet luncheon prepared by Becky Alexander, has been set out in the dining hall.

Veronica exercised every precaution to protect her future in-laws from the loathsome sentiments that had poisoned her spirit. Veronica had no doubt that Becky would remain as tight lipped as an unbreakable co-conspirator under cross-examination. Nothing could pry those deceitful sentiments from Becky's lips. Chad Harrington had been notified by the Cabot corporate attorney that a defamation of character lawsuit would be filed if the conditions enumerated within that registered letter were ever violated. The letter also assured the defamer that any future filing would have no reference to a certain incident in Madrid involving a seventeen-year-old schoolgirl.

Veronica's expertise in designing explicit strategies had also been a necessary maneuver with Bridget Radcliff and the former Regina Ellsworth. Regina accepted the explanation that only family members would be attending the intimate wedding ceremony. Regina also understood that the breadth of Veronica's inner circle had been reappraised.

Upon returning home from the Indianapolis 500 in early June and learning that Veronica and Hillard had reunited, Bridget phoned Veronica to catch up. The ladies met three days later at the same restaurant that hosted Bridget's assault upon Hillard and his family. Veronica arrived twenty minutes early. She asked the hostess for the corner table against the bay window. With her back to the glazing and with a clear view of the dining room, Veronica ordered two glasses of chardonnay, two glasses of water, a cheese tray, and the check. Bridget arrived two minutes late. Veronica waited for Bridget to settle, and then she unleashed. "The last time we met here, you imposed your unsolicited and contemptuous opinion. You defamed the man I'm going to marry. Marriage is a lifetime commitment. It's the foundation that supports a family. If you ever arrive at that conclusion, I hope you won't be too old to find a man like Hillard because men like him get snatched up by women like me. If you do change your mind about marriage, it's understood that you won't be settling down with the son of a milkman. If you ever again defame my future in-laws, you will hear from my attorney. You might want to start preparing an explanation for Edgar when he realizes no one from Cabot is ever going to return his calls." Veronica then handed Bridget the check and uttered a line she had waited years to spout. "This bill is outrageous. If I was you, I wouldn't pay it."

The couple extended two formal invitations. For reasons both sentimental and appropriate, Veronica mailed an invitation to Elizabeth Anne and Dr. Sanford Rutherford. Veronica joyfully accepted Dr. Sandy's explanation, delivered by telephone, that Elizabeth Anne is battling through morning sickness and they will not be able to attend. Had Dr. Sandy been inclined to provide details, he would have explained that two months ago, after visiting Grandmother Judith in Galway, Ireland, they climbed the Mutton Island lighthouse. Grandmother had explained, during a pot of tea, a plate of petit fours, and an extra helping of gossip, that Mutton Island's only residents were on vacation, visiting family in Salthill. Elizabeth Anne and Dr. Sandy drove across the causeway at low tide and then walked the rocky terrain to the lighthouse. Elizabeth Anne believes it happened there. The name Abigail has been floating in their morning coffee.

A second invitation had been sent to Andy Devine, host of a Saturday morning Children's television program and friends with Smilin' Ed McConnell, creator of Hillard's favorite wag, Froggy the Gremlin. During their four-month cohabitation, Hillard introduced Veronica to Froggy, a central character on Andy's TV show. "My life is now complete, Hillard. I've got you and Buster, and now I've got Froggy."

Froggy's, "Hiya, kids! Hiya, hiya!" became one of their personal public greetings; "Plunk your magic twanger!" a very private one.

Last evening, Becky and the chauffeur, Charles, rearranged the furniture in the study. Two rows of those arrogant French chairs, six chairs to a row, are stretched out across the Moroccan area rug. A simple wooden lectern, a recognizable fixture from Pastor Reed's Harlem sanctuary, stands between the chairs and the floral arrangements. The florist who decorated Bubbe's memorial service delivered the goods in his personal station wagon this morning, just after eleven.

At twelve noon, one hour before the ceremony, Mr. Cabot offered his wife his interpretation of Veronica getting married on her birthday, the twentieth of October. "She's being born again. Her second life, one as a wife and maybe someday as a mother, begins on the same day she started her first life." Mr. Cabot then reached into the top drawer of his armoire and handed his wife another fresh handkerchief.

At twenty minutes after noon, Mayor Brewster settles into the middle cushion of the leather sofa in Mr. Cabot's study. The mayor's girth infringes upon the neighboring sections. The mayor is reviewing the script for the wedding service when Dexter enters the study. The mayor's arched eyebrows and unsubtle index finger conveys his message. Dexter glides to the makeshift champagne station, grabs the bottle of Scotch by the neck, and pours the mayor a healthy dram. "I hope you will be joining me and Hillard after the ceremony," the mayor remarks just before absorbing his fortification.

"Would be my honor, sir."

Gretchen's fiancé Scotty arrives. Scottie explains to the mayor that Gretchen and Becky are helping Veronica with last-minute bride business and should be down momentarily. The mayor pats the outside of his single-breasted jacket pocket. The ring box is exactly where it was five minutes ago. At twelve-forty, the cook escorts Aunt Marjorie and Uncle Em into the study. Aunt Marge is tearing up. Steve Andres and his wife arrive a minute later and sit in the second row. A pang of anxiety invades Dexter from within, and he fakes a smile as he departs the study in a relaxed gait. *Where the hell is Hillard?*

Dexter finds the chauffeur passing through the grand foyer. "Charles, have you seen Hillard?"

"No. I was just looking for his car. He should have been here by now. Probably just traffic."

The lift descends from the second floor. "Don't say anything, Charles. Just keep smiling." Mr. and Mrs. Cabot emerge from the elevator, radiating warmth and gratitude. Mr. Cabot escorts his wife into the study. In a hushed voice, Dexter says, "I'll call his apartment from the kitchen."

"Do you think he's backing out?" Charles asks.

"No way. He loves her too much. If anyone was going to pull out, it would be Veronica, and she's upstairs."

"Not for long," Charles remarks. The elevator door closes and begins its ascent. "Maybe we should go out looking for him. What if his car broke down?"

"He would get to a phone and call. Let's give him a few more minutes. One of us has to stay here. I know the route he takes from his apartment. I'll go out and look for him if he doesn't show up." Dexter checks his watch. It's now eight minutes to one.

The lift door opens. Neither Dexter nor Charles can exercise discretion. Veronica is ravishing. Dexter quickly recovers. "Wow! I have never seen three more beautiful ladies."

Mr. Cabot returns from escorting his wife to their seats. Mr. Cabot and Gretchen exchange smiles as she passes her father and enters the study. Gretchen and Scotty sit together in the front row. Becky stands with Veronica until Mr. Cabot offers his daughter his right arm. Becky then glides into the dining hall to light the fuel canisters under the chafing dishes. "Veronica, I'm sure you know that your mother and I wish you only joy and happiness. It is my greatest honor to give you away. It is also my duty to ask if you have any doubts or reservations."

"No, Father, I have none. I'm truly in love with him."

"I know you are."

The mayor waddles out from the study. "Mr. Cabot, can we talk?" Within a few moments, everyone becomes aware of the obvious: the groom is a no-show.

The wedding party gravitates into the study. Veronica sits in the far corner of the study, on the edge of her father's leather recliner. Mr. Cabot stands in front of the lectern. "Has anyone heard from Hillard?" Tension, strain, and uncertainty are inscribed into every face. Gretchen rises from her seat and stands next to the recliner. Her hand rests upon her sister's left shoulder. Becky silently prays, *Please God, just a flat tire.*

Dexter informs everyone that he has been calling Hillard's apartment from the second line, and there's been no answer. "Veronica, is it okay with you if I go out and look for him?"

Mr. Cabot responds. "Yes, Dexter. Please do."

Aunt Marjorie surrenders a sob. Uncle Em squeezes her hand. Mr. Cabot speaks to the gathering. "I'm sure there's a logical explanation." Until this moment, Mr. Cabot had avoided scrutinizing Hillard's parents. Mr. and Mrs. Abraham are transmitting two signals: shock and bewilderment. Under different circumstances Mr. Cabot would have called the police. Such a call now would be most unwise.

Becky approaches the recliner. "Can I get you anything? A glass of water?"

"I feel so helpless, Becky. I don't know what to do. I don't want to just sit here, but what am I supposed to do?"

The group sits in silent confusion. There is no movement. A paralysis of mind and muscle has invaded the study. They await the only remedy, a phone call restoring their ransacked village. The gentlemen follow Mr. Cabot's lead. They loosen their neckties. Twenty anxious minutes pass. Mr. Cabot picks up the desk phone on the half ring. "Hello." The room is frozen, no one is breathing, Mr. Cabot is holding the black handset tight against his ear, "…are you sure? I see…I see…okay."

There is a gasp. Someone utters, "Oh, God."

Mr. Cabot re-cradles the phone. His face is sallow, and his eyes are moist. He peers over his left shoulder, seeking a connection to his earthly core. His brother issues a subtle nod of support. Chase Cabot had always been a model of adaptability, never trapped, never squeezed into the throat of a funnel. He had prepared for every conceivable twist and test his mind could conjure. He could not have been prepared for this. He walks to the back of the room and repositions the last chair in the second row. He sits across from his daughter. Clasping his hands together, he utters, "I'm so sorry I have to tell you this."

"Is he hurt?" she asks.

"Worse, much worse...there's been an accident...a terrible accident." There is a long pause. Mr. Cabot closes his eyes. "Are you sure you want to know this now?"

"Tell me."

Chase Cabot bows his head. "Hillard is gone."

Our Story

He has relived Hillard Abraham's last day on earth from every aspect and every angle, at times recalling details he had long ago forgotten, details fraught with torment and self-created persecution. One phone call, one slight change of plans, and all would be different. He survived his brother in North Carolina, scaled the seawall in Inchon Harbor, and endured the barriers of race in New York. He had always made it to the other side. But not now, not yet, not with those inescapable images seared into his gut: Hillard's lifeless body strapped to the ambulance stretcher and the crumpled TR loaded onto a flatbed.

He has replayed the police officer's deconstruction of the crash a thousand times, but he cannot alter the story or change the outcome. In every iteration, driver one, the nineteen-year-old son of a prominent rabbi, takes the curve too fast and loses control of his father's Cadillac. The Fleetwood collides head-on with the right side of the sports car. Driver two is killed instantly. Driver one and his passenger, a fifteen-year-old female, required no medical attention. If driver two's steering wheel had been on the left side, he probably would have survived. If the road wasn't so narrow, if there had been a shoulder, Hillard might have had room to swerve.

Sick to his core and numb with pain, Dexter drove to the gas station that dispatched the tow truck. Dexter dialed the Cabot residence from the pay phone. Dexter does not remember walking back to his DeSoto after making that call. Dexter came through the carnage of Korea by practicing detachment. On this day, driving back to the estate, Dexter weeps. A few gut-wrenching minutes after Dexter's phone call, Mr. Abraham asked the telephone operator to connect him to the police dispatch center. He scribbled down the address of the county morgue onto the yellow pad on Chase Cabot's desk. Twenty minutes later, Mr.

Abraham parked in front of a one-story brick building on the grounds of the county hospital. Through a voice hoarse from tear salt and tobacco, Hillard's mother pondered, "What is she going to do with the ring this time?"

Mr. Abraham ignored her question. Depressing the emergency brake pedal with his left foot, he summoned a sentence. "Wait here." Mr. Abraham walked to the ambulance parked next to the building's side door. His grief ran down his face.

The Cabot family minister and the minister's wife are in the study, standing near the lectern when Dexter returns. Mayor Brewster is slumped upon the couch; the half empty bottle of Scotch is on the coffee table next to the mayor's eyeglasses. The mayor's eyes are wet and bloodshot. Scotty and Steve Andres are sitting side-by-side on the French chairs, quietly conversing. Steve is dabbing his eyes with a cocktail napkin. His wife is comforting Aunt Marjorie in the dining hall. Uncle Em is running the water in the powder room, drowning out his whimpering. Dexter finds Charles and the cook in the kitchen. The cook is drying her tears with her apron. Charles is shaking his head. "I can't believe this, Dexter. I can't believe this."

Dexter climbs the stairs. Gretchen is in the wing of the dwelling room, leaning against Veronica's bedroom wall. Dexter hears Becky's voice filtering into the corridor. He hands Gretchen his handkerchief. She wipes her eyes and nose. "Thank you. She's tougher than all of us put together. She wants you and Becky to drive with her to Hillard's apartment. She wants to get Buster."

"Of course."

The Cabot limo pulls into the apartment parking lot. Walking to the building, Veronica digs into the pocket of her khaki cigarette pants and hands the apartment key to Dexter. Superintendent Ed greets them in the lobby. Ed had noticed the limousine from his bedroom window. Dexter explains, and Ed cries openly.

Becky, Dexter, Charles, and Ed stand aside. When Veronica enters the apartment, she finds Buster sleeping on his chair on the terrace. Until that moment, Veronica's spine had been made of graphene, her emotions held in check by a tungsten dam. She sits in Hillard's terrace chair and breaks down.

Dexter loads the trunk with Buster's litter box, food bowls, and assorted toys. He hands Hillard's tennis rackets, two tennis trophies, and Hillard's favorite fedora to Becky, who places them on the back seat between herself and Veronica. Buster curls up on Veronica's lap for the trip back to the estate. Dexter holds the two manila folders that Hillard left on the kitchen counter.

In the morning, Veronica buys a large plot behind Bubbe's resting place. She mails the cemetery director the epitaph for the headstone: *Hillard Gabriel Abraham, beloved Fiancé, Son, Grandson, Friend.* Below the inscription, a Scarlet Tanager shall forever dwell in granite and memory. At the request of owner Cindy and the staff at First Serve Tavern, Charles delivers Hillard's final tennis trophy. Cindy places the trophy on the back bar, next to the photo of Maureen Connolly.

In the quiet gloaming of the evening, thirty hours after losing her fiancé, Veronica is sitting on the Baroque bench in her bedroom. Buster is at her feet. He is sleeping inside Hillard's inverted fedora. Buster's tail and both front paws are draped across the felt brim. The Cabot Estate is encased in a vacuum. There are no sounds staining the silence, no detectable movements disturbing the stillness. Veronica opens the two manila folders Hillard left in his apartment. The thicker one contains a draft of a legal petition for Dexter and Becky to gain custody of their nephews and the paperwork for initiating the adoption. The second folder bears the title *Our Story*. Veronica reads aloud.

> *"A twelve-year-old commoner from the land of large beaks and a ten-year-old royal princess meet by chance in front of a mystic's potion tent. Fifteen years later, they dance at a royal wedding. Stealing away that night, they become lovers and decide to wed. But a jealous knight hires a wicked sorcerer who casts a poisonous spell, and she flees to distant lands. Living in a convent, pangs of love weaken the evil grip on her heart. The noble commoner seeks out the villainous knight and slays him on a red battlefield, breaking the hex. The princess returns from self-exile. The noble commoner and the royal lady negotiate a deal known as The Four Theses, a combination of Martin Luther and the Haggadah. One, they must live together in peace in the commoner's humble cottage. Two, they must pledge to eternally share the joys and hardships. Three, they must have no other lovers. Four, they must watch Froggy the Gremlin every Saturday morning. The princess and the commoner are wed, the commoners with big noses rejoice, and the blue veined aristocrats throughout the land weep for their sons. The lovers soar away on a silver bird while a powerful wizard, disguised as an orange tabby, transforms their humble cottage into a red brick ocean castle where the lovers shall live forever in peace."*

Veronica deposits her moist tissues into the wastebasket and places both folders into the top corner drawer of her bureau. She opens the French doors onto the east lawn. Swaddled in the tennis sweater Hillard gave her, she confronts the autumn chill. For as long as Veronica can remember, the night sky has inspired a humbling connection to God and creation. Those deeply seeded beliefs remain intact and uncompromised, neither buried by the sediment of time nor the tribulations of life and death. The moonless sky this evening is exceptionally clear. The clarity is extraordinary. Her window into the heavens is endless. Those shimmering messengers from that room of eternal light illuminate the room of perpetual darkness, a celestial Morse code of blinks and flickers spanning that which is known with the infinite possibilities that transcend time and dimension. "I'll find you again, Hillard," she whispers. "I will find you again."

A Note from the Author

On the day *First Token: A Story of Life, Love, & Tennis* was published, the US geological service reported a seismic event in the northeast. I knew precisely the source of that disturbance; my English teachers were spinning wildly in their graves. There were twenty-five students in my public-school classes, and the order for groupings, functions, and presentations was alphabetical. I was always last. If those teachers had been asked to compose a list of the students most likely to publish a novel, in order of probability, my position would not have changed. If the other twenty-four students had been asked that same question, I would have been last on all twenty-four submissions. If I had been asked to draft a list of the students most likely to publish a novel, I would have put myself first.

My perception of literature changed in my senior year of college. Reading assignments and term papers ceased being obligations. I fell in love with our exquisite and elegant language. In 1972, while earning a Master of Arts degree at the State University of New York, publishing a novel became an aspiration. The setting and storyline to be determined later.

I shared my ambition to publish a novel with no one. In 1997, when a catastrophic illness struck and I became a single parent, I had been told that a dad could not raise a daughter by himself. That is untrue, a dad can learn how to be a mom. The experience of raising an extraordinary child imprinted upon the writer living within.

In 2016, another extraordinary lady, my wife Elizabeth, gently reminded me that my aspiration to write and publish a novel has an expiration date. *First Token* was born. Early in the process, I discovered the similarities between a flesh and blood child and a literary creation. They are both offspring.

First Token is a hybrid novel and true to its title. The story is told in the cadence and pace of the 1950s. As comedic expression is a cardinal position on my compass, Token is infused with thoughtful wit. The novel's delivery could be construed as a contradiction in terms; a stream of consciousness narrative can be navigable; the tributaries can seamlessly flow back into the river. Enchantment, disguised as fate, elevates the tale. The characters, including an orange tabby are embraceable and endearing.

Token will resonate with readers who yearn for the positive attributes of the 1950s juxtaposed to the dysfunction of today. In 1956, faith was a guiding force, the US had two billion dollars in the bank, and baseball was unequivocally our national pastime.

My daily agenda includes applying my real estate skills on behalf of a brilliant casual dining concept, spending as much time with my family as my family can tolerate, winding up Lenny and Charlie, our two orange tabbies, planning my second novel, and watching tennis.

Made in the USA
Columbia, SC
18 January 2025

24dc5170-9543-4ab7-bb10-3caccf5d45ecR01